The Mazzard Tree

MARCIA CLAYTON

ISBN: 978-1-8383259-4-7

Published by Sunhillow Publishing

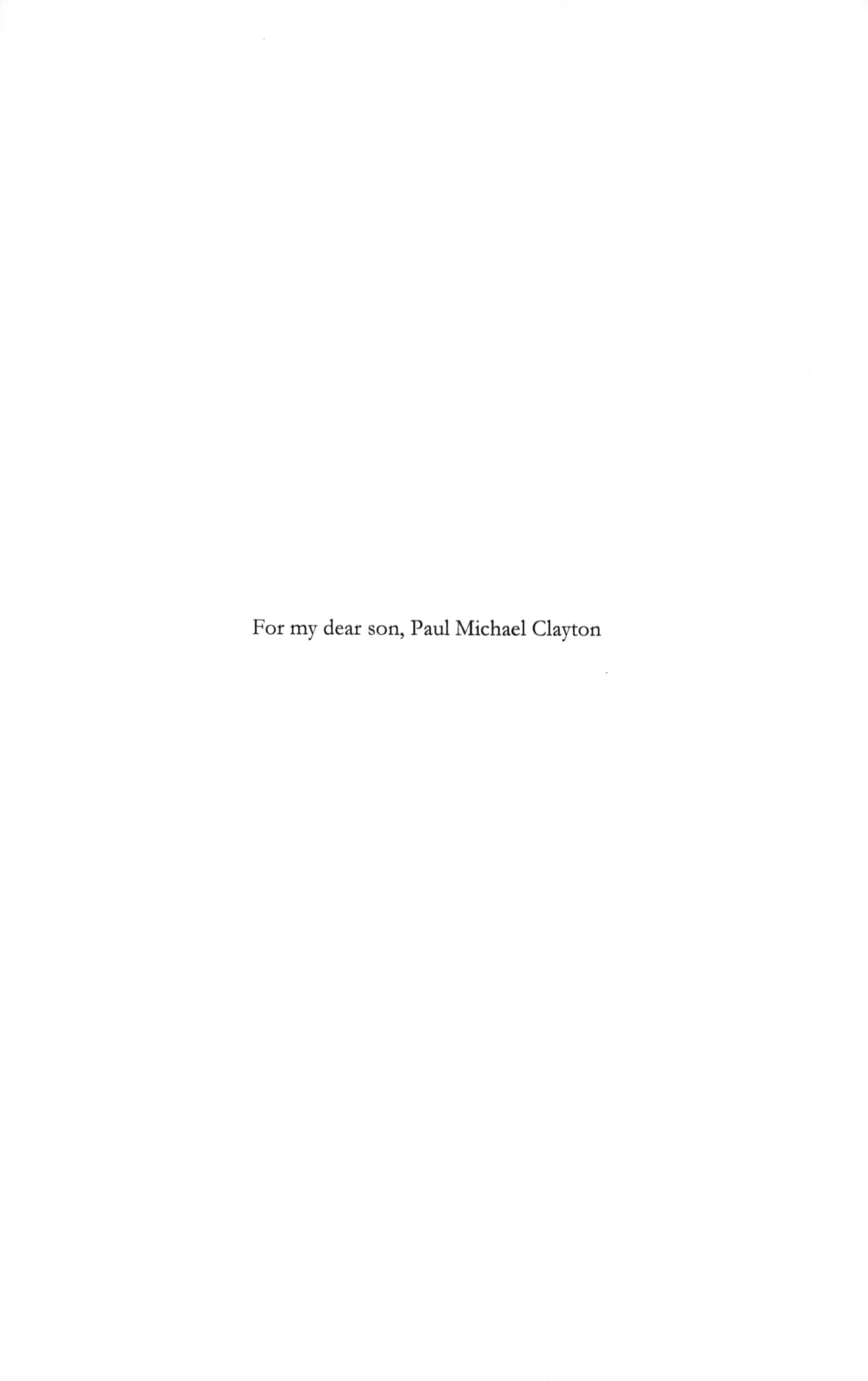

For my dear son, Paul Michael Clayton

Also by Marcia Clayton

The Hartford Manor Series

Betsey: The Prequel

The Mazzard Tree

The Angel Maker

The Rabbit's Foot

Millie's Escape

A Woman Scorned

ACKNOWLEDGEMENTS

Thank you to my husband, Bryan, for his patience and encouragement and also to my sons Stuart, Paul and David for their help along the way.

To Bryan, my sister Gill, and my nieces, Sharon and Marilyn, for being the first people to read my book and provide constructive criticism and support.

To my talented daughter-in-law, Laura, for producing a fantastic cover for the book and to Stuart for helping me to publish this book on Amazon.

Last, but not least, the biggest thank you goes to my readers. I have received some wonderful messages from readers who have told me how much they have enjoyed my books. Each and every review and message encourage me to continue writing. A simple message, particularly from a stranger, saying they loved my story helps to dispel my doubts over my ability as an author. I can't tell you how much those lovely messages mean to me.

Thank you.

The Main Characters of Hartford

The Carter Family

EDWARD CARTER (b1812)
Married **BETSEY LOVERING** (b1814)

Their children:

1. **EVELINE CARTER** (b1837)

2. **GEORGE CARTER** (b1840)
   Married Alice Brown (b1840)
   Their children:
   - Harriet (b1860)
   - Francis (b1862)
   - Alfred (1865 – 1869)
   - Theresa (b1868)

3. **FREDERICK CARTER** (b1841)
   Married **LUCY FULLER** (b1843)
   Their children:
   - Llewellyn (b1872)
   - Rosella (b1876)
   - Alfie (1877 – 1877)
   - Grace (1879 – 1879)
   - Eddie (b1880)

4. **TOM CARTER** (b1841)
   Married **SABINA BAILEY** (b1846)
   Their children:
   - **ANNIE** (b1864)
   - Mabel (1866 – 1866)
   - Willie (b1869)
   - Mary (b1871)
   - John (b1872)
   - Emma (b1874)
   - Edward (b1876)
   - Stephen (b1878)

- Helen (b1880)

5. **WILLIAM CARTER** (b1845)
   Married Lottie Chang (1850 – 1880)
   Their children:
- Identical twins Joseph (b1875) Matthew (b1875)
- Amelia (b1876)

The Hammett Family

ISAAC HAMMETT (b1806)
Married: **LIZA JONES** (b1810)

The Cutcliffe Family

JOHN CUTCLIFFE (b1842)
Married **HANNAH MATTHEWS (b1846)**
Their Children:

- Daisy (b1873)
- Mary (b1874)
- Rachael (b1876)
- Tommy (b1879)

The Chugg Family

ALFRED CHUGG (b1815)
Married **JANE WATTS** (b1820)
12 children - one son still living at home: Jimmy Chugg (b1855)

The Rudd Family

BENJAMIN RUDD (b1815)
Married **MATILDA YEO** (b1820)
Their children:

- **HARRY RUDD** (b1851)
- Jacob Rudd (b1855)
- Francis Rudd (b1860)

The Fellwood Family of Hartford Manor

LORD CHARLES FELLWOOD (b1825)
Married: **ELEANOR CHICHESTER** (b1838)
Their Children:

- David Fellwood (b1861)
- Lily Fellwood (1862 – 1864)
- **ROBERT FELLWOOD** (b1863)
- Victoria Fellwood (b1863)
- Sarah Fellwood (b1870)
- Danny (b1880)

CHAPTER 1

A small mouse poked its head out of a hole in the crumbling cob wall and rose to its hind legs. Its grey nose twitched as it sniffed the air cautiously. Finally, satisfied that it was safe, it ventured out and ran across a small mound. Annie stirred as the mouse ran over her foot. Despite being fully dressed, she shivered and snuggled closer to Mary and Emma, for the knitted blankets that covered them were thin and had seen better days. The fire had burned low, and the girl considered fetching some logs but was reluctant to brave the chilly night air. They normally slept upstairs with their four brothers, but tonight it was so cold their mother had brought their mattresses downstairs, closer to the fire.

On another straw mattress, half-hidden under the table, lay Annie's brothers, Willie, John, Edward, and Stephen. They slept top to toe, with Willie and Stephen lying one way and Edward and John the other. Her parents slept on a rickety old bed in the far corner of the room. Her father, Tom Carter, lay on his back, loud rasping snores escaping from his wide-open mouth, and Annie wondered how her mother, Sabina, ever got a wink of sleep.

It was certainly warmer in the kitchen than upstairs, where ice coated the inside of the draughty windows and the thatched roof leaked. It was January, and outside, a fierce blizzard raged across the bleak countryside. As the wind gusted, smoke billowed down the chimney and covered everything in close proximity with fine black soot. Annie slipped quietly from her bed to put three logs onto the fire, for if it went out, it would be bitterly cold in the morning, and there would be no porridge for breakfast.

"What're you doing, Annie? Lie still 'tis cold."

"Ssh, Mary, I'm putting some logs on the fire."

She peered out of the window at the snow that lay knee-deep on the ground. Thank goodness tomorrow's Sunday, she thought; at least there's no school. She snuggled under the blankets and cuddled up to her sister to get warm, but Mary shrank away, not wanting Annie's cold body near her.

"Get away, Annie, you're freezing cold."

"I know; that's why I want to cuddle you." Annie giggled and inched her freezing feet closer to Mary's warm legs.

Eventually, they drifted off to sleep, but suddenly, Annie heard a faint knocking at the door and was immediately wide awake again. She went to wake her father, but he was already at the door, the sudden exertion making him cough, and violent spasms racked his body. He flung open the door and was surprised to see Liza Hammett, one of their neighbours. Her bedraggled grey hair was white with the falling snow, and she was dressed only in a flimsy nightgown; she looked like a ghost. She was shaking violently with the cold.

"Come in, Liza, or you'll die of the cold, and so will we. What brings you here at this time of night?"

He closed the door firmly against the wind, and Sabina put her arm around the old lady.

"What's the matter, Liza? Annie, could you light a candle so we can see? There, that's better. Why Liza, your head's bleeding, and, my goodness, you've no shawl or boots and in this weather too."

Liza swayed, and the blood from a deep cut ran steadily down her ashen face. With wide eyes, she clutched frantically at Sabina and struggled to get her words out.

"Help me. Oh, please, help me. It's Isaac; I think he's dead!"

"What do you mean? Where is he?"

"He's dead! He's dead in his own bed."

Her voice broke into a sob, and tears coursed down the deep furrows in her wrinkled old cheeks, mingling with the fresh blood.

"Perhaps you'd better find out what's happened, Tom?"

Her husband nodded and reached for his coat. By this time, all the children were awake, and Stephen, the youngest, was crying.

"Willie, go with your dad, and I'll put the kettle on. We'll have a hot drink to warm us up in no time."

Stephen clung to her legs, wanting to be picked up. He was not quite two, and the sudden commotion had upset him.

"It's all right, Stevie." She gave him a quick cuddle. "Mary, hold Stevie on your knee; he's frightened."

Sabina passed the little boy to her daughter, then gently sat Liza down, poured a little warm water into a bowl, and bathed her head with a clean rag. It was a large gash, and she bandaged it tightly to stop the bleeding. Liza stared into the distance, seemingly oblivious to everything around her. Sabina made some weak tea, held the cup to Liza's chattering lips, and helped her drink.

"Annie, can you find out what's happening? Here, take my shawl. It's bitter out there."

Annie nodded, wrapped the brown shawl around her head, and gingerly stepped out onto the snow. Ahead of her, Tom and Willie were bent double against the wind, and the snow and hail made their eyes sting. As they neared the cottage, they could see that an old oak tree had fallen onto the roof, and

Tom sent the boy to summon help from the neighbours living close by in the tiny hamlet. The tree was blocking the doorway, so Tom scrambled through the branches to a broken window and cursed as he cut his hand on a jagged bit of glass. He inched his way through and was amazed that Liza had gotten out. Once inside, he mounted the stairs to find the old man and called his name. Even with the lantern, it was difficult to see through the debris, and he was relieved to hear a weak groan and know Isaac was alive.

"It's all right, Isaac. It's Tom, and I'm coming to help you," Tom shouted, to be heard above the storm.

He held the lantern aloft at the top of the stairs and surveyed a scene of terrible destruction. The roof had been crushed like an eggshell, and the massive trunk lay across the bed where the couple had been sleeping. Somehow, it had missed Liza, but Isaac was trapped.

"Don't worry, Isaac; we'll have you out of there in no time. I'll get some help and an axe and be right back."

He stumbled down the stairs and bumped into Willie and several neighbours the boy had roused. Close on their heels was Annie.

"We'll need axes because the tree has crushed the roof, and Isaac's trapped. Willie, go home and tell your Mum we're trying to get Isaac out. Annie, could you go with him and get some bandages?"

The men soon returned with axes and started hacking away at the tree trunk. Armed with rags for bandages, Annie squeezed in beside Isaac and held his hand, though he was unconscious. He had always been kind to her, and she was sorry to see him in such a bad way. The splintered beams in the broken roof creaked ominously in the wind, and Annie watched anxiously as the end wall and chimney swayed dangerously. Tom followed her gaze and pursed his lips.

"Annie, there's nothing you can do for Isaac now he's unconscious. Go back home in the warm, love."

"No, it's all right, Dad. I'll stay and bandage his leg when you get him out."

"We'll have to be quick, Tom," said Sam. "That chimney's going to collapse any minute, and when it does, the rest of the roof will go with it."

For a moment, the men stared in despair at the huge tree trunk that had snapped the beams like matchsticks, and then they began to work frantically. The snow swirled around their wet heads, and, despite the bitter cold, they were soon sweating heavily from their labours. A powerful gust of wind made the chimney sway again, and they sprang back, fearful of being buried alive.

"It's no good; it will take hours to chop through all this, and that wall's going to collapse at any minute. We'll have to take his leg off," said Tom in desperation.

They stared at him in horror.

"Well, what choice is there? We'll all die if that chimney falls, and I don't think his leg will be any use to him now, anyway. It must be crushed under all that lot. Quickly, give me that saw, Francis and you three hold him down in case he comes around. Annie, go home now."

Annie made no move to leave but held the rags ready. Tom glanced at her, noted her grim expression, and briefly nodded; his eldest daughter was made of stern stuff. He removed his scarf and tied a tourniquet around Isaac's upper thigh before placing the teeth of the saw just below his knee.

Isaac began to scream as the rusty saw bit into his soft flesh, and with grim faces, the men ignored his pleas and held him down firmly. They were thankful when he quickly lost consciousness again. Blood spurted stickily warm and red over Annie's hands and arms. It trickled between her fingers, and a scarlet rivulet ran slowly down her white forearm. Soon, the saw began to grind through bone, glistening ominously white in the light of the lantern. Fore and back went the saw in a monotonous rhythm. The men gazed in fascination, each wanting to blot the sight from their eyes and the awful sound from their ears, yet none could tear their eyes away.

Sam retched and vomited all over the bedroom floor, but none of the men jeered as they might have in other circumstances. As the saw sliced through the final bloody tatters of flesh, Annie tied rags tightly around the stump.

"Quickly, Annie, get moving." Tom Carter hurried his daughter down the stairs, then, carrying the man's bleeding body, they followed her just as the chimney creaked loudly and slowly collapsed, and with it, much of the roof. They crouched in the stairwell, covered in dust and debris, coughing as they tried to clear their lungs, knowing they had cheated death by seconds.

"Where shall we take him?"

"To my house; Liza's there already. There's nothing more we can do here tonight; we'll take a better look in daylight."

The men draped a sack over their neighbour's cold body and carried him to Tom's house, where they laid him gently on the bed. Sabina stared in horror at the blood-soaked rags and put her hand to her mouth.

"We had no choice, love, it was that, or leave him there; the roof and chimney collapsed and only just missed us as it was." Tom's face was grim.

Isaac's leg was bleeding heavily, and the wound was dirty from the rusty saw. Annie helped Sabina to wash off the dirt and bandage it tightly. The old man's face was the colour of parchment, sweat glistened on his forehead, and his breathing was shallow. Liza sat beside him, weeping silently.

"Annie put some pillows under his thigh. Perhaps if we raise his leg, the bleeding may stop."

They used every bit of cloth they could find, binding the stump tightly, and eventually, the bleeding slowed, though whether this was from their efforts at staunching it or because Isaac had none left was debatable. From the colour of his face, it was more likely to be the latter. The children gazed at the bloody mess in shocked silence. The fire was burning merrily thanks to Annie's earlier efforts, and Tom sat near it to warm himself.

"Annie, make your father some kettle broth, please, and you children, get back into bed and try to get some sleep. Liza, you get in bed beside Isaac to warm him."

Annie crumbled pieces of stale bread into a bowl, added a large lump of dripping, salt and pepper, and poured boiling water over it. She handed it to her father, who tiredly ruffled her hair in thanks.

"Are you all right, Tom?" Sabina whispered, touching his hand. Her husband, though not yet forty, was a sick man. His consumptive cough was worsening, and he'd been coughing up blood for some months, though he tried to hide it.

"Aye, I'm just tired and cold, but it's nearly dawn, and there'll be no more sleep tonight, so I'll turn into work early. We'll inspect the cottage later and shift that tree because it's blocking the lane. Why don't you get a bit more sleep here in the chair, love?"

He kissed her on the lips, and she drew him to her and held him close. He released her gently, and she felt despair wash over her. They had been happily married for sixteen years, but she had seen enough people die of consumption to know it was only a matter of time before he would be taken from her.

Picking his way across the crowded room, Tom grabbed his coat and stepped out into the snow, which lay deep on the ground. His feet sank into it until he was almost up to his knees, and within minutes, he could barely feel his feet. There was a hard frost, and long, glassy icicles hung like transparent swords from the thatched roofs. An eerie silence engulfed the countryside.

CHAPTER 2

Many local men were employed as agricultural labourers and allowed to live rent-free in tied farm cottages. The cottages that belonged to the Hartford Estate were a couple of miles from the village and half a mile from the Manor House itself. The estate covered over two thousand acres, divided into four farms. The home farm was the largest, with around eight hundred acres, and the other farms were smaller and rented out to tenant farmers.

Other men from the hamlet worked as lime burners at the three limekilns on the estate. The kilns provided a ready supply of lime, and a constant veil of smoke smothered the countryside. The quicklime was used as a dressing for the land and was in much demand on Exmoor, where the soil was too acidic to be fertile. Lime burning was a hazardous business, and not just because of the dangerous fumes. A crust would form across the top of the kiln and have to be broken before more stone could be tipped in. Folk still remembered, with horror, what had happened to old Walter Berry just a few years ago. Walter had worked as a lime burner for donkey's years and was in the habit of stepping onto the crust to break it with his feet. Unfortunately, he did this once too often and sank waist-deep into the hot coals. He was dragged out, horribly burnt, and wheeled home on a cart. Little could be done for the poor man other than ply him with copious amounts of alcohol to distract him from the pain until he died in agony a few days later.

It was a close-knit community, and families helped each other as best they could, for times were hard. The weather had been harsh in recent years, with cold, wet summers and severe winters. Harvests had been poor, and many country folk had moved to the towns, seeking work to avoid starvation. All the cottagers shared a large well, but, at present, it was frozen, so water had to be carried from the stream or snow melted in buckets by the fire.

As Tom left home on that bleak winter's morning, he was joined by the other men who had helped him free Isaac Hammett just an hour or two earlier.

"Hello, lads; I'm afraid poor Isaac's seriously injured. I'd fetch Dr Luckett, but I doubt the Hammetts would have the money to pay him, and he'd struggle to get here with all this snow."

"I'm sure Sabina will do her best for him, Tom. What a night; it will be difficult to shift that tree later," said Sam.

Tom was fond of Sam, who lived with his wife, Esther, and family at number three. The couple was in their late twenties and had four surviving children, having lost a baby to whooping cough a few years earlier. Esther was pregnant again, though they could ill afford another mouth to feed.

"Did Willie try to wake John Cutcliffe last night?" asked Sam.

"He tried but couldn't get an answer, though he could hear the children coughing and crying. I reckon John and Hannah were drunk. What do you think?"

The men laughed, and as they were passing John Cutcliffe's cottage, Tom hammered on the door. After some minutes, Hannah answered. She was about forty, with a sallow complexion and lank, dirty hair speckled with nits. She squinted against the brightness of the lantern with bloodshot eyes.

"Hello, lads, I've been trying to get him out of bed, but maybe you can get the lazy sod to move."

Tom turned his head slightly to avoid her rancid breath as the men stifled their amusement. Reluctantly, he entered the filthy cottage. The stench of unwashed bodies, stale cooking smells, and animal faeces was overpowering as he went to the bed and shook John roughly.

"Come on, man, get up. The master will sack you if you're late again, and he'll have you out of this cottage in no time. Come on, move."

John opened his bleary eyes and peered over the covers. He was a lazy, unpleasant man who had tempted fate more than once by being too drunk to work. He groaned as he rolled out of bed, staggered against the table, and drew on his coat. He fell over a chicken on his way to the door, and it flew into a corner, squawking indignantly. Reeking of cider, he shielded his eyes from the brightness of the lantern and, stepping outside, shivered as he surveyed the wintry scene before him. Tom had no time for the man, for he spent what little money he earned gambling and drinking whilst his children went hungry. His wife, Hannah, was little better, but Tom had some sympathy for her because she led a hard life, often sporting a black eye or a fat lip when she had got on the wrong side of her husband. As they trudged through the frozen snow, they told John what had happened in the night.

"Liza's all right, but we had to saw Isaac's leg off to get him out, poor man. You must have slept soundly last night, John; we couldn't get an answer from you," said Sam, grinning.

"Oh, I've got an awful cough, and I needed a drop of Scrumpy to get any sleep at all. You didn't really take off his leg, did you?"

"I'm afraid we did." Tom grimaced. "We didn't want to, but we had no choice, and the poor man's lost a lot of blood. I hope he'll pull through, but if not, at least he'll die in a warm bed with Liza beside him."

They reached the Hammett's cottage and were shocked at the sight before them. Little remained of the roof, which had been in poor repair even before the storm, and it was amazing anyone had gotten out alive. The snow would have soaked the cob walls of the bedroom by now, and maybe even the downstairs room. Most Devon cottages were built of cob, a mixture of mud, clay, straw, and water, and kept dry, they would last for hundreds of years, but it was not good for it to get too wet. With heavy hearts, the men hurried to the farm to start their day's work.

Tom and Sam were farm labourers, and, with three milkmaids to help them, they milked the sixty-odd cows morning and night. The milk was sold in the village or made into butter and cheese. John busied himself cleaning out the shippens, and when the milking was finished, Tom and Sam helped him. The dung steamed in the cold air as they transported it in wheelbarrows to the dung heap to rot down until it could be spread on the fields in the spring. The exertion of the heavy work made Tom breathless, and he had a bout of coughing, which brought tears to his eyes. Quickly, he wiped away the blood he had coughed up as a grey-haired man in his early fifties approached the men.

"Morning, lads. Rough last night, wasn't it? I'm glad the wind has died down, but I wish it would warm up a bit. I don't like this cold weather."

"Morning, Jack. I'm glad you've come along because we need a word."

Jack Bater was the estate manager and lived with his wife and six children in a cottage on the grounds of the Manor House. He had held the position for over twenty years and was highly respected, for he always treated the men fairly. Tom leaned on his shovel for a moment and eased his aching back.

"I'm afraid there was an accident last night, Jack. That huge oak tree in the hamlet blew down and crushed the roof of Isaac Hammett's cottage. Luckily, Liza escaped unharmed, but Isaac was trapped, and we had to saw off his leg to get him out!"

"Oh no, that's terrible. Will he be all right?"

"I don't know; he's in a bad way, and he and Liza are at my place at the moment. The thing is, Jack, the tree is huge, and it's blocking the lane to the Manor House. There's a lot of damage to the cottage, too."

"If that's the case, I'd better get extra help to move the tree. As it's a Sunday, the kiln isn't burning today, so there are a few men there we can call on. The master won't like it if he can't get out in the carriage."

The workforce Jack had assembled surveyed the fallen tree. Its upturned roots rose eight feet in the air, leaving a massive crater in the frozen ground. They sawed the branches, making a big pile of firewood, and used the farm horses to drag large sections of the trunk into a field. Eventually, they were able to assess the extensive damage to the cottage. The roof would need to be rebuilt, and the cob walls were soaking wet. They draped tarpaulins over what little remained of the roof to keep out the worst of the weather. However, the downstairs room was untouched, and if Liza Hammett kept the door to the stairs closed, she could safely live there until the roof was repaired.

Tom went home for his tea before starting the evening milking, and Sabina met him at the door and whispered to him.

"I'm afraid Isaac isn't going to make it, Tom. He's gasping for breath, and his lips are blue. Liza's not left his side, but he hasn't come around since last night. Anyway, come in and get warm, and eat this pasty I've made for you. You don't look well, yourself."

"Oh dear, I was afraid that might happen. I'm all right; I'm just tired, but I think I'll go right on and do the milking and give Liza some space. I'd rather finish before I sit down, or I won't want to get up again. Thanks for the pasty, love; I'll take it with me."

By the time Tom returned home, Isaac Hammett had died. They carried his body to the dilapidated cottage and laid it on a sheet on the floor to await burial, for it was not possible to put it in the devastated bedroom. Liza insisted on going with the body, so with some relief, Sabina turned her attention to her own family.

CHAPTER 3

Isaac Hammett had worked on the estate for seventy-odd years, man and boy, and was in his eighties when he died. For most of his life, he had worked as a miner, for the Hartford Estate also boasted its own silver mine and was reputed to have supplied the wherewithal to finance the wars with France. It was claimed Charles I had once visited the village and that the Crown Jewels had Hartford silver in them. The mine had been in existence for many years but had been worked intermittently, as flooding was a serious problem. The silver-lead was rich, but the veins did not run in long lodes. After a lapse of several years, the mine had reopened fourteen years earlier and was now making enough profit to employ fifty men and several children. Isaac's extensive knowledge of the mine had been invaluable in getting the mine up and running again.

Isaac and Liza had no living relatives and had struggled to survive in their old age, relying largely on the goodwill of their neighbours. Isaac had eked out an existence as a rat catcher and odd-job man for the last few years when he became too old and weak to go down the mine. The neighbours wondered what would now become of Liza, for no doubt, the tied cottage would be required for a new worker.

Over the next few days, the weather was so cold the Carter children could not play outside, and the small cottage was cramped. They had few toys, and what they did have were homemade. Sabina and Tom had little spare time as they worked long hours, but both were creative and had put their talents to good use. Sabina had sewn pieces of fabric around a few wooden clothes pegs and made them into tiny dolls. First Annie, and then Mary and Emma, had played with the five dolls for hours, and now, with the weather so bad, out they came again. Tom fashioned toys from bits of wood and made a boat and two trains that Willie, John, Edward, and Stephen played with. Sabina had also sewn material into a ball as tightly as possible and stuffed it with sawdust. All the children loved playing catch with it, so Sabina often had to sew up split seams. Ethel Potts, the cook at Hartford Manor, had given Tom a game of snakes and ladders and a pack of cards for the children. Both games were old and worn, but the Carter family treasured them and spent many hours playing Happy Families or throwing the dice and going up the ladders and sliding down the snakes.

The village school was two miles from the hamlet, and, to the children's delight, it was closed for the week because of the snow. Isaac Hammett's funeral had also been delayed because the ground was frozen too hard to dig a grave, but eventually, the weather warmed, and Benjamin Rudd, the village blacksmith, offered to transport the coffin on his cart.

Sabina had agreed to let the children have a kitten to catch the rats and mice that plagued the cottagers, and Alfred Chugg, a tenant farmer, had offered to let them take their pick of his cat's litter. On Friday morning, as there was no school, Annie took her siblings to Hollyford Farm to do just that. It was a long walk on a cold morning, but the children were glad to get out after being cooped up in the house. The melting snow had made the lanes muddy, and by the time they arrived at the farm, their hands and feet were wet and frozen. Alfred met them in the yard.

"Hello, come to choose a kitten then, have you? Well, you won't know which one to pick, I'll wager."

Alfred was a kindly man who was fond of children, and he took Edward by the hand and led them into the big barn. "My goodness, young man, your little hands are like ice. You must go inside and warm them before you go home."

A large tabby cat called Minnie and five little kittens with big blue eyes were nestled in the straw. They mewed softly as the children picked them up, and as Alfred had suspected, they took some time making up their minds.

"Let's have this one, John," pleaded Emma, cuddling a black kitten with a white nose and paws. Emma was six years old and had straight blond hair and clear grey eyes. She was a kind and caring little girl, and Sabina always thought she seemed older than her years.

"No, I like this one," said John, a wriggling ginger specimen in his arms. John was eight, with bright red hair like his elder sister, Annie, and sometimes he had a temper to match. "Mary, which one do you like?"

Nine-year-old Mary was cuddling another kitten with ginger and white markings. "I don't know. It's so difficult. I'd like to have them all."

"What about you, Edward? Which one do you like?" Alfred asked.

Edward was a handsome little boy of four with blond curls and blue eyes, but he completely ignored Alfred and seemed to be in a world of his own.

"He won't answer you, Mr Chugg. He never speaks, and Mum thinks he's deaf."

Emma joined in rather indignantly to defend her little brother. "Well, he may be deaf, but he's not stupid."

"No, of course, he isn't, but if that's the case, shall we let Edward pick the kitten?"

The old man could see the selection process could take all day, and he didn't want any squabbles.

"Oh, all right then." Mary, John, and Emma nodded. "We like them all, anyway."

Alfred was relieved and somewhat surprised at their agreement. He knelt and faced Edward.

"Which one do you like, Ed?" He pointed to the kittens.

Edward hesitated, then pointed to the lively ginger kitten that John had also favoured.

"Do you like that one, Mary and Emma?"

They hesitated, looking longingly at all the other kittens.

"He is lovely; yes, all right then, we'll have that one, please, Mr Chugg."

"Right, now, this is a little tomcat, and I need to see to him before you take him away to make sure he doesn't wander off when you get home. You go and see Mrs Chugg because she's been baking all morning, and I reckon she'd be that pleased if you would sample her cakes and biscuits. You'd be helping me out, too, because she always makes too many, and my belly's big enough already. Perhaps you'd like a cup of milk as well?"

"Oh yes, please; thanks, Mr Chugg." The four children scampered off happily to the kitchen for this unexpected treat.

Alfred quickly neutered the kitten. "Sorry, kitty, but we don't need you fathering any more cats. Annie, you go and eat too; there's nothing to you but skin and bone."

The path to the farmhouse was lined with snowdrops, just peeping through the melting snow, and a black and white collie sat outside the back door. Its tail thumped the ground enthusiastically as Annie bent to pat him. She knocked on the door timidly, and a voice from within bade her enter. Warmth and delicious smells assailed her senses and made her stomach rumble.

"Hello, Annie, what a pleasant surprise; I didn't know you were here too. What a pretty girl you're growing into. Come and sit down my dear, and have a mug of nice hot, creamy milk and a couple of my cakes. It'll stop me from eating them all."

"Thank you, Mrs Chugg, but I don't want to put you to any trouble, and I hope they've been minding their manners." Annie looked sternly at her siblings, who were cramming food into their mouths.

"Edward, John, stop putting so much food into your mouths; what will Mrs Chugg think of you?"

"Now, don't you worry, lass, they're just hungry lads who don't get much to eat. You can't blame them for making the most of an opportunity, now can you? Come on; you do the same. How are your mum and dad?"

Annie nodded, her own mouth now full of cake. "Dad's been poorly all week, and I know Mum's worried about him. He has a terrible cough, and Mum would like him to take a few days off work to rest, but he can't afford to. The rest of us are fine, though, thank you. This cake is delicious, Mrs Chugg."

"Well, have another piece, my dear. Alfred said you were coming this morning, so I did some baking. I love seeing hungry children eat, and most of my lot have left home now. Twelve I had, and they're all gone now, except Jimmy, and I can't seem to get rid of him, though he's nearly thirty-five. It's high time he found himself a wife, but I don't want him to go if the truth be known. I'm sorry to hear your dad's poorly; please tell him I hope he gets better soon. Which kitten did you pick?"

Whilst the children told Mrs Chugg about the kitten, Annie glanced around her. It was a comfortable room, and it smelt of polish. Against one wall was an old oak dresser; the wood blackened with age, and Annie thought it must have been there a long time. Its shelves were laden with fine china, painted in beautiful colours, and pewter tankards and plates. The floor was made of roughly hewn flagstones, covered with plentiful homemade rag rugs, making the room warm and cosy. The table was at least seven feet long, and the wooden surface was scrubbed so clean it was almost white. In her mind's eye, Annie pictured the twelve children sitting around it in years gone by. On the far wall was the cooking range where a fire was burning, and on the top were two huge black pots, one containing some stew and the other scraps for the pigs and chickens. To one side was a pile of logs, and on the other, a wooden crate containing two lambs. Mrs Chugg saw Annie looking at them.

"Their poor mother died giving birth, so I'm their mother now. Would you like to feed them?"

The children soon took turns feeding the lambs with bottles. Their short tails wagged as they sucked hungrily at the teat until every last drop was gone.

"Have your mum and dad gone to Isaac Hammett's funeral today?"

"Dad's gone, but Mum's looking after several children so others can go."

"What a sad business. Now, are you all full up?"

"Thank you so much, Mrs Chugg; the food was lovely. I'm not surprised Jimmy doesn't want to leave home."

"Take the rest of those cakes home with you, Annie, and there's a loaf of bread, too. I know times are hard."

Alfred handed them an old potato sack containing the ginger kitten as they left.

"Now, he'll cry for a day or two because he'll miss his mother, but rub his paws with some butter, and he'll soon settle down and be catching rats and mice. His mother's a brilliant ratter. What are you going to call him?"

It came as no surprise when they decided upon Ginger.

On the way home, they encountered the funeral procession. The cart carrying the coffin skirted the large snowdrifts as it trundled through the mud towards the church. A crowd followed, for everyone had known old Isaac and wanted to pay their respects and support Liza. Most wore everyday clothes as they had no others, but a few had put on their Sunday best.

Poor Ginger, in much discomfort in the sack, was letting everybody know about it, and as the children slowly followed the mourners, the cat repeatedly meowed loudly. This amused one or two villagers, and try as they might, they couldn't keep a straight face. Their shoulders shook as they tried to stifle their mirth. They struggled to compose themselves, for not in the world would they wish to be disrespectful, but they knew Isaac would have seen the funny side, too. The children did their best to keep the cat quiet but to no avail, and the poor creature meowed and howled for all its worth. At last, the coffin was carried shoulder-high into the church, and the children continued on home, leaving Isaac Hammett to be laid to rest with some decorum.

CHAPTER 4

In the early hours of Sunday morning, exactly a week after the great tree had been blown down, Sabina awoke suddenly. At first, she didn't know what had disturbed her but quickly became aware of a strange rattling noise by her side. She turned to Tom anxiously and, placing her hand on his brow, found it was sticky with sweat. His breath was coming in painful gasps, and his face was pale in the dim glow of the fire. She dampened a cloth to cool his fevered brow.

"Tom, are you all right?" She tried to rouse him, but he was delirious with a fever.

"'It's all right, Liza, you go home, and we'll get him out." He tossed his head from side to side. "No, not like that! Mind what you're doing, man."

The exertion made him cough violently, and Sabina pulled him onto his side to clear his lungs. At once, he coughed up blood and phlegm, and she mopped it up quickly as if removing it from sight would make it not have happened. She brought a candle nearer to the bed and sat holding his hand and mopping his brow until eventually he opened his eyes.

"Oh, Sabina," he whispered, drew her hand to his lips, and kissed it gently.

"Tom, save your strength to get well."

"I'm afraid my days are numbered, Sabina, and you know it too, don't you? Don't lie to me. If it's not today, it will be soon, won't it?"

She bowed her head, and the tears dripped unchecked onto his hand. He put his finger under her chin, raised her head, and looked at her questioningly.

"I'm afraid it may be so, Tom, but no one knows for sure, and if anyone can get better, you can."

"I love you so much, Sabina. I've always loved you, ever since you were a little girl with pigtails, even when I used to pull them." He smiled at her. "Now, don't you ever forget me, but marry again as soon as you can because you'll need someone to take care of you. Promise me, Sabina?"

"Never, Tom, there'll never be anyone else for me."

"Promise me, Sabina; you'll have to be mum and dad to our lot when I'm gone, and that won't be easy, so I'm the lucky one. It's you I'm leaving with all the worry. I'm sorry things aren't better between Father and me, but even so, I think he'll help you. Take his help if it keeps you out of the workhouse, and remember, it's no time for pride. Now climb back in here and cuddle me. No, don't kiss me; I don't want you catching it."

"Oh, Tom, if I'm going to get it, I've got it already."

She kissed him firmly on the lips and cuddled up to him as he put his arm around her. She held him tightly as they drifted off to sleep, and the candle had burned low when she awoke. By her side, Tom was quiet, and she hoped the fever had passed. However, she quickly realised it was not the fever but his life itself that was over. Sabina clung to his still-warm body for some minutes, knowing these were the last precious moments she would ever spend with her husband. Silently, she sobbed into his shirt as if her heart would break, then forced herself to release him and calmly wiped her tears as she left his side. She paused momentarily, looking at his thin, handsome face, thinking how peaceful he looked, almost like a young boy again. Gently, she covered him with a sheet and busied herself with the day's tasks.

When the children awoke, Sabina sat them in a row and faced them solemnly.

"I need you to be brave for me today." Her voice trembled, and she had to force herself to look them in the eye, but she knew she must be strong. "Poor Daddy died in the night. He was sick, and his chest hurt, but he's at peace now and not suffering anymore."

The children became round-eyed, and their attention strayed to the bed, where their father's body lay covered with a sheet.

"He will get better again, though, won't he? He will wake up one day, won't he?" said Emma.

"Course he won't, stupid," Willie snapped angrily. "She's just told you he's dead, like Isaac Hammett. He won't ever be coming back. He'll be buried six feet down in the churchyard."

Sabina knew Willie spoke harshly because he was so upset. "Ssh Willie, don't talk to her like that; she's only a little girl, and she doesn't understand. Willie's right, though, Emma. Daddy won't be coming back; he's gone to Heaven to live with Jesus. He didn't want to leave us, but Jesus needed him there. Daddy wanted you to know how much he loved you and hoped you'd be good children for me."

She gathered the children around her and hugged them, unable to say more for several minutes. "Go and play for a while now because I must tell Granny and Grandad and arrange the funeral."

Tears flowed steadily down Annie's cheeks. "Oh, Mum, I'm so sorry." For a few moments, the two women clung to each other. "What'll we do, Mum, and where will we live? We'll have to leave the cottage, won't we?"

"I don't know, Annie, but let's get your dad buried, and then we'll worry about it. Keep an eye on the children, will you? There are things I need to do."

Sabina put her shawl over her head and set off to see Tom's parents, Ned and Betsey, who kept The Red Lion Inn. The Carter family had lived there for generations, and Ned had inherited the inn from his father. It was a traditional Devon inn with a thatched roof and thick cob walls. The windows were small, making it rather dark inside but pleasantly cool on a hot day and cosy in winter when a log fire would be burning brightly. It had once been three small cottages, but many years ago, they had been converted into an inn. The floor was paved with rough flagstones, and the walls were lime-washed. In addition to providing ale and cider, the inn offered pasties, stew, and bread and cheese and was popular with travellers on their way to Exeter and London.

Ned Carter was a bit of a character with a finger in many pies. He did a bit of blacksmithing and market gardening and, if the opportunity arose, was not above dealing in contraband smuggled from France. Tom was one of five children and the fourth in line. His eldest sister was Eveline, who was still a spinster at forty-three. In her twenties, she had been betrothed to a young man, but he was killed in a mining accident, and she had shown no interest in a man since. She lived at the inn with her parents and worked in the village shop owned by her brother, George, the next in line.

George was forty-one and married to Alice. They ran a grocery shop, which his father had financed. The shop was doing nicely, and George had just expanded the business to sell clothes. His sister-in-law, Mary Ann, also worked in the shop. George was a hard worker, intent on making money, but also religious, and he taught in the Sunday school at the Baptist Chapel. He was on the parish Board of Guardians and was heavily involved in managing the workhouse and distributing poor relief. He was teetotal and abhorred drunkenness, which was somewhat at odds with his father's profession. George and Alice had three surviving children, Harriet, Francis, and Theresa, for young Alfred had perished from influenza at the age of four.

Next in the Carter family came Fred. He was a carpenter, married to Lucy, and they had three children: Llewellyn, six, Rosella, four, and a new baby called Eddie. Two other babies were born after Rosella, but sadly, they only lived a few weeks.

Ned had not wanted Tom to marry Sabina, who was from a large and impoverished family. Her father was a lime burner, and though a hard worker, with eleven children to support, the family lived at a subsistence level.

Ned and Betsey were considered well-to-do and had set George up with his shop and arranged for Fred to learn his trade as a carpenter. Fred was now fully qualified and considering taking on an apprentice of his own, but all Tom had ever wanted to do was farm work. Ned had tried to dissuade him because the pay was so poor, but Tom had been determined on both counts and had married Sabina as soon as he was twenty-one and took a job on the Hartford estate as this provided him with a tied cottage. The relationship between Tom and his parents had remained a little strained ever since, and Tom had soon discovered that his father was right and life was hard as a farm labourer, but he had vowed never to ask for help.

Ned and Betsey's youngest son, William, was even more wayward than his brother, Tom, and something of the black sheep of the family. He had run off to sea at fifteen, and his parents had heard nothing from him for many years. They had given him up for dead when they finally received a letter from him some five years after his departure. He was happily settled in China and working for the Imperial Maritime Customs Office. William had been bright at school and soon discovered that a sailor's life was not for him, but he was now doing well for himself.

Sabina hated to be the bearer of such devastating news, and when Betsey opened the door, she immediately guessed it was not a social call that had brought her daughter-in-law to see her.

"Hello, Betsey; I'm afraid I have some terrible news."

"Come in, Sabina; it's lovely to see you. There's nothing wrong with Tom or the children, is there?" Betsey anxiously eyed the younger woman's tear-stained face.

"Oh, Betsey, I'm so sorry, but Tom died in the night."

Sabina suddenly sobbed, and to her annoyance, tears ran down her cheeks once again.

Betsey went pale, and Sabina took her arm and led her to a chair.

"Oh no, he was no age, not even forty; why didn't you tell us he was so ill?"

"He's been poorly for a long time, and nothing could be done. He tried to hide it, but he's been coughing up blood for months, though I think he died of pneumonia."

"I must fetch Ned; he's outside chopping wood. Stay there a minute, and I'll pull the kettle forward, and we'll have a cup of tea."

Betsey returned with her husband, who looked shocked and upset.

"I wish he'd let us help, Sabina, but he would work on that estate, and his silly pride wouldn't let him take any help from me. Living in that damp, draughty old cottage, it's no wonder he had consumption."

Sabina wondered if that help would have been forthcoming, but when she saw the deep sorrow in his eyes, she realised it would have been.

"Well, he was independent and liked to manage on his own."

"Yes, I know he did, and some of it was my fault. I'll be honest, lass, I didn't want him to marry you; I felt he could do better, and I certainly didn't want him working as a farm labourer for a pittance. One thing I will admit, though, and that is you've been a good wife to him, so I'll thank you for making my son so happy."

"Thank you. That means a lot to me, and it would have meant the world to Tom."

"Come on, let's have this tea and Sabina, I hope you'll let us help with the funeral. We will, won't we, Ned?"

"Yes, of course. We'll see our lad properly buried with a decent send-off. Is that all right, Sabina?"

"Yes, thank you, Ned, I'd appreciate that. It's kind of you."

"Leave it all to us, then; you've enough to do with the children. I'll speak to the vicar about the funeral and ask our Fred to make a coffin, and we'll put on a spread here afterwards. The family needs to get together and support each other at a time like this."

"That's kind of you, thank you. I know Tom would like Sam Symons to be a bearer; they were good friends."

"Of course, and maybe George and Fred? If only William were here, he could have been the fourth. Do you have anyone else in mind? We could ask George's son, Francis; he's eighteen."

"I'd like to ask my brother, Charlie. He and Tom were fond of each other."

"Yes, that'll be fine, won't it, Ned?"

"Aye, of course. I'll see you later, Sabina, when I know what's happening. How are the children?"

"I don't think they've quite taken it in yet."

"What will you do? I doubt Charles Fellwood will let you stay in the cottage. He'll want it for another worker."

"I don't know yet, Ned. I'll have to speak to Jack Bater and see what he says. I need to get through the next few days and get Tom buried, and then I'll think about it."

"Quite right, don't bother the girl with that now, Ned. There will be time enough to sort all that out after the funeral."

Sabina walked home along the snowy road, wondering what they would do. Most likely, they would soon be homeless, with no money. Her parents would want to help, but they still had six children living at home, and there would be no room for Sabina and her seven to move in. Her biggest fear was the workhouse, where she would be parted from her children, but she pushed that thought firmly to the back of her mind and resolved to get through the next few days first.

By mid-morning, all the neighbours had heard the terrible news of Tom's death. He'd been a popular man, and the community was shocked, for although he had been ill with consumption, the end had come unexpectedly swiftly. One of Sabina's first visitors was Liza Hammett. In her seventies, Liza had not yet resolved her own future, for although Jack Bater, the estate manager, had said she could live in her cottage for another month, it would then be required for a new labourer. Her neighbours were kind but too poor to help, and she had seriously considered hanging herself rather than face the workhouse.

"I'm so sorry for your loss, Sabina. No doubt Tom caught his death of cold rescuing Isaac, and then he died anyway; if we could bring Tom back, I'd gladly go in his place. Now, I have something to say, and you can take it or leave it, but we're both in trouble, and I'm sure you don't fancy the workhouse any more than I do. What if I moved in here and looked after the children? You could do Tom's milking, and perhaps Annie and Willie could help you with his other jobs. I'm old but could do a few jobs and mind the babies, and I don't eat much."

"I don't know what to say, Liza. It's hard work minding children, and you've had none of your own."

"No, more's the pity, but I had fifteen brothers and sisters in Wales, and I was the eldest, so there isn't much I don't know about raising children."

"Oh, I had no idea, Liza, but can't any of them take you in? Surely they would?"

"No, I wouldn't ask. They didn't all survive, and I haven't seen the others for forty years or more. Anyway, you and I have always been friends, and this could be a solution for both of us; sleep on it and let me know."

Sabina bit her lip thoughtfully. "It doesn't take much thinking about, Liza. If Jack will let me keep Tom's job, we could give it a try, but it depends on what he says. He knows I'm reliable because I worked for him before I had the children."

"That's good enough for me, and I'm truly sorry you've lost Tom, Sabina. At least Isaac had a long and happy life, but no man should die in his thirties."

CHAPTER 5

Tom's coffin was carried on his father's horse and cart. At the church gate, the oak coffin was hoisted shoulder-high by Sam Symons, Tom's brothers, George and Fred, and Sabina's brother, Charlie, and, thankfully, this time, no kitten was serenading the cortege. The church was packed as people in the village paid their respects. Annie, Willie, Mary, and John attended, but Emma, Edward, and Stephen stayed home with Liza. The children were upset, particularly Annie, who, as his first-born, had been something of a favourite of Tom's, though he would never have admitted it, and she couldn't imagine life without her dad.

At the end of the service, the Reverend Rees announced that refreshments would be served at The Red Lion Inn, and everyone would be welcome. This was a generous offer from Ned, as none would pass up the opportunity of a free meal. Once word spread, some who didn't even attend the funeral arrived at the inn, anyway. Consequently, the inn was packed, and many a tale was told of the virtues of Tom Carter. All agreed he would be sorely missed, and many wondered what would become of Sabina and her children.

Sabina approached her brother-in-law, Fred, who had made Tom's coffin. Of the entire Carter family, she liked Fred the best, for he had always been friendly.

"Hello, Fred. Thank you for making the coffin."

"It was nothing, Sabina. I was pleased to do it for Tom; I'll miss him."

"Is Lucy here today?"

"No, she's at home with the children. She's not herself, I'm afraid. Eddie's three months old now, but it always takes her a while to get right after she's had a baby."

"I'm sorry to hear that, Fred, but many women get a bit down after having a baby. The 'baby blues' Tilly Rudd always calls it. Every time I have a baby, by the third day, I usually sit crying my eyes out, and I've no idea why. She says the shock of the milk coming in makes the mother miserable for some reason. It's never lasted more than a day or two with me, but it must be awful to still feel like that three months on."

"Yes, a few others have told me that, but Lucy wasn't herself after Llew and Rosie either, and worse still, after Alfie and Grace. She takes no interest in the baby and does nothing around the house. With Alfie and then Grace dying when they were a few weeks old, I wonder if she's afraid of getting too fond of Eddie, in case he dies too."

"Yes, I suppose that could be it, but perhaps if he continues to thrive, she'll feel better soon."

"I certainly hope so. At least her mother's staying with us for a few days to help. Lucy doesn't even feed the baby unless someone makes her do it, and I've got to work. Her mother can't stay long, though, because she's got her own family to care for."

"Oh, that's good. Having her mum around is probably just what Lucy needs."

"I'm hoping my mum might have Llew and Rosie here at the inn for a while, and possibly the baby too, though that would mean feeding him with a bottle. Anyway, you don't want to listen to my troubles today of all days; you've enough to worry about."

"That doesn't mean mine are the only troubles in the world, Fred."

"I keep telling Lucy to pull herself together, but she just looks right through me as if I'm not there, and I swear she doesn't hear a word I say."

"That's awful and a real worry for you, Fred. I could come and see her if you like. Perhaps she'd talk to me; after all, I've had seven of my own."

"I'd be grateful if you could, Sabina. She's always liked you, so perhaps she'd talk to you."

"I'll come by in a few days, then. Keep your chin up."

She scanned the room to check on her children. She had drummed it into them that she expected their best behaviour today, and they had not disappointed her.

George was the family member that Sabina liked the least, and to her dismay, she saw him approaching. He was so fortunate to have been set up in a shop by his father. It was true he had worked hard to make the business a success, but he did not seem to realise how lucky he was to have been given the opportunity. He had never wanted for anything and yet had no compassion for the poor.

"I'm sorry about Tom, Sabina. I didn't realise he was so poorly."

"Thank you, George. Tom was never one to make a fuss."

"No, quite so. I must ask, though, did he make any provision for you and the children? I mean, what are you going to do now?"

This was the question on everyone's lips, but no one else had liked to ask on the day of her husband's funeral.

"No, he never earned enough to save much, but I'm going to get today over and then decide what to do."

"I hardly like to suggest this at such a time, Sabina, but you might be able to get a position in service, possibly Annie and Mary, too. I believe there's a vacancy at Hartford Manor as we speak, and I could ask around if it would help. Willie, too, could probably earn his way. How old is he, ten or eleven? He might get work down the silver mine; he's old enough. Yes, I think all of you might earn enough to get by, but I suppose where to live will be difficult. No doubt you'll have to give up the cottage for another farm worker. The other problem, of course, will be the little ones. Now, I remember there's John and Emma, but I'm afraid the names of your two youngest quite escape me. I know it's a hard thing to do, but have you considered putting them in the workhouse? Just until you're in a position to have them back, of course. I could help you arrange everything quietly if you'd like me to?"

"I can assure you, George, that the last thing I intend to happen is for any of my children to go to the workhouse, or the mine, for that matter, but don't worry, I shan't be asking you for anything. Tom would surely turn in his grave if I did. Just because you don't drink and go to church every Sunday, you seem to think that makes you better than most. You've always turned your nose up at my family, poor as they are, but they would give me their last crust rather than see me and mine end up in the workhouse. Oh, and by the way, your youngest nephews are Edward and Stephen."

"There's no need to take that tone; I was only trying to help. I feel some responsibility for you because Tom was my brother, but there's no need to be so rude."

George was now as red in the face as Sabina, and several people turned their heads to see what was happening. Hearing the angry voices, Betsey glanced over anxiously and asked if everything was all right.

"Yes, fine, thank you," muttered Sabina. "George has kindly offered to help me find a position for Willie down the mine and for my little ones to go into the workhouse. You know how public-spirited he is, and clearly, nothing is too good for his nieces and nephews, though he can't even remember their names."

"George, what are you thinking of to talk of such things when we've barely laid Tom in the ground? Now, Sabina, don't upset yourself; we'll sort something out between us." Betsey put a kindly arm around her daughter-in-law. "Come and get some food; you must eat."

"Thank you, but I've suddenly lost my appetite."

Her brother, Charlie, came over. He was the only one of her own family at the funeral, for they lived some miles away, and several were suffering from influenza.

"What's going on? Sabina, are you all right?"

"Yes, I'm all right, but I've had enough for one day, and I'm going home. You stay a bit longer, Charlie, if you want to. Come on, children, it's time we were going. Thank you for organising the funeral, Betsey, and putting on this spread, but I must get home now."

She gathered Annie, Willie, Mary, and John to her, and they left an uncomfortable silence behind them. Charlie followed her.

"Oh, Mum, did we have to go so soon? I could have eaten a lot more yet."

"Ssh John," said Annie, "you had plenty to eat, so don't bother Mum now. You can see she's upset."

George, too, was far from happy following this exchange, for as soon as Sabina had left, his mother rounded on him and berated him for his lack of sensitivity.

"I only said what you were all thinking. Good heavens, she's got seven mouths to feed, no money, and will soon be homeless. Awkward though it is, we can hardly ignore that they're Tom's children. The least I could do was to try to find them work or organise the workhouse. I'm on the Board of Guardians, and I don't want the Parish to have to support any relatives of mine. How embarrassing would that be?"

His sister, Eveline, was listening, and she didn't like her brother, George, much either.

"You're right, George; that really was the very least you could do, though, of course, you could take some of the children in yourself," she said acidly. "After all, you're always preaching about how it is better to give than to receive. You could even let them live in that old cottage you've just bought. They do say charity begins at home."

George's wife, Alice, joined in at this point.

"Don't be ridiculous, Eveline; don't you think I've enough to do with three children of my own?"

"Well, you have servants to do the cooking, cleaning, and washing; you don't do any of it yourself. It would help if you took in the little ones and let Sabina earn a living. It's not her fault she's in this predicament."

If possible, George's face became an even deeper red. "How dare you? I'm not having my children mixing with the likes of Sabina's horde; did you not see how ragged and worn their clothes were? As for the cottage, I've bought it as an investment to do it up and rent it out. Now, I ask you, is Sabina likely to be able to pay me any rent? No, I think not."

"Yes, I did see how worn their clothes were, and I also saw that they were clean and carefully mended. Sabina's children behaved beautifully today; none grabbed at the food, though they looked half-starved. On the other hand, Harriet has been filling her mouth full ever since she arrived, even though the buttons on her coat are straining over her fat little belly."

"You forget yourself, Eveline. Be careful, or you might find yourself out of a job."

With that, he stormed off, and Eveline turned to Betsey, who was distraught.

"Mum, couldn't you and Dad help Sabina? You could take some of the children, couldn't you? There's plenty of room here at the inn."

"Oh, Eveline, I wish you hadn't said all that to George. You've upset him now, and you do have to work with him, you know. I feel for Sabina, of course, I do, but I've half promised Fred I'll look after Llew, Rosie, and Eddie for a while until Lucy's better. I'm not getting any younger, and the inn doesn't run itself. Let's wait and see what Sabina can sort out for herself. She's always had her head screwed on the right way has that one, and I know she'll fight tooth and nail to keep her family together. You're right, though; I won't see any grandchild of mine end up in the workhouse."

Jack Bater had attended Tom's funeral and witnessed the harsh words exchanged between Sabina and George. He was shocked at George's lack of compassion for his brother's family. He knew Sabina was in a desperate situation and had agreed to let her do Tom's job, but he wondered if she realised how hard the work would be. Still, anything was better than the workhouse, where the conditions were severe. He was a kindly man with no wish to turn the Carter family, or Liza Hammett, out of their cottages, though he would have had no choice if the dwellings were needed for new workers. This arrangement would solve two problems, and he would only have to employ one new worker.

CHAPTER 6

A few days after Tom's funeral, Liza moved in to look after the children, and Sabina returned to work on the farm. A purpose in life and being needed seemed to take ten years off Liza, and she was more help than Sabina could ever have imagined. It was fortunate she was, for an already difficult life had become much harder. Sabina had not taken on all of Tom's duties, just the milking morning and night, feeding the cows, and cleaning the shippens. Nevertheless, it was several hours of work every day, and in addition to caring for a large family, Sabina was exhausted by the time she fell into the bed that she now shared with Liza.

Food had always been in short supply, but now there just wasn't enough to go around, and Annie took it upon herself to find what she could to feed the family. The village of Hartford was situated in idyllic surroundings on the rugged North Devon coast, and the rolling hills of Exmoor ran on for miles. Most farmers turned a blind eye to the villagers shooting rabbits on the moors, though any man found poaching pheasants or deer on the estate would soon find himself in prison.

Early one Saturday morning, Annie gently lifted her father's gun from its home on two nails on the wall and began to clean it. Her belly was rumbling with hunger, and there was nothing to eat but a little stale bread, and that was not enough for them all. It was March, and the meagre supply of food and money, saved carefully by Tom, was long gone. Quietly though she worked, Sabina heard her.

"What are you doing, Annie? Be careful with that gun; it might go off."

"I'm hoping it will, Mum, because I'm going to try to shoot a rabbit on the moors, two if I can, or even a pigeon."

"Do you think you can?"

"Of course, Dad taught me, and I'm a good shot; he always said so. We've got to do something, for there's no food or money, and I'm starving, and I know you are, too. You can't work all the hours you do with no food. Do you feel all right, Mum? You look a bit under the weather."

"You don't miss much, do you, Annie, love? No, I'm not feeling too good, and I know why. I'm in the family way, Annie."

"Oh, Mum, why didn't you tell me? When's it due?"

"I hadn't even told your father because I didn't want to worry him until I was sure. I doubt I'll carry it all the way; I'm that tired these days, but it should be born towards the end of August."

"You're so thin it hardly shows, but at least it's a last little bit of Dad, isn't it? Don't worry, Mum, we'll manage somehow, and I'll see you later. Wish me luck."

"I do, Annie, but don't shoot anything but a rabbit, will you?"

Annie shook her head and walked briskly down the lane toward the moors. She wanted to get a couple of miles away from the village and any fear of interruption. It was a long time since she had used the gun, and she wanted to be alone to practice. The grass, white and crisp with frost, crunched beneath her feet. She could see her breath in the air, and she panted slightly as she climbed a hill. The ground became more uneven, and the grass gave way to bracken and heather.

She settled herself amid some large, weathered boulders and sat quietly to see if any rabbits appeared. It had been in this very spot that her father had taught her to shoot, and they had often gone home with a rabbit or two for their dinner. After twenty minutes, her feet were numb with the cold, and she had to clench her jaw to prevent her teeth from chattering in the biting wind. She was about to walk on and try somewhere else when a family of six rabbits appeared out of a nearby burrow. She raised the gun slowly, took aim, and gently squeezed the trigger. A loud bang echoed through the valley and made her ears ring.

She opened her eyes and rose to her feet to see what had happened. To her delight, she saw that she had hit a rabbit. Naturally, the others had bolted down the nearest burrow and would not be seen for some time. Her happiness, however, was short-lived, for as she approached the creature, its ears twitched, and it struggled unsuccessfully to regain its feet, for its back leg hung in bloody tatters.

Annie was horrified. She hated seeing the creature suffer and knew she must kill it immediately. Firmly, she grasped the rabbit's ears in one hand, its hind legs in the other, and pulled sharply just as she had seen her father do. There was a slight snick as its neck was broken, and it lay still in her arms. Her heart was beating fast, and she felt slightly sick as tears threatened, but she forced herself to think of the rabbit stew the family would soon be eating. She had been raised to be practical and knew her father would have been proud of her. All the same, she decided it was a different matter to kill a rabbit with your own bare hands than watch your father do it.

She walked briskly, going further than ever before until she eventually lay down on the ground and waited quietly. The rocks were damp and covered with yellow lichen, and they felt hard, cold, and uncomfortable beneath her. She could see a warren in the distance and resolved to shoot more carefully. She didn't have to wait long, for a few minutes later, a large buck poked its nose cautiously above ground and gradually emerged from its burrow. This time, she took careful aim and shot the rabbit cleanly through the head, thankful it had not suffered.

She wandered on for several miles, taking a few more shots without success, but she was not disappointed, for she had not expected to shoot any at all on her first attempt. At a small stream, she washed her hands and had a drink. The water was icy cold and crystal clear. She was ravenous, and her stomach rumbled, for no food had passed her lips since some thin broth at teatime the day before. A sudden noise startled her, and she jumped to her feet.

"Hello, Annie; I thought it was you. Sorry, did I give you a scare?"

"Oh, hello, Harry; yes, you did. You don't see many folk on the moors this early."

Harry Rudd, the blacksmith's son, was a tall, strapping lad of eighteen who worked with his father at the forge. He had always had a soft spot for Annie and was delighted to come across her like this.

"Looks like you've had a successful morning." He pointed at the two rabbits. "I didn't know you could shoot."

"Beginners luck, I think. Either that or I'm so hungry it's sharpened my aim."

"Hungry, are you? Well, mayhap I can do something about that." Harry reached into his bag and drew out a thick slice of bread and a piece of cheese. "Would you like to share my breakfast, Annie?"

"No, it's all right, Harry. I wasn't looking to take your food; I was just saying."

"Aw, come on, have some. Look at you; there's nothing to you. Sit beside me, and we'll have a snack together before we start back. He sat on a rock and carefully broke the bread and the cheese in half, giving Annie the slightly larger portion.

She could hold back no longer and fell gratefully onto the food, taking huge bites of the bread and nibbling at the cheese in between. She didn't speak until the food was gone and then bent down by the stream to cup her hands and drink some water.

Harry gazed at her, thinking how beautiful she was. Like most of her family, her hair was copper-red. It hung in tangled ringlets down to her waist and helped to keep her warm. The weak sun glistened on all the different hues. Her skin was pale, and her small nose was freckled. She looked so delicate and vulnerable as she looked up at him out of eyes of an intense shade of green. As he gazed into them, Harry thought they could probably drown a man. He held out his hand to help her up, and she hesitated but then took it gratefully. He pulled her to him and, before she knew what was happening, kissed her gently on the lips.

She pulled away at once, shocked. "Aw, I'm sorry, Annie, please don't run off. I shouldn't have done that, but you're so pretty."

Annie seemed surprised at the suggestion, as if she hadn't considered the matter before. There was no mirror in the cottage, and apart from trying to keep clean, she took little interest in her appearance.

"How old are you, Annie?"

"I'm nearly sixteen, and I'll be looking for a position soon. I've been helping Mum since Dad died, but we need the money now. Dad kept me at school because he wanted me to be a teacher, but I've no choice but to find work now."

"Aye, I was sorry to hear about your dad. Annie, would you like to walk out with me? I've always liked you, and the smithy will be mine one day, you know. I'm the eldest son, and it's a profitable business."

"No thanks, Harry, I'm flattered, but as I say, I'll be going into service soon, so I'm not looking for a boyfriend."

"Aye, I know, but we could take it slowly. I'd like to spend some time with you, Annie, just to get to know one another."

"I'd like us to be friends, Harry, but I'm not ready to walk out with anyone yet. It's taking me all my time to help Mum feed the family. It's been hard since Dad died."

"Aye, of course; we'll be friends then, eh? If you need anything, come and see me, Annie, and if I can help, I will. I know Willie's working a few hours on the estate, but how old is your little brother, John?"

"He's eight, why?"

"I'll have to run it past Father, but we've been talking about getting a lad to run errands, deliver things, and what have you. Would he like to work on a Saturday to earn a sixpence?"

"Ooh, yes, he would; do you mean it?"

"You haven't asked him yet. He may not want to."

"He will if he wants to eat."

"In that case, tell him to come to the smithy on Saturday. That'll give me time to talk to Father, but I think he'll agree."

They walked back to the village together, Annie feeling much better since she ate. As they parted at the stile, Annie thanked Harry again for the food and his offer of work for John.

She burst noisily and happily into the cottage. Having completed the morning milking, her mother had started on the washing.

"Hey, Mum, I've got some good news."

"We could certainly use some. Tell us, then. What is it?"

"I've got these for tea," said Annie, producing the rabbits from behind her back like some magic trick, "and I've got Johnny a Saturday job."

"You clever girl, Annie, thank goodness you've shot those rabbits. At least we can eat later. If you can gut and skin them, I can get them on the fire, and we'll eat all the sooner."

Annie nodded, for she was not squeamish and was equal to the task she had been asked to do.

"What's this job for Johnny, then? He's outside chopping logs, so you'd better tell him about it."

Johnny's face was red from the exertion of chopping logs, and he was puffing a bit as he struggled to split a particularly large one.

"John, come and have a rest; I've something to tell you."

Annie told him about the job Harry had offered, and he was thrilled to bits.

"Well, now that Dad's gone, it's only right I help Willie to keep all you women."

Annie, Liza, and her mother grinned at each other.

Annie prepared the rabbits and left them with Liza to make a stew. Unfortunately, there were only three potatoes and one turnip in the larder, and knowing more vegetables would make the stew go further, Annie gazed at the pot thoughtfully.

"Do you mind if I nip out again, Mum?"

"Yes, fine, but could you help me with the milking tonight? I'm that tired."

Annie nodded and grabbed her father's cap from a peg by the door. She found an old pair of his trousers in the shed, belted them tightly around her tiny waist, and turned them up at the ankles. She knew what she had in mind was wrong, but she couldn't let her family starve, could she?

CHAPTER 7

Following his bitter exchange with Sabina at Tom's funeral, the relationship between George and Eveline became more strained than usual. She was older than him and felt superior, but he was the owner of the shop in a male-orientated world, and they constantly rubbed each other up the wrong way. She was far more capable than his other assistant, his sister-in-law, Mary-Ann, who was a little simple-minded. Many of the new ideas in his shop had been Eveline's, including the suggestion to sell clothes. She was clever with her needle, and if any ready-made clothes did not quite fit the customers, she could make alterations for a fee, of course.

Recently, Eveline had started making rag dolls, a hobby that she enjoyed of an evening, and the dolls were beautiful. She stitched them neatly and painted their faces skilfully. She sewed horsehair to their heads and covered them with a bonnet. She also made a complete outfit of clothing for each doll. The dolls were sold in the shop, and a few weeks ago, a visitor from London had bought one for his daughter. The man was so taken with the doll that he had since written to ask if Eveline could supply half a dozen to sell in his shop in London. Eveline's quick business mind and skill had made the shop extremely profitable, and one thing George loved more dearly than any other was making money.

The shop also sold boots and shoes, a new venture, for most people visited Mr Martin, the cordwainer, and asked him to make them a new pair of boots when they needed them. Never before in the village had there been a shop stocking shoes and boots of different sizes where you could pick a pair off the shelf. It was a real novelty and was becoming ever more successful. Mr Martin was content with the arrangement as he made the boots and shoes and sold them to George for his shop.

An old tramp had recently been seen hanging around the village. He wore a brown corduroy coat full of holes, and his baggy black trousers hung off him. His face was creased and lined, and his deep wrinkles were full of grime. His teeth were brown and rotten, and his breath was rank. His hair, long, matted, and lice-ridden, was down past his shoulders. He had been begging for bread, and most people gave him something to get rid of him. Constable Folland, the village bobby, had already warned him to move on. Poor old Sam was used to being moved on, for this happened wherever he went, and he sometimes wondered where folk expected him to move on to. This time, however, Sam was less willing than usual to go anywhere. He had wandered the countryside for years, partly from choice, but just now, he had sore feet, and this wasn't helped by the fact that his boots were worn out, and one sole was hanging off completely. Sam eyed up the new boots in George's shop longingly.

Just then, several villagers went into the shop and began ordering things over the counter. It was lunchtime, and Mary Ann was alone. Eveline had gone to get some food, and George was checking how the repair work on the cottage was progressing. Mary Ann became flustered as she served customers with ham, cheese, eggs, candles, and soap and weighed the flour. Her adding up had never been up to much, and she usually relied on Eveline to do this whilst she fetched the goods for the customers. She was so heavily engrossed in her work that she barely noticed Sam slip into the shop. He calmly picked up the large pair of hobnail boots and hurried out the door.

Once outside, he grinned broadly and, slipping into an alley, quickly tried the boots on, praying they would fit. Fortunately, they were slightly on the big side, but he wasn't concerned about that, though he wished he'd had the presence of mind to pick up some thick socks as well. Looking around cautiously, he hid his old boots behind a water barrel and made off up the muddy lane that led to the next village. He whistled to himself as he went, thinking that with any luck, the boots would not be missed until later in the day. If he was fortunate, their absence might not be noticed until the next day, when he would be miles away.

Unfortunately for Sam, George returned to the shop within minutes. He was in a foul mood because work on the cottage was not going smoothly. He had known it would need a lot of repairs, but the workmen were uncovering one problem after another, and the latest was that the roof timbers were infested with deathwatch beetles. This would be costly, and the cottage was not the bargain he had first thought. His mind on these problems, he entered the shop just as Eveline returned from her break. She went to the counter and immediately noticed that the boots were gone.

"Oh, Mary Ann, you've sold the boots. Who bought them?"

"I haven't sold any boots, but I've been rushed off my feet, so I'm glad you're back. Can I get my dinner now?"

"Hang on a minute; if you haven't sold the boots, where are they? Have you moved them or put them back in the box?"

"No, I haven't left the counter. I've been serving people all dinnertime. I don't know why they always come when I'm on my own."

George overheard the conversation and joined in.

"Who's been in the shop? Someone must have stolen them."

"Well, let's see, Tilly Rudd came in and bought eggs and flour, and Mrs Luckett bought quite a few things. She really had me running around, and I had to get her some candles from out the back. Then Hannah Cutcliffe came in with her children, which was pretty noisy for a while."

"Hmm, Matilda and Mrs Luckett wouldn't have stolen the boots, though I'm not sure about Hannah. Do you think she could have taken them?"

"No, I don't think so. She was carrying her youngest child and bought flour and a few other things, so she had her hands full. No, I don't think she could have taken them."

"Did you see anyone else in the shop?"

Mary Ann frowned.

"Now I think about it, that old tramp came in, and I hoped I could get rid of him quickly because he smelled so bad, but by the time I was free, he'd gone. I suppose he could have taken the boots while I was busy."

"That's who it will be, and he's not going to get away with it, the filthy old beggar. That was an expensive pair of boots, and I'll see he's sent to jail for this, if not hanged! I'll get Constable Folland after him; he can't have gone far."

George stormed off to Constable Folland's house, for the village wasn't grand enough to host a police station. The policeman listened patiently to the angry man and agreed to endeavour to apprehend the thief. They returned to the shop together to see which way old Sam might have gone. The obvious place was the alley, and they soon found the tattered old boots stuffed behind the water barrel. George seized them triumphantly, wrinkling his nose at the smell.

"There you are; that's proof he went this way."

Unfortunately for Sam, the alley was muddy, for it had rained heavily in the night, and it was easy to see the deep footprints left by the soles of the new boots.

"See, there are his footprints; you can follow him easily enough. I'll come with you."

They set off briskly; sure, they would catch him soon enough and then woe betide him.

Half a mile ahead, Annie was on her way toward Hartford Manor. It was surrounded on three sides by a high wall, with the fourth hedged in beech and backing onto woodland. She remembered once playing in the woods with her friends and peering through a gap in the hedge, though they had not dared go inside. She spotted the opening, which seemed smaller than before, but she supposed she had gotten bigger. Tucked under her shawl, she carried the sack that Ginger the kitten had so disliked. New buds were thick on the branches, still tightly curled and waiting for the weather to warm up before unfurling and releasing their bright green foliage. She guessed the gap would be more difficult to find in a month or two. She pulled her father's cap onto her head and firmly tucked her fiery red hair under it.

As she squeezed through the thick hedge, the branches scratched her arms and tore at her face. She pushed them away impatiently. Once through, she lay quietly in the grass, listening and ensuring no one was around. When satisfied the area was deserted, she crept stealthily from one bush to another, wondering where the vegetable patch might be. The grounds were extensive, and she skirted a couple of orchards containing apple, plum, and mazzard trees before coming to a cultivated area. The plot was divided into sections, each with a low, neatly trimmed box hedge running around it with paths in between. She couldn't see what was growing at this distance, but it didn't matter, for anything edible would be welcome.

It started to rain heavily, and she sheltered under a tree, peering out cautiously. Although she could see no one, she crawled along the path between the low hedges on her belly to keep out of sight. She was soon soaking wet and cold, and the sharp stones hurt her ribs, knees, and elbows. She risked a glimpse over the hedge and saw turnips and, farther on, swedes and parsnips. She knew the potatoes, onions, and carrots would have been harvested in the autumn, and it was too early for peas or beans. In the distance, she saw two gardeners hurrying to find somewhere more sheltered to work and debated whether to turn back. It would have been better to come earlier in the day before anyone was up. Still, in this heavy rain, it was unlikely anyone would be around.

She hesitated, indecision creasing her brow into a deep frown, but eventually, she decided to risk it. Her brothers and sisters were hungry and would stay that way unless she took action. The box hedge was too thick to pull the vegetables through from the path, so, keeping at ground level, she inched her way into the plot, where she quickly lifted turnips, swedes, and parsnips. Despite the cold, she was sweating, and her heart was beating so hard she thought her chest would burst. She feared that she would be apprehended at any moment. However, she saw no one, resumed her former position on her belly, and crawled back to the bushes, pulling the sack behind her.

She panicked now, searching frantically for the gap in the hedge, and gratefully squeezed her way through and back into the woods. She ran a few hundred yards and lay in the undergrowth to get her breath back, but to her horror, she heard someone hurrying towards her. She lay still, hoping they would pass her by, but luck was not on her side, and suddenly someone fell over her.

She screamed and leapt to her feet, ready to flee, but when she saw it was just the old tramp, she heaved a sigh of relief. If anything, Sam was more shocked than she was, and he was wheezing badly.

"Are you all right, Sam? I'm sorry if I scared you, but I was having a rest."

Annie knew his name because he had tried to beg for bread from Sabina a few days before. He nodded, still unable to speak.

"Aye, I'm all right," he gasped at last. "I must get going, though, 'cos the law's after me and that chap who owns the shop, and they're not far behind. They must have guessed I'm heading for Bydown."

Sam glanced anxiously over his shoulder, and Annie noticed his new boots, which were entirely at odds with his other clothes. She guessed this was why the police and George were after him. She felt sorry for the old man and didn't like her Uncle George, so she decided to help him.

"Sam, come with me; I know where you can hide until they're gone. You can rest and get your breath back."

He followed as she led him to the gap in the hedge of Hartford Manor.

"I'm not going in there; are you mad? I'm in enough trouble already, but if I go in there, it will make matters far worse."

"No, you'll be all right, Sam. Just squeeze through and hide in the bushes; you needn't go far. Just wait in there until they're gone. You'll hear them because they're bound to come along this track, and when they've passed by, you can go a different way and shake them off. I bet it's your best chance because they'd never think you'd dare to go in there. You go in, and I'll make sure everything looks all right."

Sam was doubtful but realised it made sense, for he couldn't outrun them. He nodded his head and squeezed through the opening. Annie rearranged the branches and brushed the undergrowth with a stick. She was soaked to the skin and shivering with the cold. Her hair had escaped from under the cap and was plastered to her neck. Mud streaked her face, and her clothes were filthy, so she splashed cold water from the stream over her face and hands and ran her fingers through her hair. She also turned her shawl inside out as it was so dirty, but she didn't think George or the policeman would notice; after all, they were not looking for her. They would be, though, she thought, if they knew what I had been up to, and she hastily stuffed her sack of vegetables down a badger's sett. She was gathering a bunch of early primroses when George and Constable Folland appeared. George looked at her in surprise.

"Why hello, it's Annie, isn't it? Tom's eldest?"

"Yes, that's right, Uncle George, I saw you at Dad's funeral."

Annie wanted to say, 'when you offered to send my brothers down the silver mine and the others to the workhouse' but decided it may not be prudent.

"Have you seen anyone come this way, Annie?"

"No, sir, but I've been off the path picking primroses, so someone could have passed. Whom are you looking for?" Annie's face was a picture of innocence.

"The old tramp that's been around for a few days. He's stolen some boots from my shop, and when I catch him…."

George grew red in the face, imagining what he would do to Sam when he caught him.

"Oh dear, no, I haven't seen him, but I hope you catch him. Are you sure he went this way?"

"We followed his footsteps down the alley to this footpath, so most likely, he's heading to Bydown, and with any luck, we'll catch him. I don't think he can go that fast. He's pretty old."

"I hope you do, but I must get a few more flowers picked; we're going to sell them in the market tomorrow."

Annie continued picking primroses and decided that selling them in the market was a good idea. She waited until both men had been gone for several minutes, then retrieved her sack and called softly to Sam.

"Sam, can you hear me? Sam, they've gone."

His grimy face appeared through the hedge, and he grinned toothily at her.

"You're a kind little maid to help old Sam, my dear, and I won't forget it, especially seeing he's your uncle. I'll go the other way to Warkley now, so don't tell anyone, will you?"

"No, your secret's safe with me, Sam. There's no love lost between my family and Uncle George, I can tell you."

Annie avoided the path and carried on through the wood that would eventually bring her out behind her own cottage. The ground underfoot was marshy, and she had to cross a stream. She picked her way across cautiously, stepping on stones to avoid getting her boots wet, but unfortunately, her foot slipped and plunged into the icy water. Eventually, she came to a clearing she recognised and realised with some relief that she was nearly home. Thankfully, she let herself in through the back door, feeling exhausted.

"Why, Annie, what a state you're in. Where have you been, and what's this?"

"It's vegetables for the rabbit stew, Liza; it should last longer now, eh?"

Sabina stared at the vegetables in astonishment. "Where…?"

"Don't ask, Mum. I needn't tell you any lies then."

Sabina hugged her daughter for the second time that day. "Annie, you must be careful. If you get caught, you'll go to jail, hungry or not, and there'd be nothing I could do about it."

"I know, but I won't get caught. Now, what time's tea?"

They sat down to a wholesome meal that night, and a little colour returned to Sabina's cheeks. The children ate hungrily, mopping up the last of the gravy with chunks of bread, and even the swede, parsnip, and turnip greens were boiled and eaten along with the stew. Every morsel was eaten, and they licked their plates clean. Sabina relaxed a little for the first time since Tom died and thought they might survive after all.

CHAPTER 8

The Hartford Estate had been in the Fellwood family for generations. Charles Fellwood had become the squire twelve years earlier when his father, Joshua, died in a hunting accident. Charles' mother had died giving birth to him, and Joshua had never remarried, so Charles was an only child. Joshua Fellwood had taken a close interest in his estate and knew all of his tenants and their families. He demanded a hard day's work but knew he was more likely to get it if the men were adequately housed and fed. The tied cottages were well maintained, and the men received a fair wage. Consequently, he was well-liked and respected and genuinely mourned at his death.

His son, Charles, did not take after him, preferring to leave the running of the estate to Jack Bater, the farm manager. Charles did not share his father's sentiments about the labourers either, and there had been no repairs to the cottages or wage increases since his father's demise. Jack had much preferred working for Joshua.

Charles had been married to Eleanor for twenty years. They had barely known each other before their wedding, but she was from a wealthy family, and Charles had been encouraged to marry her for a generous dowry. They had four living children, Lily having succumbed to measles at the age of three. Their eldest son, David, was nineteen. He was a boarder at Westford public school in Exeter but would leave at the end of the year to learn how to manage the estate. He was a handsome and intelligent young man who showed little interest in an estate that would one day be his, for since childhood, he had wanted to become a soldier.

Robert and Victoria were seventeen-year-old twins, and she was the apple of her father's eye. She was a striking young woman, and it was hoped she would find herself a wealthy husband when she had her season in London next summer. Victoria had been educated at home by a governess, Prudence Rogers, and they had recently travelled to Europe to visit distant relatives.

Robert was a confident young man with a cheeky sense of humour who usually boarded at Westford School with his brother. However, he had recently been seriously ill with rheumatic fever, and the doctor advised him to stay at home until September to recover fully. The complete opposite of his brother, David, Robert loved the countryside and would have made a far more suitable heir to the estate.

Eleanor and Charles had thought that ten-year-old Sarah would be their last child. However, Eleanor had been feeling unwell for weeks, and the local doctor quickly diagnosed another pregnancy as the reason for her indisposition. Considering Eleanor's age of forty-two, the doctor was slightly concerned but reassured her that she had already given birth to five healthy babies, and there was no reason why it should be any different this time.

Prudence had recently announced her decision to retire, for she was over seventy and had been a governess to Eleanor. Charles Fellwood was frustrated that she had not informed him of this before she travelled to Europe, for by now, he could have found a replacement. On top of that, Robert had also expressed a wish not to return to school, and Charles and Eleanor discussed the situation.

"Has Robert mentioned to you that he doesn't want to return to Westford?"

"No, not recently, but I know he's wanted to leave for some time. It would be a shame, but he was seriously ill, so he may feel differently by September when he's regained his strength."

"He wants to help Bater run the estate, but David is the eldest and must inherit Hartford whether he likes it or not. I'm certainly not letting him join the army."

"No, I don't want him joining the army, either."

"Robert's too soft-hearted and so like his grandfather in that respect. If he was in charge, he'd be repairing every farm cottage for miles around and giving all the poor a pay rise, and we'd never make any money. Look how upset he was when Henry Bailey was imprisoned for poaching last week. He doesn't understand you have to make an example of these thieves; to him, it's just a pheasant or two, and we have plenty more."

The gong for lunch interrupted their conversation, and Eleanor took Charles' arm as they proceeded down the sweeping oak staircase and past the portraits of many ancestors.

" Charles, perhaps we could have a family portrait done when the baby is born. What do you think?"

"Yes, if you like, or what about a photograph? Getting Sarah to sit still long enough for anyone to paint her would be an ordeal for us all."

"Yes, maybe a photograph would be easier, but Sarah needs to learn patience, and a portrait is nicer. I'll think about it."

Sarah and Robert were racing each other down the stairs but slowed to a sedate walk and became silent as they approached their parents, for they knew better than to upset their father.

Hartford Manor was an elegant building which had been virtually rebuilt in the late eighteenth century after an extensive fire. Old manuscripts found in the library proved that a house had stood on the site for hundreds of years. A large, highly polished oak table surrounded by upright chairs stood in the centre of the elegant dining room. Charles Fellwood occupied the carver chair at the head of the table, and Eleanor sat at the other end.

A marble fireplace stood in the centre of one wall. The brass coal bucket, poker, shovel, and tongs gleamed, and there were ornaments, pictures, and brass candlesticks on the mantelpiece. Flowery wallpaper covered the upper half of the walls, and the lower half was panelled in oak. Large pictures in heavy gilt frames showed hunting and farming scenes and one or two much-loved, long-dead horses. Two sparkling crystal chandeliers hung from the ceiling. Eleanor took great pride and pleasure in the house, and the velvet burgundy curtains were a recent acquisition.

When Charles inherited the estate, the house needed refurbishment, for his father had taken little interest in it, carrying out only essential repairs. With his wife dying so many years before him, the house lacked a woman's touch, for Joshua preferred to plough the profits back into the estate. His interests lay in experimenting with new breeds of cattle to see if they gave a better yield, and he bought modern farm machinery, as well as helping the poor in any way he could. It was thanks to him that the silver mine on his land had reopened and was now providing a living for men from the village.

Following her father-in-law's death, Eleanor redecorated the house with relish. She had long wanted to make improvements, but old Joshua had been set in his ways and liked things the way they were. Once Eleanor had a free rein, the servants worked hard. Carpets were beaten, curtains washed or replaced, broken windows repaired, and experts painstakingly cleaned the old tapestries. The gardeners, too, were kept busy, growing flowers and vegetables in the hothouses, along with all sorts of exotic fruits to be enjoyed by the many guests invited to frequent dinner parties.

Charles Fellwood was not a popular landlord as he had no sympathy for the poor. He prosecuted any thief or poacher without fail, whereas his father had often turned a blind eye to minor offences. He was friendly with the local judges and insisted that all culprits were dealt with as harshly as possible. He felt that the poor could be kept in their place only by making an example of wrongdoers. He did not consider near-starvation an excuse for thieving of any kind.

He said grace, and as the family murmured, Amen raised his head and looked at them.

"Now, as you know, your mother is expecting a baby, and Doctor Luckett says she needs plenty of rest, so please remember that."

"Will I be able to hold the baby, Mama?"

"Yes, of course, Sarah; I'm sure the new nanny will appreciate your help."

"The other matter is that of a new governess. I fear it may be some weeks before a new person can be found, so in the meantime, I want you, Victoria, to help Sarah with her studies."

Victoria looked doubtful, for she was not much of a scholar, though she could sing and play the piano and was an adept seamstress. However, she murmured her agreement, for she knew challenging her father was pointless.

"We have considered your request to leave school, Robert, but have decided you must stay at least another year after you return in September. You have missed so much of your education with your illness already."

"Father, I want to work on the estate, and I don't need any more learning to do that. I know David will inherit it as the eldest, but I'm sure I could help him."

"No, there can only be one heir, and it has to be David. You will return to Westford in September for another year, and, who knows, you could achieve a scholarship to Oxford or Cambridge if you work hard. Maybe one day you'll set up a business of your own. Now, that's my last word. The subject is closed."

The meal continued in silence, and the children were glad when, at last, they were excused. The servants came to clear away the lunch, and Miss Wetherby, the housekeeper, begged a word with her master.

"If you please, sir, we have the chimney sweep here today, and if it is convenient, he'd like to sweep this chimney next."

"Yes, Wetherby, that's fine; we were just leaving anyway. I presume the job will be completed before our evening meal?"

"Oh, yes, of course, sir. I'll see to it that everything is in order. Thank you, sir."

When Charles and Eleanor left the room, Miss Wetherby ushered in a sweep master and his boy. The boy was about six years old and as skinny as a rake. He was covered in soot from head to foot. Tears ran down his cheeks from his sore eyes, but he made no sound. The sweep and the boy spread sheets around the fireplace and got their brushes ready.

"Right then, Jimmy, up you go, lad. You've not done this one before, but I did it times enough when I was your size, and it's an easy one. There are a couple of bends where the brushes won't reach, so you need to climb up and scrape away the soot from the nooks and crannies, and then when you come down, I'll put the brushes up and finish the job. Climb up, and you'll find it bends to the right; clean that bit, then up again, and there's another bend to the right because it joins another chimney from the next room. You get this one done, and then perhaps you'll get a bit of bread and cheese for your dinner."

It was illegal to send young boys up chimneys, but in rural areas, it was common practice for families who needed the money. Most chimneys were narrow and twisted, and even small children could get stuck or frozen in terror in the cramped darkness. In some cases, the sweep master had been known to light the fire beneath the boys to 'encourage' them to get on with their dangerous work. A few children had been taken out dead, having died of suffocation.

As the boy scrambled up the chimney, soot began to fall into the hearth, and Wilfred, the sweep, shouted encouragement up the chimney.

Eventually, Jimmy reappeared, his elbows and knees bleeding and tears streaming down his cheeks.

"Good boy, now I'll put the brush up and finish this one, and when we've cleaned up, we'll get ourselves a bit of dinner before we push on and do the other four. The rest can wait until tomorrow."

CHAPTER 9

Sabina went to visit Lucy a week or so after Tom's funeral. Llew and Rosie had gone to live with Betsey at the inn, and Lucy's mother had returned home, so Lucy was on her own with baby Eddie. As Sabina knocked on the door, she could hear Eddie crying lustily, but no one came to let her in. She went around the back and found Fred repairing a gate. He was hammering new nails into the wood and did not hear her approach until she touched him gently on the arm.

"Oh, Sabina, you made me jump. Have you come to see Lucy?"

"Yes, I've been knocking, but she didn't answer, though I could hear the baby crying."

"Come in the back way. I don't know why Lucy didn't answer the door; I told her you were coming."

In the kitchen, there was a huge pile of dirty washing in one corner and an even bigger pile of dirty dishes on the side. Fred sighed.

"Lucy, Sabina's here to see you."

Eddie was red-faced and screaming, and Sabina wondered why Lucy was ignoring him. They found her sitting in a chair, gazing into space. She seemed unaware of their presence and was unconcerned that her baby was crying.

"Lucy, why aren't you seeing to the lad? He's hungry."

Her face was pale and her eyes unfocused, and Fred gave her an impatient shake.

"Come on, Lucy, for goodness sake, feed the lad. I can't do everything."

"Fred, you mend your gate, and I'll chat with Lucy. Go on, I'll see to Eddie. Come on, Lucy, this little lad's hungry. You must feed him."

Lucy completely ignored her, so Sabina placed the child in the mother's arms, unbuttoned her dress, and put him to her breast. At last, Lucy stared in surprise at Sabina and then at the baby.

"Hello, Lucy, your baby's hungry. Didn't you hear him crying?"

"Yes, he cries a lot, but he'll stop eventually."

"You must feed him, Lucy, or he'll become ill like the other babies."

"I don't care. Sabina, take him home with you; he'll be much better off because I don't want him."

"Now, you mustn't talk like that; of course, you want him. He's a bonny little lad; he was just hungry, that's all. How are you feeling today?"

"No, I mean it; I don't want him. Fred doesn't believe me, but I don't want any of them, and I'm so glad they've gone to the inn. They get on my nerves."

Lucy sounded adamant, and Sabina began to think there was more wrong here than the baby blues.

"I know you've been feeling a bit down, Lucy, but it will pass, you know. You'll feel better as the baby gets older. Are you going to feed him from the other side now?"

Lucy made no effort to move the child to her other breast, so Sabina took him and put him over her shoulder to bring up his wind. He obligingly gave a big burp, and she returned him to his mother's other arm and put his mouth to her other breast. Still, Lucy took no interest, not even looking at her child. Sabina chatted to her, trying to cheer her up, but she had retreated into her own little world. Sabina took the baby again, put him on her lap, and talked to him. He smiled and gurgled, content now that his belly was full of warm milk.

"See how lovely he is. He's got your beautiful brown eyes."

"Sabina, please take him; you'd be doing him and me a real favour. Like I said, I don't want him."

Sabina didn't know what to say, so instead, she laid the baby down and changed his soiled nappy. His little bottom was sore, so she fetched water and a rag and cleaned him up. She spotted some goose grease on the table and smeared some on him to make him feel a bit better, and then laid him back in his cot. Then she went to the kitchen, took the big kettle off the fire, poured some water into a bowl, and washed the dirty dishes. She stuffed as many dirty clothes as she could carry into a sack to take them home to wash. Lucy had not moved or even buttoned her dress, and Sabina gently fastened the buttons and stroked her hair back from her forehead.

"I'll come again soon, Lucy. Eddie should sleep now, but he'll need feeding again later."

As she left the cottage, Fred looked up worriedly from his hammering.

"Did she talk to you?"

"A bit, Fred, but something's wrong here. She says she doesn't want the baby or Llew and Rosie. I put him to her breast, but she did nothing to help other than allow him to suck. I've changed him and put him back in his cot, but you'll have to make sure she feeds him again later. It's not just the blues; she needs to see the doctor. Perhaps she's worried he'll die like the last two, but I've never seen anyone behave like this. I've washed the dishes, and I'll take this washing with me, but I must get home now."

"Thanks, Sabina, I'm at my wit's end. I've got to work to earn money, so I can't do everything in the house and look after the baby. I will get the doctor to come, but he's been once already, and he just said it would take time for her to get back to normal and to be patient with her. If Doctor Luckett will call in the morning, would you come while he's here and see if we can get something sorted out?"

"Yes, of course. I have to do the milking, but I could come afterwards."

When Sabina arrived home with the washing, Liza scolded her for taking on yet more work.

"Surely Betsey or Eveline could help? I don't see why it has to fall to you. They've got servants and have never done much for you."

"I know, but I felt so sorry for Fred. Seeing Lucy like that was scary, and it was awful to hear she didn't want her children. I don't understand her."

Together, they tackled Lucy's washing and hung it out to dry. There was a strong wind, and they hoped the laundry would be dry enough for Sabina to return it the next day.

The following day, Sabina hurried through the milking, gathered the dry washing, and set off to see Lucy again. This time, she went to the backyard where Fred was making a carriage wheel, and he smiled at her.

"Thanks for doing the washing, Sabina. The doctor should be here in about half an hour. Do you want to go in and see how she is? I'll come in when he arrives. Make some tea if you like."

Sabina put the washing on the table and was pleased to see Lucy bending over the cot. However, that pleasure was short-lived when she realised Lucy was holding a pillow over the squirming baby's face. She ran at Lucy and tried to pull her away, but she held on determinedly. Sabina screamed for Fred, and he came running.

"Quick, Fred, get her off the baby; she's trying to smother him!"

Fred grabbed Lucy by the hair, hauled her away from the cot, and threw her into a chair. Sabina quickly picked up the baby, who was blue around the lips and not breathing. She blew air into his mouth and massaged his little chest. He suddenly gasped and started crying. Both Sabina and Fred heaved a sigh of relief and stared anxiously at one another, for they could not believe what they had just witnessed. Lucy sat motionlessly, and Fred shook her.

"Lucy, what were you doing to Eddie? Were you trying to kill him?"

An awful thought crossed Fred's mind, and he glanced anxiously at Sabina and saw that she was thinking the same thing, but neither wanted to voice their concern. It was too awful to contemplate, but he pulled Lucy towards him.

"Lucy, did you do this to Alfie and Grace, too?"

Her eyes focused, and a chilling smile spread across her face. "What if I did? I kept telling you I didn't want more babies, but you wouldn't listen. At least it stopped their dreadful crying. They got on my nerves crying all the time, and he's just the same." She glanced angrily at the babe in Sabina's arms.

"Lucy, you were a good mum to Llewie and Rosie, so why have you done this? I don't understand?"

However, Lucy again retreated into her trance-like state and refused to answer. They heard a noise outside and realised it was Doctor Luckett. Fred grasped Sabina's arm.

"Sabina, don't tell him. Please don't say anything. They'll put her in jail, and she'd never cope. I'll sort something out."

Dr Luckett came into the room and immediately sensed the tension in the air.

"Hello, Lucy. Are you feeling any better today?" Lucy ignored him, gazing out of the window. "Fred, I think it might be best if you leave us. Thank you."

Fred and Sabina anxiously left the room, and an uneasy silence lay between them. Neither of them wanted to speak of what they had seen.

"Fred, do you really think she killed Alfie and Grace?" said Sabina.

"Well, I never considered it at the time. I just thought they had died of something. I mean, many babies do, but now, I don't know. I can't believe what I saw with my own eyes. How could she do that?"

"I think she's ill, Fred. Perhaps there's something wrong with her mind? Animals sometimes turn on their young and kill them, don't they? Perhaps it's the same with people if something's wrong. You can't leave Eddie with her, Fred, and I think you should tell Doctor Luckett. I'm sure he'll do whatever's best."

Fred was doubtful but nodded as Doctor Luckett came outside.

"It's difficult to know what to suggest, Fred. She's suffering from some kind of mental illness, probably due to having three babies so quickly, but how to make her better is the question. How is she when you're alone? Does she talk to you? Has she behaved oddly in any other way?"

"I didn't want to tell you this, doctor, but Sabina and I caught her trying to smother the baby just before you arrived. She doesn't want him or the other children. She says she can't stand his crying and wants to stop him from suffering. Is she mad?"

"Oh dear, that's terrible. I'm so sorry, Fred, but you did the right thing in telling me. We'll have to admit her to the asylum for treatment."

He saw Fred's dismayed expression. "It may not be for long." He went on hastily. "She might suddenly snap out of it, but we can't risk her harming the children, can we? Do you think this is what happened to Alfie and Grace?"

"I don't know, but she won't want to go; I know she won't. It's a horrible place, isn't it?"

"I'm afraid there's no choice, Fred. I should alert the police to what has happened, but if you agree to have her committed, she'll no longer be a risk to the children. At least in the asylum, she'll get treatment, whereas, in prison, she wouldn't."

Not wanting to witness Lucy being taken away, Sabina offered to take Eddie home with her until Fred could make arrangements. She knew Mr Rudd's donkey had recently foaled, and it was said that donkey's milk was the nearest thing to human milk, so she would get him some of that and hope it didn't upset him. In the longer term, they would have to find a wet nurse to feed him, though, at three months, he should soon be able to manage some mashed-up food. Fred thanked her and said he would collect Eddie the next day.

With a heavy heart, Fred went to break the news to his wife, for although Doctor Luckett had assured him it might only be for a while, he knew people seldom left the asylum once they had been committed.

CHAPTER 10

It was April, and as the weather warmed, life became a little easier, and Annie quickly became adept at procuring food. In addition to her frequent rabbit shooting expeditions and vegetable stealing, she went fishing in the local pond at Shebworthy and out to sea in a rowing boat she borrowed from a neighbour. She took Willie fishing and shooting with her, for soon, she would go into service, and the family would have to rely on Willie. However, she never took him to steal vegetables because she didn't want to risk him getting caught.

One day, Annie, Willie, Mary, and John decided to catch some moles to earn a few shillings. The moles were caught in traps, then skinned, and their pelts nailed to the barn door to dry. When ready, they were sent to the fur factory, and in due course, a payment would arrive amidst much excitement.

The vicar had moles in his garden, and he hated the unsightly mounds of earth that appeared every day. The children laid traps and checked them daily until they had caught an amazing seven moles at the end of a week. The vicar was delighted and gave the children two pennies for each mole, but the best was yet to come. Being a kindly man, he sent the skins away for them, and they were rewarded with a further sixpence for each mole, making a total of four shillings and eight pence. This small fortune worked out at one shilling and two pence each.

Annie insisted they gave their shillings to their mother to buy flour, candles, and soap, and the remaining pennies they took to the village shop, which was owned by an old lady called Mrs Scott. Since George had opened his grocery shop, her little establishment had suffered, but many of the locals were loyal, and she was far more popular than George, so she just about managed to keep going. Her children had left home, and her husband had been dead so long that few remembered him. Mrs Scott was kind, and all the children loved her. She often put an extra toffee in your bag if she liked you but was quick to dish out a clip around the ear for any youngster giving her lip.

The small, dark shop was like an Aladdin's cave, stocking everything imaginable from candles, shoe polish, and soap to potatoes, corn, and porridge oats. The shelves were laden with interesting bottles, packages, and bags. A fragrance of herbs and spices assailed the nostrils of the incoming customer, with an underlying smell of linseed oil, beeswax, tea, and liquorice. Mrs Scott made delicious toffee and fudge, sold liquorice in all shapes and sizes, and huge gobstoppers, too. The sweets were weighed by the ounce and put into cone-shaped bags.

The children took a long time deciding what to buy, for it was such a rare occasion that every scrap of enjoyment had to be derived from it. Mrs Scott did not hurry them and enjoyed their anticipation. They bought enough sweets for all their brothers and sisters to have some and a small amount of fudge for Sabina and Liza.

The Carters were coping better now, though life was still hard. With Sabina's and Willie's wages, John's sixpence from his Saturday job, and Annie's efforts at finding food, Sabina felt things were looking up. The arrangement with Liza had been surprisingly successful, for the children had taken to the old lady, and she enjoyed looking after them. She was clever with her needle and set about mending their ragged clothes. Whilst they mostly got enough to eat, buying new clothes or shoes was pretty much impossible, so they relied on hand-outs from other families.

The children attended the local school with about eighty pupils, split into three classes: infants of five to seven years, juniors of eight to ten, and seniors aged eleven to thirteen. Most children left school at thirteen, or often earlier, to work on the land or go into service. One or two stayed longer to become teachers themselves, but unfortunately for Annie, the school did not need another teacher at that time. At busy times on the farms, the classrooms would be nearly empty, as the children had to help make hay or harvest corn. The harvest had to be saved, or families would starve. There was talk of compulsory education for children between the ages of five and ten, which was worrying because they needed to work.

The teachers wrote sums or spellings on a large blackboard for the children to copy onto their slates, and Annie thought what a tale those ancient slates could tell if only they could talk. The older children were allowed to use pen and ink to write in their copybooks, and each desk had an inkwell filled with blue ink by the monitors every morning. Times tables and poems were learned by rote, and every morning, after prayers, the children would recite their tables.

The three 'Rs', reading, writing, and arithmetic, were a priority, and the children learned about the countries of the empire using a globe and a map on the wall. In the afternoons, the boys and girls were sometimes taught separately. The boys learned about farming, shoemaking, and woodwork, and the girls cooking, knitting, and sewing. The children were required to jog, march, and do stretching exercises twice weekly.

The children learnt how to tell the time on a big wall clock. There was a fifteen-minute playtime mid-morning and mid-afternoon, with thirty minutes for lunch, and the older children took turns to be the bell-ringer for the week. A large brass handbell was kept under the clock, and the bell ringer would ring it at the start and end of each playtime. Timekeeping was strict, and writing lines was the punishment for ringing the bell at the wrong time. One minute late or early would result in one hundred lines.

Willie Carter dreaded his turn as a bell-ringer, for he had trouble telling the time. He would glance desperately around the classroom, whispering, 'Is it time?' His classmates invariably told him the wrong time, and poor Willie would spend most of the week writing his lines; 'I must learn to tell the time correctly.'

Discipline was harsh, and any boy misbehaving would be given a good hiding. The girls were given a smack on the hand or legs with the cane if they had been naughty. Punishments were recorded in a book, and if a child's name appeared too many times, their parents would be told. Most children felt that wearing the dunce's cap and being made to stand in the corner was worse than being caned.

The large school garden was divided into small plots, each shared by two children. Here, they learned about growing vegetables, how and when to plant, weed, thin, and harvest them. The seeds were gathered carefully for the following year. The produce was shared, and many poor families benefitted. Once a year, a farmer would bring a trailer load of dung and drop it off in the gateway, and the whole school would spend the day spreading it over the garden and digging it in. It was hard and smelly work but enjoyable, too. There was intense rivalry between plots over who could grow the largest onion or the longest runner bean.

Occasionally, on sunny afternoons, the children would be taken on nature walks to learn the names of the flowers and trees. They collected leaves and berries, fungi, and flowers for the nature table. Here lived caterpillars, ladybirds, butterflies, and frogspawn, which then became tadpoles and, eventually, frogs, toads, or newts. On the nature walks, they searched for birds' nests. The teacher would remove one egg for the children to draw from memory later. The egg was carefully replaced, and the children were warned to leave it alone. Most did, though a few boys coveted a birds' egg collection. Sometimes, there would be naked baby birds squirming around with their eyes shut, their yellow beaks wide open, as they squawked loudly.

One day, they found a wren's nest made of mosses, hair, and grass, intricately woven to form a hollow ball. Mr Atkins put his fingers into the entrance to feel for eggs but leapt back like a scalded cat when a tiny mouse ran out between his fingers, and the children squealed with laughter.

The children learned which berries were poisonous and which ones could safely be eaten. Hips and haws, the fruits of the dog rose, and the hawthorn tree were common, as were blackberries, elderberries, bryony, and spindle. The boys put the seeds from the rose hips down the girls' backs, where they caused intense itching, which the boys found extremely funny until the teacher brandished his cane.

Annie and her siblings had a four-mile return journey to school, but it was nothing for some to walk five miles or more. The boys wore corduroy shorts in all weathers, and in winter, their chapped, red knees were smeared with goose grease to soothe them. There was an annual prize for the best attendance, and sometimes, children would arrive soaking wet and cold, only to be marked present and sent home to dry out. The inadequate stove provided warmth, but only for the fortunate few seated near it. The children could barely write in cold weather because their hands were too numb to hold the chalk.

All food was carried to school and was usually bread and cheese or sometimes a pasty. Pasties contained whatever was plentiful, from potato, turnip, apple, eggs, and bacon to even kidneys at pig killing time. Mid-morning, all children had a mug of creamy milk provided by Charles Fellwood, a tradition since his grandfather's time. Many children had no breakfast, so this was a welcome treat.

The ten children from the hamlet walked to school together; there were five Carters, three Symons, and two Cutcliffes. The Cutcliffes were a scruffy bunch, and Annie felt sorry for them, for all John and Hannah Cutcliffe cared about was where their next flagon of cider was coming from. Their walk to school took them past the smithy owned by Benjamin and Matilda Rudd. They could hear Ben hammering away on his anvil long before he came into sight, and on a cold day, he would let the children come to the forge to warm themselves. The Rudds had three sons. There was Harry, who had befriended Annie and worked alongside his father at the forge. Jacob, a big strong lad but slightly retarded, or 'tuppence short of a shilling' as was the local saying, also worked at the smithy. Francis, at fourteen, was employed as a stable lad at the big house. Further on again was The Red Lion Inn, which was situated next to the church.

One day, as the children dawdled on their way home from school, Betsey came running out and shouted to her granddaughter, Annie.

"Annie, tell your mum I've news of our William. You know, the one who's in China. I've seen neither hide nor hair of him for nigh on twenty years, but a friend of his just called to tell me he's coming home soon. I can't believe it."

"Aw, Gran, I'm so pleased for you. Is he coming home to stay?"

"I don't know, Annie, but apparently, he's married, with a wife and three children, and they're all coming to see us. Don't forget to tell your Mum because she always liked William. Oh, and tell her I've got Fred's baby, as well as Llew and Rosie, now your Aunty Lucy has gone into hospital, so I've got my hands full."

"All right, Gran, I'll tell her. I expect she'll come and see you when she has five minutes."

CHAPTER 11

Robert was playing draughts with Sarah in the nursery, a pleasant room at the top of the house, well-stocked with toys. There was a grey rocking horse with dappled markings, and its mane and tail were made of real horsehair. Sarah had nearly outgrown it at age ten, but it was a big horse, and she still rode it occasionally. Her favourite toy was a doll's house, and she spent hours rearranging the furniture and playing with the dolls inside.

It was raining heavily, and Sarah was bored, as they had intended to go riding. Whilst she planned her next move, her little pink tongue sticking out between her teeth, Robert glanced out of the window, and a movement near the vegetable patch caught his eye. At first, he thought he had imagined it, but as he looked closer, he was sure someone was crawling along the path. He went to the window, wondering why anyone would crawl along the path in the mud and rain.

"Come on, Robert, it's your go, and I'm going to beat you this time."

"Sarah, look at this."

Together, they watched in amazement as a skinny boy in a large cap swarmed along the path on his stomach.

"Shall we go and ask him what he's doing?"

"No, let's just watch and see what happens."

Annie swiftly shoved the vegetables into the sack and crawled off slowly, dragging the sack behind her.

"Why on earth is he doing that? Is it some kind of game, do you think?"

"No, he's stealing vegetables, and he hasn't realised that anyone looking out of these windows can easily see him, although he's crawling. He thinks he's safe behind those little hedges. We should tell Jack, but he'll be sent to jail if they catch him."

"What for taking a few old turnips? We can't do that. Why does he want them, anyway?"

"I don't know; perhaps his family is poor and hungry. It's too late to catch him now, but if we see him again, we'll tackle him. Until then, we'll keep it a secret, right?"

Sarah nodded happily, thrilled to think they had a secret.

"Let's finish this game of draughts then. Oh, you were right; you have beaten me this time. Do you want to play again, or would you like me to read you some of your new *Alice in Wonderland* book?"

"See, I told you I'd beat you. No, thanks, I can read it myself, but I'm going to play with my dolls and my tea set now; I'll make you a cup of tea."

"All right then, thank you. I'll have two spoonsful of sugar in mine and a piece of cake to go with it, please."

Robert sat in the window seat and watched in amusement as the thief slowly crawled away from the garden, then rose to his feet and ran towards the perimeter hedge. Little did Annie know that someone had witnessed her daring excursion into the grounds of the Manor House. Indeed, she would not have enjoyed her rabbit stew later if she had known, so her ignorance was certainly bliss.

Robert and Sarah watched for the thief for the next couple of days. However, their efforts were in vain, for since her first visit, Annie had decided it was safer to go at dawn when there were fewer people around and less risk of detection. Robert walked around the vegetable plot, but it was impossible to tell if more vegetables had been stolen or picked for use in the house. He wandered along and saw the hole in the hedge.

He wondered if the thief came early in the morning or late at night and thought the morning was the most likely. He decided to get up early the next day and lie in wait behind the bushes. He was lucky that Annie chose to gather more vegetables that morning, for she didn't come every day. He saw the capped head peer cautiously through the hedge and grinned, enjoying every minute. He had no intention of reporting the culprit but wanted to give him a nasty scare and decided to tackle the boy on his return. Annie dodged from tree to tree until she reached the path, where, as before, she sank to her stomach and crawled towards the vegetables. She quickly stored her loot in the sack and retraced her steps.

"What are you doing?" Robert demanded, leaping out from behind the trees.

Annie's face blanched even whiter than usual, and she felt sick. Tears ran unchecked down her cheeks as she shook uncontrollably, so shocked she could not speak. Robert was horrified to see what a shock he had given the lad, and immediately, all the fun went out of the situation. He couldn't believe the boy was crying.

"Oh, please don't cry. I'm sorry if I scared you, but don't worry, I won't tell anyone I've seen you."

Annie gulped and decided to make a run for it, but Robert, sensing her intention, lunged out and grabbed her, and they both fell to the ground in a heap.

"It's all right; calm down. Good Lord, you're a girl!"

Annie's cap had fallen off in the scramble, and her unruly hair tumbled in disarray around her shoulders.

"Stop struggling; I'm not going to hurt you. Sit here on this tree trunk and talk to me. I was just curious to see what you were doing. I saw you crawl along the path once before from our schoolroom window, and you looked so funny. I've been watching for a few days to see if you would return. I brought some food to eat whilst I waited, so you can share it with me if you like. There's nobody else about; it's far too early, and if anyone comes, I'll say I asked you to come through the hedge."

Annie was still shocked but reassured by the boy's friendliness. She studied him as she sat beside him and silently accepted some bread and ham. He was clearly one of the gentry, for his clothes were of the finest materials, and his boots highly polished. He spoke clearly with no trace of a Devonshire accent.

"What's your name?"

"It's Polly, sir, Polly Smith, but please don't tell anyone I was here."

"No, I promise I won't, but why are you stealing vegetables and dressing as a boy? You know it's wrong to steal, don't you?"

"Yes, of course, I do, and I don't like doing it, but my family's starving. I wore my dad's cap to hide my hair because it's a bit of a giveaway, isn't it?"

"Why can't your father provide for you?"

"He's dead, and Mum can't earn enough to feed us all, so these vegetables keep us going. Anyway, I must go before someone comes. Here, take the vegetables, and thanks for not telling on me. Don't worry, I won't come again."

"No, take the turnips; I don't want them. How will you eat if you don't come again?"

"We'll just have to manage. I shoot rabbits and go fishing, which helps, and Mum works, so she gets some money. What's your name, anyway? Do you live in the big house?"

"My name's Robert Fellwood, and yes, I live in the Manor House because my father is the squire. I like talking to you; will you come again? I could bring more food with me."

"No, if I get caught, your father will send me to jail, and you might change your mind and tell on me."

"I promise I won't, and he wouldn't send you to jail just for stealing a few vegetables. Please, say you'll come again."

"Well, I'll come early on Thursday morning. It's safer when there are not many folk about."

"Right, I'll meet you here then, and don't worry, I won't tell."

Annie ran home swiftly and thankfully heaved the sack onto the table. She was frightened and had no intention of going again. She feared the boy would have the gardener waiting to apprehend her if she poked her head through that hedge again. She didn't mention the incident to her mother, for she knew she would only be worried. She hoped that having given a false name, she might avoid being identified, though with her hair being such a bright red, it always made her stand out.

However, the larder was almost bare again by Thursday, for her last rabbiting expedition had been unsuccessful. Emma, Edward, and Stephen were hungry and fretful and more difficult to care for, so poor Liza was worn out. Annie rose before dawn, planning to be in and out of the Manor House garden before Robert appeared. He, however, guessed she might do just that, for as she put her head through the hedge, she heard him whisper her name.

"Psst, Polly, I'm over here."

Robert was sitting on the fallen tree trunk, a black and white collie by his side. She went towards him, her heart in her mouth, fully expecting to be pounced on at any moment. The dog went to her, seeking attention, but she ignored the animal and glanced around anxiously, ready for flight.

"It's all right; there's no one here, I promise you. Just Jacko and myself, and he'd like to be friends. Come and see what I've brought."

Annie stroked the dog's head as Robert proudly displayed a selection of potatoes, carrots, and parsnips.

"I brought these from the storeroom. I thought it would save you that awful crawl on your stomach."

"Well, ta, I mean, thanks, but if anyone sees you, won't they wonder why you're carrying vegetables?"

"Yes, I expect so, but there was no one around. And that's not all; I've more food here that you can take home or eat some now if you're hungry."

He delved into another bag and produced two loaves of bread, a wedge of cheese, and a large ham. Annie stared in amazement.

"Ooh no, I couldn't. I'd be hanged for certain if I was caught with that lot. You must put it back; they're sure to miss it."

"No, of course, they won't. Our larders are full of cheeses and hams, and the servants must occasionally steal the odd one. Don't worry about it. I bet your mother would enjoy some decent food. How many brothers and sisters do you have?"

"Two sisters and four brothers, and then there's Mum and Liza; she's a neighbour who lives with us. I help Mum with her job now, but I'll go into service as soon as she's had the baby."

"Good heavens, no wonder you need the food. Please take it; it will be all right." He thrust the bag towards her, and she took it hesitantly. "Mind you, I do want something in return." He grinned at her concerned expression. "It's nothing to worry about, but could I go fishing with you one day? I've never been fishing or shooting rabbits. I can use a gun because we have shooting parties here, but I've never needed to shoot anything. We just shoot pheasants for the sport of it, and I think that's cruel, but shooting to feed a starving family is different, isn't it?"

"Yes, you could come, but would you be allowed? I've only ever seen you in church. You never go to the village, do you?"

"No, I'm not allowed to mix with the local children, but I'll sneak out. We'll both have a guilty secret then, won't we? I had rheumatic fever recently, and I'm not returning to school until the autumn. I should be having lessons with my sister's governess, but fortunately, she's left, and a new one hasn't been found yet, so no one will miss me. When could we go?"

"I'm going fishing at Shebworthy Pond on Saturday. The pond's on your father's land, so I shouldn't fish there, but I've never seen a bailiff, and most people take the risk. Do you know where it is?"

"Yes, I have been there, but it's quite a walk, isn't it?"

"Is it too far for you?"

"No, of course not. Shall I meet you there?"

"Yes, and thanks for the food."

She struggled home with the heavy sack, and Sabina was apprehensive when she emptied the contents onto the table.

"Oh, Annie, where did you get all this? You've gone too far this time, my girl. You'll end up in jail, and that's for certain."

Annie explained about her new friend, but this brought no comfort to Sabina, though she was glad Annie had not stolen the food. A few turnips were one thing, but hams and cheeses were quite another. However, the food could not be returned, so she decided the best thing was to destroy the evidence, and the Carters sat down to the best meal they had eaten in a long time.

Robert knew Sarah would love to go fishing with him and felt he should invite her, but he fancied an adventure alone with Polly. However, his dilemma was resolved when his sister tripped and fell down the stairs, breaking her ankle. He felt guilty, for he never wished for anything so awful to happen, but it did mean she would be inactive for some time.

It was a complicated fracture, and to ease the pain, the doctor prescribed small doses of laudanum, which made her sleepy. Robert played cards, ludo, and draughts with her to help pass the time. On Saturday, however, he made the excuse of taking his dog, Jacko, for a walk and made for Shebworthy Pond.

Annie was already there, and on the bank beside her lay two perch. As he approached her, something tugged at her line, and she immediately focused on landing the fish. She deftly grasped the wriggling fish and smacked its head with a large stone at her side, then skilfully gutted it with a sharp knife whilst Robert stared in fascination.

"What's the matter? Never seen a fish caught before?" she demanded.

"Well, yes, of course, but they're usually thrown back. It's so cruel to kill them like that."

"'It's kinder to kill them than leave them gasping and suffocating to death. People have to eat, and there's little enough else, but I don't suppose you've ever gone hungry?"

"No, you're right. I'm lucky; I never have."

"Sorry, I didn't mean to be rude. You got away, all right, then?"

Robert explained about Sarah, thinking as he gazed at Annie that she was the prettiest girl he had ever seen. Her tangled red hair hung in ringlets down to her waist, and he shuddered at the thought of anyone trying to get a brush through it. Her skin was pale, in contrast to her hair, and her green eyes seemed huge in her small, pointed face. There was a light sprinkling of freckles across her nose, and she grinned at him, showing a set of small, even white teeth.

Annie stroked Jacko, who was sitting beside her, and the dog laid his chin on her knee.

"What a friendly dog. Have you had him long?"

"Yes, we've had him since he was a puppy, and he must be about ten years old now, so he's getting on a bit. He's certainly taken to you."

"Would you like to have a go at fishing? I can make you a rod and kill the fish if you don't want to."

Robert nodded, excited at the thought. Annie found a suitable stick for a rod, tied some string to it, and then a hook. She reached into a tin at her side and hooked a worm on the end.

"There you are, just throw that in the water and wait. You must keep quiet, though, or you'll frighten the fish, and I must catch a few more before I go home. We can talk in whispers if you like."

Robert spent one of the happiest afternoons of his life. The early rain cleared up, and the sun shone brightly on Annie's hair. She had brought a thick slice of bread and a lump of cheese for each of them, and they sat side-by-side, munching the food hungrily.

"Do you know, I'd never eat just bread and cheese at home for lunch, but this is delicious." Robert was surprised at how much he was enjoying the simple meal.

"I always think food tastes much better out of doors, especially when you're hungry."

Within a couple of hours, Robert had caught three fish and Annie two more. She methodically killed and gutted the fish and showed him how to bait his hook. After a while, she stood up.

"I should go home now. Shall we walk back together?" She packed the fish into a wicker basket. "I'll let you have your fish when we reach the village."

"No, it's all right; you can have them, but I'll carry the basket. It's quite heavy now."

"Thanks, the family will eat well tonight." She glanced up at him shyly. "We could come again next Saturday if you like?"

He nodded happily and tentatively held her hand as they walked back together as far as they dared.

CHAPTER 12

Robert and Annie soon became firm friends and met as frequently as possible without raising suspicion. Their favourite meeting place was under a large mazzard tree. The village was famous for its many acres of mazzard orchards, or mazzard greens, as they were known locally. Wild cherry rootstock was used to graft new trees, and it took some fifteen years for a tree to reach maturity. When fully grown, the branches met overhead and formed a green canopy. The frothy white blossom was such a beautiful sight in spring that people came from far and wide to wonder at it. There were several varicties of mazzard, both black and red, including the Dun, the Greenstem Black, and the Hannaford, which ripened earlier than the others.

The trees were tall, often fifty feet or more, and farmers made long ladders to reach the fruit. The women skilfully picked the mazzards, leaving the stalks attached so the juice would not bleed from the cherries. The baskets had hooks on the handles, which could be crooked over a branch to leave both hands free for picking. The delicious mazzards were feasted on locally, and children went about purple-mouthed for days. The fruit was taken to the market in large panniers or maunds, sold for pies and puddings, and served with clotted cream. Merchants bought the cherries and sent them by train to London's Covent Garden. Surplus fruit was bottled for the long winter months when little fruit was available. Birds liked mazzards, too, and the children shook rattles until their arms ached to scare them away. Farmers were up before dawn, with guns ready to shoot the thieving blackbirds and thrushes in the trees, for they could strip an orchard in a day or two.

The tree favoured by Annie and Robert was in a mazzard green on the outskirts of the village. The orchard had been there for many years, and the trees were mature. The trees had a bulge around their trunks just above head height where the rootstock had been grafted long ago. A brook meandered through the orchard, and a tiny waterfall tumbled over some rocks before emptying itself into a pond in one corner. It was a deserted spot, seldom visited except at mazzard picking time or when the village children took it in their heads to seek out frogspawn or tadpoles in the pond.

It was some weeks before Annie confessed to Robert that her name was Annie Carter and not Polly Smith. She told him her family lived in one of his father's tied cottages and that her mother worked on the estate. He was saddened she had felt it necessary to lie to him but appreciated how scared she was of her family being evicted from their cottage. His father was not sympathetic to the poor, so he understood her fear and thought it was probably well-founded.

A suitable governess had been found, but unfortunately, her father was seriously ill, and she had to nurse him for a couple of months. As she was a distant, poor relative with impeccable references, Charles Fellwood decided they would wait for her. This being the case, Robert found it easy to slip away and spend time with Annie. His twin, Victoria, took little interest in his whereabouts, and his brother, David, was spending the summer holiday in Scotland with a friend and planned to return to boarding school from there. Poor Sarah was still resting her broken ankle. As often as possible, he made the excuse of going riding or walking Jacko and then meeting Annie in the mazzard green, and despite their different backgrounds, they soon became fond of each other and counted the days until they could next meet.

Most children worked on the farms in the holidays to earn a few pennies, and many stayed off school during the busy times. Robert joined in, too, mainly for an opportunity to see Annie, though he also enjoyed learning about farming at first-hand. He was careful to pay little attention to her, for they wanted no one to know of their friendship, but they both found it increasingly difficult to ignore each other. The villagers welcomed him, so he wasn't too worried about someone reporting back to his father. Farmers planted flatpolls, large, hardy, purple cabbages, and mangel-wurzels, a sort of turnip fed to cattle throughout the winter. The crops needed regular weeding until they were harvested in the autumn. Robert soon discovered weeding was backbreaking work as he learnt to identify the more common weeds such as lambs' tongue, dandelions, and thistles or dashels as they were known. The prickly dashels were unpleasant to handle and had to be weeded out carefully. He became adept at removing prickles from his hands with a needle by the light of a lamp in the evenings, and Annie taught him the old Devon verse:

"Cut a dashel in June,
'Tis a month too soon,
Cut a dashel in July,
Ee's sure to die."

Most folk kept a few ducks, geese, or hens, and four families, including the Carters, owned a pig between them. Together, they fed and cared for it. Pig-killing day was always quite an occasion as there would be plenty to eat for a while. The joints of meat would be salted and shared out, along with the offal, and nothing was wasted.

When the time came for the Carter family's pig to be slaughtered, Annie invited Robert to come along and watch. He came strolling along the path to the cottage and was welcomed by all the children as he handed out a few sweets. He ruffled their hair, kicked a ball about with the boys, and wondered where Annie was. As she came out of her cottage, their eyes met, and they exchanged a secret smile. They sat closely together on the pigsty wall, longing, but not daring, to hold hands. They giggled with the other children as Sam Symons and Edward Hooper chased Henry, a large boar, around the sty, trying to get a rope around his neck. The rope would be hoisted over a beam in the barn to hold the pig steady to have its throat cut.

"Come on, Sam, stop mucking about and grab him," Edward exclaimed as he tried and failed to get the rope over Henry's head.

Henry, squealing loudly, led them a merry dance. Cornered, he bared his teeth at Sam and promptly took a chunk out of his sleeve.

"Here, you have the rope, and I'll catch him."

Edward chased Henry around the pigsty, and the ground became increasingly slippery as Henry's bowels proved unable to cope with all the excitement. Suddenly, Edward lunged, determined to grab the pig, but slipped and landed flat on his face in all the muck. The children screamed with laughter as Henry escaped once more. Sam, too, had to turn away for fear of choking. Incensed, Edward picked himself up with as much dignity as he could muster and, with renewed determination, threw himself on Henry, crushing him to the ground and allowing Sam to slip the rope over his head.

Poor Henry was dragged to the barn and slaughtered. The pig quickly bled to death and was then butchered. Robert was physically sick, and Annie laughed at him. It didn't bother her at all, but then she had seen it many times before and was looking forward to the food Henry would provide.

To Annie's delight, her siblings begged Robert to come to tea, and with some misgivings, Sabina agreed. Robert found the cottage claustrophobic, for its cob walls were almost three feet thick, making the rooms small and dark, as the windows were tiny and let in little light. The small dwelling was full of thin, grubby children with red or fair hair. The little ones eyed the dark-haired youth curiously, and Sabina and Liza were anxious about having the squire's son to tea. Robert spoke quietly to Sabina.

"Mrs Carter, I can see my presence here worries you, so I'll go home for my tea, but it was nice to meet you. Don't worry; no one will know I've been here, and even if they did, I would take the blame."

"No, Master Robert, please stay and have your tea, for you've been so kind to us. I worry about losing my job and the cottage if I upset your father, you see."

Before Robert could answer, she clutched a hand to her rounded stomach, and her face creased with pain as she doubled over.

"Mum, what's wrong? Is it the baby?"

Sabina took a deep breath as the pain passed. "Yes, I think so. I've been getting a few twinges all day, but it will be a while yet. Come on, you lot, get on with your tea."

Robert tried not to stare as the children delved hungrily into their bowls and devoured the food with their fingers. He could see that grubby and hungry they might be but loved and cherished they certainly were. He realised what a hard life Sabina must lead and could not help but compare her to his own mother, who had so many servants. Annie smiled, knowing Robert had charmed her mother and hoped she would be able to bring him again. After tea, she walked part-way home with him. They crossed a couple of fields and climbed a stile into the mazzard green. The weather was warm, and the mazzards were formed on the trees but were not yet ripe.

"Let's sit down for a few minutes, Robert; it's so pretty here. What did you think of the Carter family? I bet it was a bit different from tea at the big house?"

"It certainly was, but I loved it; thanks for asking me. I can't believe you all live in such a small cottage; it's so crowded, and I think your mother is amazing to manage the way she does."

"I think this is my favourite place in the whole world. It's so peaceful."

He leant over and kissed her gently on the lips and, seeing no rebuke in her eyes, pressed his lips to hers again and put his arms around her. She responded immediately, and they kissed passionately for several minutes until she reluctantly pulled away from his embrace.

"Oh, Robert, I must go. I have to see how Mum is."

"Yes, I know, but I don't want you to. When can we meet again?"

"I don't know, but soon."

As she walked home, she put her fingers to her lips and wondered if she had imagined those warm kisses, and a little smile played around her mouth.

By the time Annie got home, Sabina's waters had broken, and her pains were increasing rapidly. Willie fetched Tilly Rudd, the village's nearest thing to a midwife. Sabina herself was often called upon to attend births, for none could afford a doctor. Matilda bustled up the path and took charge. She was a pleasant, motherly person who not only delivered babies but also laid out the dead.

"I take care of people at both ends of their lives and sometimes in between," she was often heard to say. She puffed a bit from walking up the hill, for she was a plump woman and proof that the blacksmith's forge was prosperous. Her cheeks were rosy by the time she got to the cottage.

"Right then, Sabina, how are you doing? You've done this more often than I have."

"Yes, that's true, Tilly, and I don't usually have much trouble. Annie and Willie, you'll have to do the milking. I meant to arrange for you to do it when this happened, but it's sooner than expected. Tell Jack the baby's on the way, and you'll do the milking for a few days until I'm on my feet again. You know what to do, don't you, Annie?"

"Yes, I can do it, Mum, but don't you want me to stay here with you?"

"No, I'll be fine. Liza can look after the little ones, and Tilly will see to me. You get the milking done, and mind that new heifer, she kicks." Sabina ended the sentence with a gasp as a strong contraction gripped her body. "Go on, go."

Sabina's labour did not last long. Within two hours, and before Annie and Willie returned from the milking, a baby girl lay in her arms. She had fair hair and blue eyes and was small, which was understandable, considering Sabina's meagre diet and her early arrival. However, she sucked hungrily at Sabina's nipple and appeared perfect in every respect. The children stared in wonder at their new little sister.

"What shall we call her? I haven't thought of a name. Liza, if you'd had a little girl, what would you have called her?"

"Well, my mother was called Helen, and I've always liked the name, but Sabina, it's your daughter, so you must choose."

"No, I like Helen, and I don't think she'd be here today if it weren't for you, Liza, so that's what we'll call her. What do the rest of you think?"

The children clambered onto the bed beside their mother and nodded in agreement.

"It's such a pity she'll never see her daddy." A sob escaped Sabina, and to her annoyance, tears trickled down her cheeks, and she brushed them away angrily. "Oh, what a silly old fool I am; take no notice of me, Tilly. I'm just tired and feeling sorry for myself."

"Right, you lot go outside and play until bedtime and give your mum some peace. You're not silly, Sabina. Yes, I know you're tired, but that's the first tears I've seen you shed since Tom died, and it's high time you had a good cry, my girl. There's nothing wrong with that, nothing whatsoever."

Matilda took the sleeping babe from her mother's arms and laid her gently in the crib, then she put her arms around Sabina and stroked her hair. Sabina cried as if her heart would break but felt so comforted by the strong, motherly arms that encircled her.

CHAPTER 13

Following their first kiss in the mazzard green, Robert and Annie could hardly bear to be apart. It was so frustrating to see each other in the village but have to hide their feelings for each other. They continued to meet secretly as often as they could, neither admitting, even to themselves, that their relationship could have no future.

A few weeks after Sabina gave birth to Helen, the village children arranged a picnic at Shebworthy Pond. Annie was delighted as Robert had agreed to come, and she was looking forward to spending the whole day in his company. It was a fine day in mid-August, hot and sunny, and many were looking forward to a swim in the cool green water, but first, they wanted to catch some fish for their lunch. At last, when there was enough fish for everyone, they stripped off to their underclothes and dived in. Most could swim, but a few just paddled near the edge. Harry, the blacksmith's son, had hoped to spend some time with Annie himself, and he resented Robert's presence because he sensed her interest in him. Harry was an excellent swimmer, and his muscular brown arms cut the water cleanly as he quickly swam from one side of the pond to the other.

The pond was too dangerous for any but the best swimmers to venture far from the edge. No matter how hot the day, the water was always icy cold, for it was heavily shaded by woodland. Years ago, it had been an old limestone quarry, and the story went that it had flooded overnight. A path had once wound around the sides down to the bottom where the horses were stabled. The men had arrived for work one morning to find the quarry half full of water. The stables were underwater, and the poor horses had drowned. It was thought that blasting from the previous day had released an underground stream, and eventually, the entire quarry filled with water. Now regarded as a local beauty spot, the pond had become the watery grave of many unwanted kittens and puppies, and even babies, over the years. A new limestone quarry nearby now offered employment to the villagers.

Some older boys began diving, trying in vain to reach the bottom. The water was clear near the top, and some interesting items rested on the old track. A fallen tree, a plough, and a large farm cart had been dumped. They swam around the old cart, only six feet below the surface and resting on an outcrop of rock. It had been there a long, long time and was rotten. As Harry swam below it, the motion caused it to shift, and it fell, pinning him to the ground. Luke Bedworth saw what had happened and tried, unsuccessfully, to pull Harry free, and he quickly surfaced and yelled for help.

Robert and Jim, a stocky farmer's son, dived to the rescue. Robert signalled to Jim and Luke to lift the cart whilst he tried to pull Harry free. Harry clutched at him in desperation, sheer panic filling his eyes as he tried not to breathe and ignored his lungs, screaming for oxygen. At last, with a look of resignation, he inhaled water, and his eyes lost focus and closed. Suddenly, he came free, and Robert swam hard, dragging him to the surface. With Jim and Luke's help, he towed him to the edge, and the cart began a long, slow descent to the murky depths and its final resting place.

They hauled Harry out, and he lay still, not breathing. His lips were blue, and some of the girls started to cry.

"Oh no, is he dead? We must fetch help."

"Harry, wake up. Can you hear me?" Annie slapped his face, but there was no response.

"There's no time to get help. It'll be too late."

Panicking now and not knowing what to do, they rolled Harry onto his front and pressed on his back, and water ran from his mouth and nose. Robert tried desperately to remember what little he had learned at school about resuscitation, and, with Jim's help, he heaved Harry into a sitting position, bent him over, and thumped his back again. Yet more water ran from his nose, but still, he did not breathe. They laid him back down, and Robert raised his chin, pinched his nose, and blew air into his mouth. At first, there was no response, but suddenly, Harry vomited a considerable amount of pond water. Everyone cheered as he sat up weakly, coughing and spluttering. He shivered violently, and they helped him nearer to the fire and wrapped dry clothes around him.

By this time, the fish was cooked and eaten with crusty bread, a delicious meal washed down with icy water from the stream. Luke and Jim told Harry how Robert had saved his life, though Robert protested at all the fuss. Harry gruffly thanked him and shook his hand.

Harry had never liked Robert, and though he was grateful to him for saving his life, it was all he could do to be civil. He could see that Annie was keen on Robert, however much she tried to hide it, and he felt it was difficult to compete with a squire's son. He vowed to find a way to discourage Robert from coming to the village. The only comfort was that Robert would never be allowed to marry a village girl, so perhaps he just needed to bide his time.

For Robert's part, he could sense Harry's animosity towards him and was puzzled. He was pleased to have been able to save the young man's life and couldn't understand why he was so unfriendly. In the end, he decided it must be because he was the squire's son, and perhaps Harry resented his easy life.

It was a hectic time of year in the countryside, and there was a lot of work to do. Farmers were busy in the fields, often stripped to the waist in the hot sun as they cut the long grass with scythes. It was left to dry for a few days before being raked up and carted into haystacks. The hay would be used throughout the winter to feed the horses and cows.

The annual Earl of Lore Hunt was traditionally held on the third Saturday in August and was a big occasion in the village. Annie asked Robert if he could come.

"Yes, I'd love to. I'll pretend I'm going for a ride over the moors. Can I leave my horse at your place?"

"Yes, if you tether him in the woods out the back, no one will see him. Have you been to the hunt before?"

"No, I've never been allowed. Papa says there is a lot of drunkenness and violence. I wouldn't be able to go this year if anyone knew."

"Well, there is a lot of drinking, but there's usually no trouble. I'm so glad you're coming."

The day of the hunt dawned bright and sunny. It was an ancient custom featuring a character called the Earl of Lore, who wore a grotesque mask, a smock coat, and a string of twelve biscuits around his neck. Legend said he had sailed from Ireland and had been shipwrecked on a local beach. He had survived by eating the biscuits he had with him from the ship.

The event began with a villager dressed as the earl being given a head start to hide in the woods. Annie and Robert joined the crowd, following youths brightly dressed as soldiers and armed with guns, ready to capture him. Eventually, they found him hidden in some brushwood. The grenadiers fired a volley of shots into the air to celebrate their find, hauled him onto a donkey laden with flowers and ribbons and paraded him back to the village.

The poor earl was forced to ride on the donkey facing the tail. He was followed by a hobbyhorse, wearing a mask and decorated with gaily painted trappings and a fool, also vividly clothed. As he was paraded through the village, pennies, halfpennies, and farthings were thrown into a bucket for the poor. Robert put a few pennies into the bucket, rattled under his nose by the fool. John Cutcliffe, standing next to him, refused to part with anything, and much to the amusement of the crowd, the fool dipped the besom he carried into a muddy puddle and shook it over John's head.

The procession passed slowly through the village, for the revellers stopped to drink a pint of ale at each inn. At length, the grenadiers fired another volley into the air as the earl was 'murdered' and thrown to the ground. There followed much wailing and lamenting by the crowd until the fool and the hobbyhorse, dancing madly, waved magic wands to heal him, and he was put back onto his donkey again. There was much merrymaking and singing from the crowd, and the streets were lined with side stalls selling pasties, cakes, fruit, and vegetables. Pedlars displayed their wares, a barrel organ played whilst a monkey danced, and there was even a Punch and Judy show. A few revellers were staggering a bit from one beer too many as the procession reached the shore, and the poor earl was thrown back into the sea from whence he had allegedly come.

Another antic of the day was the pig chase. A young pig donated by Lord Fellwood was delivered to the inn each year. Thickly greased to make it slippery, it was released in the main street. Whoever caught the pig could keep it, so it was an attractive prize. However, catching and holding onto the greasy, squealing piglet was difficult, though entertaining. Robert would have loved to catch the pig for Annie but didn't dare risk his father hearing he had been at the festivities, let alone taken part in such an event. As it was, Sam Symons carried off the prize. Robert and Annie enjoyed their day, and late in the afternoon, she walked with him to retrieve his horse. He wanted to stay for the hog roast and celebrations that would continue long into the night, but he knew he would be missed. There would, no doubt, be some sore heads in the morning. Before climbing into the saddle, he pulled Annie to him and kissed her tenderly, but she was uneasy.

"Not here, Robert."

"Don't you like me kissing you, then?"

"You know I do, but what if someone sees us? You'll be off to school soon, and I'll miss you so much."

"Let's not think about that now. Let's enjoy the next few weeks."

She sighed and returned his kiss. When she released him, he reluctantly mounted his horse to return home.

CHAPTER 14

Following the incident at the pond, Robert had become a hero in the village, and he worried about his family hearing of his exploits. A few days later, Harry went to the Manor House to return a horse he had shod, and Jack Bater stopped for a chat.

"Hello, Harry, lad, how are you? Goodness, look at the size of you. You'll be bigger than your dad soon, and young Francis is catching up, too."

"Hello, Jack. Yes, we're all big in our family. Mind you, I wouldn't be here at all if it weren't for young Master Robert; he saved my life last week."

"Master Robert? How did he come to save your life, Harry? I'm surprised he even knows you."

"Well, he doesn't really know me, but we've met a few times since he started working on the farms. Anyway, he joined a few of us swimming in Shebworthy Pond and rescued me when an old cart fell and trapped me underwater. If it weren't for him, I'd have been a goner, a strong swimmer, though I am."

Jack Bater stared at Harry in surprise, knowing that Charles Fellwood, and particularly Eleanor, would never allow Robert to mix with the locals, let alone swim in Shebworthy Pond. She was from a wealthy family and would have been appalled at him mixing with the villagers, never mind swimming in the dirty pond water.

"Are you sure it was Master Robert, Harry?"

"Oh aye, it was him all right and very grateful I am to him too. I'd stopped breathing, but he got me going again. He's kind-hearted too, giving food to the needy as he does."

"Well, I'm glad you're all right, Harry. Give my regards to your mum and dad, will you?"

Jack pondered this news, a troubled expression on his face. Should he tell the master? He had no wish to get the lad in trouble, but if the master ever found out that he, Jack, knew and didn't tell him, there'd be hell to pay. He had a prestigious job and a comfortable cottage, and with six children to feed, he couldn't risk putting all that in jeopardy for the lad getting a telling-off. He went indoors and knocked on the door of his master's study.

"Good morning, Jack. Nothing wrong, is there?"

"No, sir, but there's something I think you should know. To tell you the truth, I'm in a bit of a predicament. I don't like telling tales, but if I tell you, it's up to you what you do then, isn't it?"

"Well, get on with it, man; what is it?"

"It's Master Robert, sir. He's been taking food to the poor and working on the farms. I didn't know if you knew this, sir, but I thought I should tell you."

"Are you sure, Jack? Why would he do that, and how do you know anyway?"

"Harry Rudd, the blacksmith's son, returned a horse he'd shod this morning, and he told me Master Robert saved his life when he nearly drowned in Shebworthy Pond. I think it's right enough, sir, for he'd no reason to lie."

"I see. Thank you for telling me, Jack. I'll have a word with Master Robert."

"Yes, sir, I'm sure he meant no harm, and he's something of a hero in the village for saving Harry's life."

As Jack left, Eleanor entered the room and overheard part of the conversation.

"Jack doesn't normally see you at this time of day. Is something wrong, dear?"

Charles had not planned to burden her with the news, for he knew she would overreact. However, he told her what Jack had said, and predictably, she was horrified.

"Oh no, he could have caught all sorts of diseases. We must get Doctor Luckett to check him over. How could he be so thoughtless and disobedient? Fancy swimming in that filthy cold water when he's only just got over rheumatic fever."

"I'll send for him. Do you want to stay?"

She nodded, and he rang the bell to summon a maid to fetch Robert, who arrived looking somewhat apprehensive. His father asked him straight away if he had been visiting the village.

"Yes, sir, I have."

"Well, at least you're honest, but why? What is there to interest you in the village?"

"I love going to the village and meeting the people. They're so poor and lead such hard lives, Father. I'm not sure you realise how terrible their living conditions are. Their cottages are desperately in need of repair; some of the roofs are even stuffed with rags to keep out the rain. They're our cottages, aren't they, so could we have them repaired? Some of the families are near to starving, they..."

"Enough; this is not your concern, Robert. There are too many villagers for us to help them all, and they breed like rabbits. They're dirty, for the most part lazy, and worst of all, disease and vermin-ridden. You may have brought all manner of illnesses home to the family. How could you be so thoughtless?"

"I'm sorry. I never thought of that, but if we improved their living conditions, there wouldn't be so much illness, would there? They work so hard, father; I know because I've been working with them. Look, I've even had blisters."

He proudly held out hands that now bore callouses, but his father was not impressed.

"What could you possibly want with a few shillings that you don't have already? You have never wanted for anything, so why did you feel the need to lower yourself and work for a pittance?"

"I didn't want the money; I gave it to a poor family. The father died of consumption a few months ago, and there are eight young children. The mother has just given birth prematurely and is almost killing herself, trying to earn enough to feed them. I enjoyed the work because it made me feel useful, and they were ridiculously grateful. Please could we help some of the poorest families in the village? It wouldn't cost..."

His father slammed his hand on the desk, his face red and angry.

"I've heard enough. Your grandfather entertained these silly notions of helping the poor. Indeed, he spent so much money on them that he neglected this house and almost ran the estate into debt, re-opening the silver mine. I will never allow such a thing to happen again. You will not leave the grounds again without my permission, and if you disobey, I'll have you whipped. People will never respect you if you mix with them like a common labourer. I am glad David will be the next squire and not you, for you would have seriously undermined your position through this foolishness. I shall arrange for you to return to school tomorrow. The summer holidays are nearly over, and I think you're fit enough to go back, though how long you will stay so after swimming in the filthy water at Shebworthy Pond, I do not know."

"Yes, sir. I'm sorry, sir."

Throughout all this, Eleanor stood silently, not daring to interrupt her husband. He had a vicious temper, and she knew when to hold her tongue. She, too, thought it best for Robert to return to school, mainly to escape his father's attention. Hopefully, the company of other young people of the same standing as himself would help rid him of these strange ideas.

Robert sat miserably in his room and knew he was lucky to have gotten away with it all for as long as he had. He had never thought his father ruthless but could now believe that families would be evicted from their cottages and put in the workhouse if they displeased him. If only he could see Annie again to explain and warn her to stop stealing vegetables, but with the mood his father was in, it was far too risky, and there was so little time. He pondered the matter and decided to go to the gap in the hedge at dawn the next day and hope she arrived. His father had forbidden him to leave the grounds, but he would not need to. He settled down to wait for the morning.

CHAPTER 15

Eleanor went into labour later that morning. Her other children had been born relatively easily, but this birth was difficult, for the cord was wrapped not once, but twice, around the baby's neck. It was many hours before the child was born, but at last, she sank back against the pillows, glad it was all over and relieved to hear the child cry.

"Is it all right? Is it a boy or a girl, Andrew?"

"It's a boy, ma'am. I need to check him over, and then you can hold him."

Eleanor sensed from his hesitant tone that something was wrong and caught a glance between the doctor and nurse.

"What is it? Is there something wrong? Let me see him."

Silently, Andrew Luckett handed the baby to her. The boy had a fine head of hair, dark and curly, just like his siblings. His skin was perfect, soft, and downy, and his eyes were large and clear. He cried weakly, and one glance was enough to see he was not normal. His poor little mouth was deformed. His top lip was split by a cleft that ran up to his nose, and his tongue, hanging over his bottom lip, seemed too big to fit into his mouth. As if that wasn't enough, both legs were deformed, and the ankles turned in at ridiculous angles. Eleanor stared at her newborn son in horror, for the child was ugly. There was no other word for it; he was ugly and deformed. Silently, she passed him back to the doctor, tears shining in her eyes. Andrew placed the child in its cot and left the room. He slowly descended the magnificent staircase, wondering how best to break the news to Charles. He met him at the foot of the stairs.

"Is Eleanor all right, Andrew, and the child? What is it?"

"Yes, Eleanor is fine, and it's a boy, but just a minute, Charles, before you go up." Andrew laid a hand on his arm. "There's no easy way to tell you this, but I'm afraid the child is deformed. He has a cleft palate and club feet. Now, there may be a surgeon in London who can help. I don't know, but we can find out. The only thing is..." He hesitated.

"Well, go on, man. What is it? Isn't that enough?"

"Well, I can't be sure, but I suspect the child may be mentally retarded. Eleanor had a difficult labour, and the cord was wrapped tightly around his neck twice, and he may have been starved of air. I'm so sorry, Charles, but I've seen this before, and often the children are not as they should be."

"Good God. How sure are you?"

"Well, as I say, I can't be sure, but his tongue hangs out of his mouth, and his head is rather too large, which is not a good sign. Of course, that was not caused by the birth, though it's probably why it was so difficult. I'm only mentioning it because there may be no point in making him suffer surgery. I suspect his heart could be weak, too. We will know much more in the coming months, and it may not be nearly as serious as we fear, but I wanted to be frank with you."

Charles proceeded up the stairs slowly and reluctantly opened his wife's bedroom door. He didn't want to see the child but knew he must. He went to his wife and gathered her into his arms. She wept bitterly, and he kissed her gently, then went to the crib. The child's deformities were far worse than he had expected.

"Eleanor, what shall we do?"

"Send him away, Charles. I don't ever want to see him again."

"Andrew says we may be able to get a surgeon to operate on him; it's too soon to say, but he is our son after all."

"No, I shan't change my mind, Charles. He looks just like my little brother, Sydney, did when he was born, and he just got worse as he grew older. He was an idiot and dribbled constantly. I could never understand mother letting him stay in the house, but she doted on him. He died when he was ten, but I thought it was a pity he lived that long. Charles, I don't want this baby, and I certainly don't want to watch him suffering for years."

"Andrew, do you know anywhere we could send the child to be cared for? Is there any other solution?"

Robert was just about to knock on the half-open door and overheard this last statement. He wondered what they were discussing and put his head around the door.

"Please, may I come in and see Mother?"

His father nodded, and Robert sat on the edge of the bed. Eleanor hugged him, needing to know that this son, at least, was whole.

"Are you all right, Mother? May I see the baby?"

"No, wait..."

Without waiting to be told, he looked in the crib and gasped. "What's wrong with it?"

"Robert, he's deformed and unlikely to live, so we shall have him fostered. I was too old to have another baby. I'm glad Victoria and Sarah are staying with Aunty Margery for a few days; they need never know he lived."

"But Mother, you can't give him away. He's your baby."

"Robert, listen to me; please forget you ever saw him because I want everyone to think he was born dead like he should have been. You are not to tell anyone, do you understand?"

Charles put his arm around Robert's shoulders and led him from the room and out of Eleanor's hearing.

"It's a pity you saw the baby, Robert, and you must forget about him. We'll find someone to wet nurse him, and I'll ensure he's cared for, but as your mother said, he'll likely die anyway. You can see how deformed he is. His feet are no use to him, poor child, and how can he feed properly with a mouth like that? I want you to promise me you'll tell everyone he was stillborn."

"I know someone who would look after him."

"Whom do you know that would look after him?"

"It's the woman I told you about this morning. Her husband died of consumption recently, and she had a baby a few weeks ago. Helen, the baby's called, and Sabina must still be feeding her. I'm sure she would take him, especially if you could pay her. It would help them, too, because they're living on the breadline."

"What do you think, Andrew? Do you know this woman? Would she keep her mouth shut?"

"Yes, I know the family, and they're struggling to make ends meet, but they're one of the cleaner families, and Sabina loves her children. He'd be well cared for, and I'm sure they could be trusted to be discreet. It could work, Charles, but are you sure you want to do this? It's far too soon after the birth for such a decision, and Eleanor may feel differently when she's rested. She wanted the child sent further away, too, not cared for locally, where his identity might come out one day."

"It will have to be now if we are going to pretend the child was stillborn. We can't risk the servants seeing him or hearing him cry. Can the nurse be trusted to keep a secret?"

"Yes, she's completely trustworthy; you have no worries on that score. If Sabina took the child in and Eleanor changed her mind, we could always get him back somehow, though I'm not sure how we could explain it."

"I know the family well, Papa. Please may I see if they will take the baby before I return to school? I know how angry you were with me earlier, but this would come better from me."

Reluctantly, Charles Fellwood allowed Robert to visit Annie's cottage once more.

"You must make it clear, Robert, that if the truth about the baby's identity ever comes out, they will be evicted from their cottage and lose their jobs."

When Robert later spoke privately to Sabina and Annie, they could not believe what he was telling them.

"But it's her son, even if he is deformed. No, she'll change her mind in a day or two; you'll see."

"No, I'm sure she won't, Sabina. I wish she would, but her brother was mentally impaired and died young, and the baby reminds her of him. She's adamant she doesn't want the child, so please, will you take him? Father found out I've been hanging around the village, and he's furious. It's only because of the baby that he's let me come here now. I have to return to school tomorrow, and I won't be able to come again."

At these words, Annie stared at him in dismay but could say nothing with her mother present. Robert continued hastily, carefully avoiding Annie's eyes.

"Until yesterday, I thought I knew my parents, but not anymore; they disgust me. They'd pay you, though, Sabina, so it would make life easier for you, but no one must ever know it's his son. My father would send you packing if the truth ever came out, but you'll always be safe if you care for the baby. Please, Sabina, I'd be so grateful if you would take him. I think they'll just let him die otherwise."

Sabina slowly nodded her head, and Robert embraced her. "Thank you. I knew you wouldn't let me down. If I fetch the baby, could you meet me by the gap in the hedge, Annie?"

She nodded sadly, thinking this might be the last time she would ever see him alone.

Robert gave the news to his parents, and Andrew Luckett and the nurse were sworn to secrecy. With the child wrapped in a piece of sacking, Robert carried him to the door.

"Do you want to hold him just once more, Mother?" He asked, still hoping she might change her mind, but she firmly shook her head.

He met Annie as arranged and carefully passed the bundle to her.

"They'll send money, Annie, but remember you must keep your mouths shut. My father will be ruthless if anyone discovers it's their baby." He put his arms around both her and the child and kissed her. "Father was furious when he found out I'd been spending time in the village. I don't know who told him, but I'm being sent back to school tomorrow. You must make sure no one suspects our friendship, for it would go badly for your family. At least you won't need to steal vegetables now with the extra money for keeping the baby."

"Oh, Robert, I'm going to miss you so much. Do you have to go so soon?"

"I'm afraid I have no choice, but I love you, Annie Carter, and don't you ever forget it. I'll be back for Christmas before you know it."

"I love you, too, but we've been fooling ourselves, Robert; we can never be together, can we? If your father won't even let you come to the village, we have no future."

"Somehow, we'll find a way. For now, I must do as I'm told, but I promise you, we'll find a way. I must go now, though."

Still, Annie clung to him, but gently, he took his arms from around her and the baby and kissed her fingers before quickly walking away.

Blinded by tears, Annie stumbled through the woods and arrived at her door without glancing at the baby. Hastily, she rubbed the tears from her cheeks and called to her mother for the benefit of anyone listening.

"Mum, I've found a baby in the woods! It must have been abandoned, but there was no one around."

Her mother and Liza entered the room, and as Annie pulled back the sacking, they gasped.

"Oh, the poor little mite, what a shame."

The child cried feebly, and without more ado, Sabina unbuttoned her dress and settled down to feed him. However, he could not latch on to her breast properly with his split lip, though he was hungry. A lot of the milk just ran out of his mouth, and Sabina was dismayed, thinking he might starve to death. However, she allowed him to continue to feed as best he could, put a small dish under his chin, and wedged it close to her breast to catch the spilt milk. After a while, she removed the baby from her breast and spooned the milk from the dish into his mouth. It was a painfully slow business, but gradually, he took a little milk and seemed satisfied. Annie found some baby clothes, and they made him comfortable in the crib beside Helen.

Everyone in the Manor House was saddened to hear that the child had only lived for an hour. He had been placed in his tiny white coffin, and the lid put firmly in place immediately, for it upset Lady Fellwood to see his poor face. A private funeral was quickly arranged in a few days when the coffin would be laid to rest in the family vault.

Later that night, Robert put his arm around his mother's shoulders. They had been close, but her recent actions had upset him, and he no longer felt he knew her.

"Mother, if you change your mind about the baby, I'm sure I could get him back for you."

"I won't change my mind, Robert. I know you think I'm hard, but you would understand if you had seen my little brother. He was a dribbling idiot and an embarrassment, for he had no idea how to behave. My mother aged watching him suffer, and it drove my father to drink. I've never told anyone else that, but I want you to understand. Your father has sent the child to someone Dr Luckett knows who will care for him. Let's talk of happier things; are you looking forward to returning to Westford?"

"Yes, it will be good to see David and all my friends again. I wonder if he enjoyed himself in Scotland with James. In his letter, he said they climbed Ben Nevis."

"Yes, apparently so. You do feel well enough to go, don't you, and you will write to me?"

"I'm fine now, and, yes, of course, I'll write, Mother, every week."

"I doubt that, but I'll say goodbye now because you'll be gone early in the morning, probably long before I'm up."

She hugged him and would have kissed him, but he pulled away, hating all the fuss.

He was up at half-past seven in the morning and boarded the carriage which would take him to Eggleston station. It was a fifty-mile train journey to Exeter, and usually, he would have been looking forward to returning to school. However, he was miserable this time, for all he could think about was how long it would be before he could hold Annie in his arms again. As the carriage swept down the drive, he saw Mrs Potts waving from the kitchen window, and he waved back with a grim expression.

CHAPTER 16

Robert enjoyed the journey to Eggleston station, and although he was sorry to be leaving Annie, he liked Westford School. The carriage was driven by Dodger Watkins, who himself was only sixteen. Robert soon knocked on the side of the carriage for it to stop, and when it did so, he alighted from the carriage and climbed up next to Dodger.

"That's better. You can see where you're going up here, can't you?"

"Yes, sir, but you're supposed to ride inside."

"Well, there's only the two of us here, Watkins, and I won't tell anyone if you don't. What's your first name anyway? I can't keep calling you, Watkins."

"My real name is Donald, sir, but most folk call me Dodger."

"And why is that, Dodger? What is it that you dodge?"

"Well, sir, you won't know the schoolmaster, Mr Atkins, at Hartford School, but he has no patience with children who aren't good at their lessons, and, unfortunately, I wasn't. He reckoned I was just being awkward when I didn't know the answers to his questions, but I didn't understand what he was on about half the time. Anyway, he was a bit handy with his cane or clipping people around the ear, and I soon learned when to duck and keep out of his way, so everyone started calling me Dodger, and the name stuck. He used to get that mad when he missed hitting me, especially when the class laughed about it, but I always suffered for it when he finally did catch me. It made no difference, and I still can't read. It doesn't matter, though, because I can drive carriages and groom horses well enough, and that's all I'm ever likely to need to do."

Robert had been laughing at Dodger's tale but then felt sorry for this young man, who was only a year or so younger than himself and who had so little ambition in his life.

"You never know, Dodger; perhaps you'll learn to read one day and get a better job. You should be more ambitious."

"It's no good for the likes of me to be ambitious, sir; it would only lead to trouble. Even if I were to learn to read and write, I don't talk properly, and folk would say I was trying to get above my station. No, I don't like bookwork, and I'm happy with my horses. Now you, that's a different matter; being the squire's son, you need to learn all you can. Mind you, I don't envy you going to that big school. Do you like it?"

"Yes, I do, and I'm looking forward to seeing my brother, David, there, though he's leaving at the end of this year. He stayed with a friend in Scotland during the holidays and returned to school from there, so I haven't seen him for months. He'd like to be a soldier, but my father won't hear of it."

"It might be best if your father let him be a soldier if that's what he wants. Master David never spends time on the estate like you've done this summer. If he became a soldier, you could run the estate, and that would suit everyone."

"Well, I expect David will enjoy running the estate when he's ready, and it will be his one day, as he's the eldest son. Anyway, I shouldn't be discussing all this with you, Dodger, but I am enjoying talking to you. You won't repeat what we've been talking about, will you? My father doesn't like me conversing with the servants. Sorry, I didn't mean to be rude."

"No, you're not rude. I am a servant, and no doubt always will be. Mind you, I still think you'd be best at running the estate, and most villagers would welcome it, too. You've made a lot of friends this summer, mucking in and getting your hands dirty, just like the rest of us. What's more, you've been generous to the poor, which doesn't go unnoticed. I'll tell you something else for nothing, too; Annie Carter will miss you something awful. Took a proper shine to you, she has."

"I don't know what you mean, Dodger. We're friendly, it's true, and I have tried to help the family since Tom Carter died."

"Aye, well, you have it your own way, but I couldn't see your father or brother, David, helping out like you've been doing. Anyway, you can say what you like; I still reckon Annie's got a soft spot for you. I wish it were me she was sweet on, and that's a fact, for she's a pretty maid and nice with it and all."

Robert was anxious to change the subject and asked Dodger to stop to let him get his snack from inside the carriage. Soon, both boys were munching on crusty bread, boiled eggs, and ham, washed down with lemonade, and Dodger enjoyed every mouthful. The snack had been intended for Robert to eat on the train, but he felt it was worth sharing it to divert the conversation. At the station, Dodger helped Robert board the train with his luggage.

"Goodbye, sir, enjoy yourself at school, and I'll pick you up when you come home for Christmas."

"Goodbye, Dodger, and thanks. I enjoyed the journey."

Two other boys were on the train bound for Westford School, and the three soon introduced themselves, their uniforms giving away their destination. Archie Bowden was a plump, sandy-haired twelve-year-old with a somewhat spotty complexion. He lost no time telling the others that his mother, a widow, had just inherited land and money from a distant relative, thus making it possible for Archie to attend a private school. Stephen Turner was a doctor's son, aged seventeen, and had recently moved to Devon from London.

Robert was pleased to meet Stephen because he was the same age, and they would likely be in the same class. Archie, however, was another matter. He didn't speak well, and his education had obviously been limited until his mother's recent inheritance. Robert and Stephen would not have held that against him, but his continual boasting about his family's newfound wealth was somewhat wearing.

The train travelled through the pleasant Devon countryside, and in a few hours, they were dismounting at Westford station. Other pupils had joined the train at various stops along the way, and about a dozen or so alighted from the train. A horse and cart were waiting in the station yard, and Robert, Stephen, and Archie collected their luggage from the guard and followed the other boys in putting it onto the cart. The cart driver introduced himself to the new boys as Taffy Jones. He had a singsong Welsh voice and clapped Robert heartily on the back.

"I'm pleased to see you back, sir. Is your brother not with you?"

"Thank you, Taffy; no, David's been to Scotland for the summer and is coming straight back here. In fact, I thought he'd be here before me. Haven't you seen him?"

"No, I don't think he's arrived yet."

"Oh, he'll probably be on a later train, then."

Taffy offered the boys a lift to the school, but Stephen and Archie decided to walk and get their bearings, so Robert joined them. The high hedges of the steep lane obscured much of the scenery, but the odd gateway revealed stunning countryside views. Their legs began to ache, and they realised why most had opted to ride on the cart. After a mile, the lane levelled out, and they had their first glimpse of Westford School. It was constructed of pale grey stone, erected over a hundred years before, and built in the shape of a square with a small tower at each corner. Extensive grounds surrounded the building, and an avenue of sycamore trees led from the impressive gateway to the front of the house. A massive oak door, blackened with age, stood open and was reached by a dozen steps.

Two senior students, charged with caring for newcomers, greeted Stephen and Archie at the door, and one of them introduced himself.

"Hello, I'm George Winters, and I'm here to tell you what to do and where to go. So, name, please?"

Stephen and Archie gave their names. Stephen was assigned to Montgomery Hall, the same as Robert, but Archie was directed to Sandford Hall. Robert and Stephen exchanged relieved glances, and Archie began to protest.

"No, I don't want to go to a different hall. I want to go with my new friends."

"I'm sorry, but students of your age reside in Sandford Hall. Montgomery is only for students of sixteen and upwards, but don't worry, you'll soon make friends with someone else. Many new boys are starting today, so come with me, and I'll show you where to go."

George took Archie's elbow to direct him along the corridor.

"Take your hands off me. Do you know whom you're talking to? I'm from a rich family, and my mother will not allow me to be put somewhere I don't want to go. Just change your list, and we'll say no more about it."

George Winters stared in amazement and surprise at Archie's outburst, and then his jaw tightened.

"I'm afraid it doesn't matter how rich or titled your family is; whilst you are at Westford School, you'll do as you're told. You will reside in Sandford Hall like all the other boys your age, and you will not utter one more word on the subject, or you'll be sorry. Do you understand?"

George shoved him along the corridor before a surprised Archie could say any more. Grinning, Robert and Stephen entered the main entrance hall, which was laid with huge flagstones. The walls were panelled, and paintings, flags, and rolls of honour were hung with pride. There was a large fireplace at one end, though the fire was not lit. The corridors were cold and draughty and had bare stone floors, and their dormitory was a long, plain room already occupied by several boys. The walls were half panelled to dado height, the upper portion whitewashed and decorated with religious pictures and crucifixes. There were thirty beds in the room, fifteen on each side, and they all had an identical cover, with a shelf and a small cupboard. Soap bags were hooked on a nail on the wall. There was a fireplace at one end of the room, and the two beds nearest to it were assigned to the two dormitory monitors, who were always the two eldest students.

The other boys welcomed Robert back, and he introduced Stephen and showed him to the only empty bed in the room. They had just unpacked and made themselves at home when a bell sounded for afternoon tea.

In the dining room, long tables were laid for a meal of jam, crusty bread and butter, and a cup of tea. They ate hungrily and then assembled in the hall for a welcome talk by the Head of the School, Professor Franklin. In his address, he welcomed all the students, new and old, to the school. He was an old, white-haired gentleman who looked like he had been in the job for too long. However, when an unfortunate scholar in the front row caught his eye whispering to his neighbour, he was off the podium with impressive agility and yanked the lad to his feet by the ear. He dragged the boy, scarlet with embarrassment and pain, up to the raised dais at the front of the hall.

"What's your name, lad?"

"Archie Bowden."

"Archie Bowden, sir."

"Yes, sir, you're hurting my ear, sir."

"It's lucky you're a new boy, Bowden because I'll put your rudeness down to ignorance just this once. However, let me assure you that any boy found talking during assembly, and particularly when I am speaking myself, is normally whipped. Do I make myself clear?"

"Yes, sir."

"Right, now sit down and behave yourself."

If Robert had dared, he would have nudged Stephen, who was also enjoying the episode. Normally, he would have felt sorry for any boy in Archie's predicament, but he needed to be taken down a peg or two.

After tea, the students attended their first lesson, but Robert was summoned to the headmaster's room within minutes. Puzzled and slightly concerned, he knocked on the polished oak door, which bore a brass plaque with the headmaster's name.

"Come in, Fellwood."

The room was decorated with ornate wallpaper and furnishings, and a thick carpet covered the floor. A cheerful fire burned brightly in the vast marble fireplace, and a large bronze bust stood on a plinth in one corner. It was a pleasant room.

"So, Fellwood, are you fully recovered now?"

"Yes, sir, I'm fine, thank you."

"Good, I'm pleased to hear it. I wanted to ask you when David would return to school. I understood from your father's letter that he spent the summer in Scotland with his friend, James MacNamee, and would return directly to the school from there. I rather got the impression that he would be here before now."

The headmaster raised his piercingly blue eyes questioningly at Robert, who shook his head.

"I'm afraid I don't know, sir. He's not been home for some time and didn't reply to my last letter. Like you, I thought he was coming here directly from Scotland and would be here before me."

"I see. Well, I'm sure there will be a perfectly reasonable explanation. James left school at the end of the summer to join the army, so perhaps David stayed with him for a few more days until he was posted away. Don't worry, I'll write to your father to tell him of David's absence. Do you enjoy rugby, Fellwood?"

"Not as much as David, sir; I prefer cricket."

"Well, that's a fine sport too. Now, don't worry about David; I'm sure we'll soon sort the matter out. Goodnight, Fellwood."

As he left the room and returned to his dormitory, Robert puzzled over his brother's whereabouts. David was usually so reliable, and he was sure his father would have no more idea than he about where his brother was. James accompanied David to Devon last summer, and Robert had gotten to know him well. He was from a highly respected Scottish family with strong military traditions, and sons were expected to follow their fathers and grandfathers into the army. Having always wanted to be a soldier, it was from listening to James' tales of glory that David had plucked up the courage to ask his father if he, too, could join the army. However, Charles Fellwood would not hear of it, for as his first-born son, David would inherit the estate, and in the meantime, he needed to learn all he could about it.

CHAPTER 17

There was quite a stir at The Red Lion Inn when William Carter walked in unannounced one morning. Betsey was on a stepladder, dusting bottles on the top shelf, a job she did not entrust to clumsy servants, as brandy did not come cheap. Well, only if it was smuggled from France, as occasionally happened. She heard the door unlatch and was about to say they were closed when she looked down and into the blue eyes of her long-lost son, William. Her hand flew to her mouth, and tears glistened in her eyes. With a wide grin, he lifted her off the ladder and swung her into his arms.

"Hey, Mum, it's so good to see you."

"Oh, Willie, is it really you? I don't know whether to scold you or hug you, you bad lad. The nights I've laid awake, worrying about you."

"Oh, Mum, I'm sorry, but I knew you and Dad would never let me sail off to sea, and so I just went. Then it was difficult to send word to you, and the longer I was away, the harder it got."

Upon hearing voices, Ned entered the room and stared in surprise at his wayward son, now a tall, strong man and no longer the skinny whippersnapper he had last laid eyes on. William released his mother and, unsure of his welcome, held out his hand to his father. However, Ned knocked it away impatiently and hugged his son. Neither could speak for several moments.

"So, how are you both? You don't look much different. Perhaps just a few more grey hairs than when I left, and I suppose they're down to me."

"Yes, indeed, they are, and is it any wonder? You're looking well, too, William, and so much bigger than when you left."

"Where's your wife? I don't even know her name."

William's expression changed to one of sadness.

"Just after I asked Bill Reynolds to let you know I'd be coming home, Lottie became ill, and that's why I was delayed; she wasn't fit to travel."

"But she's better now? I can't wait to meet her,"

"No, I'm afraid not. She'd been plagued with malaria for years, and this was a bad bout. She had a high fever for days and never recovered. After the funeral, I booked us on a later ship."

"Oh, I'm so sorry, but what about the children? They didn't…"

No, they're fine. They're outside in the passageway. I wanted to tell you about their mother before they came in because they're still upset."

With that, a small face framed with black hair peered around the door. The little girl had an olive complexion and slightly slanted eyes. She was a pretty child of about three or four, with an upturned nose and a curious expression. Betsey and Ned exchanged a glance; all their children were blonds or redheads.

"Come on then, Miss Nosey Parker, and you two lads, meet your granny and grandad."

The little girl and two slightly bigger boys sidled shyly into the room. The boys had the same complexion, hair colour, and slanted eyes as the little girl and were exactly alike, for they were identical twins.

"This is Amelia; she's four, and this is Joe and Matthew, or it could be Matthew and Joe. I can never tell them apart, and they're five."

"Hello, I'm your granny. Would you like a drink of milk and a biscuit?"

The three children nodded, and Betsey busied herself with getting the food and drink for the children. Ned looked enquiringly at William.

"Yes, Lottie was Chinese. Her real name was Lotus Flower, but I called her Lottie. She was so beautiful and kind; you would have loved her. I certainly did, and I still can't believe she's gone."

There was a catch in William's voice as he struggled to control his emotions. The young man explained that he soon discovered a sailor's life was not for him, and when the ship docked in China, he escaped. At first, he struggled to survive, but then he obtained a job working in a shop, where he served the customers and helped with the books. Two years later, an opportunity arose to work for the Chinese Imperial Maritime Customs. There was an entrance test, which he passed with flying colours and had worked there ever since. He met Lottie through her father, who also worked for the Customs Service, and they had married six years earlier.

"Where are you planning to live, William? You can stay here for a few nights, but we don't have any spare rooms because we take in lodgers. Ernest is away this week, though, so you can have his room; he won't mind."

"Thanks, Dad. I'd like to stay for a night or two, but then I'll find somewhere to rent. I'll be here for a few months, so we'll need our own place, and I want the children to attend the local school. I earn a decent wage, and Lottie's parents have been generous, so I'm not short of money."

William turned his attention to the three children, who had made short work of the milk and biscuits and were beginning to fidget at the table.

"Mum, do you think the children could play in the garden?

Or perhaps you still have some toys here?"

"Yes, of course, I expect they're tired of sitting still. What would you like to do? Play in the garden on the swing, or I could find you a box of old toys I have here in this cupboard."

She reached into a cupboard under the stairs and dragged out a large wooden box. The children slid from the table and peered into the box with interest.

"Could we have a swing and then come back and play with the toys?" asked Joe.

"Yes, of course, come with me, and I'll show you where the swing is." Betsey held out her hand to Amelia, and the little girl took it shyly.

When his mother returned, William continued his conversation.

"How are the others? I can't wait to see them all."

"Well, Eveline's still a spinster and works in George's shop. Since Jimmy was killed in a mining accident, she's not looked at another man. George runs the grocery shop and also sells clothes and boots. His wife, Alice, is fine, and their children, Harriet, Francis, and Theresa, are almost grown up now. They lost one little boy called Alfred; he died of influenza when he was four."

"What about Fred and Tom? They'll have a few tales to tell, I'm sure."

"Oh, William, I'm afraid Tom died a few months ago. He had consumption, and then on top of that, pneumonia, poor lad. He left Sabina with eight children to support; she was expecting the youngest when he died. It's not an easy life for her, I can tell you. She took on Tom's job at Hartford Manor so she could keep the tied cottage, and Liza Hammett moved in with her after her husband, Isaac, was killed last winter. Sabina's worked hard to keep her family out of the workhouse."

"Oh no! Poor Tom, how awful to think I shall never see him again, but I would hope there was no chance of the children being sent to the workhouse. Surely you, or George, or Fred, would have helped?"

"Well, yes, of course, we would, but Sabina's managing surprisingly well, and she's even taken in an abandoned baby. I'm afraid Fred has his own problems."

"Oh dear, what's the matter with Fred?"

"He's fine; it's his wife, Lucy, that's the trouble. I think they may have been courting before you left?"

"Yes, that's right. If I remember correctly, she came from Wales. I struggled to understand her Welsh accent."

"Yes, we all did, and she was always homesick for Wales. They were married for years before they had any children, but then along came Llewellyn and Rosella. Lucy struggled with severe depression after both births, and it was hard for Fred, but eventually, she improved. Then she had Alfie, but he died at just six weeks, poor little mite, and before you knew it, she was expecting Grace, and she only lived a fortnight. It was a terrible time, and I shall never forget those tiny coffins. Anyway, she had Eddie a few months ago, and her depression's been so serious this time she's been put in the asylum for treatment. I feel so sorry for her. They say the patients have a terrible time with the doctors doing experiments on them. We've got the three children living here with us for now so that Fred can work, but it isn't easy because we're not getting any younger. It would have been impossible to take on Sabina's family as well."

"That's awful, poor Fred. I think I'll go and see him now."

"You could call in at the shop on your way and see George and Eveline. He recently bought a little cottage down by the sea to rent out. I think the workmen have finished, so you may be able to have that for a few months. Leave the children here, if you like, and they can play with Llew and Rosie until teatime. They'll be back soon from playing with the children next door, and baby Eddie is having his nap. It will be nice to see your brothers and sister on your own to catch up with their news."

CHAPTER 18

William left The Red Lion and strolled through the village, the memories flooding back. He walked through the churchyard and noticed a few new graves, including that of his brother, Tom. Removing his cap, he stood momentarily with his head bowed and tears in his eyes.

He moved on and smiled as he passed the village green with its huge chestnut tree in the centre. The same swing he had played on as a child still hung from its branches. The ropes must have been replaced over the years, but the old wooden seat was still the same one, for he recognised the names carved into it and ran his hand over it fondly.

As he approached his brother's shop, he smiled as he saw the name above the door. 'George W Carter, Grocer and Outfitter'. Very grand, he thought to himself. He caught sight of his brother and sister through the window and studied them for a moment before he went in, thinking Eveline looked old and George miserable. His sister glanced up as he entered, then took a second look.

"Willie, is it really you? My goodness, you've changed so much. Fancy you having a beard, and you're so tanned. When I last saw you, you were a skinny, spotty lad with just a few stray whiskers. I can't believe you've come back after all these years. We thought you were dead, you naughty boy."

"I'm sorry, but I'm so pleased to see you again, Evie. You always spoilt me, you know." He hugged her and held his hand out to George, who looked less welcoming.

"So, the wanderer returns. Are you here to stay?"

"No, not forever, but I've got twelve months' leave of absence from work, though a couple of months of that's gone already. I planned to bring my wife, Lottie, and our three children, but she died of malaria a few weeks back."

"Oh, how awful for you, Willie. I'm so sorry to hear that. Are the children all right?"

"Yes, they're fine, thanks, Evie. There's four-year-old Amelia and five-year-old twins Joseph and Matthew. They're identical and as much trouble as a barrow load of monkeys. Mum's looking after them at the moment. George, I'm looking for somewhere to live for a few months, and Mum thought perhaps I could rent your cottage?"

"Why yes, I would advertise it next week, anyway. Do you want to see it?"

"Yes, we could go now if you like."

The two men left the shop and strolled through the village towards the beach. For brothers who had not seen each other for many years, they found it surprisingly difficult to keep the conversation going, and an awkward silence fell between them. William suspected George disapproved that the family had welcomed him back so readily when he had run off to sea without a word. Both men were relieved when they reached the cottage.

George's workmen had done an excellent job of repairing the pretty little cottage, and it now had gleaming white walls and bright blue paintwork. Fortunately, there had been a plant lover amongst the workmen, and he had carefully pruned a pink rambling rose, detaching it from the front wall whilst they painted behind it. When he had finished, he tied the rose back to a series of hooks and wires on the wall, and it was now in full bloom, all the more vigorous for being trimmed. A low, white picket fence surrounded the front garden, and honeysuckle scrambled over it, giving off the most fragrant scent and attracting many bees.

"Oh, George, what a lovely little cottage. You've done wonders with it. It was always a ramshackle old place, even before I left. The children are going to love living here right beside the beach. I couldn't wish for anything better. How much rent do you want?"

George found this question difficult, for, in truth, he wanted as much rent as possible to cover the cost of all the repairs, but on the other hand, William was his brother. He pondered briefly and then suggested a figure that William seemed to find reasonable. Predictably, this left George wishing he had asked for a bit more. They agreed William would move in as soon as he had some furniture, and George handed over the key before returning to the shop. William walked on to Fred's yard, where, after a hearty greeting, he heard all about the problems with Lucy.

"I've only been to see her once in the asylum. It's so awful there, William, and I hated leaving her. She begged me to bring her home, and when I said I couldn't, she wouldn't speak to me. The doctor says she's seriously ill and not to visit too often, as it will only upset her. The children don't understand, and it's hard on Mum looking after them all, but what else can I do?"

William told Fred about Lottie, and sharing their problems brought them closer.

"I was so sorry to hear about Tom, and I can't quite believe it. I'm going to see Sabina now; I always liked her. Life's so hard for some, yet George has it all, doesn't he? A healthy wife and family and a business doing nicely, too."

"Aye, that's true, William, but he doesn't seem content, and I can't remember the last time I saw him smile. I'm afraid Tom was ill for quite some time, and as we all know, there's no cure for consumption, so 'twas always a matter of time."

When William arrived at Sabina's door, they hugged each other tightly, and neither could speak for several moments.

"Oh, Sabina, I'm so sorry about Tom; I was so looking forward to seeing him again."

"Yes, it's a sad business, and we all miss him terribly. He would have loved to see you again, William. We often spoke of you and hoped you were all right. Between you and me, we often wished George had run away and not you. It was hard on your mother, you know. Imagine how you would feel if one of your children did the same to you."

"Yes, you're right, Sabina. It was selfish, but I was young and foolish and didn't realise the hurt I caused. Anyway, I'm here now, so you'd better introduce me to my nieces and nephews."

Sabina introduced the children and Liza to William. Edward seemed to take to him immediately, and when William lifted him onto his knee, he sat there contentedly.

"Well, you've made a new friend there; I think you remind him of his dad, for you resemble him. Anyway, tell us all your news. Where are your wife and children? I thought you would have brought them with you. What is it, William? Are they all right?"

"No, I'm afraid I have sad news too, Sabina."

William explained about Lottie, and Sabina expressed her sympathy.

"I'm sorry to hear that, William; I know only too well how hard it is. You must bring the children here soon; I'd love to meet them."

"Well, Mum's planning a bit of a party tomorrow night at the inn, so I'm hoping you can all come. I've already asked George and Fred, and they'll be there with their families."

"What an excellent idea. We could all do with something to cheer us up. Yes, we'll see you tomorrow, then."

The party was held in Betsey's Kitchen, a separate food outlet housed in the old shippen of the inn. It was a prosperous venture which had been Betsey's idea way back in the thirties and where food could be purchased and taken away to eat. The large room was ideal for the family get-together. Sabina's children were excited about the party, where there would be plenty of food and the chance to play with their cousins. George and Alice and their three children were the first to arrive, followed by Sabina and her seven; she had left the babies at home with Liza. Fred had been working on an urgent job mending a broken cartwheel but came as soon as he could, and his children were already at the inn. William held up his hands for quiet.

"Hello, everyone; I'm so pleased to see you all and relieved you've taken me back after my appalling behaviour in running off to sea. I want to introduce you to my children."

He beckoned them through the door, and they shyly entered with Eveline.

"This is Joe and Matthew. They are five and like two peas in a pod, and this is Amelia, who is four."

George gasped as he took in their foreign appearance and realised they were half-Chinese, and his shocked expression did not escape William's notice. Betsey and Eveline had been expecting such a reaction, and this was why Betsey had suggested they stay with her whilst William sorted out the cottage rental. She knew her eldest son would disapprove of the mixed marriage. William spoke quickly to cover the awkward moment.

"Now, as you can see, they are half Chinese and exceedingly clever because they can speak Chinese and English, which I bet is more than any of you can do. I love them dearly, so I hope you'll take them to your hearts as you have me."

"Of course, we will. Hello, you three, come in; we won't eat you. I'm your Aunty Sabina; come and meet John, Emma, and Edward; they're all about your age."

George's face was like thunder as he hissed at his wife. "He kept that quiet, didn't he? He never told me they were half-Chinese. Goodness knows what religion they've been brought up in. I certainly wouldn't have rented the cottage to him if I'd known."

Alice murmured something and moved off. She did not want to discuss this with George, for she knew anything she said would only make him angrier. He was not an easy man to live with. His sister, however, was not so much in awe of George as his wife.

"Aren't they charming children, George?".

"You knew, didn't you, Eveline? You, and Mother and Father, must have known, but you didn't tell me, did you? Oh no, let George find out for himself after he's agreed to rent the cottage."

"I didn't know, but what does it matter? They're William's children, and they seem delightful. Surely you would have rented the cottage to him, anyway?"

"I would not, but it's a bit difficult now that he's paid me rent, isn't it? The sooner he returns to China with his mongrels, the better."

"Don't be so despicable, George; they can't help their appearance, and they've just lost their mother, so how about a bit of compassion? You're fast enough to preach your sermons in the chapel, but it takes a real man to abide by them."

Before he could respond, she turned swiftly on her heel and went to help her mother with the food. The two women spoke together quietly.

"It's as we thought, he's furious."

None of this was lost on William, and he was not surprised, for his brother had always been a hypocrite. He caught a glance between his mother and Eveline and realised they had guessed how George would react. Oh, well, he thought, I'm paying a fair rent, and I won't be here for long. My children will never want anything from him.

Betsey was in her element that night, for it was many years since all her children had been under one roof, and she just wished Tom could have been there too. She had been baking all day with the help of the two kitchen maids she employed. A trestle table, covered with a snowy white cloth, was laden with pies and pasties, sandwiches, sausage rolls, and cakes. She had made a large pot of chicken and leek soup and baked some crusty bread to go with it. There were two trifles and scones piled high with clotted cream and strawberry jam. In one corner of the room was an old piano, which Eveline was persuaded to play. The instrument had been recently acquired second-hand by Ned, for the venue was sometimes used for Christmas and New Year's Eve parties. A retired schoolmaster had taught Eveline to play years earlier, and although she was a bit out of practice, she soon had the family singing along to all their favourite tunes.

Betsey was determined to get all the children playing together and give them a night to remember, so she and Eveline organised games. First, they played blind man's buff, where one child was blindfolded with a scarf and had to try to catch someone and guess who it was, an almost impossible challenge with identical twins present. The next game was hunting the thimble, where all the children left the room whilst one of them hid the thimble, and then they all returned and tried to find it. They all enjoyed this game and shouted, 'warmer, warmer,' when someone got near the thimble, and 'colder, colder' as they moved away.

Next was musical chairs. The chairs were lined up in a double row back-to-back, and the children had to dance around them as Eveline played the piano. There was one chair less than the number of children, and they had to sit on a chair when the music stopped. The child who failed to get a chair was out of the game. Willie won, and to his delight, his granny gave him a penny.

CHAPTER 19

Life seemed dull without Robert, and his mother, Victoria, Sarah, and even Sabina missed him, but Annie missed him most of all. She busied herself looking after the new baby, whom they had called Danny, and she soon became fond of him. The villagers were curious about whose child it could be, but Annie kept to her tale of finding him in the woods. The old women shook their heads and speculated who could have hidden their pregnancy so successfully. No one was surprised that Sabina had taken him in, for she had always been soft-hearted. She nursed birds with broken wings, children with bruised knees, and men with wounds. They all sought Sabina when they were hurting, and invariably, she made them feel better. If anyone could make the foundling whole, it would be her. However, Sabina thought there was little to be done for this child besides loving and nurturing it. She studied the baby's deformed feet and tried binding them with splints to straighten them.

Sabina had secured the position of kitchen maid for Annie at the Manor House, and she was to start in a couple of weeks. The arrangements had been made before the arrival of Danny, and despite the money she received for looking after him, Sabina knew Annie's earnings would be useful. It might even allow the family to save a little, for one never knew what was around the corner. In the meantime, Annie helped her mother with the milking and the housework. She also helped Liza care for Danny, for he was a fretful child and was always hungry with his feeding difficulties.

Sabina and Annie were leaning over the washtub one morning when their neighbour, Hannah Cutcliffe, called to them. Her greasy hair was plastered to her head and infested with head lice. Annie could see the eggs hanging from the strands of hair. The woman's hands were dirty, and she reeked of cider.

"Sabina, could you have a look at our Mary? The poor maid's got a terrible sore throat, and she's feverish."

Sabina dried her hands and signalled Annie to do the same, and then they followed Hannah into her house. Chickens ran in and out, leaving a mess all over the floor. Tommy, the youngest child, was crawling around in all the filth, for although he was two, he had rickets and could not walk. His face was covered in sores, and his nose was running. Rachael, at four, was sitting by her sick sister's bed, tugging her hand.

"Come an' play with me, Mary."

Annie picked up Rachael and settled her on her knee. Rachael loved the attention, and Tommy crawled up to sit on the other knee. Annie wiped his nose, brushed his brown curly hair out of his eyes, and cuddled them. She wondered if her own hair would be crawling with lice by the time she went home.

Sabina put her hand on Mary's forehead, which was hot, and the child was pale and listless. "What's the matter, Mary? Where does it hurt?"

Mary pointed to her throat and whispered hoarsely, "It hurts in there, and my head, and everywhere."

"Never mind, we'll soon have you better, don't worry. Could you eat some stew?"

Mary shook her head miserably. She was six but small for her age, and Sabina could see many clusters of nits stuck to her wispy brown hair.

"Sabina, I could eat some stew if you've any to spare, and I'll bet Rachael and Tommy could manage some too."

Hannah and her husband, John, were fat and lazy, but the children were thin, dirty, and ill-kempt. Sabina's eyes flashed with anger.

"I've plenty of food in my kitchen, Hannah because I work hard. I'll take Rachael and Tommy home with me to have some, and I'll bathe them, too, because they're filthy. I know you're poor but look at the state of this place. When did you last clean up or do any cooking? Or does all your money go on that bloody scrumpy? I'm sorry, but it's time someone told you a few home truths; you should be ashamed of yourself. Now, I could leave Annie here with you, if she'll stay, to help you clean up. I'll come back at teatime, and if the place is clean, I'll bring rabbit stew for all of you. Just this once, though, for you have a man to provide for you, which is more than I have."

"How dare you! It's none of your business how I keep my house. Things have got on top of me a bit, that's all."

"Please yourself then; it's no odds to me. Mary certainly isn't well, but it might be a nasty cold. Now, do you want Annie's help or not? It's up to you."

"Aye, I suppose the place could do with a bit of a clean, and you'll bring enough supper for all of us?"

"Yes, I'll bring some later and see how Mary is. Annie, would you mind helping Hannah?"

Annie, facing away from Hannah, pulled a face and screwed up her nose, but she nodded. Sabina grinned as she left with the two children. As she entered her own cottage, Sabina called to Liza.

"Liza, could you put a couple of pans of water on the fire, please? I want to bathe these two. I don't suppose they've ever had a bath, so they may not think much to it, but they certainly need one."

Sabina explained about Mary and how Annie was helping Hannah to clean up.

"She's a lazy slut, that woman, and it will soon be like it again, you know. She's too lazy to lift a finger to care for that family properly, and her mother was just the same. They don't deserve to have children, and they don't deserve your help either, Sabina. Goodness, you've enough to do to feed and look after your own."

"Aye, you're right, of course, but I felt so sorry for the children. It isn't their fault, and Mary, poor little thing, was so poorly."

Liza pulled the old tin bath in front of the fire and filled it with warm water. Rachael and Tommy sat wide-eyed, anxiously watching the activity around them. Sabina decided to start with Rachael and sat her on her knee.

"Now, Rachael, I'm going to take off these dirty clothes and bathe you. You'll like it in that lovely warm water, and afterwards, you'll feel much better. Then we'll see if we can find you something clean to wear while I wash your clothes."

Sabina gently undressed the little girl, chatting all the time as she lowered her into the bath. Rachael went stiff with fright and kept her legs rigid. She started to thrash about and scream.

"No, no, don't. I don't wanna get wet. No, don't. Let me go! Mummy, I want my mummy. Don't."

Sabina held her gently but firmly. "Come on, Rachael; I want you to show Tommy what a big, brave girl you are. You'll like it in the water when you sit down, and if you let me wash you, I'll find you a bowl of rabbit stew with a big slice of bread. Are you hungry?"

Rachael immediately became more cooperative and sat down gingerly at the mention of food. She still seemed frightened, but as Sabina gently splashed the warm water over her tiny body, she began to relax. It saddened Sabina to see that she was covered in flea bites, and her hair was crawling with lice. There were also a few suspicious bruises.

Gently, Sabina soaped the grime from the child's body, cut her hair short, and then washed what was left to get rid of the lice. Rachael began to enjoy herself and suddenly grinned at Sabina.

"This is nice, like you said. I like it in here. Can I stay a bit longer?"

Sabina let her stay a few minutes longer, then lifted her out and dried her. She reached for an old blue dress and popped it over Rachael's head.

"There, you look beautiful now. Liza will give you some stew for being so brave. Right then, Tommy, it's your turn now, but I think we'll need some clean water first."

Tommy was in a similar condition to his sister, and after some initial reluctance, he enjoyed his bath, too. His legs were bowed with rickets, and his bottom was sore from being wet all the time. Sabina applied some goose grease to soothe it, then dressed him in clean clothes and fed him with some of the stew. By this time, she needed to feed and change Helen and Danny, and before she knew it, the morning was gone. Once fed, Rachael and Tommy fell asleep on the mattress on the floor, and Helen and Danny in their crib.

Next door, Annie washed Mary all over, then nipped home to find something clean for the child to wear and left her dirty clothes with Liza to wash. She gave her a little warm milk, which she struggled to swallow, and then cuddled her until she fell asleep in her arms. She laid her down gently and covered her up to keep her warm. All this time, Hannah sat and watched.

"Right, let's get these chickens out of here first, Hannah. John should make a pen for them because they make far too much mess in here."

"Oh, there is a pen, but they got out the other day, and I haven't had time to put them back."

Annie stared at her in amazement. How could anyone be so lazy? She shooed the chickens outside, lured them into the pen with a handful of corn, and then returned to the cottage. The floor was covered with dirty straw and chicken droppings, so she raked it all up with a fork, carried it outside, and swept up the remainder. The floor was roughly made of uneven flagstones, and on her hands and knees, she began to scrub them. Cleaning the floor thoroughly at one attempt was impossible, but it was much better when she finished. Hannah remained comfortably seated beside Mary and watched.

"Hannah, I'm not doing all the work on my own. It's a warm sunny day with a stiff breeze, so why don't you do some washing? It will be dry in no time at all. Those sheets are filthy, and is that a pile of dirty clothes over in the corner?"

"You mind your tongue, young lady. I'm not taking orders from a slip of a girl like you, even if you have got yourself a fancy boyfriend. You're no better than the rest of us. He's gone away now, and no doubt he's forgotten you already. I hope he hasn't left you in the family way; that's what the gentry usually do."

"Now look, Hannah, you leave Robert out of this. If you don't want my help, that's fine, and I'll go home, but I'll tell Mum you didn't lift a finger to help, and you'll get no food from us. I'm only trying to help."

The smirk on Hannah's face changed to one of concern as she realised that the free supper she was looking forward to may not be forthcoming after all.

"Aye, I suppose you are. I'm sorry, love. Don't tell your mum I haven't been helping you. Come on then, let's do this washing together."

By teatime, the Cutcliffe cottage was cleaner than it had been for many a year. Indignant spiders had been ousted from their grimy, soot-laden webs, where they had thrived undisturbed for generations. Annie took the straw-filled mattresses to the back garden and emptied the dirty straw onto the compost heap. She beat the sacking to remove the dust and fleas, filled the mattresses with clean new straw from their own shed, and then left them in the hot sunshine. Clean clothes, blankets, sheets, and rags billowed in the breeze on the long washing line, and Annie was exhausted. She had done the elephant's share of the work, although she had kept Hannah going as best she could. Each time Hannah sank down and put her feet up, Annie did the same and made it clear she would sit there just as long as Hannah.

"I don't know. I'm being bullied in my own house and aching all over."

"Well, don't you think your house looks nice now, and doesn't it smell better? What about you, Hannah? Would you like a bath? The fire's burning well, and we could easily heat some more water, and there's nothing like a hot bath to ease your aching bones."

So, Annie persuaded Hannah to have a bath, and she cut and washed her hair for her before thankfully returning home.

"Well, Mum, I've finished, thank goodness. It was filthy, but it looks much better now, and even Hannah's had a bath. Mind you, I think Mary's worse. She's had nothing to eat all day apart from a drop of warm milk, and she struggled to swallow that. Are you going to see her?"

"Aye, I'll take the stew now, like I promised. Can you bring Rachael and Tommy?"

Annie took Rachael by the hand and carried Tommy on her hip.

"Here's the stew I promised you, Hannah. My goodness, this place looks clean, and you look lovely, Hannah; short hair suits you. How do you feel?"

"Well, I must admit I feel better for that bath, and thanks for the stew, Sabina; it's kind of you. You too, Annie, you've worked hard today despite all my moaning, and I am grateful, but I'm worried about Mary."

The little girl was deathly pale and did not respond when Sabina spoke to her. Her breathing was laboured, and she had a fever. Sabina felt her forehead, then looked in her mouth and turned away abruptly.

"What's the matter, Mum? What's wrong with Mary?"

"I hope to God I'm wrong, but I think she has diphtheria. There's a grey film over her throat. Two of my sisters died of it when I was little, nearly me too, apparently, but I recovered. We'll have to get Doctor Luckett."

"We can't afford a doctor, Sabina; you know we can't. Can't you give her something?"

"I've nothing to give her, but we need to know if it is diphtheria, and only the doctor can tell us that. We'll have a whip-round to pay him because we all need to hear what he has to say, and you can go without your cider for a day or two. Hannah, feed the children with the stew while it's warm, and Annie, you get Willie to fetch Dr Luckett. I'll bathe Mary's forehead and come home before I start the milking."

Sabina gently laid a cool cloth on Mary's brow, and she began to cough and gasp for breath, going red in the face.

"Hannah, I have to go, but try to keep her cool, and I'll call again later to hear what the doctor said."

Sabina hoped and prayed she was wrong, for whole families could be wiped out by diphtheria, and she had unwittingly exposed them all to infection. She fed Helen and Danny before going off to do the milking. Annie went with her mother to help despite being so tired.

Together, they hurried through the milking and, on the way home, called at the Cutcliffe house and found the doctor had just arrived. Mary was much worse; her little face was nearly blue as she struggled for each painful breath, and evil-smelling blood ran from her nose. The doctor probed in her mouth, trying to clear the membrane that kept forming over her windpipe, but eventually, Mary's struggles ceased, and she lay still. Hannah cuddled her daughter, tears running down her cheeks.

"I'm so sorry, but there was nothing I could do for the poor child. You must move her body to an outhouse and ensure she's buried tomorrow. I'm afraid diphtheria is infectious, and the other children may also become ill."

"Isn't there any treatment, doctor?"

"I'm afraid there's little anyone can do, Mrs Carter, apart from keeping healthy people away from infected houses to limit the spread. Patients must be kept warm and persuaded to drink, if possible, and rest to prevent the toxins from spreading to the heart. I'm afraid nature will take its course, but people do not always die from the disease. Sadly, children are usually at the greatest risk."

"Whilst you're here, doctor, would you look at my little boy? Well, he's not mine; he's a foundling, and I call him Danny. He's a couple of months old now."

Andrew Luckett willingly accompanied Sabina to her cottage, for knowing where Danny had come from, he was curious to see how the child was progressing. He was pleased to see the boy was gaining weight despite the difficulties he must have feeding with such a disfigurement, and he noted with interest the splints Sabina had attached to his legs.

"This baby is very fortunate to be cared for by you, Sabina. He's thriving, and it can't be easy. He must take a long time to feed with that deformed lip."

"Yes, he does, but he's got such lovely eyes and smiles as best he can. Will his mouth improve, do you think?"

"It's difficult to say, but I doubt it. His club feet, though, they don't seem to be as deformed as they, well as they might have been." He hesitated as he realised he had nearly given away the fact he had seen this baby before.

Sabina noticed his hesitation and smiled inwardly. She was aware they both knew where Danny had come from, but neither dared discuss the matter, and her face gave nothing away.

The doctor continued. "Binding them may help, and perhaps one day, he will walk after all. The way he smiles is encouraging, too. Sometimes babies with these sorts of disabilities are also retarded, but from the look in his eyes, I would say he'll be intelligent. You're doing a wonderful job, anyway. The diphtheria outbreak is worrying, though, because he's not strong. You should steer clear of the Cutcliffe house, though you may already be infected, having been in and out of there all day."

"It's Annie and the children I'm worried about. I nearly died of diphtheria when I was little, so I doubt I'll get it again."

"Oh, I see. In that case, I don't suppose you will. Let's keep our fingers crossed it's an isolated case and tell Hannah I don't want to be paid; I couldn't do anything for the poor child anyway."

CHAPTER 20

Hannah called to see Sabina again early the following day. "I'm sorry to bother you again, Sabina, but Rachael isn't well, and after losing Mary, I'm worried. Could you have a look at her?"

"Well, Hannah, it's a bit difficult because I'm worried about bringing it home to my lot."

"Of course, I'm sorry I asked. I don't suppose there's much anybody can do anyway."

"No, wait, I will come. Seeing I was in and out yesterday, I don't suppose it will make much difference."

It was obvious that Rachael was seriously ill. She was feverish, pale, and listless and a different child to the one that Sabina had bathed only the day before.

"What do you think, Sabina?"

"I'm so sorry, Hannah, but I think she has diphtheria too. Poor little maid."

Hannah took the limp child from Sabina and hugged her, tears flowing down her cheeks. "Surely I won't lose Rachael, as well as Mary?"

Sabina put her arm around her as John Cutcliffe appeared at the door. He took in the scene at a glance and went to comfort his wife. Sabina was pleased to see they were both sober and turned her attention to little Tommy. His forehead was hot, and his eyes a little too bright, but he held out his arms to Sabina, so she picked him up and cuddled him.

"Come on, Tommy, I'll just change your nappy. Would you like a drink?"

The little boy shook his head. "All right then, you lie down and have a little sleep, and I'll see you later."

"Hannah, keep an eye on Tommy because he doesn't seem himself. Keep them both warm and give them some milk if they can manage it."

During the next six weeks, diphtheria tore through the village, and the school was closed to try to halt the spread of the disease. The teachers were shunned because they had been in contact with pupils who had died, and the servants at Hartford Manor were not allowed to go home for fear they would carry the disease back to the gentry. Annie could not start her new job at Hartford Manor, and nearly every family suffered losses.

Of John and Hannah's four children, only two survived. Mary was the first to die, and two-year-old Tommy, already weak from rickets, also perished. Rachael hovered at death's door for days but somehow pulled through, and Daisy, aged seven, was not even ill. Then, just as it seemed the poor family would, at last, be left in peace, Hannah herself became sick and died within a matter of days. The villagers were sorry for Daisy and Rachael because they had never been well cared for when their mother was alive, but goodness only knew what would happen to them now. Their father could not look after them and earn a living, and there were no willing relatives to help, so within a week of their mother's death, poor Daisy and Rachael found themselves in the workhouse.

Edmund Lovering's wife, Jane, died, leaving him with two daughters, Emily and Sarah, both in their teens. Both the girls were in service at Dr Luckett's house and were not allowed home to visit their mother. Francis and Jane Bedworth lost their two-year-old daughter, Matilda, and funerals became a daily occurrence. However, the worst tragedy was that of Sam and Esther Symons, for their entire family was wiped out in a few weeks. Lydia, aged four, was the first to die, followed the next day by eight-year-old twins, Katie and Elizabeth. Then, two-year-old Freddie passed away during the night, leaving only Sam, just a few months old. It was hoped he might be spared, for he showed no sign of illness, but a fortnight later, he, too, had joined his siblings. The couple was distraught, and Sabina visited them but had no words of comfort. So many had died, and so many more still might.

The Carter family had not escaped the disease. John, who was so proud of his Saturday job at the smithy, died first, and within hours, Emma, too, lost her battle for life. Willie, Mary, and Edward were seriously ill, but thankfully they all pulled through. Strangely, Annie, Stephen, Helen, and Danny all remained healthy. Sabina found this surprising, particularly in Annie's case, as she had been more exposed to Mary Cutcliffe than anyone. She wondered if the two babies were unaffected because she was breastfeeding them. She had heard that if a mother survived a disease, some resistance could be passed on in the milk. Whether this was true or not, she would feed the babies for as long as possible.

Just as the outbreak seemed to have run its course, Alice Carter, George's wife, took ill and died within days. Neither George nor any of his children caught the disease, and he was mystified as to how Alice had caught it, for he had been so careful to keep his family as isolated as possible. If anyone were likely to catch it, you would think it would be him serving in the shop, but no, instead, it had been Alice. There did not seem to be any rhyme or reason as to why some people were victims, and some were not.

Eventually, with the diphtheria outbreak apparently over, Annie walked to the Manor House carrying a small bag with her few belongings. She went to the tradesman's entrance and, with her heart in her mouth, timidly lifted the heavy brass doorknocker. Her call was answered by Maisie Jones, another young girl from the village with whom Annie had gone to school.

"Hello, Annie, don't look so worried; we won't eat you." Annie was relieved to see a friendly, familiar face and relaxed a little.

"Come in, and I'll introduce you to everybody."

Annie was taken to a large kitchen with flagstones on the floor. In the centre of the room was an enormous oak table around which several people were hard at work. A cooking range occupied the whole of one wall, the brass knobs gleaming. Under the windows, which looked out over the kitchen garden, were two large sinks, and on racks around the walls were rows of plates and dishes and shining copper saucepans. Other shelves were laden with jelly moulds, mincers, grinders, knives, ladles, and many other implements, of whose purpose Annie could only guess. Maisie led Annie to the table and introduced her.

"This is Annie Carter. Her mum, Sabina, does the milking like her dad did before he died, and I went to school with her. Annie, this is Mrs Potts; she's the cook and an excellent one, too."

Annie, unsure what was expected, bobbed a curtsey, and Mrs Potts laughed.

"There's no need to curtsey to me, my dear. Just keep a civil tongue in your head and a smile on your face, and we'll get on just fine."

Annie took to Mrs Potts straight away. She looked every inch the way a cook should look. Her bright blue dress strained at the seams to cover her voluptuous figure. Over her dress, she wore a snowy white apron, and on her head, a frilly, white cap covered her greying hair. Her bare forearms were lightly dusted with flour from the bread she was kneading, and Annie thought she had a beautiful face. It was plump and lined, but when she smiled, two dimples appeared on her cheeks, and her violet eyes twinkled merrily.

"This is young Molly, the tweeny. Molly's only ten and has no family, so she's lucky to be here instead of in the workhouse, aren't you, Molly, my girl?"

"I am that, Maisie, and even luckier to work with you. I'm pleased to meet you, Annie."

Maisie ruffled Molly's dark, curly hair fondly, and it was clear the two were friends.

"Molly does all sorts of jobs that no one else has the time to do. She irons the master's newspaper if it's crumpled, washes his small change, polishes the silver, cleans the windows, and does all sorts of things, don't you, Moll?"

"This is Fred Baker, Mr Fellwood's valet. He helps the master to dress and attends to his clothes, shoes, and everything. He sees to his every comfort."

"I'm pleased to meet you, Annie, and I hope you'll be happy here."

Fred was about twenty and was good-looking, apart from his rather large nose. He seemed friendly, so Annie smiled at him as Maisie moved her on.

"Now, you and I are the kitchen maids, and here are Emily, Susan, and Patsy, the three laundry maids. They're kept busy morning, noon, and night doing all the washing and ironing."

The three girls came forward to meet Annie, drying their hands. Their faces were red and gleaming with perspiration, for the room was hot and steamy. Annie noticed their hands were sore and chapped from constant contact with hot water and harsh soap. They were about seventeen or eighteen, and Annie remembered Susan and Patsy from school. Maisie, however, did not let her stay long enough for a chat.

"Come on, I'll take you to meet the outdoor servants, and then you'll know everybody. It's sunny, so I'll show you the gardens if we have time."

Annie did not like to tell Maisie that she probably knew far more about the gardens than she did and could take her straight to the swedes or turnips with no trouble at all.

"The master keeps several horses because all the family ride, and sometimes they have visitors join them and go hunting. There are four stable boys and two grooms. Come on, I expect they're around somewhere."

They crossed a clean and tidy yard and entered the largest stable, where they found Francis Rudd, Harry's younger brother.

"Hello, Annie; Harry said you were coming to work here. I hope you like it. There's plenty of food, anyway."

"Thanks, Francis, I'm sure I will."

Annie studied Francis, for she hadn't seen him since he left school. He was about fifteen, but to look at him, you would have thought he was at least twenty. His hair was jet black, and he had thick beetling eyebrows, and, like his father and brothers, he was broadly built and immensely strong.

"Come and see the horses and meet the other stable lads. This here's Jimmy, he's twelve, and this is Ross, his brother, he's fourteen, and Dodger over there, is sixteen." They all nodded their greetings, and Francis moved down the row of horses.

"Some lovely horses there are here, Annie. It's a real pleasure to work with them. This chestnut mare is called Lady, and Miss Victoria rides her. The next one is Snowdrop, Lady Fellwood's favourite, and you can see how she got her name. The black stallion is Galahad, and he belongs to the master."

A dark brown horse nuzzled Annie as she leaned over the gate to stroke his nose.

"Well, now, Prince doesn't usually take to strangers, but he's certainly taken a fancy to you, Annie; you'd think he knew you already. He's Master

Robert's horse, so he's missing him, now he's returned to school. This stallion next to him is Lancelot, and he belongs to Master David, who's also away at school. Then, this last little pony is Miss Sarah's, and she's called Jenny. That's all the family horses, but there are another ten used for the guests and the carriages, and then, of course, there are the shire horses for the farm work. I won't tell you all their names now because you'll never remember them, but come back and see them again when you have a minute."

Maisie took Annie's arm. "Come on, Annie, we'd best get a move on; there's a lot of work to do. Arthur Potts, the head groom, is not here at the moment, but he's in charge of the stables, and he's Mrs Potts' husband. They've been here for years. Now, you have to see Miss Wetherby at ten o'clock. She's the housekeeper and gives the orders around here, not that Ethel Potts takes much notice of her, but the rest of us have to. She doesn't stand any nonsense, so don't get on the wrong side of her. Then you've just got to meet Sid Hobbs, the butler; he's a bit stuck up, and you'd think he owned the place the way he carries on sometimes."

Back in the kitchen, everyone was enjoying a mug of tea and one of Ethel Potts' freshly baked muffins. Maisie and Annie took their places at the table, and after her first heavenly mouthful of muffin, Annie knew she would like working at the Manor. Later, Maisie took her to the housekeeper's room. She knocked timidly on the door, and when bidden, they entered the room.

"This is Annie Carter, the new kitchen maid, ma'am." Maisie bobbed a small curtsey and left the room, winking at Annie.

Annie stood uncomfortably in front of a large desk where Miss Wetherby was busy writing. The woman continued to write for some five minutes, and Annie wondered if she had forgotten she was there and whether to risk a slight cough. She was plucking up the courage to do so when Miss Wetherby raised her head.

"So, Carter, you have come to join us at Hartford Manor. Has Jones shown you around?"

"Yes, ma'am."

"Well, I expect you to work hard and be willing and polite. As long as you behave and do as you are told, we shall get along fine. You will be paid quarterly and have one half-day off a week. You will rise at half-past five every morning and not finish until the work is done. Do you have any questions?"

"No, ma'am. Thank you, ma'am."

"Right then, you may go. Jones will find you a uniform that you will wear at all times."

Miss Wetherby rang the bell, and Annie quickly left the room to find Maisie waiting outside.

"Cor blimey, what an old misery; her face looked like she'd eaten a lemon."

Maisie giggled. "Ssh Annie, she'll hear you. I'm glad you've come. I can see you'll liven things up a bit."

CHAPTER 21

Robert had been at Westford School for some weeks and had quickly settled back into the disciplined routine. The building had become a public school in 1850, and virtually all the boys attending were boarders aged eight to nineteen years. There was a broad curriculum, including music and piano tuition. The teachers were strict, the lessons were demanding, and life, in general, was challenging. Marks were given for good behaviour, punctuality, and tidiness. The reward for the highest achievers was to be excused for the evening roll call, which was highly valued. At the end of the summer term, an examiner from Cambridge University would visit the school and select the best pupils to study there.

Pupils rose at half-past six each morning, and breakfast, usually porridge, was served an hour later and preceded by prayers. Lessons started at half past eight and continued until one o'clock when the boys had an hour for dinner, their main meal of the day. Classes then continued until five o'clock, when the boys would have some free time until their tea at six. In the evening, the boys settled down to do their homework until a supper of bread and cheese. They then went to their dormitories to prepare for bed, and lamps were extinguished at ten o'clock. It was a busy and structured day, designed to give them little time to get into mischief.

The boys washed in basins in their dormitories and dried themselves on rough towels. They bathed once a week, or if they were muddy, after games. Their collars were changed regularly, but not their shirts, so they had to be careful to keep them clean. Sports were important, with cricket and rugby taking priority, and the masters often joined in the matches to make up the numbers. A lake on the grounds was used for swimming lessons and competitions during the summer. Cross-country runs were frequent all year round, and the hare and hounds race took place in the spring. One boy, carrying a bag with pieces of torn-up paper, was given a head start, and he would run off, throwing down the odd bit of paper, to provide a trail for the rest of the boys to follow. He would aim to run in a circular route and return to the school before being caught.

The younger boys had to fag for the older ones, cleaning boots and rugby kits, making beds, and tidying the dormitories. Bullying was rife and largely ignored. The previous term, a serious incident occurred when a young boy was grabbed at night and carried to the stables. He was doused with freezing water from the pump, blindfolded, put in a barrel, spun round and round and rolled down a slope. The poor lad was then hauled out, dazed and soaking wet, and tied to some railings, where he remained until morning. He was fortunate it was early summer, or he could have died of exposure. Despite an investigation, the culprits had never been identified, for not one pupil would risk telling tales for fear the same fate, or worse, would befall them one dark night.

Occasionally, visitors would be invited to the school to perform plays and concerts, give missionary talks, or show lantern slides. Musical evenings were organised where the masters joined the older students, singing and playing the piano. Girls from a nearby private school were sometimes invited for these strictly supervised social evenings to enable the boys to learn to dance correctly, for Westford School aimed to turn out young gentlemen.

One morning, Robert was again summoned to the headmaster's study and was surprised to see his father talking to Professor Franklin.

"Hello, Robert, how are you? I had to come to Exeter on business, so I thought I'd call in and see you."

"I'm fine, sir, thank you. Is everything all right at home? Have you found David?"

"Well, yes, to your first question, and no to the second, I'm afraid. Are you sure David didn't tell you of his plans?"

"No, he didn't reply to my last letter, and I assumed he decided not to bother writing as he'd be seeing me here soon. What does Mama think?"

"Naturally, she's beside herself with worry and convinced something terrible has happened to him. However, I think I can guess where he is, and if I'm right, that young man will be in serious trouble when I catch up with him."

"Now, Lord Fellwood, David is a responsible young man, and I'm sure there will be a perfectly reasonable explanation."

"Where do you think he is, Papa?"

"I think you know, don't you? I think he's joined the army with James McNamee, but I can assure you he'll be returned home before he knows it."

Robert was sure his father was right, for David had desperately wanted to join the army. He had tried to convince his father that it was the right career for him, but his pleas were ignored, and the matter had become such a sore point that his father refused to discuss it further. Since their disagreement, David had barely been home, instead choosing to spend almost all his holidays with his friend in Scotland.

"Well, I know he wanted to sign up with James. Perhaps if he stayed in the army for a year or two, he'd be ready to manage the estate."

"That's not the point. If he's joined the army when I expressly forbade him to do so, then that type of behaviour cannot go unpunished, and I shall insist he returns home."

"Yes, sir."

"I shall return to Hartford now to await a reply to my letter to McNamee's parents. Hopefully, they should have some information as to the whereabouts of my son. However, before I leave, I'd like to take Robert to the village for lunch. Would that be all right with you, Professor?"

"Yes, of course, Lord Fellwood, that will be a splendid opportunity for you to spend some time with your son. He's a promising student, and we're pleased to have him back with us after his dreadful illness. I think he has a bright future ahead of him."

Robert was surprised but pleased to hear this from his father, for whilst the school food was adequate, it offered little variety. They decided to walk the short distance into the village and go to The Castle Inn. Over lunch, Robert enquired after the family.

"Well, Sarah's ankle is fully mended, thank goodness, and she's up and about again, and the new governess started a couple of weeks ago. She's called Jane Leworthy and seems capable. She's mainly teaching Sarah, but Victoria is sitting in on a few lessons each week."

"How is Mama? Is she fully recovered from the birth now?"

"Yes, physically, she's recovered, but she's been unsettled by the whole matter. If I'm honest, she's still not quite herself, and, of course, she's worried about David."

"Have you heard how the baby is doing?"

"No, and beyond knowing he's being cared for, I don't want to. Doctor Luckett has assured me that the woman is looking after him, and I've ensured that additional money is put in with her wages, so the matter is being dealt with. I think it's best left to that for all concerned."

"You know, Father, perhaps Mama has second thoughts about giving him up? When I come home at Christmas, I could get the baby back from Sabina. I think she half expects that to happen anyway, for she couldn't understand any mother giving up her baby, even if he was disabled."

"No, that's not the case, Robert. I know you don't understand, but your mother doesn't regret her decision to give him up and won't change her mind. However, that doesn't stop her from missing the child and wishing he had been born whole. Anyway, let's move on to a happier topic. In one of your letters, you mentioned you had made a new friend. Stephen, I think you said he was called?"

"Yes, I met him on the train. He's a pleasant fellow; his father is a doctor in Harley Street in London. I might ask him to come and stay at some point if that would be all right?"

"Yes, of course. That wouldn't be a problem; I'd like to meet him."

They continued chatting over lunch, and then Robert accompanied his father to the train station. He saw him off on his train before hurriedly returning to the school, for it had begun to rain heavily.

CHAPTER 22

Annie was getting on well at the Manor. She had worked hard all her life, particularly in the last few months, so she took the long hours in her stride. She rose at five o'clock and, if she had time, would grab a quick glass of milk from the kitchen. For the first hour, she helped Maisie stoke the fires in the downstairs rooms or relight them if they had gone out during the night. Then, she cleaned herself up and helped Mrs Potts prepare breakfast. Her next task was to take hot water to the bedrooms for the family to wash and attend to the fires there.

Breakfast was served in the dining room at eight o'clock, and by the time the dishes were cleared away, it would be at least half past nine and Annie would be ravenous. This was her favourite time of day, for the cook insisted the servants sit around the kitchen table and eat a hearty breakfast. The full-time outdoor servants joined them, so it was a large party and a sociable meal. Annie wished the invitation to breakfast was extended to part-time workers, for her mother would be included then, and Annie would have loved to see her enjoy such a wonderful meal. The servants worked long hours, but Mrs Potts always saw they had plenty to eat. She had been at the house when the old master was alive and still commanded enough respect to be left to run the kitchen as she saw fit. Most mornings, there would be thick creamy porridge, followed by fried bacon, eggs, and crusty bread, washed down with a couple of mugs of hot sweet tea.

Annie thoroughly enjoyed her breakfasts and began to put on weight. Her flat breasts became fuller, and she developed hips for the first time in her life. As her figure matured into a more curvaceous form, she looked much the better for it. Her cheeks became rosy, and her green eyes sparkled, yet she had no idea how beautiful she was. There had been no mirror at the cottage, but Annie now enjoyed looking at her reflection in the cracked mirror in the attic room she shared with Maisie, and she brushed her long, curly red hair until it shone.

"My word, Annie, you're so pretty with your hair down; it's down to your waist, and your ringlets are amazing," Maisie exclaimed one day. "It's a pity to hide it under your cap."

All the servant girls wore their hair tucked up under a mobcap. Their uniform consisted of a plain, ankle-length, black dress covered with a white pinafore and cap. On their legs, they wore warm black stockings, and on their feet, laced-up boots. Annie had never been so warmly clad. The others moaned how old-fashioned their uniform was and how hot the stockings were in fine weather, but Annie thought they didn't know when they were well off. They should try keeping warm with no stockings and worn-out shoes on their feet in winter, and even then, they would be lucky, for some children had no shoes at all. Frostbite was not uncommon.

The rest of Annie's day was spent scrubbing and polishing, preparing vegetables, tending fires, and, indeed, any job that needed to be done. She was glad she worked with Maisie, for they had become firm friends. Their day did not finish until about ten at night, though sometimes they managed to sneak off to bed a little earlier. The laundry maids also worked hard, washing and ironing all day long, and Annie was glad she didn't work in the laundry, for the atmosphere there was hot and steamy and unbearable in summer.

The cleaning, too, seemed endless, with silver to clean, brass doorknobs and knockers to shine, heavy wooden furniture to polish with beeswax, lamps to clean, wicks to trim, and floors to scrub. The list went on and on, yet Annie loved it. She enjoyed working with such beautiful things around her and took pride in her work. The staff teased her that she was becoming Miss Wetherby's favourite, but in fact, she was popular with everyone.

She looked forward to her weekly half-day off, for it was a relief to get out of the Manor House for a few hours and visit her family. However, she'd had no time off the previous week because some of the servants were ill with a stomach bug and not allowed near the food. Annie had remained healthy, so Mrs Potts had told her to help in the kitchen. Annie didn't mind because it meant she could have a whole Sunday off this week.

"Right then, Miss, if you're going home today, there are a few leftovers your mother might be glad of."

Ethel Potts often sent Annie home with a stale loaf of bread or a chunk of hard cheese, for she knew the family was in dire straits. Only Jack Bater knew of the extra money added to Sabina's wages, and even he didn't know it was for looking after Danny. However, the food was always welcome, with so many mouths to feed.

"Oh, thanks, Mrs Potts. Are you sure it's all right? I'm grateful but wouldn't want to get you or me in trouble."

"Don't you worry, my dear; they're only leftovers that would go for pig food. That bread is a bit hard, but it would make a nice bread pudding."

"Yes, I'll tell Mum, Mrs Potts. The children, especially our Willie, are always hungry. Honestly, he'll eat anything; I've never known him to leave a scrap on his plate."

"He's a growing lad, so it's only natural. Now, don't be late back because there are a lot of visitors coming next weekend, and we'll be busy preparing for them. You'd better warn your mum you won't be able to see her next week. There won't be any time off for any of us for the next week or two."

"Oh, I didn't know we were having visitors. Who are they? Are they staying long?"

"Now then, all these questions. You need to know the ins and outs of everything, don't you? Ah, well, I don't suppose there's anything wrong with that. How else can you learn, eh? I don't know any names, but I understand most are rich, and a few are titled. It will be an opportunity for Miss Victoria to get to know a few eligible young men before her season in London next year. Anyway, it'll mean a lot of hard work for all of us, and that I do know. Everywhere will need an extra spring clean if I know Miss Wetherby, and all the bedrooms will need the fire lighting, and I can hardly bring myself to think about the food that must be prepared and cooked. Go on now, off, and enjoy your day. I'm going for a walk around the lake while I can."

As Annie strolled home, the chilly October wind made her shiver, but the sun shone brightly, and she was in high spirits. She could hear the children squabbling from a distance and smiled, thinking some things never changed. Being away from home during the week, she took more notice of how fast they were growing. Helen and Danny now chuckled, and Danny, though smaller than Helen, seemed healthy enough. Sabina still had his feet bound, and when she removed the bandages, she was sure his feet were a bit straighter. Helen was a placid child who rarely cried and slept soundly, but Danny's difficulties in feeding did not stop him from feeling hungry, and he took up a lot of Sabina's time. However, she had no regrets and loved him just as much as her own children.

"Harry Rudd called on Wednesday to ask when you were coming home."

"Did he? What did you say?"

"Well, I said you'd be here today, of course, so I expect he'll be here later to see you. He's a pleasant lad, you know, Annie. You could take the babies out in the pram and go for a walk with him this afternoon if you like."

"No, I don't think so. I'm only sixteen and not looking for a husband just yet."

"Maybe not, but getting to know him better wouldn't hurt. He'd be a good catch, you know; that smithy will be his one day."

"Well, if he calls, I'll take the babies for a walk, but I'm not interested in him or anyone else at the moment."

"Hmm, are you sure about that, Annie? Are you sure there isn't someone else you have set your sights on?"

Annie blushed. "I don't know what you mean, Mum. When do I have the time to meet anyone? Anyway, as I said, I won't marry for ages."

"Annie, I know you and Robert became close during the summer, but I hope you realise you could never have a future together."

"Yes, of course I do, but you're right; we love each other. My head knows nothing can come of it, but unfortunately, my heart doesn't listen. Anyway, I'm not courting anyone else."

Sabina hugged her daughter. "It's a pity because he's a nice lad, but you'll get over him. Come on, it's time we went to church."

Liza pushed Helen and Danny in the pram as they strolled to the church, and Sabina enjoyed talking with other villagers bound for the same destination. The Reverend Rees welcomed his flock at the church door and shook Sabina's hand warmly. He told her she should be proud of herself for coping so admirably since Tom died. William Carter and his three children arrived just behind Sabina, and they all entered the church and sat together.

Sitting in the pew opposite was Mr Martin, the cordwainer, who made the shoes and boots for George's shop, and with him, his four daughters and three sons. His wife, Mary, had died giving birth to the youngest child, Harry, who was now twelve, and Sarah, the eldest, had cared for the family ever since. She was now considered an old maid, still a spinster at thirty-two. Not a particularly pretty girl, she had never attracted the attention of any suitors, and her father was more than happy to keep her at home running the house.

William Carter and Sarah were the same age and had been at school together, though they had little to do with each other at the time, William preferring the company of her brothers. However, when William caught Sarah's eye and smiled at her, she blushed, and her eyes dropped to her lap. A few minutes later, she also smiled when she glanced in his direction and saw him still looking at her with a slight grin.

The Reverend Rees preached an interesting sermon which held the congregation's attention, and the service ended with a few familiar hymns, so most people enjoyed their visit to church. At the end of the service, William quickly gathered his children and ensured they were out of the church first. He waited outside until the Martin family appeared and introduced himself to Mr Martin.

"Hello, Mr Martin. I don't know if you remember me, but I'm William Carter. I used to live at The Red Lion, but I've been working in China for several years."

"Aye, I remember you and how upset your poor mother was with you going off like that. Still, I'm glad you're all right." Mr Martin eyed the children curiously.

"These are my children, Amelia, Joseph, and Matthew. I wanted to have a word with you, Mr Martin, because we all need new shoes. If I come along tomorrow, could you help us out?"

"Yes, of course, William, always glad of a bit of business, come whenever you like. I have a few pairs already made that might do the job, or if not, I can easily make some. I'll see you on the morrow."

As they moved away, William caught Sarah's eye and gave a broad wink, and the little smile hovered around her mouth again as she followed her family home.

Sabina and her family returned home to a lunch made all the more enjoyable by the food Annie brought. No sooner had they finished than Harry Rudd called for Annie. He was delighted Robert had returned to school, for this left the way clear for him to get to know her better.

"Hello, Annie. I saw you pass the smithy earlier, and I was hoping perhaps we could go for a walk. I'd like to hear how you're getting on at the Manor House."

"Hello, Harry. I was about to take the babies for a walk, so we could go together if you like, but I don't have much time until I have to be back."

"Shall we walk to the smithy? I know Mum would like to see the babies, and we could have a cup of tea whilst we're there."

Annie nodded, and they set off for the village.

"I've looked forward to seeing you all week, Annie. Do you think we could do this every Sunday?"

"Look, Harry, I don't want to lead you on because I don't plan on getting married for years, if ever. I don't want you to waste your time on me when plenty of other maids would jump at the chance of going out with you."

"Now, you let me worry about that, Annie and I have to say you're a bit forward; I've not asked you to marry me, have I?"

"Well, no, Harry, sorry, I er..."

Her face was flushed with embarrassment, and he laughed at her.

"I'm happy to enjoy your company for now, and if things develop, well, so be it. Whatever happens, I'd rather be with you than anyone else, so I don't see it as wasting my time. I love you, Annie, but if you'll just spend some time with me, we needn't rush things."

"Yes, all right, Harry and I am fond of you. You can push the pram up this hill if you like; it weighs a ton with these two in it."

They arrived at the smithy, and Matilda was soon cooing over the babies. She was pleased to see Harry out with Annie, for she had delivered her at birth and was fond of the girl. She made them a pot of tea and insisted they sample her freshly baked scones. They spread the scones thickly with cream and spooned a generous amount of strawberry jam on top. This was the customary way to eat scones in Devon, though over the border in Cornwall, they insisted the jam should go on first.

"What a pity about Danny's poor little mouth; will it ever get any better, do you think?"

"No, I don't think so, Mrs Rudd. It takes ages to feed him, and of course, it doesn't look nice, but he's gaining weight. His legs aren't as deformed as we first thought, and Mum thinks he may walk eventually."

"Did you ever find out whose baby he is? It was strange, wasn't it, just finding him like that? Of course, people do abandon babies in these hard times, but no one I know was expecting about that time, except your mum, of course. I usually know all about babies in the village because I deliver most of them."

"No, it's a mystery, and it could be someone from another village, but I don't suppose we'll ever know. Anyway, it doesn't matter; Danny's one of us now."

"Aye, well, he's a lucky lad, despite his deformities, for at least he's loved and cared for. As if your mum hasn't enough to worry about, but it's just like her to take him in; she always did have a soft heart."

"I'd better be going now, Mrs Rudd. Thanks for the tea and scones; they were delicious."

Annie tucked the two babies back into the pram and headed for the front door, which Harry held open, smiling brightly at her. As they neared Annie's cottage, Harry took her hand, raised it to his lips, and kissed it gently.

"Thanks for walking with me, Annie. Can I see you again next week?"

"No, I'm sorry, Harry, but I can't have any time off for the next couple of weeks because a lot of visitors are coming to the house, and we'll be busy." She noted the disappointment on his face.

"Oh, never mind, see you in a couple of weeks then?"

Annie nodded. "Yes, fine. Bye for now."

She felt vaguely guilty, although she had been honest with him. She wondered if she was making a big mistake, for Harry was clean, not likely to mistreat her, and he wasn't bad-looking. She sighed. The trouble was none of that stopped her from loving Robert. Just the thought of him made her heart race, and she longed for even a glimpse of him in a couple of months.

The next day, William and the children presented themselves at Mr Martin's cottage to buy shoes. Sarah laid out all the ready-made stock that might fit. She found suitable boots for William and the two boys, but nothing was small enough for Amelia. Mr Martin asked the little girl to stand on a piece of slate, and he drew around each foot to give him a template for the boots.

"I can make these in a few days; will that suit you?"

"Yes, that's fine, thank you. I wondered if I could call on Miss Sarah later; that's if she'd like me to, of course. We used to be at school together, and I'd like to catch up on all the news."

Richard Martin was most surprised and glanced at Sarah, who was blushing.

"Well, yes, all right, if you don't mind, Dad?"

"Aye, 'tis no odds to me."

So, William started to court Sarah Martin, for though he knew no one could ever replace his beloved Lottie, he intended to find an English wife to return to China with him. Sarah was about the right age and had no attachments. Though no oil painting, she seemed pleasant enough, and there was no harm in getting to know her a bit better.

CHAPTER 23

There was to be a grand ball on Halloween Night, and Hartford Manor had been a hive of activity the entire week. The servants were dog-tired, for every nook and cranny had been cleaned, and fenders, doorknobs, furniture, and chandeliers gleamed. Carpets had been beaten, cobwebs removed, and windows opened to let in the fresh air. The kitchen table groaned with food, and the larders were bursting with hams, cheeses, pheasants, grouse, and suckling pigs. Mrs Potts had excelled herself in preparing soups, sauces, and desserts fit for royalty. The silver cutlery shone, and the crystal glasses sparkled. Molly had been busy scooping the ripe, yellow flesh out of numerous pumpkins and cutting weird and ghoulish faces into them. They were placed all around the hall with a lighted candle inside to add to the atmosphere. A few figures of witches, complete with grotesque papier-mâché faces, pointed hats, and wooden broomsticks, had been retrieved from the attics and spruced up for use once again.

The four gardeners had been hard at work in the grounds, too, for the gardens were extensive. There were rolling lawns enhanced by fountains and statues, fragrant rose beds, long herbaceous borders, and, of course, the vegetable patch and orchards so familiar to Annie. The lake, loved by Mrs Potts, was a particular feature. Three small rowing boats, tied to a jetty at one end, were used by the family and visitors for trips out onto the water. The grass was mowed, shrubs were pruned, and weeds were removed. In the hothouses, flowers, exotic fruits, and vegetables were ready to be picked at the last moment.

Among the twenty-six guests were eight eligible young men, all keen to make Victoria's acquaintance. Some were local, whilst others were from London or even further afield, but all were rich and a suitable match for Victoria. It was fashionable for women to change their clothes several times throughout the day, and the ladies visiting Hartford would not dream of being seen in the same outfit more than once. For a long weekend, a lady would need, at the minimum, sixteen or more changes of clothes. Most ladies brought their maid with them, but keeping all the clothes, underwear, and accessories in perfect condition was challenging, and they often required help from the household staff. Shawls, cloaks, mantles, scarves, and little aprons were popular accessories, and gloves and parasols were also in demand, as pale skin was a mark of gentility. Large brooches were worn at the throat, with earrings to match, and fur or feather boas often completed an outfit. A vast amount of luggage was required for even a short visit, and the servants worked hard.

A range of beautifully decorated, elaborate masks was available for guests to choose from, and everyone attending the ball was traditionally expected to wear one to add to the mystery and excitement of Halloween. At midnight, the guests would remove their masks and reveal their identities. Victoria could barely wait to wear the stylish scarlet bustle gown made especially for her, and she chose a vivid gold and silver mask to complete her outfit. With her raven black hair piled high on her head, she knew she looked stunning. This was her favourite dress, but it was only one of six new gowns made for her by a seamstress in Exeter.

Miss Wetherby called the servants together on the morning of the ball to give them their instructions. "Thank you for your hard work over the last few days. The house looks magnificent, and Mrs Potts has prepared so much food it is hard to believe it will ever all be eaten, but I am sure it will. This party is important to Lord and Lady Fellwood and, of course, to Miss Victoria, and I'm sure you will each do your best to ensure it is a huge success. If there are any problems, I want to hear about them in good time. Be polite and helpful, and ensure you are always tidy, even when you are tired at the end of the day. Remember, the ball will not be the end of the entertainment because many guests are staying for several days. Everything must be cleared up thoroughly, and normal service resume first thing in the morning. Some guests have brought their own maids, and of course, they will help, but they will not know the layout of the house or our ways, so you must make them feel at home. Now, are there any questions?"

She was greeted by silence and continued, "Good, then please get on with your duties."

The guests started arriving at midday, and Annie was rushed off her feet, fetching and carrying for them, taking tea, coffee, and cakes to their rooms.

"I shouldn't think they'll need a meal tonight with all these cakes and sandwiches," she mumbled to Maisie as they passed each other in the kitchen.

"Ah, Annie, there you are; take this tray to the fourth bedroom on the second floor, will you, and then come back for another, for the fifth bedroom, next to it. The first one's for a Mr and Mrs Eastleigh, and their son, Frank, is next door. Go on now, and be quick because there's a sink full of dishes here that needs doing."

Annie carried the heavy tray up the back stairs, and as she struggled to open a door at the top, a young man of about twenty held it open for her, and she smiled her thanks. The passage was narrow and the tray wide, and she had to squeeze past him. Somewhat embarrassed, she blushed as she turned to thank him. He was closer than she thought, and she found herself staring into a pair of deep blue eyes. He had dark curly hair and was smartly dressed in a navy blue velvet jacket and cream trousers. Around his neck, he wore a yellow cravat, and she thought he was the most handsome man she had ever seen.

"Tha, thanks very much," she stammered. "I can manage now." However, he followed her.

"Here, let me knock and open the door for you; that tray looks heavy." She nodded her thanks and entered the room with the tray. When she came out, he was waiting outside.

"I was wondering if you could bring me a tray of tea and sandwiches, too; I'm rather hungry."

"Yes, sir, of course. I was going to fetch your tray next, anyway."

"You needn't knock because I know you're coming."

She ran down the stairs and bumped into Maisie. "Hey Maisie, have you seen that man in the fifth bedroom? Frank Eastleigh, I think he's called. Good looking, isn't he?"

"Good looking? He's gorgeous and can pay me a visit anytime he likes. I'm going to ask Mrs Potts if I can take his tray when I've delivered this one."

"Too late; she's already asked me to do it."

"Oh, she would ask you, wouldn't she? Well, I'm taking his hot water later."

Annie quickly fetched his tray and mounted the stairs again, but she didn't like to go in without knocking and was about to put the tray down when he opened the door.

"I knew you wouldn't come in without knocking, but you must learn to do as you're told. Put the tray down there, look. What's your name, girl?"

"Annie, sir." She bobbed a small curtsey.

"Well, Annie, could you pour me a cup of tea, please?"

"Yes, sir. I'll fetch it straight away." She poured his tea and took it over to him. "Will that be all, sir?"

"For now, Annie, but I would like you to bring my hot water later, not the other girl. I would also like you to attend to my fire and bring my breakfast. In fact, to cater to my every need. Is that understood?"

Annie blushed deeply, realising he had overheard the conversation between her and Maisie.

"I'm sorry, sir. We were just gossiping as servants do, you know. We didn't mean to be rude or offend."

"No harm done, Annie. Just do as I have asked."

The young man looked at her sternly, but she could see amusement dancing in his eyes.

"Yes, sir, I'm sorry, sir." She bobbed another curtsey and left the room sharply.

She grabbed Maisie in the scullery. "Oh, Maisie, he heard what you said about him coming to your room and being good-looking."

"Did he now? Is he coming then? Does he fancy me?"

"Oh, you're awful," said Annie, nudging her in the ribs. "He could complain to Miss Wetherby, and then we'd be in trouble."

"Nah, he won't. He's been here before, and he's a proper flirt. I bet he loved every minute of it, and anyway, he shouldn't eavesdrop. I wonder what he'll say when I take his water up."

"No, you can't. He's asked me to do it and see to his fire, breakfast, and everything.

"Well, be careful, Annie. I was joking, you know; I wouldn't really let him in my bed, though he is handsome. There's no future with someone like him. He'd have fun with you, then be off and most likely leave you with a belly full of baby. You keep him at arm's length."

"Maisie, I'm only taking his hot water; I'm not going to stay the night."

However, she felt quite nervous later as she carried hot water to his room. She knocked timidly on the door, and he bade her come in.

"Ah, there you are, Annie. Could you make up the fire, please? It's a little chilly, and then pour the water for me to wash. Unfortunately, my valet could not accompany me on this visit as he went down with pneumonia, silly man. Could you lay out my clothes for me, too? They're in that cupboard."

"Well, maybe it would be best if I sent one of our manservants to help you dress, sir. I'm sure there will be one available."

"No need for that. I'm quite capable, and with your help, I'm sure we'll manage perfectly. You don't mind, do you?"

Annie glanced at him anxiously, and as their eyes met, she immediately lowered hers away from his piercingly blue ones.

"Of course not, sir." She took the necessary items of clothing from the cupboard and laid them on the bed. "Will that be all, sir?"

When she turned back to him, she saw he had stripped to the waist to wash, and she hastened to the door.

"Now, Annie, have I said you can go? Come here. You don't want me to report you to that miserable housekeeper of yours, do you?"

Frank looked at her provocatively, his eyes lingering a few moments too long on her breasts, a glimmer of a smile playing around his mouth.

"No, sir."

"Right, now come here and wash my back. Come on, I won't bite, you know."

Timidly, Annie took the flannel and washed his back, but as she reached for the towel, he swiftly put his arms around her, pinning her arms to her sides. She struggled furiously, but he was too strong for her. He pushed her back against the wall and kissed her. Holding her against the wall with one arm, he nuzzled her neck, and she felt his hand glide down over her body and begin gathering up her skirt. She began to panic and debated whether to knee him in the crotch when there was a knock at the door. He released her immediately and reached for his shirt. She straightened her cap and picked up the tray, glaring at him as she did so.

"Don't you ever try that again," she hissed at him, and he grinned as he opened the door to find Maisie outside.

"I've brought your hot water, sir."

"I've already got my hot water, you stupid girl; see, Annie is just clearing my tray."

"Oh, I'm sorry, sir, my mistake. I didn't realise Annie had brought it. I'll take this away again."

The two girls exchanged glances, and Maisie noted Annie's obvious discomfort. "Are you coming, Annie? Mrs Potts is looking for you."

"Yes, I'm right behind you, Maisie."

As Annie left the room, she shot a look of contempt in Frank's direction and was annoyed to see the smirk on his face. Once outside, they hurried down the stairs before they spoke.

"Oh, Maisie, I was that glad to see you. He kissed me, and his hands were everywhere; I don't know what would have happened if you hadn't come."

"It's all right, Annie. You're all right now."

Annie was shaking with anger and emotion, and to her disgust, tears slid down her cheeks.

"Oh, look at me, crying when I'm so angry. Just who does he think he is? I'm going to tell Miss Wetherby."

Maisie put her arm around her. "Annie, it wouldn't do any good. Why do you think I came with the hot water? I knew he'd try it on. One of the other maids warned me earlier what he's like, and there's no point in complaining to Miss Wetherby because she wouldn't want to know."

Annie sobbed with rage. "Well, it's time someone taught him a lesson. If you hadn't come when you did, I was about to knee him hard in the crotch. My dad always told me to do that if a man tried it on."

"Well, I needn't have worried about you then, need I? In fact, I wish you had; it would have served him right. Seriously though, Annie, he's a big, strong man, so steer clear of him. From now on, we'll send one of the lads up with his trays."

In addition to all the Halloween trimmings, the great hall was decorated with exotic flowers from the hothouses, and a snowy white tablecloth covered the immense table, laden with the best china, cutlery, and glass. Eleanor surveyed the scene with satisfaction, for everything was perfect, and it promised to be a wonderful weekend. What with Sarah breaking her ankle, Robert mixing with the locals, the birth of the deformed baby, and David going missing, it had been such a stressful time recently, and she hoped this weekend would take her mind off it all.

A letter from James McNamee's parents confirmed that David had joined the army. Worse, he had completed his training and was already in South Africa, waiting to play his part in the unrest there. The McNamees were unaware that David had joined the army against his father's wishes, and they tried to reassure the Fellwoods that there was no finer occupation for a young man, but their words of comfort fell on deaf ears. Charles Fellwood had written to the army headquarters to ask for David to be returned as soon as possible and was awaiting a reply.

Eleanor had not regretted parting with her baby, but it somehow left a gap in her life. All her preparations, the new nursery, the baby clothes, and the new nanny, were no longer required, and she found it difficult to fill her time. Charles had been supportive and had even suggested they try for another baby, but that was the last thing Eleanor wanted. So determined was she to never run the risk of producing another deformed child that she had not allowed her husband to share her bed since the birth and had made it clear, despite his pleas, that she had no intention of letting him do so in the future.

Although Eleanor had been looking forward to the weekend, entertaining her guests and showing off the recent refurbishments to the Manor House, she was quite nervous on the night of the ball in case everything did not run smoothly. However, the food was delicious and the wine excellent, and she began to relax and enjoy herself. Many women, particularly the ones from London, wore the latest fashions. Mrs Eastleigh, Frank's mother, was dressed in a peacock-blue bustle, a dress which had all but replaced the crinoline. It was made of a heavy, luxurious fabric that clung tightly to her slim body, accentuating her bottom. Her hair was piled high on the top of her head and was dressed with combs and ornaments, an arrangement which had taken her maid some considerable time.

Her friend, Mrs Raleigh, also wore her hair piled up on the top of her head, and ringlets cascaded down her neck. She wore a fringe frizzled over her forehead. This was the latest fashion, a style known as 'Josephine Curls'. She also wore a bustle of emerald green and had such a tiny waist some wondered how she could breathe.

All ladies wore their corsets as tight as possible, and even girls as young as three or four were often laced up into bodices. The corsets were sometimes drawn in so tightly and for such long periods that the internal organs became deformed, and women could not draw in a deep breath, even when they took them off. This led to women fainting or getting the vapours; a condition put down to their delicate breeding. Wearing corsets was particularly difficult for pregnant women and led to many miscarriages. Some babies were born with deformities or respiratory problems because they had insufficient room to develop properly. Doctor Luckett suspected that Lady Fellwood's insistence on wearing a tight corset during her pregnancy may have contributed to her baby's deformities, but wisely, he kept his thoughts to himself.

The servants had been hard at work since before dawn, and there was little chance of them getting to bed until the early hours. Maisie and Annie ran to and fro, collecting empty glasses and carrying them to the kitchen.

"Is that the lot, now, lass?" Mrs Potts yawned loudly. "I'll be that glad to get to my bed tonight."

"No, there are still a few more, Mrs Potts, but go to bed if you like; I'll finish up here."

"Oh, thank you, Annie. Well, if you can manage, I think I will. It won't be long before I have to start the breakfasts, and I'm not as young as I used to be. I can't take these late nights anymore."

Annie could barely keep her eyes open. She unloaded the last tray of dirty glasses onto the draining board and then returned to the hall to put out the lamps. She extinguished each lamp in the passageway as she retraced her steps towards the distant glow of light radiating from the open kitchen door. She sighed and debated whether to leave the dishes until morning but decided she had better do them. She wondered where Maisie had got to. It wasn't like her to leave everything to Annie.

She carried a kettle from the range to the sink, filled a bowl with hot, soapy water, and washed the glasses, thinking she would leave them to drip dry. She heard a sound behind her and, without turning, said, "Is that you, Maisie? I wondered where you'd got to?"

"No, it's not Maisie, Annie, it's me, and I thought you might still be here. Dry your hands and come here; you've done enough dishes for one day. You deserve a little fun, too, you know."

Annie gasped and spun around to find Frank Eastleigh standing in the doorway.

"What are you doing here, Mr Eastleigh? I thought all the guests had gone to bed."

"I came looking for you, Annie. You're such a pretty girl, and I want to know you better, much better, in fact. What do you say?"

"No, I must get these finished and get to bed. I have to be up again in three hours."

"Well, a couple of hours in bed sounds like an excellent idea. Now, don't play hard to get; I know you don't mean it."

Frank was drunk. His eyes were glassy, and he swayed as he grinned at her.

"You keep away from me, Frank Eastleigh. I thought you were keen on Miss Victoria, anyway?"

"Oh, I am, but she's not likely to share my bed tonight now, is she? And I'd love to share my bed with you, Annie, and that's just what I'm going to do."

He staggered across the room and lurched towards Annie, but she was far too quick for him and darted around the big kitchen table. Frank roared with laughter.

"So, you want to play games first, do you? That's fine, but I will catch you, you know."

He sprinted around the table, and Annie ran to the other side.

"You're wasting your time; Maisie will be here any minute."

He chuckled. "No, she won't. I upset my tray of tea things and also broke a pillow, so she's busy clearing up the feathers, and it will take her at least half an hour. I've told her it has to be done tonight. Now, come here, you little minx."

He suddenly leapt across the table and grabbed Annie. She could smell the ale and wine on his breath as he crushed his mouth to hers and kissed her, his hand pawing roughly at her breast. Annie struggled furiously but quickly realised it was useless, for he was too strong to throw off. Suddenly, she relaxed, making him think she would comply. He loosened his grip slightly and smiled.

"That's better; see, it's not so bad, is it?" She tilted her weight onto her back foot, then brought her other knee up as sharply as she could. It struck him hard between the legs, and he doubled up and groaned in agony.

"You wait till I catch you," he gasped.

"No, I don't think so."

Annie beat a hasty retreat up the staircase to her room, then suddenly remembered Maisie and decided she must warn her. The door to Frank's room was open, and Maisie was on her hands and knees, gathering feathers from the broken pillow.

"Maisie, leave that. Come on, quick. Don't argue. Just come with me."

Maisie recognised the urgency in Annie's voice and followed her swiftly from the room. They heard footsteps on the stairs and ran to a dark alcove and hid behind a curtain. Frank Eastleigh, cursing, staggered into his room and slammed the door. The two girls crept to their bedroom, where Annie told Maisie what had happened.

"Keep out of his way tomorrow, Annie. He'll be furious, and I can't believe you hit him in the crotch." She giggled. "Serves him right; I hope it hurt."

"Oh, it hurt all right. He was bent double and red in the face." She started to laugh. "Come on, we'd better get to bed; we must be up again in a couple of hours."

As soon as their heads touched the pillows, they fell fast asleep, and it seemed only two minutes later that the early bell rang to wake them. They both groaned.

"Oh no, it can't be morning already. I can't go through all that again."

"Well, at least there's no ball tonight, and most of them will go home tomorrow."

"What am I going to do about Frank Eastleigh? He told me to do his fire and take his water, meals, and everything, but I daren't."

"We'll go together. He won't try anything with two of us there."

"All right, I bet he's angry, though."

They helped to prepare the breakfasts and then attended to the bedroom fires. Only a few guests wanted a fire because the weather was mild, but some of the bigger rooms were always cold, even in the sunniest weather.

They knocked timidly on Frank Eastleigh's door and heard him mutter, 'Come in.'

Annie peered around the door and saw Frank lying in bed, the bedclothes barely covering him. It was apparent he had nothing on.

She blushed. "I'm sorry, I'll come back later."

"Oh no, now is fine, Annie; we have a little unfinished business to attend to, do we not? Come here and apologise for your bad manners last night."

Maisie followed Annie into the room, and Frank pulled the covers over himself.

"What are you doing here, girl? It doesn't take two servants to bring my breakfast. Go away unless you would like to join in the fun?"

"No, I don't think so, sir. I'm here to look after Annie, and you wouldn't want us both to start screaming with your dear mama next door, would you? I assure you, I can scream extremely loudly when I want to."

"Get out of my sight, the pair of you, but Annie, I intend to bed you, young lady, and I always get my way in the end, so you mark my words. Go on now, get out."

The two girls left the room shaking.

"You're certainly going to have to watch your step, Annie. I think you've made him keener by turning him down, but at least he goes home tomorrow. We'll wait on him together until then, and don't go anywhere on your own."

"No, I won't. Thanks, Maisie."

CHAPTER 24

A couple of weeks after all the guests had left the Manor House and life had returned to normal, Mrs Potts entered the kitchen one morning and clapped her hands.

"Right then, girls, do you know what day it is?"

"Well, yes, of course, Mrs Potts, it's Sunday."

She sighed. "Yes, I know that, but what is special about today?"

The girls looked at her blankly.

"I don't know what young people are coming to these days; you know nothing about tradition. Today is the last Sunday before Advent, so it's Stir Up Sunday. Maisie, you should have remembered that from last year. Today, we'll make the Christmas puddings to give the flavour time to develop before they're eaten. You three can prepare the ingredients for me."

The morning was spent chopping apples and weighing the ingredients for fifteen puddings. When it was ready, Mrs Potts called them for a lucky stir.

"Now, there are thirteen ingredients in this pudding mix, and this represents Jesus and all his disciples. We must stir the mixture from the east to the west in honour of the Three Wise Men, who visited the baby Jesus. Come on then, Molly, you can go first."

Mrs Potts handed her the large spoon.

"No, silly, the other way. Don't you know which way is east? That's it. Now make a wish, but don't tell us what it is, or it won't come true."

They made their wishes one by one and then put the mixture into the pudding basins, ready for steaming.

"Now, there is just one job left to do, and that's to put a silver sixpenny bit in each one. Whoever finds that sixpenny bit in their helping will become rich. Mind you, I found one last year, and I'm still waiting, but you never know."

Robert counted the days until he could return home for Christmas as he longed to see Annie. He'd thought about writing to her, but it was too risky. Any messenger would be puzzled by a letter from the squire's son to a village girl, and Annie would have difficulty explaining it to Sabina. It wasn't until they were apart that he realised just how much she had come to mean to him. He knew his parents would never consent to him marrying Annie, but he had decided that was what he wanted to do. He wondered if she had started working at the Manor House yet.

There was no news of David, and Robert knew he would be in serious trouble when he did return. He had given the matter a lot of thought. One day, David would inherit the estate, and once his father handed the reins over to him, he would ask David to let him rent one of the farms. A couple of the tenants, Alfred Chugg, for one, were getting on a bit and may like to retire to a farm cottage. Well, perhaps not Alfred, because he might want one of his sons to carry on, but Tom Houle, now that was more likely. He was over seventy and had no children, and his farm would do nicely. The more Robert thought about it, the more he liked the idea and wished he could discuss it with David.

Eventually, the last day of term arrived, and Robert caught the train back to Eggleston. He was pleased to see that Dodger had come to collect him.

"Hello, Dodger. How are you?"

"Hello, Master Robert. I'm well, thanks, and yourself?"

"Yes, I'm fine. Now, tell me all the news from home. What's been happening?"

"Oh, not much, sir. Prince had a nasty bout of colic just after you went. Right worried about him I was, but he pulled through, and now he's as good as new."

"Splendid; anything else?"

Robert wanted to ask how Annie was and if she had missed him, but of course, he couldn't, so he tried to lead the conversation around to it.

"My father visited me the other day and mentioned that an abandoned baby had been found. He seemed to think the Carters had taken it in. Is that right? Mrs Carter has a lot of children already."

"Yes, Annie found a little boy, and the Carters have taken him in even though he's deformed. I believe he's doing all right. There was a serious outbreak of diphtheria, which was terrible, and there were a lot of deaths. All the Symons children died, and Matilda Bedworth, Hannah, Mary, and Tommy Cutcliffe, Jane Lovering, even George Carter's wife, Alice, and they have the best of everything."

"Oh no, that's awful. Did any of the Carter family die?" exclaimed Robert, unable to help himself. He was suddenly petrified in case Annie had died.

"Yes, John and Emma both died within a few hours of each other, I believe. It was a sad time."

"Were the rest of the Carters all right?"

"Yes, they were fine. It was strange how some people caught it and others didn't."

Robert tried to hide his relief.

"What about your family, Dodger? I hope you didn't lose anyone?"

"No, we were fortunate as none of us caught it. Mind you, we kept to ourselves. The worst of it was in the hamlet. Those cottages are damp and draughty, and the folk there are often ill."

"Has it finished now, do you think?"

"It seems to be at an end now. There haven't been any new cases for a month or more, anyway."

Try as he might, Robert could not direct the conversation to Annie, and eventually, he asked.

"How about Annie Carter, Dodger? Is she all right? I know she was hoping to start work at the Manor House."

"Yes, she's working at Hartford and prettier than ever now she's eating decent meals. She'll be pleased to see you."

When they arrived at Hartford Manor, Robert went to see his parents. He shook his father's hand, and his mother hugged him and held him at arm's length.

"Why, Robert, you've grown. You're quite the young gentleman now."

"Well, I am nearly eighteen, you know. Victoria wrote to me about her coming out ball in London next spring. She said we might have a joint birthday party, too; is that right?"

"Yes, of course, you are twins, and we thought we could combine the two. We'll explain to Professor Franklin that you need to go to London for a few weeks."

"Is there any news of David? I received a letter telling me he was in South Africa, but the letter took a long time to get to me."

"I wrote to the army and explained he did not have my permission to join and that he must be returned at once," said his father. "However, he had already left for South Africa. They will advise him of my wishes, but it was unclear whether they would release him until he's served his time. I do not know how he could have been so stupid as to sign up."

Robert wished he hadn't asked because his father was getting agitated.

"I'm sure he'll be fine. Anyway, I must go and see the girls."

Victoria and Sarah were delighted to see him and told him all their news, but he couldn't wait to see Annie. He strolled nonchalantly into the kitchen for a chat with Mrs Potts. She had spoiled him for years, and her face beamed with pleasure as she hugged him to her ample bosom.

"Master Robert, my, how you've grown. Pull up the settle by the fire and have one of my fresh scones. I made them especially for you when Miss Wetherby said you were arriving today."

Robert smiled and sat down. As a child, he had often retreated to the sanctuary of the warm kitchen, where Mrs Potts' fat, motherly arms had held him tight and usually put right whatever it was that troubled him.

"So, what's new then, Mrs Potts? I do believe you've lost some weight. Been working you too hard, have they?"

"Oh, you tell a wicked lie, Master Robert. You know I'm bigger than ever, but I was surely never meant to be thin. It's a cook's job to test the food before letting the gentry eat it, and I take my job seriously, as you know."

Her eyes twinkled, and her plump cheeks dimpled as she smiled.

"Mrs Potts, I love you just the way you are. Any new servants since I left?"

The question was not unusual, for Robert took an interest in the staff. However, Ethel Potts had heard of his friendship with Annie and smiled.

"Well, now, Annie Carter's working alongside Maisie as our second kitchen maid. They're just turning down the beds and lighting the lamps and should be back soon to help me with the evening meal. Know Annie, do you?"

"I've seen her in church, I think. Is she good?"

"Yes, she's an excellent worker and a pleasant young girl. We've been teasing her that she's Miss Wetherby's favourite. I think I can hear them coming now."

The sound of chatter and laughter drifted down the passageway, and Robert's heart leapt as he caught his first glimpse of Annie. Dodger was right; she was even more beautiful than ever. The extra food had rounded her body, and she now had breasts and hips. Her face had filled out, and in each cheek was a dimple that danced in and out as she laughed. She looked stunning even in her uniform, with her hair tucked under her cap.

When she saw Robert, she stopped in her tracks and stared. Mrs Potts stepped in to rescue the awkward situation.

"Well, now, here's our new kitchen maid, Annie Carter. Annie, this is Master Robert; he's come home for the holidays. Master Robert, you already know Maisie, don't you?"

"Yes, of course I do. How are you, Maisie? Hello Annie, do you like working at Hartford? I know Mrs Potts can be a terrible trial. I certainly wouldn't want to work for her."

"Hello, Master Robert, I'm fine, thanks," said Maisie.

"Hello, Master Robert. Yes, I like working here, and Mrs Potts is a pleasure to work for," said Annie.

"Well said, my dear." Mrs Potts beamed at the compliment. "Maisie, pull the kettle over and make us a cup of tea with our scones. Will you join us, Master Robert?"

"Yes, please, I can't resist your cooking, Mrs Potts. It's a good job I'm not home for long, or I'd be so fat I couldn't walk."

Robert could not have paid Mrs Potts a greater compliment, and they enjoyed their tea and thickly buttered scones. Robert and Annie could not take their eyes off each other and left most of the talking to the other two. Oh, dear, thought Mrs Potts, I'm afraid this will end in tears.

Mrs Potts surpassed herself that evening by providing a wonderful meal. The Fellwood family was first served with a lightly poached salmon smothered in a prawn sauce. This was followed by a sirloin of beef and Yorkshire puddings, accompanied by roast potatoes, carrots, and cabbage. Desserts included gooseberry fool, syllabub, apple crumble, and spotted dick. Robert fidgeted throughout the meal, thinking how he might see Annie alone. However, the opportunity arose sooner than he had expected. After enjoying a glass of port with his father, he retired early, saying he was tired after the journey. He had only been in his room a few minutes when someone knocked on the door. He opened it, and outside stood Annie with a jug of water and a glass on a tray.

"Excuse me, sir, Mrs Potts told me to bring this tray to your room. I'm sorry if I've disturbed you." Annie grinned broadly and bobbed a curtsey.

"Yes, you most definitely have disturbed me, wench, so bring that tray in quickly, please."

Robert waited until she had put the tray down and then pulled her into his arms.

"Oh, Annie, I've missed you so much, you wouldn't believe it." He kissed her tenderly, and Annie clung to him, never wanting the moment to end. "I can't believe how you've changed. You were lovely before, but now you're beautiful. What have you done to yourself?"

"Well, I've put on a lot of weight. Mrs Potts' cooking has much to answer for, and I'll be as plump as her soon if I'm not careful."

"No, it suits you. You have curves now where you didn't have any before," said Robert, his eyes twinkling mischievously.

"I must go, but I've missed you so much."

"Me too. We must meet soon."

"No, we can't. Your parents would be furious, and they'd sack me. You know they would."

"They mustn't find out then. Annie, I have to see you. We must meet at least once to catch up on all the news."

He saw her waver. "Go on, it will be all right. Just once, that's all, then you can call me Master Robert as much as you like and bob a curtsey when I pass."

"Well, I have a half-day off on Sunday. Shall we meet in the mazzard green like we used to?"

"Of course, what time?"

"I'll have to see the family first, so about four o'clock?"

"Yes, fine, I'll have three hours then before our evening meal."

"I know." Annie giggled. "I have to help cook it. Now, I must go before I'm missed. I'm sure Mrs Potts sent me up here on purpose."

"She's an angel, that Mrs Potts. Come here and give me one little kiss, and then I'll let you go."

This time, Robert kissed her passionately, and Annie felt weak at the knees. Reluctantly, she pulled away and ran to the door, straightening her cap as she descended the stairs. Maisie and Mrs Potts glanced up as she came in and noticed her flushed face. They said nothing as Sid Hobbs was sitting at the table drinking a cup of tea.

CHAPTER 25

The rest of the week dragged on slowly for Annie and Robert. It was so difficult seeing one another around the house and unable to speak to each other properly. They tried to snatch odd moments together in empty rooms and deserted corridors, and it didn't take Maisie and Mrs Potts long to suss out the situation. Both women warned Annie to cool it. She feigned innocence, but they were not fooled and were worried about her. Mrs Potts forbade her to wait on Robert and sent Maisie instead. Robert could not complain without causing suspicion, so they saw little of each other.

Annie went home as usual on Sunday afternoon but pleaded a headache when Harry called to take her for a walk. Sabina eyed her suspiciously.

"You didn't mention a headache, Annie? A walk might have done it good."

"I don't have a headache, Mum, but I don't want to encourage Harry too much. I'd like a walk on my own, and then I'll head straight back to the House. Is there anything you want me to do before I go?"

"No, that's all right. We all need time on our own sometimes. Don't be late back, though, will you? I know Miss Wetherby's always singing your praises, but it doesn't take much to get on the wrong side of her. Harry was disappointed; you know he thinks the world of you."

"I know, and I'll see him soon, but I only get a half-day off, and he doesn't own me."

"No, fair enough. I've made a cottage pie for dinner, and it's ready, so we'll eat it now, and that will give you time for a decent walk. The fresh air will do you good."

Annie slipped away quickly as she didn't want any of her siblings tagging along. However, they were too busy mopping up their gravy with the crusty bread provided by Mrs Potts. It was a cold day, and a thick frost still sparkled on the grass. The leafless trees stood out starkly against the weak winter sun.

Sabina sighed as she watched her daughter walk into the woods. She knew Robert was home and guessed Annie was probably going to meet him.

"Annie, I'm over here."

"I didn't expect you to be here yet. I thought I was early."

"Yes, you are, but that's good because we'll have a bit longer together. Come here."

Robert drew her to him, holding her tightly and kissing her passionately. She kissed him back, her hands caressing his strong muscles through his shirt. Finally, she pulled away from him.

"Oh, Robert, I've missed you so much. How was school?"

"All right, I suppose. I was sorry to hear about the diphtheria outbreak, especially losing John and Emma. It must have been awful."

"Yes, it was terrible, and the worst thing was, there was nothing we could do. I was worried Helen and Danny would catch it, but they didn't. You must come and see your little brother, Robert. He laughs and chuckles away, and we all love him just as much as Helen."

"How are his mouth and his legs?"

"Well, his mouth's no different, and he still has trouble feeding. Patience isn't his strong suit either, and he yells when he's hungry. You can tell he was meant to be a gentleman and waited on hand and foot, but his legs aren't too bad. Mum's been binding them with splints to make them grow straight, but I don't know if it will help. Dr Luckett went to see Mary Cutcliffe when she had diphtheria, and Mum asked him to examine Danny. It was funny because we knew he'd delivered him, and Mum pretended he was a foundling. Anyway, he thought Danny was doing remarkably well and might walk eventually."

"Oh, I'm glad. Would your mother let me see him?"

"I'm sure she would, but what about your father?"

"Hmm, I could ask if he'd like me to come to see how he's doing, but he'd probably say no. I think I'll come once without asking him, just in case he says no, then, if he agrees, I could come again with a clear conscience. I think he would have kept the baby; it was Mother who was dead against it. My father came to see me at school a few weeks ago and said he had arranged for Sabina to get paid. Is she getting the money all right?"

"Yes, the extra money gets put in with her wages every week. Jack must wonder why she gets paid so much unless he's in on the secret. It's made life a bit easier for Mum, but I think she'd keep him for nothing; you know what she's like where babies are concerned."

"How are you getting on at Hartford?"

"Well, it's hard work, but I love it and adore Mrs Potts' cooking. When I tasted her creamy porridge the first morning, I thought I'd died and gone to heaven. I've never had so much to eat, and she always sends me home with a couple of loaves of bread, some stale cakes, or whatever is left over."

"What about Miss Wetherby and Sid Hobbs?"

"I've kept on the right side of them so far, and that's where I intend to stay, but I wouldn't want to upset either of them. I love working with Maisie, though. We have a real laugh, even when we're rushed off our feet. I hope your family doesn't have too many parties; that last one wore us out."

"Well, there will be several parties over Christmas. I know we have a lot of visitors coming to stay again over the next few days. With Victoria and I turning eighteen in the spring, Mother and Father are searching for a suitable husband for her, so they're being rather more sociable than usual. I hope they don't try to organise a marriage for me because they would certainly disapprove of my intended bride." He grinned, and Annie blushed in embarrassment.

"Now, did I say it was you? You are such a forward hussy."

Annie slapped him, and laughing, he pulled her to him and kissed her. She tried to pull away, but he held her firmly, suddenly serious.

"I love you, Annie. Will you marry me?"

"Don't be ridiculous. You know I can't; don't tease."

"I'm not teasing; I mean it. If you could, would you marry me?"

"You know I would. I love you, too, but it can never happen, so it's no use pretending."

"Well, I have a few plans up my sleeve, so wait for me, and I promise I will marry you one day."

"Whom do you think Miss Victoria will marry?

"Well, she seems keen on Frank Eastleigh. I haven't seen him for ages, though we played together as children, and he was always into mischief."

"Hmm, no change there then."

"What do you mean?"

"Oh, nothing. I just didn't take to him when he was here in October, that's all."

"No, come on, there's more to it, isn't there? I saw the expression on your face when I mentioned his name. What's he done to upset you?"

"It's nothing. It's just that he tried it on a couple of times when he was here. He'd had too much to drink, but you needn't worry; I can take care of myself. I'm just not sure he'd be faithful for long."

"He's coming again for Christmas. I wish I'd been here last time; I'd have sorted him out."

"Don't be daft. Like I said, I can look after myself, and Maisie and Mrs Potts take care of me anyway. You mustn't show any interest in what happens to me, or people will be suspicious. Why should you concern yourself with a lowly kitchen maid?"

"Well, just be careful, and I shall keep an eye on him anyway. Come on, we'd better get back, or you'll be in trouble, and I shan't get any dinner."

It was almost dark as Annie struggled to find her way over the rough ground, but the visibility improved at the top of the hill, and she hurried towards the Manor House. Robert gave her a five-minute start and then followed. He approached the front door while she went through the servant's entrance to the kitchen, where everyone was busy with the evening meal.

"Ah, there you are, Annie. Can you help Maisie with the carrots, please, and then make the batter for the Yorkshire puddings? Did you have a nice time?"

"Yes, thanks, Mrs Potts. Mum was pleased with the bread. She says she doesn't know what she'd do without you."

"She's welcome. Now, it will be busy over Christmas, so not much time off for any of us, I'm afraid. We'll all have to work on Christmas Day, though most of us will have some time off on Boxing Day. Mind you, there's the staff party to look forward to. You'll enjoy that, Annie. Do you have a dress to wear?"

"No, nothing suitable."

"Well, no doubt we can find you something to wear. Two days before Christmas Eve, we have our party. It's a tradition the old master started, and Mr Charles has carried on with it, though it's not quite like it used to be. We have a slap-up meal, and then the family joins us for the singing and dancing. We've had some good parties over the years, and you enjoyed it last year, didn't you, Maisie?"

"Yes, it was a delicious meal, Annie, and so wonderful to dance to the music, and on Boxing Day, we get our Christmas boxes. Last year, I was given a new shawl; you know, that blue one I keep for best. I've got a dress you can wear; it's too small for me, and I blame Mrs Potts' cooking for that. It will be plenty big enough for you, though; I'll show it to you later."

They stopped talking then, for the meal was nearly ready, and there was much to do. However, later in their room, Maisie took an emerald green dress from her cupboard.

"Here's the dress, look. It's an old one of Miss Victoria's that Miss Wetherby gave me."

The dress was low cut with lace around the neck, gathered tightly at the waist, with a full skirt.

"Oh, Maisie, it's beautiful. Are you sure you don't want to wear it yourself?"

"Well, I'd love to, but see that tiny waist, I've no chance of squeezing into that anymore. No, it will look lovely on you, and I have this one."

Maisie took a deep blue dress of a less fitting style from the cupboard.

"She gave me the two dresses last year, and I've never had an occasion to wear this one, but I think it will fit. What do you think?"

"Yes, I think it will look lovely. Shall we try them on?"

"Go on, then. It's a bit cold, though."

They stripped off their uniforms, put on their dresses, and grinned at each other.

"We look just like ladies, don't we?" Maisie giggled. "Annie, you look so beautiful."

"You do, too, and don't they feel soft? Perhaps we could get some matching ribbon for our hair?"

"Yes, we'll see what we can find because we're allowed to wear our hair down for the party."

"Brr, I'm freezing." They took off the fine dresses and dived thankfully into their warm nightgowns and straight into bed.

CHAPTER 26

As the days sped by to Christmas, Annie and Robert continued to meet in concealed passageways and corners of the garden. It was difficult, for Annie's job was demanding, and she was soon missed if she wasn't where she was supposed to be. With Sabina's permission, Robert went with Annie to see Danny. He was amazed at how much his little brother had grown and pleased he was so contented.

"Mrs Carter, you've worked wonders," he said, thankfully. "I'm so glad you took him in. I've got some money left from last term, so get a few things for Christmas."

"No need for that, but thank you, Master Robert. He's an adorable little boy, and it's a shame his mother didn't want him; she doesn't know what she's missing. He's made up a bit for losing John and Emma with diphtheria, though he can never replace them. The extra money has made all the difference, too. I think he'll walk, eventually, though for certain he'll limp, but that doesn't matter."

"Please take it. I don't need it, and I'm sure it will be useful. Buy some new clothes if you don't need the money for food."

"Well, that is kind of you. The children need some warmer clothes, and shoes are always a problem. Do you think your mother would like to see Danny?"

"No, she wanted him sent far away, and she'd be angry if she knew he lived so close. She must never find out he lives here with you."

Annie spotted Harry Rudd walking towards the cottage. "Here comes Harry, and he'd better not see you here, Robert. I'm sure he told tales about you swimming in Shebworthy Pond. I'll go for a walk with him. I have to be back soon, anyway."

Robert stood outside the back door while Annie greeted Harry at the front.

"Hello, Harry, how are you? I was just going for a walk around the village on my way back to the house. Do you want to walk with me?"

Harry beamed with pleasure. "Well, that was good timing then, and yes, I'd like to."

When they had gone, Sabina let Robert back in.

"Right, I'll give them a head start, and then I'd better go too."

"I'm glad to have the chance to speak to you alone, Master Robert. You're a fine lad, and any mother would be pleased for her daughter to be courting you, but it's no good, is it? I may be speaking out of turn here, and you can deny you have feelings for Annie if you like, but I've seen the way you look at each other, and it's obvious you're in love, but you are the squire's son. Your father will never let you marry Annie, and I know you wouldn't shame her by asking for less. Can't you see it's better to end it now before you both get hurt?"

"I can't deny it, Mrs Carter; I've loved Annie since the first day I saw her. That may sound ridiculous, but it's true. It's not just that she's so beautiful, she's also kind, funny and good-natured. I can't stop seeing her, anyway; for one thing, she works in my house."

"I know, and that's why I'm going to seek a new position for her after Christmas." He opened his mouth to protest, but she held up her hand. "It's for the best, and I don't want you to tell her because it will be hard enough to convince her, as it is."

"Please, don't do that; there's no need. The situation seems impossible now, but I'll ask my father to let me rent one of the farms in a couple of years. Old Mr Houle is over seventy and widowed, with no children, so he'll have to retire soon. I'd love to take over his farm, and once I've done that, I'll ask Father's permission to marry Annie. I expect he'll say no, but we're young and can afford to wait if we have to. I can marry whomever I like once I'm twenty-one. It's not as if I'm the heir to the estate because that will be David, as you know."

"You make it sound so simple, Robert, but your father will never allow it. Good heavens, he won't even let Master David stay in the army, and that's not nearly as shocking as marrying a kitchen maid. No, I shall find a new position for Annie, and with any luck, Harry will ask her to marry him. I'm sorry, but I'm sure it's the best thing for both of you. You're high-born, Robert, and you'd be shunned by all the gentry if you married our Annie."

Robert tried to keep the impatience from his voice and remain calm. "I don't about care about that. I understand what you're saying, and I know you mean it for the best, but I am determined to marry her, with or without my father's permission. I only hope she'll wait for me."

"Well, please think carefully about what I've said, Robert. You're both so young, and you'll meet someone else, really you will."

As she watched him walk away, Sabina's face was solemn, for despite her assurances that he would find someone else, she was not so sure. She had loved

Tom since they started school and married him at sixteen. He had always been the only man for her, and despite her promise to him as he lay dying, she knew he always would be.

The hall at Hartford Manor was decorated with holly, mistletoe, and ivy, and a large Christmas tree was festooned with shiny glass baubles and paper lanterns. On the day of the staff party, the family had a large meal at midday and a cold buffet for their dinner, leaving Mrs Potts free to cook a Christmas meal for the staff. They sat down at six o'clock to leek and potato soup, served with a swirl of cream and freshly made warm bread rolls, followed by roast turkey and all the trimmings. Mr Potts carved the turkey, though his wife kept interfering, telling him to put an extra slice on each plate. Then, although they felt they could not possibly eat another mouthful, no one could refuse a portion of Mrs Potts' Christmas pudding, smothered in Devonshire clotted cream. They were all pleased for Molly when she suddenly squealed excitedly as she found the sixpenny bit. A barrel of cider for the men and mulled wine for the ladies accompanied the meal. At eight o'clock, precisely as every year, Charles and Eleanor Fellwood, followed by Robert, Victoria, and Sarah, entered the room. The servants rose respectfully to their feet until the family was seated at the end of the room.

Sid Hobbs, speaking gruffly, as he had a heavy cold, thanked their employers for such a delicious meal and Mrs Potts for cooking it. Robert gasped when he saw Annie and tried not to stare. Annie had brushed her hair until it shone, and fiery ringlets reaching to her waist were held back by a single green ribbon that matched the dress and her eyes. The well-tailored dress accentuated her breasts and provided the perfect contrast to her pale skin. Victoria, recognising the dress, was dismayed it had never looked as elegant on her.

The family traditionally danced the first few dances with the servants, and when the musicians started to play, Sid Hobbs, as was expected of him, asked Lady Fellwood if she would care to dance. Charles Fellwood took Miss Wetherby by the hand, and Fred Baker accompanied Victoria. Dodger Watkins smiled kindly at Sarah as he led her onto the floor, and she was thrilled. Robert gallantly asked Mrs Potts to dance. None of the staff danced with each other until all the family had a partner. Robert waltzed Mrs Potts around the room, surprised at how light she was on her feet, bearing in mind her considerable size. When the dance ended, Robert escorted his partner to her seat and kissed her on the cheek, telling her she'd always be the only one for him.

"Get away with you, Master Robert; you're such a tease," she gasped, out of breath, but her old eyes twinkled fondly. "Go on, I know who you really want to dance with."

Robert thought he wouldn't make his desire to dance with Annie too obvious, so he held out his hand to Maisie, and she smiled and accepted gracefully. As they whirled around the room, she saw him watching every move Annie made as she danced with Sid Hobbs.

"Annie looks beautiful tonight, doesn't she, sir?"

"Yes, she does, Maisie, and so do you. I might dance with her next."

"I rather thought you might."

"Sorry, is it that obvious?"

"Well, it is to me and possibly a few others, but she's a pretty girl, so why shouldn't you dance with her? Go on, you know, you want to."

Maisie was looking past him, and he wondered what had captured her attention. Sid Hobbs was still on the dance floor, talking to Annie, and when the music started up again, instead of returning her to her seat, he continued to dance with her. Robert was surprised by this and could not imagine what had possessed the man as everyone focused on the couple as they danced around the room. Some of the staff began to smirk, and Annie was most uncomfortable. It was so out of character for Sid Hobbs to dance at all, let alone dance twice with a maid.

As the dance ended, Robert tapped Sid on the shoulder to ask Annie for the next one. Sid did not look pleased about the intervention, but Annie took his hand gratefully. Sid then dutifully went to ask Miss Wetherby to dance.

Robert skilfully manoeuvred Annie around the dance floor, trying to find a space to talk without being overheard. Sid scowled at him as he waltzed past with Miss Wetherby, and Annie became aware that several people in the room were watching closely as she danced with Robert.

"Well, what was all that about?" said Robert.

"I don't know. I was surprised Mr Hobbs danced with me at all, never mind twice. He's an excellent dancer, though, and it's a pity I'm not because I kept stepping on his toes. Hopefully, he'll never ask me again."

"I should hope not; he shouldn't have asked you more than once, anyway," Robert whispered to avoid being overheard.

"Shouldn't he?"

"Well, I can understand why he did, the way you look in that dress, but he should have danced with the older women first. Mind you, I think every man in the room is hoping to have a dance with you."

"Oh no, don't say that. I couldn't refuse to dance with him, could I? The dress was Miss Victoria's, you know, and she gave it to Maisie, and she gave it to me."

"No, you couldn't refuse to dance with him but keep out of his way for the rest of the party, would you? I see Ethel Potts is having a word with him. Do you know, I think he's had too much to drink, and I've never known that happen before either?"

Their dance ended too soon, and Robert suggested another dance to Annie, saying if Sid Hobbs could dance with her twice, then so could he. However, Annie begged him to lead her back to her seat as she already felt the object of too much attention. Dodger Watkins was quickly on the scene and asked her to accompany him in the barn dance, so Robert danced instead with young Molly. The party was going with a real swing, and even Charles Fellwood had enjoyed dancing with several women, including Annie herself, much to her embarrassment. Some of the servants thought it was about time the Fellwoods left so they could get down to some serious drinking. Eleanor Fellwood, too, was eager to go and pulled at her husband's sleeve.

"Come on, Charles, it's time we left. The servants can relax and enjoy themselves more after we've gone."

"Oh, let's stay a little longer, Eleanor. The musicians are good, and I'm enjoying it this year. Let's have a dance together, and then we'll go." Charles rose to his feet and held out his hand to her.

"No, I'm not dancing with you before all the servants. It's bad enough having to dance with them, thanks to your father's stupid traditions, and I think you've had too much wine."

Charles gave her a stern glance and went to ask Mrs Potts for a dance. Francis Rudd was about to ask Annie to dance when Sid Hobbs appeared on the scene again.

"Now then, young man, you can have your dance a bit later. I'm sure you won't mind me having another dance with young Annie here."

"No, of course not, sir; I'll see you later, Annie."

Sid held out his hand, and Annie paused, feeling everyone's eyes on her again.

"Would you mind if I sat this one out, sir? I've not stopped dancing all night, and I could do with getting my breath back."

"I don't think you should refuse me a dance, do you, Annie? Come on, you can sit out the next one."

The dance was a waltz, and Sid held Annie far too tightly and occasionally stumbled. She was embarrassed, and it was fortunate she could not see the thunderous expression on Robert's face, but it was noted by several others in the room.

Charles went back to Eleanor and took her arm.

"Come along then, my dear, we'll leave these good people to enjoy themselves. Merry Christmas, everyone. Come, Robert, Victoria, and you too, Sarah."

As soon as they left the room, Eleanor shook her arm free from his and stormed down the corridor. The children hurriedly made themselves scarce. He followed her up the grand staircase to their bedroom.

"What's the matter?"

"You need to ask? You made a complete fool of yourself in front of all the staff. I can't believe you danced so many times. What on earth possessed you?"

"It's my house, and I can dance as often as I like, can't I? You've never complained when I've danced before?"

"You know how I hate these stupid evenings, but you took it too far this year, and I believe you're drunk."

"I am not drunk. I've had a glass or two of wine and danced a few times, but it is Christmas after all, and it's not like my wife would dance with me, is it? Or do anything else with me, for that matter," he muttered.

He suddenly reached out and pulled her to him.

"Eleanor, it's months since the child was born. You're better now, and it's unlikely you'll get pregnant again at your age. I still love you, and we're not that old. You can't expect me to live like a monk the rest of my life."

"I'm sorry, Charles, but I can't risk it. I love you too, of course, but Dr Luckett says I shouldn't rush things." She started to cry.

"No, I'm sorry, don't cry. I shouldn't have spoken to you like that. Maybe you're right, and I've had one glass of wine too many."

Back in the hall, Miss Wetherby beckoned Annie. "Carter, you should leave the party now and change into something more suitable. You're making an exhibition of yourself and attracting far too much attention. Jones, you go with her. In fact, you should change too. Neither of you is dressed appropriately."

"But Miss, you gave Maisie these dresses for last year's Christmas party, and she passed this one on to me. I've nothing else suitable to wear, so please can we stay a bit longer? It's early yet."

Mrs Potts overheard what was said.

"It's a bit early, Miss Wetherby. Perhaps they could stay just a little longer? I promise I'll keep an eye on them and see them to their quarters later myself. They can't get into any trouble then, and it's only Christmas once a year."

"Oh, very well, Potts, on your head be it, but I'm going to my room for I have such a headache. I shall hold you responsible for any wrongdoing."

So, thanks to Mrs Potts, Annie and Maisie stayed until the end of the party and enjoyed every moment. However, the cook was true to her word and escorted them to their bedroom and insisted they lock the door. She had seen how most of the men present had looked at Annie that night and decided it would be advisable to see her safely to her bed.

CHAPTER 27

There were a few thick heads the following day, and Fred Baker was subdued, begging Molly to be quiet at breakfast. Sid Hobbs, too, looked much the worse for wear when he came in for a cup of tea and steadfastly ignored everyone, perhaps somewhat embarrassed by his unusual behaviour the night before.

"Thanks for letting Maisie and I stay last night, Mrs Potts. I couldn't believe it when Miss Wetherby said we had to leave so early."

"Oh, that's all right, my dear; I could see how much you were enjoying yourselves. Now, we've had our turn, and there are about twenty guests expected today, so look lively."

For the next few days, they were rushed off their feet. The Eastleighs were guests again, and Annie made sure she went nowhere near Frank's room. Mrs Potts had heard from Maisie that he wasn't to be trusted, and she waited on him herself or sent Fred Baker.

"I don't think there's much danger of him fancying me at my age, but if he does, I'll eat him for breakfast."

Frank was not amused at the elderly cook delivering his tray and asked why Maisie and Annie no longer attended to him. "Oh, they're busy in the kitchen, sir, but it doesn't matter who brings it as long as it gets here, does it?"

"No, I suppose not." He scowled but could hardly argue.

Mrs Potts cooked a delicious meal for Christmas Day and was congratulated by Charles Fellwood when he unexpectedly visited the kitchen. Following the meal, Robert and Victoria entertained the family and guests by playing the piano and singing songs. Both had pleasant voices, and Victoria was a talented pianist. Sarah was persuaded to recite a poem about Father Christmas by Clement Moore that she had recently learnt. She was a little self-conscious as, haltingly at first, she repeated it without error and was applauded for her efforts.

As the evening progressed, Sarah was sent to bed, and the younger people played a game of charades in the drawing room whilst some of the men played cards. It was late when the household finally retired to bed, and Annie and Maisie made sure they were not alone in the kitchen and at risk of Frank Eastleigh's unwelcome advances. They had confided their fears to Mrs Potts, and she suggested they get up a little earlier in the morning when it was safer and complete the clearing up.

After the festivities of Christmas Day, the servants were tired and glad that on Boxing Day, most could go home to see their own families. They lined up in the hall, and Charles and Eleanor thanked each of them for their services and handed them their pay. Robert, Victoria, and Sarah followed behind carrying presents and gave each servant their Christmas Box, carefully selected by Mrs Potts and Miss Wetherby. Molly, the tweeny, was excited, for she had never had a present before, and eagerly tore the paper from her gift. Inside, she found some bright red gloves and beamed with pleasure.

"Oh, Maisie, look, aren't they pretty? I shan't have cold hands now. What have you got?"

Maisie had a warm blue scarf and hat. "Oh, it's so soft; you feel it, Molly."

As Robert handed Annie her present, their eyes met with a knowing look, and he smiled as she bobbed him a curtsey and thanked him. Inside was a warm, pale grey shawl, and she swung it around her shoulders.

"Well, what do you think? Do I look like an old granny? It's so warm; I think I shall even wear it in bed."

"No, you certainly don't look like a granny, Annie," said Robert.

"Well, it will always be my Granny Annie shawl now, won't it? Never mind, I love it, and I shall wear it home today. Thank you."

Annie and her fellow workers left in high spirits. She carefully packed the presents she had bought for the family into her basket. There were sweets for her brothers and sisters, a shawl for Liza, and a thick coat for her mother. The garments weren't new but were of fine quality. Annie gave most of her wages to Sabina, but she had saved for months from the few pence her mother insisted she keep. She had bought the clothes from a travelling pedlar and couldn't wait to hand out the presents and show off her new shawl.

As she crossed the yard, someone whispered her name, and she was relieved to see it was Robert.

"Oh, you gave me a scare, then."

"Sorry, but I wanted to catch you before you left. Could we meet later? I go back to school the day after tomorrow. I usually stay for the New Year's Eve party, but Father says I must return early; I wonder if Miss Wetherby suspects we are friends and has said anything about us? Anyway, could we meet before I go?"

"Why don't you come home with me? Mrs Potts has given me loads of food, and I know Mum would like to see you."

"No, I'd better not because your mum's asked me to stop seeing you. I don't blame her; she's just worried about you."

"It's none of her business, and I shall tell her so. If I'm old enough to work, I'm old enough to pick my friends."

Robert took her hand and pulled her gently out of sight. He put his arms around her and kissed her.

"No, don't upset her, but could we meet this afternoon? I must see you again before I leave."

She pulled away from him reluctantly. "Not here, Robert. Someone might see us, but yes, I'll see you in the mazzard green about three o'clock."

Sabina and Liza were delighted with their gifts, and Annie was thrilled with a new dress Liza had made for her. She took the older children to the beach, played games with them, and let them enjoy some of the sweets she had bought. Then they returned home to eat a huge egg, cheese, and bacon pie, which Sabina had made, mostly with ingredients sent by Mrs Potts. After lunch, Annie put Helen and Danny in the pram and went to visit Harry. He was delighted to see her, and Matilda gave them some tea and mince pies.

Annie confided in her mother that she was meeting Robert to say goodbye. Sabina disapproved but was glad to hear he was returning to school. Annie strolled to the mazzard green and went to the pond to search for frogspawn, but it was far too early in the year. She knew the village children would soon be collecting the slimy clumps of jelly dotted with little black specks that would grow into tadpoles and, eventually, change into frogs, toads, or newts.

Her favourite tree was the tallest in the orchard, and Annie had been almost to the top on a long ladder to pick the mazzards. However, there was no fruit now, nor even any leaves. She heard a twig snap as Robert hurried towards her, grinning broadly.

"Hello, Annie, so we're alone at last. You'd never believe it could be so difficult to meet when we live in the same house, would you?"

He put his arms around her and kissed her.

"I asked Papa if I could come and see Danny, but he said it was best left alone. Still, I'll be back at Easter, and I'll come and see him again then. I wish I could write to you, Annie, but I can't, can I?"

"No, it would be suspicious if I got a letter, wouldn't it? I'll be thinking of you, though."

Robert reached into his pocket. "I've got a Christmas present for you." He handed her something wrapped in soft tissue paper.

Annie beamed, for presents seldom came her way. She carefully pulled the paper apart to reveal a gold locket and gasped.

"Oh, Robert, I love it, but I can't take it. Everyone would wonder where I got it from."

"Of course, you can; wear it under your uniform, then only Maisie will see it, and she won't mind. Here, let me put it on for you." He fastened it around her neck. "It looks lovely on you."

"Where did you get it?"

"Well, I could pretend it's a priceless family heirloom, but I'm afraid it's not. I bought it in Exeter on a shopping trip from school. It is real gold, though, but nothing to what I'll buy you when we're married."

"You know what I think about that, don't you?"

"I do. But would you like to marry me?"

"You know I would, but how could it ever be possible?"

"Well, as I told your mum the other day, I hope to persuade my father to let me rent Mr Houle's farm when he retires. It's two hundred acres of fertile land, and I'd love to farm it. David will inherit the estate, and rightly so, but Papa could let me rent that farm. Once I'm there, we'll wait until I'm twenty-one, and then I can marry whom I like. Oh, I know there'd be a lot of trouble, but people would come around eventually. What do you think? Would you wait that long for me?"

"You know I would, but I still think it's wishful thinking. You'd better have this necklace back and keep it for me."

"I certainly will not. I can't buy you an engagement ring, but I shall feel we are betrothed if you wear my necklace. Would you do that?"

Tears sprung to Annie's eyes. "Oh Robert, you know there's nothing I would like better. Do you mean it?"

He kissed her passionately, his hand gently fondling her breast through her dress, and hers crept inside his shirt and caressed his bare flesh. At last, he pulled away in frustration, not daring to allow this to go any further.

"There's nothing I want more, but it must be one step at a time."

They kissed again, and reluctantly, Annie returned to the Manor House. Robert followed discreetly, and they entered by separate doors as before.

The following day, Mrs Potts asked Annie to pick some parsley. "There should be a bit in the kitchen garden. Just go along the path, and you'll find it by the wall. It's sheltered there and usually survives unless we've had a cold spell."

"Yes, I know where you mean."

Right opposite the swedes that I used to pinch, she thought to herself. It was raining heavily, so she hurried along with her new shawl over her head and took a shortcut through the barn. She quickly picked the parsley and hurried back the way she had come. As she ran into the barn, someone jumped out from behind the door and grabbed her. Annie squealed in shock and dropped the parsley.

"Get off me! Get off!"

She found herself staring into Frank Eastleigh's blue eyes.

"Oh, it's you. I might have guessed. Let me go, or I'll scream."

"Oh, don't be such a little spoilsport. I only want a kiss and a cuddle, and I know you find me irresistible. You maids are all the same, always saying no when you really mean yes."

"When I say no, I mean no. Now let me go." Annie wriggled and tried to knee him, but he was wise to that little trick and held her too tightly to allow her to manoeuvre. He kissed her and fondled her breast, easily holding her arms with one of his, for he was a strong man. She was furious and stamped hard on his foot.

"Now, that wasn't very friendly, was it? What a little spitfire you are. How about we go up into the loft and get better acquainted? The hay's soft and comfy up there. I know, you see, because I've been there before."

He swung her over his shoulder and started to climb the ladder, and Annie screamed.

He hastened his step, but when he was almost at the top, Dodger appeared in the doorway.

"What's the matter?" His voice trailed off as he quickly read the situation. "Sir, I think Annie would like you to put her down."

"Sod off, boy! Just go about your work and mind your own business."

"I can't do that, sir. Annie's a friend of mine, you see."

"Oh, I'll bet she is, and you're jealous because I'm about to do what you would like to, or probably already have. Here's half a crown, now clear off."

He tossed the coin at Dodger and threw Annie onto the hay. Annie heard his footsteps running away and couldn't believe Dodger would abandon her.

Quickly, Frank was on top of her, one hand groping her breast and his other gathering up her skirt. She fought fiercely with the man for several minutes, but slowly, he got the better of her, pulling down her underwear and exposing her naked flesh. Suddenly, strong hands grabbed Frank and threw him to one side, and Robert stood there, glowering with anger. Annie hastily adjusted her clothing and covered herself up.

"What the hell are you doing, Eastleigh? Leave her alone."

"Oh, for goodness sake, Robert, she's only a maid. I expect you've had her already, and it's just a bit of fun. You can join in if you want." He winked broadly.

Robert hit his former friend squarely on the chin. Frank staggered back but recovered himself and lunged at Robert. They exchanged heavy blows, each giving as good as the other. Eventually, blood pouring from their faces, they stopped for breath and glared at each other.

"Annie, go to the kitchen," Robert panted.

She ran behind Robert, climbed down the ladder and found Dodger waiting below.

"Come on, Annie. I'll see you back."

"Oh, Dodger, I thought you'd left me, but I knew you wouldn't."

"I thought I'd better fetch Master Robert because that man could have made a lot of trouble for me, Annie, if I'd hit him. I wanted to, though. There, you go on in. I'm going back to make sure Master Robert's all right."

He ran back to the barn just in time to see Frank leaving. He scowled at Dodger. "You've not heard the last of this; you'd better watch your back." Dodger ran into the barn where Robert was dusting himself down.

"I'm fine. Is Annie safe?"

"Yes, sir, I took her to the kitchen."

"You were right to fetch me, Dodger. Keep an eye on her for me, will you? I don't think he'll try it on again, but you never know."

Ethel Potts and Maisie looked up in surprise as a dishevelled Annie entered the kitchen.

"What's the matter, Annie? Where's the parsley?" asked Mrs Potts.

Annie burst into tears.

"Come on now, what's wrong?"

Annie blurted out the story to them.

"Oh, Annie, thank goodness Dodger came along, but you'll have to watch out for that young man from now on; he's a real menace. I'd report it to Miss Wetherby, but she'd say it was your own fault for leading him on. He left a maid in the family way last Christmas, and she got the sack."

Robert entered the room, blood pouring from his nose.

"Oh, my goodness." Mrs Potts sat him on a stool and quickly pressed a damp cloth to his nose. "How are you going to explain this to your mother, Master Robert?"

"Well, I might just tell her the truth." Impatiently, he pushed the cloth away. "Annie, are you all right? He didn't hurt you, did he?"

Robert gazed anxiously into her eyes, distraught to see the tears brimming there. He longed to take her into his arms and comfort her properly. Annie sensed this and made a considerable effort to pull herself together in case he did just that.

"I'm fine, thanks to you, but don't tell anyone what happened, or I might get the sack."

"I don't see how you can get the sack for something that rogue did."

"No, she's right, Master Robert," said Mrs Potts. "It's best to say nothing. I know it's not Annie's fault, but that doesn't mean she won't get the blame. It's happened before, and no doubt, it will happen again. The trouble is, she's far too pretty for her own good. We'll have to take care of her until the visitors have gone."

Robert took Annie's hands in his. "Are you sure you're not hurt? He shouldn't come near you again after the hiding I just gave him."

Maisie and Mrs Potts exchanged glances as Robert held onto Annie's hands, and she made no move to pull them away.

"No, thanks to you, but I was that angry. I wish I could have given him a hiding like you did."

"Frank will be gone in a few days, so keep out of his way until then. I wish I didn't have to go back to school tomorrow. I could keep an eye on you, then."

Suddenly, they both became aware of Mrs Potts' and Maisie's eyes on them.

"I'd better go then," said Robert, and he reluctantly released Annie's hands, took one long last look at her, and left the room.

CHAPTER 28

George Carter had been miserable since his wife, Alice, died of diphtheria. He had never been passionately in love with his wife, but, nevertheless, he missed her. She had obeyed him without question, managed his house efficiently, and bore his children willingly, so he genuinely mourned her. In fact, he was surprised that he missed her so much. All domestic matters had been left to Alice, and only now did he realise how capably she had dealt with everything. Also, after twenty-odd years of marriage, he was not used to being alone in his bed. It would be improper even to consider taking another wife until at least a year had passed. However, he found his attention straying to his sister-in-law, Mary Ann, thinking that maybe a solution was just under his nose.

Mary Ann was Alice's younger sister and had initially come to help with the children and had never gone home. As the children grew up, she assisted in the shop, relying on Eveline for support. The two sisters were close, and Mary Ann missed Alice.

George pondered the problem of how to approach Mary Ann without causing offence. She had a pleasant and willing disposition, already lived in his house, and was used to the children. It would be an ideal solution, but it was a nuisance having to wait a year, and he decided to tackle the problem by seeking sympathy for his loss. Mary Ann had always taken her meals in the kitchen with the servants, and George thought it might be a start to suggest she now ate with him and the children. He called to her one morning as she passed the dining room.

"Good morning, Mary Ann. How are you today?"

"Good morning, George, I'm fine, and thank you for asking," said Mary Ann in surprise. George usually barely acknowledged her existence, speaking to her only to complain when something was not to his liking.

"That's good because I've something to ask you. I hope you don't mind?"

"No, of course not; what is it, George?"

"Well, I miss Alice so much," George managed to engineer a little break in his voice, making it sound like he was stifling a sob, "and I wondered if you would eat your meals with the children and me? We hate seeing Alice's empty chair, so why don't you sit there? I'm sure Alice would approve."

The children were surprised as they had never spoken of this, but they said nothing.

"Yes, of course; thank you. Alice asked me to join you often, but I always felt a family needs some time to themselves. Shall I join you for breakfast?"

"Yes, please do. We must discuss the running of this house too. Do you think you could manage it if you did fewer hours at the shop?"

"Yes, I'm sure I could, George, but I've been meaning to talk to you about the situation we find ourselves in. Now Alice is no longer with us. I'm not sure it's right and proper for me to be here alone with you."

"Oh, I see. Well, I think we can both be trusted, and we're hardly alone; after all, Harriet and Francis are teenagers and can act as chaperones to ensure we behave. That should keep tongues from wagging."

"Well, if you think that will be all right? I just wonder what the people at the chapel will think."

"As long as you're happy with the arrangement, it will be fine. Harriet, I want you to take over Mary Ann's duties in the shop and leave her free to act as housekeeper."

"Well, I'm not sure I want to work in the shop, Father."

"Nonsense, Harriet, we all have to pull together at a time like this, and you need something to occupy you now that you've left school. Mary Ann can work with you for a week or two until you've learnt the ropes, and then she can concentrate on running the house. Is that all right with you, Mary Ann?"

"Yes, I'd like that, if you're sure?" said Mary Ann, delighted at the thought of not having to struggle with the adding up in the shop anymore.

George was not the only Carter contemplating marriage, for William had been courting Sarah Martin for a couple of months. They were becoming fond of each other, though she hadn't taken to the children as well as he would have liked. When they were alone, she was all sweetness and light, but it was plain to see that she preferred not to spend time with the children. This sentiment was reciprocated, and the children dreaded the times when they had to visit Aunty Sarah with their dad. They would beg to see Aunty Sabina or Granny Betsey instead, but William knew that if he were to make a go of it with Sarah, they would all have to get used to each other. The twins, Joe and Matthew, were mischievous and keen to deter Sarah from seeing their dad, if possible.

One day, when Sarah came to tea, the boys were playing under the table with marbles and tied her bootlaces together. Stifling their giggles, they manoeuvred the marbles away and were innocently playing in the far corner when Sarah rose to leave. As soon as she took a step, she fell flat on her face, and the twins stuffed their fists into their mouths, trying not to make a sound. Amelia didn't know whether to laugh or cry, but on hearing the loud exclamation from Sarah, she decided upon the latter.

William rushed to help Sarah up, and as soon as he saw the laces tied together, it was clear what had happened. The boys were making a quick exit, but William grabbed them both.

"Oh no, you don't. Come here and apologise to Sarah. She could have hurt herself, you naughty boys. There'll be no supper for you tonight, and I'll tan your hides before bed."

He marched them over to Sarah, who was rubbing her arm as she had knocked it on the table as she fell. She had soot smudged across her face as she had fallen near the fireplace.

"We're sorry, Aunty Sarah; it was just a joke."

"Well, it wasn't funny. If I had done that to someone, my father would have beaten me with a stick."

"They will be punished, Sarah, I promise you. Now, go to your bedroom, you two, and I'll deal with you later. Come on, Sarah, I'll walk you home."

William was annoyed with the boys, for he had planned to propose to Sarah when the children had gone to bed, and now the moment had been ruined. However, he thought it over and decided to go ahead. If she wanted to be his wife, she would have to take on his children, too, so now was as good a time as any to hear her thoughts.

"Children, you will stay in your rooms while I walk Sarah home, and don't you dare come down until I tell you to."

They set off down the lane, hand in hand, Sarah still seething.

"Come on, it's not quite so cold this evening, and it's stopped raining. Are you hurt anywhere?"

"No, I'm all right. It's just my pride that's hurt."

"They're not bad boys, you know, just a bit naughty, and it's been a difficult time for them recently losing their mum."

They strolled around the churchyard, commenting on the graves of people they had known and criticising a few that were ill-kept. William suggested they sit on the bench for a few minutes, and once they were settled, he dropped to one knee and took Sarah's hand.

"Sarah, will you marry me? I've fallen in love with you, and I'd like you to go to China with me as my wife."

"This is rather sudden, William, and it would be a big step to leave my family and move to China. I'm not sure. Could I think about it for a few days?"

"Yes, of course, and I would have to ask your father's permission, but I need to know if you would like to marry me first."

"I'm fond of you, William, and I'd love to visit China, but I'm not sure I'd want to stay there forever or that I could cope with the children. Would I have any help?"

"Well, Lottie looked after the children and the house herself, but I can see it's more difficult when they aren't your own, so yes, I think we could find someone to help you. I'm sure they will come to love you, Sarah. They just need a bit of time. The boys are at school most of the day, and it won't be long before Amelia goes, too. My job is well paid, and you'd want for nothing, and other English people live locally."

He took her hand and kissed it, then pulled her to him and kissed her gently.

"I love you, Sarah, and I hope you'll say yes, but there's no rush, so think about it, and we'll talk again. Come on; I'd better get you home."

They met Annie on her way back to the Manor House after running an errand for Mrs Potts.

"Hello, Uncle William, hello, Sarah, the weather's a bit better this evening, isn't it?"

"Hello, Annie, yes, it is. I don't like the cold weather, you know. Living in China for so many years has made me soft."

"How are the children?"

"They're fine, thanks. I've just left them for a few minutes to walk Sarah home, but I must get back, or they'll be up to mischief."

"They're lovely children, and I've never seen two boys so alike. I have to get back to the Manor myself to help with the evening meal, so bye for now; see you soon."

"Yes, bye Annie, take care."

CHAPTER 29

The next few days continued to be busy for Annie and the other servants. With guests at the house, there were more fires to light, more washing and cleaning, and more food to prepare. There was to be a New Year's Eve party, and as well as the dozen or so guests already staying at the manor, another twenty had been invited. Mrs Potts told Annie that, after the party, the visitors would depart, and she wouldn't be sorry, for her poor old feet and legs couldn't take much more.

Annie was careful not to provide an opportunity for Frank to accost her again, for, despite her bravado, she was frightened of him. She had felt his strength and knew she would be at his mercy unless someone intervened, a thought that made her shiver. So far, she had avoided contact with him and hoped this would continue until he left.

The party was a huge success and naturally ran on into the early hours of the morning, as everyone wanted to welcome in the New Year. Annie and Maisie could barely keep their eyes open. Annie gathered the dirty crockery and carried it to the kitchen, where Maisie was washing up.

"Is that the lot now, Annie? Please tell me it is, for I'm desperate to get to my bed."

"No, there are just a few more, Maisie. I'll fetch them while you finish washing that lot. We'll do the rest in the morning. I don't want to risk Frank turning up again, and Mrs Potts won't mind as long as the hall has been cleared."

The long corridor to the hall was dimly lit as most of the lamps had been extinguished for the night. Other passages joined the one along which she was walking, and as she passed one, the nearest lamp suddenly went out, and she was plunged into darkness. She retraced her steps cautiously towards the distant glow of light from the open kitchen door, thinking she would fetch a candle when suddenly someone grabbed her. She started to scream, but a hand was quickly clamped tightly across her mouth. She kicked hard and tried to bite, but the person holding her was strong, and her struggles were useless.

His hand across her mouth, her captor carried her along various corridors and into the uninhabited west wing. As he struggled to open a door, she succeeded in biting his hand and kicked him hard in the shins, but a sharp blow sent her reeling. He quickly picked her up again, and they descended some steps. She guessed she was being taken to the cellars as the air grew colder. He threw her to the ground, and she screamed, but he laughed as he lay beside her.

"There's no point screaming in here; no one can hear you, so shut up, or I'll hit you again."

He hissed these words quietly in her ear. Then she felt his hands on her as he began to pull up her dress. She fought hard, punching, kicking and biting, but he was too strong for her. He tore the front of her dress and grasped her breasts. She turned her head to the side as he tried to force his mouth on hers.

"Please don't do this! Just let me go, and I'll say nothing. Who are you, anyway? Please, just let me go!"

He ignored her pleas, and as she continued fighting, he once again slapped her hard across the face. She fell back, stunned, as he ripped her petticoat from her. Tearing off his clothes, he was swiftly on top of her, forcing her legs apart. As he entered her, she screamed in pain, but this seemed to excite him, and he treated her roughly. Annie was terrified, and her heart pounded loudly in her chest. She felt sick and dizzy and longed for him to be finished with her but wondered what would happen when he was. Would he kill her?

She didn't know how long her ordeal lasted, for minutes seemed like hours. When her assailant eventually moved away, she lay still, too frightened to move or speak in case he hit her again. A small beam of moonlight shone through a grill high up in the wall, but there was not enough light to see her attacker's face. He had not spoken aloud, and she could not think who he was from the few words he had whispered. The rapist moved away, and she heard his footsteps retreating. As her senses slowly returned, she staggered to her feet, pulled her dress across her chest, and ran up the steps. She was glad to find the door open and relieved he hadn't locked her in. She wasn't sure where she was and felt her way cautiously along the corridor until she came to a lamp and got her bearings. She paused to peep in the kitchen and saw the time was half past four, and she needed to be at work in an hour. Slowly, she climbed the stairs to her attic room and opened the door quietly. Maisie was wide awake, and a candle was still burning.

"Annie, where have you been? Oh, my God, look at your face. What's happened?"

Silently, the tears slid down Annie's cheeks in a river of shame and humiliation, for she felt so dirty, used, and ashamed. Her head throbbed, and her whole body ached; she felt violated.

"Annie, who did this? Annie, speak to me."

"I don't know who did it, but what does it matter? Whoever did it, it's done."

"But what happened? You just vanished into thin air, Annie. I searched everywhere, but I couldn't find you. Where were you?"

"I went towards the hall, but most of the lamps had been put out, and it was dark. Then, just as I got to that corridor that leads to the West wing, the last lamp went out, and it was pitch black. A man grabbed me and put his hand across my mouth so I couldn't scream. He carried me to the west wing cellars, and it was bitterly cold and dark. He raped me, Maisie, and there was nothing I could do, nothing!" Annie sobbed. "I was helpless, and it was awful. He hit me, and then he raped me!"

"Oh, Annie, come here." Maisie put her arms around her friend and stroked her hair. "It'll be all right, but don't you know who it was?"

"No, I know it sounds stupid, but it was so dark, and he only whispered. He smelt funny too, like he was wearing some perfume."

"Do you think it was Frank? After all, he's been determined to get hold of you."

"I don't know; it could have been, but I don't think so. He's grabbed me before, as you know, so I think I would have known if it was him. Oh, Maisie, I'm so tired. How can I get through another day? It must be five o'clock by now. Should I tell Miss Wetherby what happened?"

"She won't listen; she'll just say you brought it on yourself and sack you. There was that poor maid last year who got herself in the family way and was thrown out, though God forbid that should happen to you. Get into my warm bed and get some sleep, and I'll tell Miss Wetherby you're ill."

Maisie quickly dressed, tucked the bedclothes around Annie's cold body and kissed the top of her head. She left the room and went to work, though she was tired too. Annie could not sleep, exhausted though she was. She felt sick and couldn't believe what had happened to her. Who would do such an awful thing? It must have been planned, and what could she do now? With all these thoughts going around and around in her head, she eventually fell into a deep sleep, and it seemed like only five minutes later that Maisie woke her, shaking her shoulder gently, but in fact, it was ten o'clock.

"Annie, wake up. Miss Wetherby is furious you haven't come to work. I have to get back because we're busy, so come as quickly as you can. Here you are; I've found some spare clothes because yours are ripped."

Gingerly, Annie crawled out of bed. Her head hurt, and her body ached, but the horror in her mind troubled her the most. She felt so dirty. She thought of going to her mother but dismissed the thought. What could Sabina do other than worry? She stared in the mirror and saw that her lip was split and her eye was swollen. As she relieved herself in the chamber pot, she saw that her thighs were bruised and noticed blood on her petticoat. She splashed cold water on her face, put on the clothes Maisie had supplied, and wearily walked to the kitchen.

"Annie, what's the matter, my dear? You look terrible. Your face is swollen, and I swear you have a black eye." Mrs Potts, busy though she was, put her floury arms around Annie. "What's happened? Has someone hurt you?"

"No, I'm all right, but I tripped last night and fell against the door and hurt my face. Now I've got a headache, and I feel sick."

Mrs Potts was suspicious but was too busy to investigate further.

"Oh, Annie, I'm sorry, my dear, but we're so busy we need you; can you help us?"

"Yes, I'll be all right, but could I just get a quick cup of tea before I start?"

"Of course, you can, my love, help yourself. Then start on those spuds, would you?"

How Annie got through the day, she would never know. Perhaps it was for the best that she was too busy to think about what had happened, but she would have given anything to put the clock back twenty-four hours.

CHAPTER 30

Eveline was surprised to hear that George wanted Harriet to replace Mary Ann in the shop, though it was true she might do a better job. Mary Ann was willing enough but so slow with her arithmetic that folk got impatient, and goodness only knew what she cost them in mistakes. George still hadn't forgiven her for the loss of the stolen boots. He and Constable Folland had never caught Sam or understood how he had shaken them off. She was even more surprised to learn that Mary Ann would be managing George's house. What was George up to?

Eveline called at George's house one evening after the shop had closed. He had left early to prepare an order for a new supplier he would visit in Exeter the next day. A maid greeted her at the door and led her to the parlour, where she found Mary Ann seated in an armchair on one side of the fire and George on the other; it was a cosy scene.

"Hello, Eveline, what are you doing here? Is everything all right?"

"Yes, everything's fine, thanks, George. I'm going to visit Fred, but I've thought of a few more things we need from the supplier. I won't see you before you leave in the morning, so I've made a list. Hello, Mary Ann. How are you getting on as a housekeeper? It must seem strange here without Alice."

"Hello, Eveline, yes, I'm getting used to running the house, thank you, and I always helped Alice anyway, but I miss her. How's Harriet getting on?"

"Well, she's got a lot to learn and tends to think she knows it all, but she's coming along nicely. George, would you like to visit Fred with me? I might see William too, as the cottage is just down the road."

"No, I'm too tired tonight and have a long day tomorrow. I expect the journey will take ages with the muddy roads, so I'll stay the night in Exeter and return the day after."

George had some other rather more personal needs that he hoped to satisfy whilst in the city.

"Well, here's the list. I hope you didn't mind me calling unexpectedly?"

"No, of course not; call at any time."

Eveline guessed George was making a play for Mary Ann, with poor Alice barely cold in her grave. No wonder Mary Ann looked uncomfortable. At Fred's house, hearing hammering, she went around the back to his workshop.

"Hello, Fred. Don't you think it's time you stopped work for the day?"

"Hello, Eveline. I'd rather be busy, but what brings you here at this time of night? You should be at home in the warm."

"I had to take George a list of stock we need in the shop because he's going to the suppliers tomorrow, so I thought I'd call in on you as I was out and about. Shall I put the kettle on and make us a cup of tea whilst you put away your tools and finish up?"

"Yes, please; I was about to stop anyway. You go in, and I'll be there in a few minutes."

Eveline pulled the kettle forward onto the stove, and by the time it was beginning to boil, Fred entered the room and went to the fire to warm his hands, for it was a cold January night.

"I haven't seen much of you lately, Fred. How are you managing without Lucy?"

"I'm all right, but I miss her and the children. I'm lucky Mum's looking after them, and I see them every day, but I miss us all being together as a family, and I don't think there's much hope of that changing anytime soon."

"How is Lucy? Could I visit?"

"I think she's worse since she went to that awful place. You don't want to go there, Evie. It's horrible, and what they're doing to her is even worse. I wish I could bring her home."

"What's it like there, Fred?"

"Well, I've only visited a few times because they'd rather she had no visitors, but I can't just abandon her. The building's old and grey with dirty windows, and the inside's no better. There are long corridors and big, cold rooms with high ceilings, and the patients seem to sit around doing nothing most of the time. The dangerous ones are locked up, of course, and goodness knows what their living conditions are like. At least Lucy is with other people, but some of them are in a terrible state, rambling to themselves, twitching, and dribbling. It's so distressing, and I don't know how she stands it, but then, she has no choice."

"Does she talk to you?"

"Sometimes she does, but mostly she just clings to me and begs me to take her home, and, of course, I can't. It breaks my heart. Other times, she looks right through me, and I can't get a word out of her. I don't know which is worse."

"Oh, Fred, how awful for you to see her like that."

"I spoke to the doctor the last time I went because her head had been shaved, and there were two burn marks. He said they had tried some new electrical treatment to remove the negative impulses from her brain. He went with me to see her, and she was terrified as soon as she saw him. I so wanted to bring her home, but I'm afraid she's seriously ill. I've told very few people this, Evie, but I think she killed Alfie and Grace! Sabina came to see her one morning and found her trying to smother Eddie. Doctor Luckett arrived just after, so we had to tell him what had happened, and that's why he sent her to Stockton's. It was that or go to jail."

"Oh, Fred, how awful. Surely she didn't? She was a good mum to Llewie and Rosie, wasn't she?"

"She was as they got older, but she had no patience with them as babies. I looked after them when they were tiny because she was terribly depressed after the births. Evie, you won't tell anyone, will you? Sabina and Doctor Luckett agreed to keep it to themselves."

"No, of course not, but does the doctor think she'll get better?"

"It's not looking promising, and I think she's given up. To be honest, if I was in there, I think I would. I feel so sorry for her, but it's come to light now that her granny ended her days in a lunatic asylum in Wales. I had no idea, and I don't think Lucy knew either, but her mum told me when she came to see the children the other day."

"I'm so sorry, Fred. It's almost worse for you than it is for George. With Alice having died of diphtheria, at least he knows she's at peace. Mind you, I don't think he's missing her too much."

"Evie, that's a terrible thing to say. They were married for over twenty years, so he must miss her."

"Well, maybe he's missing her too much, then. I think he's lining Mary Ann up as a substitute. He's replaced her in the shop with Harriet, leaving her free to run the house, and when I called earlier, they were sitting together in the parlour looking very cosy."

"Eveline, you are wicked, and poor Alice has only been dead a few months. It wouldn't be right for him to be courting so soon."

"I know, but you wait and see. I'll bet I'm right and trust George not to practice what he preaches. He's so judgemental, but when it comes down to it, he's no better than anyone else. Why don't you come to the inn on Sunday and have lunch? It would be nice for the children to spend some time with you, and it would do you good, too. I know you keep busy to stop thinking about Lucy, but you'll make yourself ill if you don't have a break. Have the whole day off; take the children to church, then come to lunch and spend the afternoon with all of us. Will you? To please me?"

"Go on then, you always could twist me around your little finger, and I know Mum's struggling to cope. I'm glad you came to see me, Evie; I feel better for talking to you."

"I'm going to see William now to invite him to Sunday lunch, too. It would be nice for all the children to play together. Do you see much of him?"

"Yes, he often calls in for a chat. He occasionally does a few jobs for me if I have a lot of work, which helps him earn a few shillings. It's a shame the way things have worked out for him. The children are certainly different, aren't they, with their strange appearance, but they're his just the same. George doesn't see it that way, mind. He's disapproving of them, but they didn't ask to be born into a mixed marriage. I think he worries about their souls because I don't suppose Lottie was a Christian."

"Oh, he makes me cross. Live and let live, that's my motto. When he saw the children, he didn't want to rent the cottage to William. His own nieces and nephews, I ask you. Anyway, I'll see you on Sunday, Fred."

Evie gave her brother a quick peck on the cheek as she left and walked the short distance to William's cottage, just across the road from the seashore. The views from its windows were magnificent. Eveline knocked on the door, and William smiled when he saw who it was.

"Hello, Evie. This is a pleasant surprise. What brings you here?"

"Well, I seem to be having a night of visiting all my brothers. I saw George first about some stock for the shop, then Fred, and now you."

"Good; I've just got the children to bed, and it's nice to have some company. I don't get many visitors, though I see quite a bit of Fred. I feel so sorry for him. What a difficult situation with Lucy; I think it's even worse than my Lottie dying."

"Yes, I'd rather be dead than in Stockton's. Our family has suffered this year, hasn't it? Still, we must carry on. Life's for the living, you know. Did I hear you've been seeing Sarah Martin?"

"Do you think it's awful of me? It's not even been a year since Lottie died, but Sarah and I seem to have hit it off and to be honest, I'd like to take an English wife back to China with me. I'll have to return there in a few months, and that's made me start looking around sooner than I'd like. I'll never replace Lottie, and I wouldn't want to, but you're right; life must go on. I haven't told anyone else, but I've asked Sarah to marry me."

"It is a bit quick, Will, but I don't blame you under the circumstances. No one here knew Lottie or when she died, and you'll be back in China soon. Goodness, Alice has only been dead a matter of months, and I swear George has already set his sights on Mary Ann. Did Sarah say yes?"

"She hasn't given me her answer yet. I'm fond of her and think she has feelings for me, but the children are making her hesitate. She's not taken to them, or they to her, to be honest. I've promised she can have some help with them when we return to China because servants are cheap over there. I thought going to China might concern her, but it seems to be more the thought of taking on three children."

"Well, I hope she says yes, but if not, there are plenty of other women around, so don't rush into marriage unless you're sure you love her. You know what they say; marry in haste, repent at leisure."

"Good advice, Evie, but I think we'd be all right. It would be a big step for her, taking on three children and moving to the other side of the world, so she'd be silly not to take her time to think about it. I haven't mentioned it to her father yet because there's no point until I know if she wants to marry me. I doubt he'll approve because he would lose his housekeeper."

"Fingers crossed then, Will."

CHAPTER 31

Sarah had given the matter of marriage much thought and was still undecided. She was fond of William; he was handsome, from a decent family, and earned good money. She was thirty-two and unlikely to find anyone else at her age, for she was not particularly pretty and had never attracted much attention from men. Her father had not helped by keeping her at home to care for the family since her mother had died. She knew he would disapprove if she accepted William's offer of marriage but decided she was old enough to do as she pleased. Then again, there were the children. She had never liked children much, and these were no exceptions. She'd had no choice but to care for her siblings over the years, but they were growing up now, and life was becoming easier. If she was honest, the last thing she wanted was to be lumbered with three more.

She tossed and turned in her bed every night, considering William's proposal. What should she do? He had promised to provide help with the children, and it would be interesting to see another part of the world. She was fond of him, though not sure she loved him, but finally, she decided to accept his offer. After all, she could make sure the children behaved themselves when she was in charge. The decision made, she was eager to get things sorted, so the following day, she hurried to William's cottage. He was tidying the front garden, and the three children were playing on the beach. He saw her approaching and smiled.

"Hello, Sarah, what a nice surprise." He took her hand and kissed it.

"Hello, William. It looks like the children are enjoying themselves."

"Yes, they're hunting for crabs. An endless pastime, isn't it? We spent hours trying to find them as children and then let them go again after all that. I'll get the kettle on."

"Just a minute, William, I've something to say. I want to marry you if the offer is still open, of course?"

"Yes, of course, it is; that's wonderful, Sarah. I'm so pleased." He smiled and hugged her. "I hope your father will approve."

"I doubt it. I'm too useful looking after the house and children, but I'm old enough to please myself, and that's what I shall do. I'm a bit wary of taking on three children, having spent so many years bringing up my brothers and sisters, but if you get me some help as you promised, I think it will be all right. I'm not a maternal person, though I'll do my best, but I wouldn't want to mislead you."

"I'm sure you'll grow to love them in time, Sarah. They usually behave themselves, but all children are naughty sometimes. When we've had some tea, I'll visit your father. It shouldn't come as too much of a shock because he knows we've been courting. Could you mind the children? It would be better if I saw him on my own."

Sarah felt doubtful but realised she would have to get used to looking after them.

"Yes, all right then."

William made a pot of tea and called to the children to come in from the beach. They entered the room reluctantly, for they had been having fun. William told them to sit at the table as he fetched them a glass of milk each and made some bread and jam.

"Now, I have to go out for a little while, and Aunty Sarah is going to look after you, so I want you all to be good. Is that understood?"

"Can we play on the beach again, Daddy?" asked Amelia.

"Yes, but just do as Aunty Sarah says. It will be good for you to spend some time with her because we might be seeing a lot more of her in the next few weeks."

William grinned at Sarah over their heads and missed the dismayed expression on his children's faces, but it was not lost on Sarah.

He walked briskly to Richard Martin's house, feeling happier than he had in weeks, and as soon as Richard saw him striding purposefully towards his door, he guessed what was on his mind.

"Could I have a word with you, Mr Martin?"

"Aye, come in, lad. I think I can guess what you've come about."

"I thought you might, Mr Martin. I've been seeing Sarah for a while now, and I've come to ask you for her hand in marriage."

"I thought that might be the case. I'm afraid I've little to offer as a dowry, for times are hard, and she's run the house since my Mary passed away, so I'll miss her help."

"I'm not worried about a dowry, Mr Martin, because I have a steady, well-paid job in China. I can provide for her, and she'll want for nothing."

"Well, I don't know why she'd want to travel to them hot foreign lands, but if that's what she wants, I don't suppose I can stop her. I've nothing against you, William, but I never expected her to marry now she's in her thirties and especially to take on three children. I'll tell you now, they'd better behave themselves, for she has no patience, or at least, she never had with her brothers and sisters. I felt quite sorry for them sometimes."

"I know she's not too fond of children, but I'm sure she'll come to love them. Do I have your permission, then?"

"Yes, I suppose so. My children are older now, and Ellen, my second daughter, moved back in with her two babies last month because her husband died of diphtheria. She couldn't make ends meet living on her own. If Sarah's moving out, at least it will give us more room because it's pretty cramped. When were you thinking of having the wedding?"

"We haven't discussed it yet, but I would have thought sometime in the spring. That would give Sarah time to get used to the children before we sail to China."

"All right, then, you have my blessing. I'm pleased for her. She hasn't had much of a life since her mother died."

Happily, William returned to Sarah, and they agreed to see the Reverend Rees without delay.

CHAPTER 32

It was several weeks since the guests had left Hartford Manor. The Christmas festivities had been successful, and Charles and Eleanor were delighted that three eligible young men had shown an interest in Victoria. She favoured the rich and handsome Frank Eastleigh, and they were to meet in London in the spring when the twins would celebrate their eighteenth birthday. Although the Hartford estate was prosperous, the refurbishment of the house, the lavish parties, and the school fees did not come cheaply, so a wealthy match was desirable.

David, of course, was not at school, and Eleanor was worried about him. He had written, apologising for his deceit and telling them that he and James were in the same regiment. They were stationed in South Africa, where there had been unrest with the Boers. However, it was clear he had no intention of returning any time soon, and Charles decided to cancel his place at Westford School.

Annie was worried. Her periods were always as regular as clockwork. They had started on a Sunday when she was thirteen and had arrived every four weeks since. She had never needed to keep track of them but was aware that it was some time since the monthly curse had occurred. Hopefully, she was just late, but she was afraid she knew the reason and could not believe she could be that unlucky. However, when she was sick after her breakfast on two consecutive days, and her breasts felt tender, she knew there was little doubt but that she was pregnant.

Maisie shared this worry with Annie and followed her to the orchard after breakfast. When Annie had finished retching, Maisie put her arms around her and pulled her close.

"Oh, Annie, you're so unlucky for this to happen after just once. Have you told your mum yet?"

"No, I didn't want to worry her, but I'll have to now. Oh, Maisie, I feel so ashamed to be pregnant and unmarried, and I don't even know who the father is. Who's going to believe me?"

"It's your half-day off tomorrow, so tell Sabina what's happened. She won't turn her back on you, will she?"

"Oh, no, I'm sure she won't, but I'll have to leave here, and I don't know how we'll manage for money and with yet another baby. We have a houseful already, but at least they're not bastards."

Tears ran down Annie's cheeks, and she wiped them away impatiently. Maisie quickly offered her a rag to dry them.

"Ssh, it'll be all right. These things always sort themselves out, and you never know if Sabina will look after the baby; they might let you come back. After all, it's not your fault."

"Hmm, I doubt it, but I'll have to tell Mum. Do you think it is Frank's?"

"It could have been any of the visitors, couldn't it?

The others probably knew he had tried it on with you before, and that would make him the obvious suspect, but yes, I think he has to be the most likely."

"All I know is that he wore perfume, and I'd probably recognise it again, but then loads of men might use the same one. It was too dark to see his face, but it sounds so lame."

"Come on, let's get back before we're missed. People will soon put two and two together, though, if you're sick every morning."

Annie went home the next day with her basket heavily laden, but her heart was even heavier. The children came running to see her, and Sabina took the basket and surveyed her anxiously.

"Are you all right, Annie? You look a bit peaky?" Annie shook her head, and tears were shining in her eyes. Sabina hugged her. "Come on, I want to show you something in the garden."

They went to the bottom of the garden where Willie had built a pen, now housing six squawking chickens.

"I bought these from Alfie Chugg last week. He's such a kind man; he let me have them for next to nothing, and they should keep us in eggs for a while. Willie's done an excellent job on the pen, hasn't he? What's wrong, Annie?"

"Oh, Mum, I don't know how to tell you this, but I'm in the family way."

"Oh, Annie, are you sure? Who's the father?"

"That's the worst part, I don't know."

"Annie, surely you haven't slept with more than one man! I can't believe you've even slept with one. Is it Robert's?"

"No, of course, it isn't."

"Harry's then?"

Annie glared at her mother indignantly.

"No, what do you think of me? I was raped! Do you remember I couldn't come home at Christmas because of all the guests? Well, after the New Year's Eve party, Maisie and I were clearing up, and I went to the hall collecting glasses. I was walking down the corridor when someone put out the lamp and grabbed me. He put his hand across my mouth and carried me to the cellars under the west wing. It's a part of the house that isn't used. I tried to scream, and I kicked and punched, but he hit me hard, and then he raped me. It was so dark I don't even know who it was."

Annie sobbed bitterly. She had kept her worries bottled up for so long, but now she couldn't stem the tears. Sabina, too, was weeping.

"Oh, Annie, I'm so sorry. Who else knows?" Sabina hugged her daughter tightly and gently smoothed her hair from her face.

"Only Maisie, but I think Mrs Potts is suspicious because I've been sick the last two mornings. No doubt I'll get the sack when Miss Wetherby finds out."

"It's not your fault, and you mustn't blame yourself, but you're not the first, and you won't be the last. A similar thing happened to my granny when she was a maid at the house, and she was thrown out on her ear. She knew who had done it too, but, of course, the gentry think they can do just as they like. Are you sure you're pregnant?"

"Well, I've missed two of my monthlies and been sick in the mornings, so it doesn't take a genius to work it out, does it?"

"Sounds like it, then, but let's go inside in the warm and think what to do. Do you mind if we tell Liza? She won't tell anyone, and she's bound to wonder what's going on."

The children were enjoying dripping, spread thickly on the bread Annie had brought. Sabina gave Helen and Danny a crust to chew on, and they both gave her a big, toothy grin. The children ate their fill, and then Sabina sent them out to play so she could tell Liza the news.

"I'm so sorry to hear that, Annie. I doubt you'll get any sympathy from the big house, and they'll certainly sack you. Still, if you're only a few weeks gone, you can work a bit longer, earn as much as possible, and then come home to live. Most folk will believe what you say, and those who don't are not important. Helen and Danny are easier to manage now, so I'll look after the baby, and you can find work somewhere else."

"Oh, Liza, thank you. I was dreading telling you both."

Annie felt better for having told her mother and Liza and was grateful for their support, for some families would have disowned her because of the shame. However, her relief was short-lived, for the following day, she once again had to dash from the breakfast table to be sick. The staff exchanged knowing glances, and one or two eyebrows were raised, though no one said anything. Miss Wetherby later summoned Annie, and she knocked timidly on the door.

"Come in."

"Good morning, Miss Wetherby, you sent for me?"

"Yes, Carter. I'm told you have left the breakfast table to vomit for the last few days. Can you explain this to me? Are you ill?"

"Well, the thing is... What I mean is."

"You're pregnant, aren't you, Carter? Just a simple yes or no will do."

"Well, yes, I am, but it's not like you think, Miss Wetherby."

"I do not want to know the sordid details, Carter, but I am disappointed in you, very disappointed indeed. I thought you had higher morals than to get yourself into this condition. You are an excellent worker, and we'll be sorry to see you go, but go, you must. You received your pay at Christmas, but what you have earned since will be forfeited for behaving so disgracefully. Fetch your things and leave the house immediately."

"But Miss Wetherby, I was forced, and there was nothing I could do. It was one of the guests, and I don't even know who it was because it was so dark."

"How dare you suggest that one of our guests would do such a thing?"

Miss Wetherby's face wore a haughty expression, and she gave Annie a look of sheer disgust.

"It's the truth, nevertheless."

"A likely tale and one I've heard before, but it makes no difference. Even if it was true, you are still pregnant and unmarried, a disgraceful state to be in. I will be unable to provide you with a reference, and you should be ashamed of yourself for tarnishing the name of this house."

"I won't show for weeks yet, Miss Wetherby; could I carry on until you find someone else? I could do with the extra money, and Mrs Potts needs the help."

"You certainly cannot; do you not understand how disgraceful this is? Good heavens, you're little more than a child yourself, and the family has its reputation to think of. I don't suppose one more baby will make much difference in your mother's house; apparently, it's full of children already."

"It's you that don't, or won't, understand."

Annie's green eyes suddenly sparkled with anger. "I was taken against my will. I fought and kicked and screamed, but it made no difference, and there was nothing I could do. You don't want to understand, do you? It was one of the so-called gentlemen staying in this house, and you're trying to tell me I'm a disgrace. Well, I don't think so."

"How dare you speak to me like that. Get out of this house immediately and return to the hovel where you belong."

"Don't you worry, I'm going. It may be a hovel full of children, but it's also full of love, and that's something you know nothing about, do you? I wouldn't wish what happened to me on anyone, but you have no idea what you're talking about. God forbid it should ever happen to you, but you'd see things differently if it did. Mind you, it's not likely, a dried-up old stick like you; who would want you?"

Annie strode out of the room, for she was so angry she was afraid she might hit the woman if she stayed any longer. She went straight to her room and packed her few belongings. She wondered whether to say goodbye to everyone but felt she couldn't face them, especially Sid Hobbs, whom she knew would have some nasty remark. It was probably he who had reported her sickness to Miss Wetherby. Since the Christmas party, he had been unpleasant, and it seemed he blamed her for his drunkenness and inappropriate behaviour in dancing with her more than he should.

She tried to sneak out of a side door quietly, but Maisie had been watching for her and came running.

"Annie, Annie, wait. Where are you going?"

"That silly old cow has sacked me. She said it was my own fault, but at least I had my say. I told her she'd see it differently if she'd been raped, but no one would want to."

"You didn't? Oh, Annie, I wish I'd been there. It's a wonder she didn't faint."

"She's lucky I didn't hit her, the ignorant woman."

"That's the way, Annie. Give 'em as good as you get, girl. I'm sorry you're leaving, though; I'll miss you. We all will. Come and say goodbye to everyone. They'll all be on your side, you know."

"No, I can't face them just now, but explain my side of things, will you?"

"Of course, I will, and I'll come and see you on my next day off. Bye, Annie, take care of yourself."

Annie sadly made her way home, and as soon as Sabina and Liza saw her, they guessed what had happened.

"Never mind, we're pleased to have you home, so sit yourself down, and I'll put the kettle on. It'll be all right, you'll see."

"No, I'm going for a walk, Mum; I need time to think. I'll take the gun and shoot a rabbit whilst I'm out."

"Now, Annie, you won't do anything silly, will you?"

"What? Oh no, of course, I won't. You're not going to get rid of me that easily. See you later."

Annie loved the moors, and even today, she found her bleak surroundings calming. In the open countryside, it didn't matter who she was or what had happened. She walked to the coast and sank down on a pile of rocks to rest. It was a mild day for February, and the sea was calm and blue. The gulls wheeled and screamed above her head, and out at sea, she could see a couple of seals swimming.

She fingered the gold locket around her neck and thought of Robert. She wished she could tell him of her troubles, and tears began trickling down her cheeks. She had always known there was no chance of them marrying, yet he had been so confident there had been the tiniest glimmer of hope in her heart. She wondered if even he would believe her tale of being raped. It made little difference, for he could never marry a pregnant servant girl, as if he would want to, anyway. So deep in thought was she that she did not see or hear Harry Rudd until he was beside her, and she had no time to disguise the tears glistening on her cheeks.

"Hello, Annie, I'm sorry if I made you jump, but what's wrong? I've never seen you cry before, not even when you were a little maid, so it must be something bad. Is there anything I can do to help?"

"No, there's nothing anyone can do, thanks, Harry. I'm sorry you saw me like this, but I didn't see you coming."

"I've been to see my Aunty Jane and took a shortcut across the beach. It's quicker than the road and a pleasant walk, too."

"If you're going home now, I could walk back with you. I was going to shoot some rabbits, but I haven't seen any today."

"Yes, all right, but why aren't you at the big house? You're not poorly, are you?"

"I might as well tell you, for it will soon be common knowledge. I've had the sack."

"What! I can't believe that. Why would they sack you? I bet you do twice the work of all the others."

"I'd rather not say at the moment, Harry."

"I don't want to pry, but how can anyone help you if you won't say what the trouble is? It must be a misunderstanding. Let's talk to the vicar and ask him to put in a word for you. They might listen to him, you know."

"No, I think he's probably the last person who would want to help." She sighed, "All right then, I'll tell you, though, then you'll want nothing more to do with me. I'm going to have a baby, Harry. There, now, do you still want to be friends with me?"

"I don't believe it! Are you sure?"

"Oh yes, I'm sure, and I don't even know who the father is."

With this, Annie started sobbing again, and Harry put his arms around her, stroking her hair gently.

"Hey, come on, it'll be all right, but how can you not know who the father is? Is it Robert's, and you don't like to say?"

"No, it's not Robert's; he'd already returned to school when this happened. What do you take me for, Harry?"

"I'm sorry, I just couldn't think of anyone else it might be. How can you not know?"

Annie told him the whole story.

"That's awful, but didn't you tell the housekeeper what happened? I mean, it's not your fault, is it?"

"Oh yes, I told her, but she wasn't interested. She said I must have encouraged it. I told her no one would want to rape her, the old misery."

"Good for you. What are you going to do, though, Annie?"

"Well, that's what I was trying to think through when I got interrupted." She glanced at him and smiled. "Sorry, Harry, you're a loyal friend, but you must find yourself another girl now. I'm glad we met today because you're the first one I've told apart from Maisie, Mum, and Liza, and I wouldn't have wanted you to hear it from someone else. Would you keep it to yourself for a few days, though? I'm not ready to face the Reverend Rees or the old busybodies in the village just yet."

"I won't say a word, but come on, let's get back; it's a fair step from here." He picked up the gun and carried it for her, and they trudged on in silence for some minutes.

"When's the baby due?"

"Well, it happened on New Year's Eve, so around the end of September."

"So, you're only a couple of months gone?"

"Yes."

He put down the gun and took both her hands in his. "Annie, please think hard before you answer this question, but I know what I'm saying, and I mean it. Will you marry me, and preferably, as quickly as possible?"

"Don't be ridiculous, Harry. You can't seriously want to marry me when I'm carrying another man's baby. Your parents would be horrified."

"If we marry quickly, everyone will think the baby is mine. It happens all the time. As long as we're wed before the baby's born, it's respectable enough, and people know we've been seeing each other. I love you, Annie, and I promise I'd be good to you. What about it? I know you don't love me, but you might come to in time, and you do like me a bit, don't you?"

"Of course, I like you, Harry. I like you a lot, but I don't love you, and I couldn't let you do this."

"Annie, it would make me the happiest man on earth, so will you just think about it, please? See what Sabina thinks. If you like, I could get a special licence to speed things up."

He raised her hands to his lips and kissed them. "You're so beautiful, Annie Carter and the best thing is, you don't even know it. You're kind and funny, so what more could any man want in a wife?"

"Well, no bastard in her belly, for a start."

"Hey, don't think of it like that. It's not the child's fault, and it's better we don't know the father because I'll have no one to be jealous of. I'll love it as if it were my own, and maybe one day, we'll have one of mine."

"Oh, Harry, you're far too good for me." Tears ran down Annie's cheeks once more. "I can't thank you enough for your offer, and I will think about it, but I can't promise. It doesn't seem right to marry a man unless you love him, and I don't think it's fair on you."

"You let me worry about that, but if you decide not to marry me, I'll help in any way I can. Come on now, it's time we went back because it's getting cold."

They walked back together in companionable silence and parted at the edge of the moor.

"I'll call for you on Sunday to take the babies for a walk. Will that give you long enough to decide? If you say yes, we must get things arranged quickly."

"Yes, fine, and thanks, Harry."

"Until then, just pretend you're poorly and have come home for a few days. There's no need to let the cat out of the bag unless you need to, is there?"

"Yes, I will, and no, I'll keep my condition a secret for now. I was thinking that if we did marry, I might have been able to go back to work for a few months, but there's no way Miss Wetherby will have me back after the way I spoke to her. I suppose it serves me right for speaking my mind. It would have given me a chance to save a bit of money, though."

"There's no need, and you'd every reason to say what you did. I earn enough to look after you, and, anyway, I would want my wife living at home with me, so don't give that awful woman another thought. I'll see you on Sunday, bye."

CHAPTER 33

David Fellwood and Jim McNamee were in high spirits as they travelled to South Africa with their regiment. They were dressed in their new red jackets, black trousers with red piping down the side seams, white pith helmets, and black leather boots and were proud of their uniforms. Armed with Martini-Henry rifles with a long bayonet, they longed for action.

Since 1835, some 15,000 Dutch Voortrekkers had moved out of the British Cape Colony across the Orange River and into the interior of South Africa. Their Great Trek illustrated their rejection of the British policy with its equalisation of black and white at the Cape. They established two republics: the Transvaal and the Orange Free State. Lord Carnarvon, the British Colonial Secretary, had proposed a confederation of South African states in 1875, hoping to create a settled environment under British supremacy, particularly after discovering diamonds in 1867 near the Orange and Vaal Rivers.

However, the Boers revolted against the British annexation of 1877. Initially, they offered only passive resistance, but when the British government made clear its determination to uphold the annexation, the Boers turned to an armed offensive. There had been a skirmish between the British garrison in Potchefstroom and a Boer commando under General Cronje before Christmas, and more troops, including David's regiment, were sent from Britain with orders to quell the uprising.

David and Jim were officers in the 58th Regiment, serving under Major-General Sir George Pomeroy Colley. Their youthful enthusiasm for war quickly evaporated when they realised they were up against a deadly enemy and fighting for their lives. The farming Boers had grown up in the saddle, with rifles in their hands, and were skilled marksmen able to judge distances accurately. They were mostly armed with German Mauser rifles, accurate enough to hit a man at eight hundred yards. In contrast, the British Martini rifles, used by David and Jim's regiment, were almost as accurate but had a lesser range. However, they quickly learned that their greatest disadvantage was that the Martini could only be loaded one round at a time, whilst the Mauser, with bolt action and a magazine, could fire more than three shots to the Martini's one.

They had first encountered the Boers during Colley's attempt to enter the Transvaal on 28 January. This foray had been thwarted by Piet Joubert at Laing's Nek and again by General Nicolaas Smit at Ingogo on 8 February. Their regiment sustained heavy losses, and they lost several friends. The pride David had felt when he first donned his uniform now turned to fear and disgust, for the brightly coloured garb of their uniforms stood out against the stark African landscape, making the men an easy target. The Boers, on the other hand, being essentially a citizen militia, wore what they liked, mainly drably coloured jackets and trousers and slouch hats with bandoliers.

Major-General Colley issued his regiment with orders to occupy the summit of Majuba Hill. The men were puzzled by this request. Some thought he might be attempting to outflank the Boer positions at Laing's Nek or that he thought the sight of his men occupying Majuba would encourage the Boers to withdraw, thus opening the road to the Transvaal.

"I hope he knows what he's doing?" said Jim. "It's a steep climb, and I'm tired to death already."

"I know," David grumbled. "Goodness knows why I let you talk me into this army lark. I didn't know how lucky I was, and I'll tell you now, if I get out of this lot alive, I'll be more than happy to go back and run our estate. I hate to say it, but my father was right; I'm not cut out for this."

"Ah, it's not that bad, and you'll see it differently when we've won and return home as heroes."

"Well, I'll take your word for it, but I can't believe he wants us to start climbing such a steep hill in the dark; it would be difficult enough in daylight."

They assembled their men and set out under the cover of darkness. Their planned route would take them from their camp at Mount Prospect, up the south eastern slopes of the Newel Mountain, and along a connecting ridge to the south side of Majuba. The troops were ordered to move as silently as possible and to use no lights. That was easier said than done, for each man carried his rifle, bayonet, ammunition, three days' rations, a greatcoat, blankets, and tools to dig trenches. Their load weighed around fifty pounds.

The last few hundred yards of the climb were steep, and the men struggled with their heavy loads. David whispered words of encouragement to his men, but he, too, was exhausted. Finally, at around half past three, they breasted the summit and fell to the ground, but their relief was short-lived when Colley barked orders for them to move to the perimeter.

"Should we spread out to occupy the whole perimeter?" Jim asked David.

"Well, he's not said so, and he should know."

"I haven't seen any artillery coming up here, have you?

"No, but I hope they're not far behind because we'll be sitting ducks if not. I wonder if the Boers know we're here yet."

They didn't have to wait long to find out. As soon as dawn broke, some of the soldiers on the summit began to hurl abuse at the Boers, presumably hoping to scare them away. However, far from fleeing, the Boers steadily advanced up the hill. Armed with weapons of longer range, they kept their enemy pinned down while others crossed the open ground to attack an exposed knoll protected by only a handful of British soldiers.

"We're in real trouble now, Jim. Look, they're coming over the ridge. Where, for heaven's sake, is the artillery? We'll be slaughtered!"

Within an hour, the Boers poured over the summit and engaged the British at long range. They avoided hand-to-hand combat at all costs, for they knew they would be disadvantaged without bayonets. Unable to see their opponents clearly and helplessly watching their companions picked off one by one, the troops began to panic. David and Jim shouted orders to their men to hold fast, but more and more Boers were spotted encircling the mountain.

Over the next hour, the Boers continued to engage the British soldiers at long range, taking advantage of the scrub and long grass which covered the hill. The panicky British troops were being given little direction, and when hundreds more Boers were spotted, the British line collapsed, and the soldiers deserted their posts and fled pell-mell down the hill. The Boers then launched an attack that shattered the crumbling British line. As the soldiers fled, Colley himself was shot, and it was only then that David and Jim decided the battle was lost, and, unable to rally their men, followed them and ran for their lives.

"Come on, Jim, this is hopeless; we can't win this one,"

"You're right. Come on."

As they ran down the slope, Jim was shot in the hip, and blood spurted from an artery as David bent to help his friend.

"No, David, I'm done for. Run and save yourself; you can't help me now."

David quickly hoisted his friend over his shoulder and staggered down the steep hill with his heavy load. However, he was immediately spotted by the Boer marksmen and went down in a hail of gunfire. As James reached across to David's lifeless body, the Boers ran towards him to finish the job.

CHAPTER 34

Annie's head was spinning. She liked Harry, and he had offered an easy solution, but she didn't love him, and despite his protests, it wouldn't be fair to marry him. How she longed to talk to Robert, for although marriage to him was now out of the question, to tell him of her predicament would have helped.

"Are you all right, Annie? You've been so long we were worried."

"Yes, I'm fine, Mum. I didn't get any rabbits, but I'll try again tomorrow."

"Never mind, come and get warm; you're as white as a sheet. I'll get you a bowl of stew, and you can sit near the fire and eat it up."

"I bumped into Harry Rudd on the moor, and he made me tell him what was wrong. He's asked me to marry him. Isn't he daft?"

"Annie, that's wonderful. Harry's a kind man, and you could do far worse, but does he understand the situation? It's no use marrying him if he doesn't know you're pregnant. The truth always comes out between man and wife eventually, and lies can ruin a marriage."

"Oh yes, he knows, but he says it doesn't matter. He thinks he loves me enough for both of us, and he'd need to because I certainly don't love him. I like him, and he's kind, but I don't love him."

"Well, as long as you've been honest with him, that's all he can ask, but Annie, do think carefully before you turn him down. This is the best chance of happiness you'll ever get. Harry will inherit the smithy one day, and you know how close I am to Matilda. My goodness, she even delivered you."

"I knew you'd say that, but I must think about it. I promised him an answer on Sunday. Until then, if anyone asks why I'm home, it's because I'm poorly. I'll get Maisie to ask the other servants to keep quiet about the truth if I decide to pass the baby off as Harry's."

"Fine, and Annie… there's no point waiting for Robert. I know you love each other, but there's no future in it, and you know it, so grab this chance while you can."

Annie spent an unsettled week in more ways than one. She was repeatedly sick, so her tale of feeling ill was not questioned. She crept to the back door of the Manor House one evening and beckoned Maisie. Annie told her what had happened with Harry and asked if she would get the servants to keep quiet about her condition. Maisie assured her they would and gave her the same advice as her mother.

"Annie, be sensible; this is an ideal solution. As far as most folk are concerned, Harry could be the father, for you've been seen walking out with him. He's a good man who'll care for you and the baby. Goodness, if he asked me, I'd say yes straight away. What's stopping you? Oh, it's Robert, isn't it? Annie, forget him; you and he could never marry."

Annie lay awake at night, trying to decide what to do. Her mother had not mentioned the subject again, feeling it best to let her make up her own mind. Eventually, she realised she had no choice but to accept Harry's offer. She could never marry Robert, and there was no one else she was interested in, so she was lucky to have this way out.

Harry called on Sunday morning, and they took Danny and Helen for a walk together. The babies loved going out and were full of smiles. Harry and Annie chatted until he laid his hand on hers.

"I can't stand this any longer, Annie. Please tell me what you've decided."

"Well, the answer is yes, Harry, I want to marry you. I still think you're stupid to want to marry me, but unless you've changed your mind, then the answer is yes."

"Oh, Annie, you've made me the happiest man alive, and of course, I still want to marry you. It will be all right, you know; I won't rush things, and I'll be so kind to you that you'll have to love me eventually. Does Sabina know?"

"No, I wanted to be sure you hadn't changed your mind first. We don't have to tell your mum and dad what's happened to me, do we?"

"No, there's no need. If we can get married quickly, no one need know the baby isn't mine."

"Well, I don't want a special licence because that just draws attention, but if the vicar starts calling the banns next week, we could be married three weeks from now. I don't think I'll be showing by then. I'm not very big and won't eat much until after the wedding."

"You'll eat properly, young lady, especially in your condition, but you're right about the licence. Shall we tell Sabina now and then my mum and dad? We could probably see the vicar this evening if you like."

"My goodness, there's no stopping you now, is there? Yes, come on then, I know Mum will be pleased, and Harry, although I don't love you, I will try to be a good wife to you. It's so kind of you to do this for me."

"Aw, don't be daft. Come here."

He hugged her, grinning widely.

Sabina and the Rudds were delighted, and if the vicar was a little suspicious, he said nothing, pleased they were getting wed, even if it was with haste. He agreed to call the banns for the next three Sundays and marry them the following Saturday.

William and Sarah had also been to see the Reverend Rees, and their wedding was to be a few weeks after Annie and Harry's. Matilda, Sarah's younger sister, and Amelia would be bridesmaids, and the reception would be held at the inn. There would be no honeymoon as the couple would travel to China in a few months.

Sarah called to see William one morning to discuss the wedding arrangements. It was high tide and windy, and the sea was rough. The children ran to the sea's edge and then back across the beach, dodging the huge waves as they broke almost onto the road. Laughing loudly and enjoying the game, Joe ran backwards to avoid an enormous wave and didn't see or hear the approach of the mail cart coming around the corner. The driver reined in the horse as quickly as possible, but poor Joe disappeared under its hooves, and the cartwheel went over his middle.

Hearing the screams of the other children, William and Sarah rushed outside to find Matthew and Amelia in tears and the driver ashen-faced. Joe lay unconscious on the road.

"What's happened? Peter, what have you done?"

His face white and full of horror, William rushed over to the still body of his son and, kneeling, took him in his arms.

"I'm so sorry, but he ran backwards, avoiding a wave, and went straight under the horse. I couldn't stop in time, and I think the wheel went right over him; yes, you can see the marks on his clothes. Luckily, I have the small cart today, and it's almost empty."

William's face was grim as he examined his son. Joe had a nasty gash on his head, which was bleeding heavily.

"Joe, can you hear me? Are you all right? It's Dad. Can you hear me, Joe?" He picked him up gently and carried him to the cottage, shouting over his shoulder to Sarah. "Sarah, can you get Doctor Luckett to come quickly, please? Tell him it's an emergency."

Matthew, Amelia, and Peter followed William into the cottage, where he laid Joe on the table and put a pillow under his head. He left Peter watching him while he fetched water and a cloth to bathe his head.

When Doctor Luckett arrived, Joe was still unconscious, and he examined the child carefully.

"Well, his head's stopped bleeding, and I can't see any other injuries, but there's no knowing what damage the cartwheel did running over him like that, and he could be bleeding internally. The head wound doesn't look serious, but it's worrying that he's still unconscious. I suggest you put him to bed and watch for any change. With a head injury, he could remain unconscious for days or come around quite soon; it's impossible to tell. If he's no better in a day or two, we'll send him to the hospital, but I think it's advisable not to move him at the moment and just let him rest. I'll return in the morning, but send for me if you need me before."

"Thank you, Doctor; do you think he'll be all right? I mean, he's just a child. He will be all right, won't he?" William's face was full of concern for his son.

"Well, he's a strong, healthy boy, so I hope so, but I'm afraid we'll just have to wait and see."

All thoughts of wedding plans had vanished from William's mind as he sat with his son and prayed; please don't let Joe die. I've lost Lottie, and I don't want to lose him too. Sarah hovered around, ill at ease and not knowing what to do.

"William, I'm going home now, but I'll come back later to see how Joe is. I don't think I can do anything here at the moment. Is that all right?"

"Yes, that's fine, but could you just get Matthew and Amelia some dinner before you go? I don't want to leave Joe's side at the moment."

"Oh yes, of course. Come on, you two, let's find you something to eat."

Peter left when Doctor Luckett arrived. The incident had shaken him, and he knew he would never forgive himself if the little boy died, though there was nothing he could have done differently. He knew he must get on and deliver the mail to the Manor House. As he drove up the drive, he hoped he was not the bearer of more bad news, for one letter looked important. He gave Mrs Potts the letters, and she passed them on to Sid Hobbs. As usual, she offered Peter a piece of cake and a cup of tea, for they had gone to school together and enjoyed a chat. However, poor Peter couldn't face any cake this morning. As he told her about the accident with young Joe Carter, Ethel noticed that his hands were still trembling.

Sid put the letters on a small silver tray and took them to Charles Fellwood. Charles frowned when he saw the official-looking envelope and opened it anxiously. He grew pale as he read the contents and immediately went to find his wife, who was in the sitting room, working on some embroidery.

"Eleanor, my dear, we have received a letter from the army with the most terrible news. There's no easy way to tell you this, but I'm afraid the letter says David has been killed in action in South Africa."

Eleanor rose unsteadily to her feet, and Charles put his arms around her.

"Oh no, Charles, are they sure? I can't believe it. He's so young."

Her voice trailed off as she sobbed and clung to him. When she had composed herself a little, she said, "What does it say? Please let me see."

He handed her the letter.

"It says he was killed fighting the Boers in a battle at Majuba Hill in South Africa. It seems there was a huge loss of life on the British side; a complete disaster."

"We must tell Victoria and Sarah, and what about Robert? We can't wait until he comes home for Easter; will you go and tell him?"

"Yes, we must break the news to Victoria and Sarah first, and then I'd better tell Sid Hobbs and Miss Wetherby. Poor Robert was close to David, and this will hit him hard. I'll travel to the school tomorrow and tell him myself."

Eleanor and Charles clung to each other, unable to take in that their first-born son was dead. As he moved away from her, Charles suddenly stumbled and sank to a chair.

"Charles, are you all right? Charles, what's wrong?"

Eleanor was quickly at his side. The left side of his mouth suddenly drooped, and his eyes looked pleadingly at his wife as if to say, what's happening to me? He tried to get up but found he couldn't, and his left arm hung uselessly at his side. He said nothing.

She fetched a footstool, covered him with a blanket, and then rang the bell. She told the maid to send for the doctor as the master had been taken ill.

CHAPTER 35

Harry insisted on buying material for a wedding dress for Annie and a bridesmaid's dress for Mary. Annie's Aunty Eveline was an excellent seamstress who offered to make both dresses. This was quite a challenge in the short time available, but Matilda, Annie's future mother-in-law, was also skilled with her needle and pleased to help. The villagers were a little suspicious about the haste of the marriage, but Annie and Harry were well-liked, so little was said.

It was late March, and the wedding day dawned dry and clear. Annie wore a pale green gown. The dress was stylishly cut and fell away from her bosom, successfully disguising the small bump that was now evident. Her fiery red hair had been brushed until it shone and hung in ringlets under her veil, and she carried a small posy of primroses. Mary's dress was a slightly darker shade of green, and she looked pretty. She'd been so excited for the last few weeks; she could hardly believe the day had finally arrived.

Sam Symons was to give Annie away, and she smiled at him as they made their way up the church path to the sound of the wedding march being pounded out on the old organ. She was sad that her father could not be there to give her away but knew he would have been pleased she had asked Sam, especially as he had lost all his children in the diphtheria outbreak.

As she walked up the aisle with Sam, Harry smiled at her, and she could not help but smile back at him, though in her heart, she longed for Robert to be standing there instead. They recited their vows perfectly, and the crowd clapped as Harry kissed his new wife.

The reception was held at the smithy, and Matilda had done them proud, for there was plenty of food and drink and a lively band. Sabina's eyes brimmed with tears as she watched Annie and Harry dance. She wished Tom could have seen her, for he would have been so proud. Thank goodness she had agreed to marry Harry, for he was a kind man with a steady income. The attack on her daughter had been terrible, but perhaps it would work out all right in the end after all.

Sabina had insisted that Liza attend the wedding so the babies were also present. Helen was nearly nine months old and crawling everywhere. She was a contented child, happy as long as her belly was full. Danny was seven months old and a different kettle of fish altogether. He was affectionate and loved to be cuddled but was rather demanding and fractious. He struggled to eat, and Sabina was still breastfeeding him, though she had weaned Helen, as she didn't have enough milk for both of them. His lip was ugly, and his smile grotesque, but he had adorable big brown eyes that would melt the hardest heart. She had taken the splints off his feet now that he was rolling around because he didn't like them. One foot turned in worse than the other, and she didn't know if he would ever walk; only time would tell. The family was interested to see how Danny was developing, and Sabina thought it was curious that he attracted more attention than any of her other children.

It was with enormous relief that William and Sarah could attend with Matthew and Amelia and a now fully recovered Joe. He had lain unconscious for two days following his accident with the mail cart but had then opened his eyes and, within a short time, asked for something to eat because he was so hungry. Poor William had been beside himself with worry and had barely slept for the entire time. Joe did not remember anything about the accident but seemed none the worse for his experience, and William felt he could now turn his attention to his wedding.

William, in particular, was interested in Danny, for he knew what it was like to have children who looked different.

"Hello, Sabina, it's good to see you." William hugged her. "Annie looks beautiful."

"Yes, she does, doesn't she? I wish Tom could have been here to see her."

"Yes, of course. I know he would have been proud. It was kind of you to take on another baby, Sabina, for I'm sure you had enough to cope with. Did you ever find out who abandoned Danny?"

"No, Annie found him outside our back door, as if someone had left him there for us to find. I guess whoever it was knew I wouldn't turn a baby away."

"You always did have a soft heart. He was lucky to be left outside your door, for with his problems, some would have dumped him in Shebworthy Pond. I've heard it's happened before."

"How's Joe?"

"He seems fine now and none the worse for his accident, but he frightened me, I can tell you. For two days, he lay there and barely moved a muscle. I thought I would lose him, and so soon after Lottie, it would have been awful. I think poor Matthew suffered just as much as I did. Being twins, they're close, and I don't know what he would have done if Joe had died. Anyway, thank God he's all right, so now I can think about my wedding. You are coming, aren't you?"

"Yes, of course, and congratulations. I'm pleased for you. Now, if you'll excuse me, I'll see if I can give Matilda a hand. I can see George approaching, and I don't want to speak to him. I know he's your brother, but I'm afraid we don't see eye to eye."

"Don't worry, you're not alone there. Go on, make your escape; I wish I could."

George had asked Mary Ann if she would like to accompany him and the children to the wedding, and though somewhat surprised, she had been pleased to accept. He felt it was an opportunity for them to be seen in public together and let people get used to seeing them as a couple.

However, the main topic of conversation was the news that young Master David had been killed in South Africa, and it seemed the shock had caused the master to have a stroke. The poor man could no longer speak, and the left side of his body was paralysed. Doctor Luckett said little could be done, though sometimes the speech could return and some use of the limbs; only time would tell. The menfolk of the village were concerned for their master but also for themselves, for who would run the estate now? Following his stroke, Charles Fellwood could not travel to Westford School as he intended, and Eleanor had sent Sid Hobbs to break the news to Master Robert instead. As it was so close to the Easter holidays, she had insisted he stay at the school and take his examinations before travelling home, as there was little he could do, anyway. He was expected in the next few weeks, so perhaps something would be sorted out then.

There was a small cottage next to the smithy, where Harry's paternal grandfather had lived until he died at the ripe old age of ninety-three. Benjamin and Matilda had agreed that Annie and Harry could live there, and they had spent the few weeks before their wedding smartening it up and giving it a lick of paint. As the reception neared the end, Harry whisked Annie into his arms and strode through the crowd, still dancing the night away. To many raucous cheers and laughs, he carried her to the cottage and over the threshold and, with a broad wink, firmly shut the door behind them. This was the moment Annie had been dreading. Since she had been attacked and raped, she had wanted to shrink from any man's touch. She had forced herself to hide these feelings when Harry held her hand or gently kissed her, but now she felt the panic within her rising uncontrollably. He carried her upstairs as if she weighed nothing and gently placed her on the bed, then leaned over and kissed her softly. He noticed that she was trembling and smiled at her.

"Now then, Mrs Rudd, I'll sleep in the other room. You should be warm enough because I lit the fire in the bedroom this morning, and Mum's kept it going all day. There's no need for you to get up early in the morning because it's been a long day, and I know you're tired. You stay there until I bring you a cup of tea. Don't get used to it, mind, because I shan't be doing it every day."

Annie's heart was beating so fast she thought it would surely jump out of her chest, but she placed her hand over his and held it there.

"Harry, you don't need to sleep in the other room; you've just married me. Don't you want to share my bed?"

"Are you joking? Of course, I'd love to share your bed, but I promised not to rush things, and from the way you're shaking, I can see you're not ready after what happened. We can move on if and when you want to, but I expect nothing from you except for you to live here as my wife. I love you dearly, Annie, but I won't make you do anything you don't want to. Now go to sleep, and don't worry about anything."

But still, she kept her hand on his.

"No, I don't think leaving it will help, so I want you to stay because I want this marriage to work. We've not had the best of starts, but I'm fond of you, Harry, and I will fulfil all my wifely duties. I wouldn't have agreed to marry you otherwise; it wouldn't be fair. That is unless you don't want to sleep here. I'd understand if you didn't want to under the circumstances."

Annie began to stammer as her face turned bright red, and she was thankful for the dim lamplight. Harry's grin became even broader.

"Ssh, that's enough. Annie, there's nothing I want more, but are you sure? You don't have to; I wasn't expecting it."

Silently, she nodded, with tears bright in her eyes. She had not expected him to be so kind. With a sigh, he lay beside her, kissing her gently and stroking her hair. She tried not to shy away from him, for she was sure delaying this would not help, and she was determined to let him make love to her. He didn't rush things and slowly helped her to undress, spending a long time just cuddling, kissing, and holding her, and gradually she began to relax. Afterwards, they lay in each other's arms for a long time, both relieved this awkward time was behind them. Annie felt happier than she had for some time, and as she drifted off to sleep, she thought that perhaps everything would be all right after all.

CHAPTER 36

Robert was devastated to hear of his brother's death and his father's subsequent illness. He could not believe he would never see David again. They had squabbled and fought as all brothers do, but despite that, they were close. As soon as Sid Hobbs broke the news, he wanted to return home. However, his mother had sent Hobbs with a letter for him, insisting he must stay until the end of term. She explained that his father was being cared for, and there was nothing more Robert could do. It was more important to stay and sit his examinations, as they were only held once a year. Robert found this extremely frustrating, but his mother's letter was so insistent he did not like to disobey, particularly as she had also made her wishes known to Professor Franklin, and he completely agreed with her.

However, a few weeks later, he caught the early train from Exeter, and Dodger met him at Eggleston Station with the carriage. Again, he discreetly tried to prise some information about Annie from Dodger, but he seemed strangely reticent and not as talkative as usual. Robert thought he probably felt awkward about David's death and his father's illness. When the carriage arrived at the Manor, Robert went to find his parents. His mother hugged him, unable to speak, and Robert had tears shining in his eyes as they thought about David.

"How is Papa? Is he in bed?"

"No, he's in the sitting room; you must prepare yourself, Robert. He can't speak, and his left side is paralysed. He gets so frustrated because he can only communicate by writing things down, and even that isn't easy because he's always been left-handed. I'm going to have a walk around the grounds whilst you are with him. I don't like to leave him alone too much, but I could do with some fresh air. We need to talk about what is going to happen. Perhaps we could meet in the drawing room around seven o'clock to discuss matters?"

"Yes, of course, Mama. Enjoy your walk, and I'll see you later."

Charles Fellwood was seated in an armchair near a roaring fire. His feet rested on a footstool, a blanket was draped over his legs, and his eyes were closed. He had always been a big man, but he appeared to have shrunk in the short time since Robert last saw him. His hair was grey, his face pale, and he looked at least ten years older than a man in his early fifties. Robert sat quietly, not wishing to disturb him, but his father opened his eyes within minutes. At first, he seemed slightly bewildered, and then recognition dawned on his face as he saw his son. He gave a lop-sided smile and grunted as Robert went to him and took his hand.

"Hello, Papa. I'm so sorry you're poorly, but it's good to see you."

Charles attempted to speak, and unintelligible grunts emanated from his mouth. Robert could see that his father was fully alert but unable to communicate.

"Don't worry, Papa, I know you can't speak, and I'm so sorry about David; I still can't believe it, but I'm glad I'm here to support Mama and the girls now. I wanted to come straight away, but Mama insisted I sit my exams first."

Charles nodded as a tear slid down his cheek, and he brushed it away impatiently with his right hand. Robert told him what he had been doing at school and how he had got on with his examinations. However, it was difficult to hold a one-sided conversation for long, and Robert could see the effort was tiring his father, so he left him to rest, saying he needed to see Victoria and Sarah.

He searched for Victoria and found her in the stables, where she had just returned from a long ride. Robert hugged his twin, and for a few moments, they clung to each other for comfort, unable to speak. He moved back to arm's length and looked at his sister. Tears were running down her cheeks, and she brushed them away impatiently.

"I'm sorry. What must you think of me? It's weeks since we had the news about David, and Papa had his stroke, and here I am, still sobbing like a child."

"No, don't be silly. I'm not far from tears, myself. I've just seen Father, and he isn't at all well, is he?"

"No, and it's been so difficult because Mama's not used to dealing with any of the day-to-day matters of the estate, and so she has simply ignored them. On occasion, Jack Bater has even sought me out to ask about things I have no knowledge of. I'm so glad you're back, Robert. You've always been interested in the estate, so I hope you'll know what to do."

"Well, I'm glad I'm here now to help, and yes, I'm more than happy to work with Jack. Where's Sarah? I thought she might have been out here with you. I don't usually have to look for her; she finds me."

"Oh, she's gone over to her friend, Mabel's, for the day. They've been seeing quite a bit of each other recently. Either Mabel is here, or Sarah's at her house. I think Sarah has been glad to get out of the house. It's not been much fun here lately, but she's coped well. She's certainly growing up."

"I'm pleased to hear she's found a friend to spend time with; she needs some company of her own age. I'll see you later at dinner, but I want to see Mrs Potts now. If I know her, she'll have made a cake for my return home, and I could certainly eat a piece at the moment."

Mrs Potts' cake was not the only reason Robert wanted to visit the kitchen, for he longed to see Annie. When Mrs Potts spotted him at the door, she stopped what she was doing and hugged him.

"Why, Master Robert, I'm so pleased to see you; it's been such a difficult time here, as you can imagine. With young Master David getting killed in the war and then your poor father taken ill, your mama has been quite beside herself with grief. I'm so glad you're here now to be with Miss Victoria and Miss Sarah. They've been like two lost souls, poor dears."

"Hello, Mrs Potts; I'm glad to be here, too. Now, how about a cup of tea and a piece of your best cake? I've travelled a long way, and I'm looking forward to it."

"Bless you, lad, of course; what am I thinking about? Maisie, pull that kettle onto the fire. Now, fruit cake, ginger cake, or chocolate sponge? They're all freshly made, and you can have a bit of each if you like, a growing lad like you."

"Well, I've no doubt I'll try them all, but for now, I'll have a piece of that chocolate cake, please. Maisie, how are you, and where's Annie?"

"I'm fine, thanks, Master Robert, but Annie left a few weeks ago."

"Did she? Why was that? I thought she liked it here." Robert was astounded and immediately thought Sabina had found a new post for Annie.

"Well, now she's married Harry Rudd; he doesn't want her living in as a servant."

"What did you say? She's married to Harry Rudd?"

Robert had an incredulous expression on his face. He had only been gone a few months, and he and Annie had, at the very least, had an understanding. He couldn't believe she would marry Harry Rudd as soon as his back was turned.

"Why yes, Master Robert, she married him last month. I didn't realise you didn't know."

Robert could not betray his true feelings and tried to make light of it.

"Oh, well, good luck to them. I'm just a bit surprised; I didn't know they were courting."

"Well, Harry's been sweet on Annie for a long time, so he must have eventually won her round. He'll be a good husband, and the smithy will be his one day, so she'll want for nothing."

"I didn't even know he was fond of Annie," said Robert, suddenly understanding Harry's hostility towards him. "It just seems rather sudden. You must miss her; have you taken on anyone else yet?"

"No, not yet, though goodness knows, we need someone."

Sid Hobbs overheard all this and opened his mouth to speak, but Ethel Potts fixed him with such a steely glare that he thought better of it. Ethel wanted Robert to accept Annie's marriage before he heard she was carrying a child, far less the sordid details. Ethel was a better manager than Robert gave her credit for, and, but for her, the cheeses and hams he had given to the Carters from time to time would have soon been missed. Miss Wetherby kept a strict list of everything in the larders to ensure there was no pilfering. However, Ethel had managed to keep the books straight, for she doted on Robert and was glad he was helping such a needy family.

Ethel was fond of Annie and knew she had grown close to Robert. She wondered if the baby Annie was carrying was, in fact, Robert's. If he had found out it was his, Ethel was sure he would have wanted to marry her. Then again, Maisie had told her how Annie had been raped. There was no doubt the girl had been in a terrible state that morning, with a black eye and split lip. Whomever the father was, perhaps Harry's proposal had offered the best solution to her dilemma. Of course, there was always the possibility that the baby was Harry's anyway. When Ethel heard that Annie was to marry Harry, she warned the kitchen staff to keep their mouths shut about Annie's condition. She suspected Annie would keep out of Robert's way whilst he was at home, and hopefully, he would return to school in a couple of weeks, none the wiser.

Robert was devastated at the news. He couldn't understand why Annie would have married Harry so suddenly and without telling him. He sighed as he munched his chocolate cake and wondered how to see her, for he knew he must, despite his father's wishes.

The next day, he slipped out through the now-familiar hole in the hedge that Annie had used to sneak in and steal vegetables. Although late April, there had been a hard frost the night before, and the grass was crisp beneath his feet. He smiled as he remembered Annie's head poking through the hole, with her dad's cap covering her hair; he really had thought she was a boy.

He squeezed through the hedge and walked briskly to Sabina's cottage, wanting to chat with her before seeing Annie. He paused at the edge of the woods, not wanting to be seen, and quickly slipped from the cover of the trees through the back gate and knocked gently on the back door. Sabina answered the door, her face tense when she saw who it was.

"Hello, Master Robert; how are you? You'd better come in."

The cottage was warm and clean, with delicious smells of home baking, and the children were pleased to see him. He reached into his pocket for some sweets and enjoyed seeing the smiling faces around him. He passed a parcel to Sabina.

"There's some cheese and ham in there, Sabina; it will make a pleasant change from rabbit or fish."

She opened her mouth to protest, but he held up his hand.

"Don't argue; you know it's pointless. I need to talk to you about Annie."

"She's married to Harry Rudd, Robert, and you must move on. He's always liked Annie and started calling on her soon after you returned to school."

"I know, but I…"

"I'm sorry, Robert. I know you cared for her, and she was fond of you, too, but there was never any future in it, was there? You're from different walks of life, and I thought your father had forbidden you to come here?"

"What? Oh, yes, he has, but he doesn't know I'm here. Sabina, I love Annie, and she agreed to wait and marry me. I can't believe she'd do this. I've missed her so much, and I must talk to her."

"No, Robert, it can change nothing, so please leave her alone. She's married to Harry now, and that's an end to it. She didn't want to hurt you but realised the relationship was impossible. I know it doesn't seem like it now, but in time, you'll see it was for the best. Trust me, you'll soon meet a young lady from your own class and be happy again."

"I think that's unlikely. Where's Annie living now, at the forge?"

"She and Harry are living in the cottage next to the smithy. It's small, but they've made it cosy, and they're content, so please leave her alone, Robert. She's married, and that must be an end to it."

"How long have they been married?"

"Four weeks."

"I still can't believe she would marry him without talking to me first. What was the hurry?"

"I think she married him quickly because she knew you would try to talk her out of it, and maybe she was afraid you would succeed. I know it's hard for you, Robert, and it's been hard for her, too, but she's determined to make a go of this marriage, so please leave them alone and give them a chance. Now, what do you think of young Danny?"

Robert studied his little brother, who until now had been asleep in his cot. The baby gave Robert a wide grin, revealing some uneven teeth with a large gap in the middle where his palate was deformed. Despite his unhappiness, Robert smiled back and held out his arms. Danny went to him readily enough and started playing with his cravat.

"He's thriving, Sabina. Thank you for taking care of him. Do you think he'll ever walk?"

"I don't know. Dr Luckett examined him during the diphtheria epidemic, and he thought he might. I've taken the splints off because he's trying to crawl, and I don't think his feet are quite so twisted now. Even if he walks with a limp, it will be better than not at all. He's eating solids now and putting on more weight."

"Well, I'd better be going. I still can't believe Annie's married, and I'd like to talk to her. Could you ask her if she'll meet me? I could call next week to see what she says."

"I'll tell her, Robert, though I don't think she'll meet you. You're welcome to come and see Danny whenever you like, though."

Robert walked home past the smithy on the chance he might see Annie. He strolled past the cottage with its bright blue curtains at the windows. Smoke was coming from the chimney, and he guessed Annie would have made it cosy inside. He saw a curtain twitch slightly and hoped that Annie would appear, but she didn't. He could see Harry working inside the forge and was tempted to go in and speak to him. Eventually, he decided against it, for he knew he would pick a fight with him if he did.

Ben Rudd saw Robert walking past and hoped Harry wouldn't notice him. However, Harry must have sensed something, for he glanced at his father and then out the door and just glimpsed Robert. He went to the door, watched Robert walk past the cottage, and then returned to work. Ben said nothing but noticed Harry's mouth was pressed into a thin line, and the horseshoe he was working on was certainly taking some punishment.

Annie saw Robert pass, and tears ran down her cheeks, for she longed to explain to him what had happened but didn't dare. She knew Harry and Ben would be watching, and what good could it do? The situation could not be changed, but she felt so guilty. She had betrayed Robert and knew he would be so hurt, especially as he didn't know the whole story. Sobbing, she went back to her mending.

When Annie next saw her mother, Sabina told her of Robert's visit and how much he would like to see her.

"Don't you even think of meeting him, Annie. You're married to a good man now, so let it rest and think of the baby."

"Mum, did you tell him about the baby? Did you tell him why I married Harry?"

"No, I didn't because it would only stir up more trouble. Just forget what happened and concentrate on Harry and the baby."

"That's easier said than done. I want to tell him what happened because he must think he meant so little to me. I can't bear for him to be hurting like this."

"Annie, if you tell him, no doubt he'll make a big fuss trying to find out who attacked you, and people will soon figure out the baby's not Harry's. I know it's hard, but it's better for everyone if you don't see Robert. I expect he's only here for a couple of weeks over Easter, so keep out of his way. Things will settle down once the baby's born, and by then, he'll have met someone else."

"Oh, I suppose you're right, but I feel so awful."

"Come on, the worst is over, and you're lucky to be married to Harry. He's kind to you, isn't he?"

"Yes, he is."

If it weren't that she loved Robert, she would have been content with Harry, for he did everything he could to make life easier for her. He lit the fires before leaving for work and ensured there was a supply of logs, chopped and ready for use, during the day. He gave her money to buy food and was appreciative of her cooking. She enjoyed preparing his meals and keeping the cottage spick and span. It all seemed so ridiculously easy just looking after one man. She had worked long, hard hours all her life, but sometimes now she looked around for something to do, though she knew she would be busier after the baby was born. In the meantime, she visited her mother and helped Liza with the children, often taking Danny and Helen for walks in the old pram.

Matilda had wondered about the hasty wedding and was not surprised when Annie confided that she was pregnant. Annie said she wasn't sure when the baby was due, but Matilda's practised eye could tell that the growing bump had been there before the wedding day. She didn't mind, for they were married now, and the baby would be born with its father's name, and that was all that mattered. Knowing how fond of Robert Annie had been, her only concern was whether Harry was the baby's father. However, she told herself, it was no use speculating. Harry was a grown man old enough to make his own decisions, so she said nothing and welcomed Annie into the family with open arms. Indeed, she enjoyed her company because, with a husband and three sons, female company was something she'd had little of over the years.

Annie lay low over Easter and didn't even visit Sabina in case Robert should turn up. She didn't think he would come to the cottage, and he didn't, though he very much wanted to. If Harry wondered why she didn't go out much, he didn't ask, and she thought perhaps he had guessed the reason why.

CHAPTER 37

Sarah was delighted to see Robert when she returned home from her visit to Mabel. He hugged his little sister and realised she was not so little anymore.

"I can't believe how much you've grown whilst I've been away."

"I'm so pleased you're home, at last, Robert. It's been awful here since we heard David was killed and Papa was taken ill. How long are you home for?"

Victoria, who was also present, looked up in interest.

"I'm not sure until I talk to Mama, but I'd rather not return to school at all. Of course, we were to visit London next month to celebrate our eighteenth birthday, but I don't think that will be possible now."

"No, Mama has already said we can't go to London, and I agree. It wouldn't be right to celebrate after what's happened to David and Papa."

"I expect you're a bit disappointed, though, aren't you, Vic? It doesn't matter so much to me, but it would have been your coming-out ball, as well as our birthday."

"Don't worry, I don't mind; I'm not in the mood for celebrating after what's happened. Although I would have enjoyed a season in London, with all the grand balls and new dresses, Frank Eastleigh has already proposed to me, so it would have been a bit of a waste of time."

"Oh, has he? Have you accepted?"

"No, not yet, so don't tell anyone, but I will. I'm fond of him, and we seem to get on well together."

"Do you think I could be a bridesmaid?"

"Yes, of course, Sarah, but remember it's a secret because I haven't even accepted his proposal yet."

"Are you sure you aren't being a little hasty? Perhaps you should wait and see what other young men are interested in you. You're a pretty girl, you know, and I think you'll have many more proposals to consider if you wait a while, and you could certainly have a season in London next year."

"No, my mind is made up. I think I'm already half in love with Frank, and he's so handsome. You don't seem pleased, though, and I thought you would be because he's always been your friend."

"I'm just not sure he's ready to settle down yet."

"Well, surely he wouldn't have asked me to marry him if he wasn't."

"No, I suppose not. Anyway, if you're sure, congratulations, and I hope you'll both be happy together. Now, if you'll excuse me, Mother wants to talk to me before dinner."

Walking to the drawing room, Robert rehearsed what he would say to his mother. He had wanted to leave school for some time and fervently hoped his parents would agree. As he entered the room, his mother glanced up from the book she was reading and smiled at him.

"Ah, there you are, Robert; we need to talk about what will happen now that David has died. The estate will now pass to you, and if your father had been in good health, that would not have been for some time. However, as he is so ill, we must consider the best way forward. Doctor Luckett hopes Papa's condition may improve, but it's unlikely he'll ever fully recover. I've given this a lot of thought, and, as you will be eighteen next month, I think perhaps, with Jack's help, you're old enough to take control. What do you think?"

"I've never made any secret of the fact that I'm interested in the estate, but I never wanted to inherit it at David's expense."

"No, of course not, but it's only right it comes to you now. Are you ready to take it on, or do you want to spend longer at school?"

"I wish it were under happier circumstances, but yes, I'd love to take it on. I've always wanted to do it but never expected it to happen. I was going to ask if I could leave school, but I never thought Papa would agree."

"Well, I haven't discussed it with him yet, but I can't see any other solution. We must sort something out soon because I can't deal with some of the things Jack's been asking me about. I'll have a word with your father, but I'll leave it until the morning because I don't want him worrying about it all night. It's strange how things work out, isn't it? I wish David were still with us, but I'm sure you'll do a good job. Come on, you can escort me into dinner."

Eleanor broached the subject of Robert leaving school with her husband the following day. It was clear from his reactions that he fully understood but was extremely reluctant to hand control of the estate over to Robert. However, he could see it was the obvious solution under the circumstances. His main concern was that Robert would spend too much money improving the living conditions of the workers and paying them higher wages. Lord Fellwood was frustrated that he could not hold a proper conversation and explain himself fully, but he felt so weak and tired that eventually, he nodded his agreement. Eleanor sent for their son so they could tell him together. Robert was delighted, for he'd enjoyed himself immensely the previous summer, and not just because of his relationship with Annie. It felt so rewarding to do an honest day's work, and he loved everything to do with farming. He took his father's good hand and promised to do his best to run the estate with Jack. His father nodded tiredly and smiled his now-familiar lop-sided smile.

Eleanor and Robert told Jack the news together, and he was not surprised, for it was the logical step to take. He was pleased because he liked Robert, and it had been not easy over the last few weeks for both him and Lady Fellwood. They agreed Robert would shadow Jack to learn as much as possible. Robert could not help but wonder at the irony of the situation, for once the estate was formally handed over to him, he could marry whom he liked. No doubt some would shun him if he married below his station, but he didn't care about that. If only Annie hadn't already married Harry.

The knowledge that he would soon be managing the estate made Robert long to see Annie and tell her, though he knew that, sadly, it would probably make no difference. He was sure Annie loved him, and he couldn't understand her actions. The only reason he could think of was that she had married Harry before he could dissuade her because she didn't believe they had a future together. How he wished she would talk to him. He pondered for some time to think of a way to see her. Then he remembered she often visited her father's grave early on a Sunday morning when fewer people were around.

He decided that would be his best opportunity to see her alone. On the following Sunday, he loitered around at the back of the church, keeping an eye on Tom Carter's grave. He didn't have to wait long, for after about fifteen minutes, Annie appeared. Her grey 'Granny Annie' shawl was wrapped around her, for it was a chilly morning, and she carried a bunch of wild daffodils in her hand. She read the names on the familiar gravestones as she passed them. Sydney Grigg and Martha, William Handford, John Kentisbeare. She smiled to herself, for she had not known any of these people as they were long dead, but she had walked this path so often since her father's death that they almost felt like old friends. Robert walked swiftly towards her.

"Hello, Annie. I hoped you might still visit your dad's grave. How are you?"

"Oh, Robert, you made me jump. I thought you would have gone back to school by now."

"No, I've left school. Now David has died, and Papa is so ill, I will manage the estate. It's mine now, Annie."

Annie was surprised, and a look of resignation briefly crossed her face. He moved towards her and would have taken her in his arms, but she stepped back swiftly, pulling her shawl across her chest and crossing her arms. Her body language made it clear she wanted no contact with him. He looked at her intently, trying to read what was going through her mind.

"Oh, I'm so pleased for you, Robert. Of course, I'm sorry about your brother and your father, but you'll have Jack to help you, won't you? I know it's what you've always wanted to do."

"Oh, Annie, why did you marry Harry? Now the estate is mine; I could marry you when I'm twenty-one if only you had waited."

"I had my reasons, Robert, and I'm so sorry, but it's done now, and there's no going back. There was no way I could know this would happen."

"No, of course, you couldn't, but Annie, why did you marry him so quickly and without even telling me? I thought you loved me?"

"All I can tell you is that I had my reasons. I did love you, Robert, more than you'll ever know, but it wasn't to be. We must put this behind us now, but I'm so glad to have seen you. I've hated not being able to tell you."

"No, that's not good enough, Annie. I deserve better than that. What was the great hurry that you couldn't wait to talk to me first? I think I have a right to know; we had an understanding."

He reached out and pulled her towards him, but still, she resisted.

"Robert, please just let it go." Annie now raised her eyes to his, and he saw they were bright with tears.

"I have to know, Annie; please tell me, and then I'll leave you alone."

She took a deep breath and led him into the church porch, where there was a stone bench they could sit on. She carefully kept her shawl loosely wrapped across her stomach, for her pregnancy was evident, and she wanted to explain the circumstances to him before he realised.

"Well, you remember how Frank Eastleigh attacked me at Christmas, and you drove him off? Then, a day or so later, you returned to school?"

"Yes, of course, but what has that to do with anything?"

"Well, there was a New Year's Eve party which went on into the early hours, and we were all shattered because we'd been working since dawn. There was a lot of clearing up, and poor Mrs Potts was dead on her feet, so Maisie and I said we would finish up. I went to the hall to collect the last dirty dishes, but as I went along the corridor, someone put out the lamp, grabbed me from behind, and put a hand around my mouth."

Robert's eyes narrowed, and his face wore a grim expression. "Go on."

"Well, of course, I struggled and kicked like mad, but I couldn't scream. I was taken to the cellars under the west wing and raped."

A sob broke from her as she relived the ordeal, and at once, his arms were around her, but again, she tried to push him away.

"Don't, someone will see."

"I don't care if they do."

"No, but I do. If Harry found out I was seeing you, he'd be devastated."

However, he held on this time, and at last, she relented and melted into his embrace.

"So, who was it?"

"That's just it; I don't know. That sounds ridiculous, but whoever it was hit me hard, and I was stunned. It was so dark I couldn't see, and I screamed and screamed, but no one could hear me in the cellar, and it was so cold."

Robert's face took on a thunderous expression, and there were angry tears in his eyes as he held her.

"Oh, Annie, I'm so sorry." He kissed the top of her head. "What an awful thing to happen. Do you think it was Frank?"

"Well, he's the obvious suspect, but he was so open about trying it on before that I don't think he would have cared if I had known it was him. I think he'd have enjoyed the fact that he'd got his way in the end. I've no idea who it was, but Frank has grabbed me before, and I think I would have known if it was him. All I know is that whoever it was wore a strange perfume. I've never smelt it before, but I would know it again."

"I still don't see why you had to marry Harry?" Then his gaze fell to the shawl that had fallen open, and the penny dropped.

"Oh, Annie, you're not pregnant?"

She hung her head in shame. "Yes, I am. I kept being sick at breakfast, and Miss Wetherby got to hear of it and sacked me. I think Sid Hobbs told her. I tried to explain what had happened, but she said it was my fault for leading men on. Anyway, I had to leave, so I moved back home, where, luckily, I knew Mum would support me. I went for a walk to think things through and bumped into Harry. He saw I was upset about something and made me tell him all my troubles, and you can guess the rest."

"I'd never have let him marry you if I'd been here. You wait until I see him; I'll soon put him straight. He took advantage of you at a difficult time. If only you had waited until I got home. I would have married you, myself, Annie."

"No, you must leave him alone, Robert; he's been so kind to me. He says he'll bring the child up as his own, and I think he will; after all, it's not the child's fault. I knew you'd want to marry me, but there didn't seem any possibility of that ever happening, and I had to make a quick decision if I was to pass the baby off as Harry's. I'm afraid it's too late now. Harry's a good man, and I will try to make him happy. You'll meet someone else, Robert, someone from your own class. It would have been difficult if we had wed; you know it would. It's probably for the best."

"I'll never see it like that, Annie. Would you move away and live with me as my wife if I sold the estate? Once it's formally mine, I can do as I like."

"Oh, Robert, I can't do that to Harry after he's been so kind. Think how upset your family would be after all that's happened. No, I'm sorry, but we have to move on. I'll always love you, Robert, and I'm so glad to have had the chance to explain all this to you myself, but we can't see each other again. Please keep away from me; it's just too painful otherwise."

Reluctantly but firmly, she pulled away from him and walked quickly down the path. The smithy backed onto the graveyard, and as she entered the cottage, she knew instinctively that Harry had seen the exchange.

"I've just seen Robert in the graveyard."

"I know; I saw you talking to him."

"I had to explain to him, Harry. We had feelings for each other, though we knew nothing could come of it, and I owed him an explanation. I hope you understand why I had to speak to him?"

"Aye, I understand that, but what will happen now?" Harry looked anxiously into her eyes, fearful of what she might say.

"Nothing, nothing at all, will happen. I'm so glad to have explained everything to Robert myself, but that's an end to it. I'm your wife now, Harry, and I take my vows seriously, so I'm afraid you're stuck with me." She put her arms around his neck. "Please don't be angry with me, Harry."

"I'm not angry, and I knew you'd have to see him sometime, but are you sure that's an end to it?"

"Yes, it is. Robert's upset, but he understands."

"I'm so glad, Annie. You know how I feel about you, but this has been hanging over us. I'm glad Robert knows the score now."

"Harry, it's not his fault he was born a gentleman. Could you try to get on with him if you should meet?"

"I'll try, but the fact that I know he loves my wife makes it a little difficult, you know."

"Good. Now I'll get some dinner for you, or you'll grumble about how hungry you are."

CHAPTER 38

It was a sunny morning in early May when William Carter and Sarah Martin married. She wore a white lacy dress and looked radiant as her father proudly led her up the aisle to give her away, a pleasure he had never expected to happen. Amelia and Matilda, Sarah's youngest sister, were bridesmaids. They wore pretty dresses of pale blue and carried small posies of violets. Joseph and Matthew were page boys, dressed in navy suits with white shirts, and for once, the twins behaved themselves, much to William's relief. The wedding reception was held at The Red Lion Inn, and the villagers enjoyed yet another free meal.

There would be no honeymoon as the family would travel to China in the next few weeks. After the wedding, Sarah moved into the cottage with William and the children, but her new role as a stepmother did not come naturally to her, for she had little maternal instinct, and she was glad William had agreed to employ a nanny in China. The children sensed her lack of interest in them, and the boys were naughty to attract attention. William tried to coax the children to accept Sarah and behave better. However, they missed their mother and resented this new person ordering them about. Sarah, for her part, stood no nonsense and felt the sooner they understood she was the boss, the better it would be. Poor William was divided between loyalty to his children, whom he adored, and his new bride, so the first weeks of married life were not exactly full of wedded bliss.

The newlyweds and the children were to travel to London in the middle of June as William had some business to attend to before they sailed to China. The children liked the heat of China and found the cold, damp climate of North Devon unpleasant. They were excited about returning home to see all their friends and relatives. However, Betsey was sorry that her son would leave her again, for she enjoyed having him around.

In the meantime, William was earning a few shillings helping his brother, Fred, with his carpentry or lending a hand behind the bar at the inn. His mother was glad of the help, for she still cared for Fred's three little ones and found it hard going at her age. Poor Lucy was no better, and Fred found his visits to her upsetting.

Fred had secured a job at a remote dwelling on Exmoor, and William had been helping him. The derelict cottage had stood empty for many years, but Mr Southbrook, a visitor to the area, had fallen in love with the place and decided to buy it. He was a distinguished old gentleman with incredibly bushy white eyebrows and a thick beard. He was an author and loved the isolation of the rugged moors. He felt it was just the right place to stimulate his imagination and allow him to concentrate on his work.

The cottage needed a new roof, floorboards, staircase and windows, so there was plenty of work to keep Fred busy for some weeks. The only downside to the job was the time spent travelling to it. Some days, he needed his horse and cart to carry new materials to the cottage, but on others, he travelled on horseback, which was much quicker. William borrowed his father's horse so he could come and go as he liked.

The brothers were making progress with the work and enjoyed spending time together. It took Fred's mind off his problems with Lucy, and William was glad to earn some money. One afternoon, Fred went to buy more timber from the sawmills and left William working on the roof, for they needed to get the cottage watertight as soon as possible.

"Don't stay too long, Will. I can smell rain, and it's blowing up for quite a storm. You don't want to get caught in that on the moor."

"No, all right, I won't be too long, but I'd like to see this roof finished before I go off on my travels again; you should be able to do the rest of the work on your own then. I'll be quicker on horseback anyway; I might even get back before you in the horse and cart."

"Well, I'll see you at the inn later, and we'll have a jar or two."

William carried on happily, determined to finish his work, but when the wind rose to gale force, and it started to rain in torrents, he decided to call it a day, annoying though it was not to complete the job. He climbed carefully down the ladder, thinking it had suddenly become cold. That was the problem with the moors; they could be bathed in golden sunshine one minute but turn wintry in no time and present a very different landscape. That was the case now, for he could hear thunder in the distance. He went to the kitchen, the only fully dry room, to get his coat. He had been too hot earlier when he was hard at work, but he would certainly need it now. He searched the entire cottage but could not find it. Eventually, he concluded that he must have left it on the cart, and Fred had driven off with it.

He considered waiting until the storm had passed, but it looked like it was in for the night. He was cold and hungry and decided there was nothing for it but to ride home as fast as he could. He tied an old sack around his shoulders, mounted his horse, and set off. The rain was so heavy he could barely see his way, and within minutes, he was wet through and wishing he'd made a fire at the cottage. The ride usually took about half an hour, so with a determined set to his jaw, he urged his horse on. About halfway home, his horse stumbled, and he was nearly thrown from the saddle, but he was an experienced rider and managed to hold on.

"Come on, lass, it's not much further." He spoke aloud to his horse to encourage her, but within a few paces, he could tell she was limping and dismounted to have a look. She had thrown a shoe and was lame. He knew he could no longer ride her without risking permanent damage. He couldn't believe his bad luck, as, most unhappy now, he trudged along on foot, leading the poor horse, and by the time he reached the inn, he was shaking with the cold. He took the horse to the stables and asked one of his father's servants to attend to her before making his way home, tired, cold, and hungry.

Sarah exclaimed aloud when she saw him. "Why, William, you're soaked through; what were you thinking of to get in this state on such a cold day?"

"Oh, Fred went to the sawmills with the horse and cart, and I didn't realise I'd left my coat in it. The weather came in really bad, and as if that wasn't enough, old Bess threw a shoe, and I had to walk her home. Let me get near the fire, will you? I'm frozen." He could barely talk with his teeth chattering.

"Yes, do, and get those wet things off, or you'll catch your death of cold. I'll get you a bowl of broth to warm you up."

Shivering, William took off his clothes and put on his nightshirt. The children were amused to see him in his bedclothes so early and gathered around him.

"Now, children, let your dad eat his broth and give him a bit of peace."

"Oh, they're all right, Sarah; I like them around me. What have you been up to today?"

"Daddy, Aunty Sarah smacked Amelia hard. She left red finger marks on her leg and made her cry."

William was shocked, for Amelia was such a placid little girl who was seldom naughty, and he was surprised she could have done anything to warrant such a blow. Amelia's lip trembled when reminded of the incident, and William put his broth to one side and gently picked her up.

"Now then, missy, what did you do to upset Aunty Sarah like that?"

"I didn't mean to do it, Daddy; honest, I didn't mean to," sobbed Amelia.

"She broke one of my best dishes, William, and had to be punished. She had no business even touching it."

"Well, I'm sure she didn't mean to break it, did you, Amelia?"

"No, Daddy. It was so pretty I just wanted a better look, but Aunty Sarah shouted at me, and I dropped it."

"I see. Well, say you're sorry to Aunty Sarah, and then we'll forget all about it. I'll buy another dish for you, Sarah, but I think we need to talk about this later."

William sat beside the fire all evening but couldn't get warm, for the cold seemed to have seeped into his bones. He told the children a bedtime story before tucking them in for the night.

"Sarah, I've bitten my tongue so far, but I'm not having you hitting my children for no real reason. Amelia is seldom naughty, and I expect it was the shock of you shouting at her that made her drop that dish. I know you're finding it difficult to cope with them, but it's not easy for them either, and it will take time for them to accept you. If you could just be more patient and meet them halfway."

"Well, I might have known you'd take their part. I don't know what sort of a mother Lottie was, but it's clear they've had little or no discipline, and you spoil them."

This criticism of Lottie angered William further, and they had their first serious row since their marriage. They went to bed not speaking and lay back-to-back, ignoring each other. In the night, William awoke feeling ill, and although shivering with the cold, his forehead was burning hot. His body ached, and his throat was sore. Nevertheless, he rose early the next morning and went to Fred's cottage.

"Good morning, William, you look a bit rough; are you all right?"

"Morning, Fred, no, I don't feel too good, but it's my own silly fault. You probably didn't notice, but I left my coat in the cart yesterday, so I had to ride home without it."

"Oh, no, I didn't see it. Mind you, I never expected the weather to turn as quickly as it did. You must have got soaked?"

"Yes, I did. It was pouring with rain and blowing a gale, and then, to top it all, old Bess threw a shoe and went lame, so I had to walk her home. I've never been so cold; in fact, I don't think I've thawed out yet."

"You must have been. Anyone would have thought it was winter. Why don't you leave it to me today and get some rest?"

"No, my throat's sore, and my head's throbbing, but it's just a cold. I want to see the job finished before the end of the week, so I'll come if there's another horse I can use."

Ned said William could use his other horse, Bonny. William felt unwell all day, but he soldiered on, and together, they finished the roof and made the building watertight.

"There, I'm glad that's finished. Hopefully, you can finish the rest of the work on your own now, Fred."

"Aye, that's the worst of it. Thanks so much for your help, William; I would have struggled without you and haven't paid you much, but I've loved working together. Are you sure you won't stay in England? We could go into partnership?"

"Now, don't you start; I've already had enough from Mum. I'd love that in some ways, but I'm better at paperwork and earning good money in China.

Besides, it's what the children know, and they're looking forward to going home and seeing all their friends and Lottie's family. I'll come back again one day, though, and now I've married Sarah, I'm sure she'll want to come back and see her family. I'm going to miss you all."

"Come on, then, I think we've earned an ale or two; let's lubricate that sore throat of yours."

CHAPTER 39

A couple of days later, William, Sarah, and the children said their goodbyes and boarded the stagecoach for London. Poor William was still ill, and his mother pleaded with him to delay his departure.

"Will, just stay a few more days until you're better. I know you think I don't want you to go, and that's true enough, but you're not fit to travel; you should rest for a few days first."

"I'm not well, Mum, and I won't lie about it, but I must clear up some business in London before our ship sails, and if I don't go today, I won't have enough time. I shall only just get back before my leave is up as it is. I promise I'll rest every day as soon as I'm on that ship."

He hugged her. "I promise I'll write too, and I'll be back to see you again one day. Thanks for everything, Mum; I love you."

Betsey clung to him with tears in her eyes, then pushed him away and hugged the children.

"Go on then, take care of yourselves, and don't forget us."

Eveline was also there to say goodbye, for she had become fond of the children over the last few months. She hugged each one and thrust a present into their hands.

"Here's a little present from me to send you on your way. Matthew and Joe, you have some sweets from Mrs Scott's sweet shop, and she tells me these are your favourites. Amelia, you have a few sweets, but not as many as the boys because eating too many is not ladylike, and I've made you a dolly. I hope you like her?"

The doll was skilfully made and would have fetched a handsome price in the London shop where they were now sold. It was fifteen inches long and had a pretty face framed with brown hair. A blue bonnet was tied under its chin with a cream ribbon, and the blue velvet dress was trimmed with delicate cream lace. Underneath the dress, the doll had a white lawn petticoat and pantaloons.

Evie had even made some little boots from scraps of thin leather given to her by Mr Martin, and the crocheted laces were tied up tightly. She had gone to a lot of trouble and was pleased with the result.

"Ooh, thanks, Aunty Evie," chimed the boys.

"Yes, thank you so much, Aunty Evie. Oh, I love my dolly. I shall call her Evie after you, and then I shall never forget you."

Amelia hugged her Aunty Evie, and William quickly ushered them all into the stagecoach before the situation became any more emotional.

"Thanks, Evie; I'm going to miss you so much. Take care of Mum and Dad for me, won't you?"

"Of course, and make sure you come back and see us again, and don't forget to write."

Although William was putting on a brave face, he couldn't remember ever feeling so ill, and once they were settled in the stagecoach, Sarah told him to get some sleep. He was sweating profusely one minute and shivering the next, and his cough was so bad that his sore ribs felt as if they had been kicked by a mule.

The roads were in a terrible state, and the journey to London took nearly three days, with the stagecoach stopping at wayside inns for overnight stops. The journey seemed never-ending, and the jolting of the carriage made William's head stab with pain. Sarah could see he was poorly, but she was still cross from their row a few days earlier. At first, the children enjoyed looking out of the window, but they soon got bored, and their squabbling tried Sarah's patience. When they reached London, Sarah was amazed at the crowds of people and the size of the buildings. She had never imagined it would be like this. William took them to an inn where they would stay for a few days until the ship sailed. He turned wearily to Sarah.

"I'm sorry, love, but do you mind if I go straight to bed? I feel so awful. If I get some rest, perhaps I'll be better tomorrow. Get something for yourself and the children to eat, and come up when you're ready; we're all in the same room."

"Yes, all right, but do you think we should find a doctor for you?"

"No, I just need my bed, and we'll see how I am tomorrow."

However, when Sarah went upstairs after their meal, she could see William was far worse. The sweat was rolling off his body, and the sheets were soaked, yet he was shivering with the cold. She asked the innkeeper to send for a doctor, and Doctor Brown arrived an hour later. He was an elderly man with kindly blue eyes, and he spoke to the children for a few minutes and heard how excited they were to return to China. After examining William, he took Sarah to one side.

"Mrs Carter, I'm afraid your husband is seriously ill with pneumonia; has he had it before?"

"I don't know, doctor, we've only been married a short time, but his mother said he had a weak chest, so maybe. The children are from his previous marriage."

"It's unlikely he'll be well enough to sail to China for some time. He must be kept in a warm bed and given as much fluid as possible. I'll call back again tomorrow."

Through the night, William became delirious and tossed and turned in his bed. The children could not understand what was wrong with their daddy. Sarah was worried and knew the ship would have to sail without them.

Over the next few days, he became weaker and was seldom conscious. The weight fell from him, and his eyes looked sunken in his face. The doctor warned Sarah to expect the worst. At one point, William woke and called hoarsely to Sarah. She came to him immediately from the couch where she had been sleeping and sat on the edge of the bed.

"Are you feeling any better?"

"No, not really. Has the ship sailed?"

"Yes, I'm afraid so. I didn't know what to do, but there was no way you could travel; we can go on a later ship when you're better, though, can't we?"

"I hope so. Sarah, you must find the letters in my coat pocket and go to the address on them." He closed his eyes and gasped for breath, the effort of talking draining what little strength he had. After a few moments, he continued. "Tell the people there I'm ill and ask them when the next ship will sail. Hopefully, we'll be able to go on that one. Take the children with you and use a carriage."

He sank back on his pillows but caught her hand as she went to move away.

"Come here a minute."

She sat back on the bed and wiped his forehead with a damp cloth.

"Sarah, if I don't get better, you will look after the children, won't you?"

"Of course, you'll get better; the doctor says the worst is over."

"Maybe, but promise me you'll care for them?" He closed his eyes again and rested for a few moments before he continued, his voice faltering with emotion and exhaustion. "If you feel you can't bring them up, take them to Mum or Evie. I know you're not keen on them, but please, promise me you'll see they're all right?"

"Hush now, you'll get better, and we'll be off to China in a week or two. Now, you must rest, and we'll talk again in the morning."

William sighed and lay back on the pillows, exhausted by even this short conversation.

In the morning, Sarah roused the children and got them dressed. She found the papers in William's coat pocket and went downstairs to get a carriage. William was sound asleep, so she didn't disturb him. At the offices, she explained what had happened to the manager. He was not best pleased, for the passage to China had been paid for and was now wasted. She apologised for not letting him know sooner but explained that William had been unconscious and she hadn't known what to do. She promised to let him know when William could travel so that passages could be booked on another ship.

Unfortunately, however, William's condition worsened, and a few days later, he passed away in his sleep. Sarah was horrified, for she had become fond of him and had been looking forward to a new life in China. The children were heartbroken, for they knew what this meant. When their mother died, they did not understand the concept of death and, at first, thought she would wake up again. As time passed, and William explained they would never see her again, they were devastated. This time, they did not even have their daddy to console them. Sarah spoke kindly to them, but it was beyond her to kiss and cuddle them as their father would have, and they were bitterly unhappy. They squabbled and fought, and their stepmother, worried about the future, found them difficult to deal with.

Sarah had barely slept since her husband's death. She knew she should contact William's family to let them know what had happened and was sure they would want the body taken back to Devon for burial in the local churchyard. However, she could not bring herself to contemplate bringing up the three children single-handedly and spent hours trying to think of a solution to avoid this.

Without William, she had no idea where they could live, for there was no room at her father's cottage, and whilst she had no knowledge of William's financial situation in China, she had no intention of going there without him. Eventually, she devised a desperate plan and went over it in her head. It would mean she could not tell William's family of his death. Therefore, only Sarah, the children, the innkeeper, and his wife attended the funeral. After the funeral, Betty, the innkeeper's wife, gently took Sarah to one side.

"Sarah, I'm so sorry for your loss. If it helps, I can watch the children if you have things to sort out. What a shame he had no family to come to his funeral, and my heart goes out to those poor children. Thank goodness they still have you to care for them."

Sarah nodded and forced a reassuring smile onto her face.

"Well, we won't be going to China now, and that's for certain. Is it all right for us to stay here for another day or two?"

"Why yes, of course, and like I say, if you need me to look after the children, I'm willing to help."

"Thank you, that is kind. I'd be grateful if you could keep an eye on them tomorrow morning, as I need to sort out a few things."

Sarah spent another restless night. Paying for William's funeral had used up most of his money, and she couldn't stay at the inn indefinitely. She knew if she took the children home to Devon, she would be expected to care for them, but where could they live, and what on? After hours of indecision, she decided to go ahead with her plan to leave the children in London and return on her own. She packed a bag with some belongings, took all William's paperwork and anything that could be used to trace her, and then left the children with Betty. She went to the Customs Office to tell them of William's death and explained the family would no longer be sailing to China. The man offered his condolences and said he would inform the officials in China. He asked what Sarah would do now.

"My family lives in Bristol, and I plan to return there with the children."

As she boarded the stagecoach for the South West, she felt as if a load had been lifted from her shoulders, knowing she would not be burdened with the children for years to come. She felt a bit guilty, considering William had asked her to look after them, but fortunately, she hadn't promised him. She had avoided that by leading the conversation in a different direction. She comforted herself that the innkeeper's wife was a kindly soul who had taken to the children, and most likely, she would keep them, and they would be fine.

However, as the stagecoach rumbled along the rutted lanes, Sarah became ever more nervous as she rehearsed the story in her head. She dreaded lying to Betsey, but even this was preferable to raising three young children alone. Fortunately, it was dark when she arrived in Hartford, and when she alighted from the stagecoach, she saw no one. She was about to open the back door when her father stepped out and stared at her in amazement.

"Why, Sarah, what are you doing here?"

"Hello, Dad. I'm sorry if I gave you a shock."

"I thought you'd be halfway to China by now."

"I couldn't go, Dad. I feel terrible about it, but when it came to getting on that ship, I couldn't do it. I've never liked the hot weather, even here, and it's not like I could come home if I wanted to."

"What about William, though? You married him, after all. Didn't he mind?"

"Yes, of course, he did, but he wouldn't take me there against my will. I worried about it for days, but I know I've done the right thing, though I do miss him."

"Well, it's a shame and no mistake. He needed a wife and a mother for those children, and now I suppose you want to come home to live?"

Richard Martin's voice was sharp.

"Yes, I was hoping you'd let me because I've nowhere else to go and no money. William gave me a little to get home, but it's all gone now."

"Well, you'll have to share with Matilda and Sophie because I've let Ellen and her babies have your old room. You'll have to find work, too. I can't be expected to keep you all your life."

"Oh, thanks, Dad." She hugged him.

He was surprised, for Sarah seldom showed her feelings, but he had no idea how relieved she was.

"I'll look for work, honest I will, and I don't care where I sleep; I'm just so glad to be home."

"Aye, well, I don't envy you telling Betsey and Ned. You've left their son to cope with those young children all the way to China, and after marrying him as well. Go on, get yourself inside and find something to eat; time enough to face the music tomorrow."

The following day, Sarah walked briskly to the inn, keen to get the ordeal over. There was a knot in her stomach, and she felt sick. Her sisters thought she had taken leave of her senses, passing up an opportunity to see the world, and were not best pleased to have her back in the overcrowded cottage.

Timidly, she knocked on the door and saw surprise turn to hope and then disappointment as Betsey glanced behind her, looking for William.

"Why, Sarah, this is unexpected. Is William all right?"

Betsey was anxious as she searched her daughter-in-law's face for the answer, but Sarah carefully avoided eye contact.

"Yes, he's fine, but not here with me, Betsey. I decided not to go to China, and he's sailed with the children."

"But why? I thought you loved him? Why on earth did you marry him?"

"I do love him, and I feel so bad about it, but when it came to it, I just couldn't go to China. I tried to convince myself it would be all right, but it was no good, and William didn't want me to go unless I was willing."

"Oh, Sarah, you silly girl. Now he's married you, he can't take another wife. You should be ashamed of yourself."

"I know, and I'm so sorry, but I just couldn't bear to live in such a hot and foreign country."

"Well, you always knew that was the plan, so you should never have married him. How was he when you left him, anyway? Was he better? I know he was poorly, although he denied it."

"He was ill for a time, but when the ship sailed, he was much better."

"So, what will you do now?"

"Dad's said I can go home to live, thank goodness, but I'll need to find a job."

"Well, I'm not happy about this, Sarah, but if you hear from William, you will let me know straight away, won't you?"

"Yes, of course, and I am sorry."

"Aye, but unfortunately, that doesn't make it right, does it?"

CHAPTER 40

Matthew, Joe, and Amelia waited all day with Betty, and to their delight, she played cards with them and bought them a muffin from the bakery. As the day went on, Betty was surprised Sarah was gone so long. She gave the children their dinner, telling them that their stepmother would, no doubt, be back soon, but by evening, she was concerned as she read them a story and put them to bed.

When morning came and still no Sarah, she searched the room for clues about where she might have gone but found nothing. She asked the children where they came from, and they told her China, which she already knew. They also told her they had lived in the country near their granny for a while and had travelled to London by stagecoach. As she gently questioned them, they explained that their real mummy had died in China and that daddy had recently married the lady they called Aunty Sarah.

As the days passed, Betty realised Sarah must have had an accident that prevented her from returning, or she had abandoned the children. There were no clues about where the family had come from or where they were going, which made her suspect the latter. She called the police, who interviewed the children and the undertaker who had arranged William's funeral. However, the only address given was that of the inn, and Sarah had paid for the burial in cash. Knowing the family planned to sail to China, the police made enquiries at the customs office. The man there told them Mrs Carter had reported her husband's death and intended to take the children to Bristol, where she had relatives.

The police reported this to Betty and her husband, Jim, who were still looking after the three children, and the policeman asked if they would like to keep them. Betty and Jim were in their late sixties, and their six children had left home. They had fifteen grandchildren dotted around London. Even so, Betty wanted to keep the children because she had grown fond of them and knew the alternative. However, in the end, Jim put his foot down and insisted they were too old to take them on, never mind the expense, and they would have to go to the workhouse.

Betty had never been inside the workhouse herself but knew enough about it to know that no one would ever go there willingly. So, knowing what the future likely held in store for them, it was with a heavy heart she explained to Matthew, Joe, and Amelia that, as Aunty Sarah had not returned, she would have to take them to their new home. The policeman offered to take them, but Betty thought the least she could do was to see them settled in. As she approached Moorfield Workhouse, she felt sick and wished she had let the police deal with the matter after all. She almost turned tail and took them back home; only the thought of Jim's wrath prevented her.

The entrance to the workhouse was through a pair of tall wrought iron gates. Betty urged the children down the driveway towards the formidable black front door of an imposing dirty grey building with large windows. The paint was peeling, and the whole place was neglected. Betty pulled sharply on the doorbell, and eventually, a maid opened the door. Betty explained she had come to deliver the children into the care of the workhouse and was asked to wait in the hallway.

The décor was harsh. The walls were bare stone, the wood unvarnished, and the floor laid with large flagstones. There was a strong smell of carbolic soap. They sat on a wooden settle just inside the front door, and Betty wondered how many poor unfortunates had waited where they now sat. The maid returned and took them to meet Mr Parsons, the Beadle.

"Good Morning, Mrs Drew; I understand you wish to entrust these children to our care?"

"Yes, sir, that's right. I believe the policeman, Mr James, told you to expect us?"

"Indeed, he did, dear lady, indeed he did. What are these children called, and can you tell me what you know about them?"

"Well, sir, this little girl is Amelia Carter, and her twin brothers are Joseph and Matthew, though which is which I never can tell. I'm afraid I know little more about them, except that they arrived by stagecoach with their father and stepmother to stay at our inn a week or two ago, as I understand it, en route to China. Unfortunately, their father was taken ill and died, and their stepmother went out one day and never returned. They're unable to tell me where they're from or where their relatives live, though they have mentioned grandparents, aunts, and uncles, who live a long way off near the sea."

"I see. Well, as the police cannot trace their relatives, we can take care of them here. If you'd like to say goodbye to the children, Mrs Drew, I'll get Matron to see to them."

"If it's all right with you, sir, I thought I'd stay a little while to help them get accustomed to their new surroundings because they're a bit nervous like you'd expect. Could I see where they will be sleeping? I've brought their spare clothes, and Amelia goes nowhere without her dolly."

"No, I'm afraid you must bid them farewell here. Prolonging the matter only worsens the situation, and you can rest assured they will be cared for. Children say goodbye to this kind lady, and we'll get you settled in."

Betty looked down at three sets of wide, frightened eyes. She put her arms around them all and drew them to her.

"Now then, Amelia, and you too, Joe and Matthew, I have to go back and help Mister Jim now, but you'll be all right here. Mr Parsons will care for you now, and I expect there will be lots of other children to play with. Amelia, here's your dolly; keep her with you, and cuddle her when you go to bed tonight. I'll come back and see you one day to see how you're getting on."

The children clung to Betty, and Amelia started to sob. Fortunately for Mr Parsons, Florence Williams, the matron, arrived and immediately took charge of the situation, for she had seen it all many times before.

"Right, that's enough now. Come along, children, wave goodbye to this lady, and come with me."

She positioned herself between the children and Betty and briskly marched them down the corridor. Mr Parsons took Betty's arm and skilfully steered her towards the door, ushering her out.

"I can see it pains you to leave the children, Mrs Drew, but they will soon forget you. I suggest you do not visit again, as it will upset you and them. Now, rest assured you have done all you can for them, and leave them safely in our hands."

Sadly, Betty retraced her steps down the drive and out through the large gates. Tears were running down her old cheeks, and she was still crying when she reached home.

The matron marched Amelia and her twin brothers down the long corridor and into a washroom, where she handed them over to a large woman. "Here you go, Nellie, three new arrivals for you."

Nellie took in their foreign appearance with a disapproving glance. Pursing her lips, she mumbled something to herself about there being enough poor in the country already, without half-castes adding to the problem.

"Now, I have to cut your hair and give you a wash, and then you'll put on some new clothes. Don't give me any trouble, because I haven't the time for it. Come here, lad, you can be first."

She sat Joe firmly on a chair and began cutting off his long curls. Tears shone brightly in his eyes, but he did not complain. When most of his hair was on the floor, Nellie took a razor and shaved his head. Matthew and Amelia stood close together and watched in horror. Their mother had loved their thick, curly hair. Nellie then beckoned Matthew.

"Come on then, lad, you next. Show your little sister there's nothing to be frightened about."

She pulled Matthew onto the chair, and he received the same treatment as his brother. By this time, Amelia's eyes were round with fear.

"Please don't cut off my hair. I'm a little girl, and girls don't have short hair. Please don't cut off my hair. My daddy loved my curly hair."

"Now, it's no use you making a fuss. Your daddy's gone, and you must do as you're told. Your hair will soon grow again, but this is the only way I can be sure you don't have nits. We have enough trouble with them, so sit still and be a good girl."

"I don't have nits. I don't have nits. My hair is clean."

Amelia had no intention of being a good girl, and she struggled and refused to sit on the chair. Nellie smacked her legs and tried to sit her on the chair, but Amelia was having none of it, and she kicked Nellie hard in the shins and bit her hand.

"Ouch, now look what you've done, you little devil; you've drawn blood." Nellie slapped Amelia hard across the side of the head, and she fell to the floor, stunned.

At this, Matthew and Joe leapt up and ran to her. "Come on, Meely. It will be all right. Let her cut your hair off, and then you'll look just like us. It's not so bad."

Nellie was furious. She dragged the dazed child to the chair and tied her to it with a bandage.

"Right then, madam, now you just sit still and let me cut your hair, or I'll give you such a hiding you won't sit down for a week."

Amelia sat still, tears rolling down her face, and decided she would hate this woman for as long as she lived. When their hair was cut, the children were taken to the pump and made to stand underneath the stream of cold water. By the time Nellie allowed Amelia to get dried, she was shaking with the cold and fright. The new clothes that their daddy had bought them were taken away, and in their place, the boys were given rough grey tweed shorts and a coarse shirt and jersey. Amelia was given a grey woollen dress with a white apron. Amelia's doll lay on the floor next to her clothes, and she eyed it wistfully, debating whether to risk picking it up. Just as she was plucking up the courage to grab the doll, another maid appeared.

"Ah, there you are, Lizzie, just in time. Take these three to the refectory, will you, though this little madam is not to have any tea. Bit me, she did. She's lucky I don't have her beaten. Put their clothes in the storeroom; fine quality they are and should fetch a few bob. That doll, too."

Lizzie gathered up their clothes and the doll and led the children away. Amelia pulled at Lizzie's arm.

"Please, may I have my dolly? I always sleep with her. Please, may I have my dolly? My aunty made her for me."

Lizzie looked down at the small, tear-stained face, the bright red finger marks still vivid across her bald head and cheek, and could see what had happened.

"Well, now, little girl. You won't be able to keep your dolly. Even if I let you keep her, the bigger girls would take her off you in no time, and you'd never see her again. I'll tell you what, though, how about if I keep her for you, and maybe, just maybe, I might be able to let you see her sometimes?"

Sadly, Amelia nodded. "Yes, please, she's called Evie after my aunty who made her."

"All right, now, will you behave yourself for me if I do that? It's not easy living here, but you'll get on better if you do as you're told. Here, give your dolly one last cuddle and say goodbye."

They entered a large room with long tables surrounded by seemingly hundreds of children, all dressed in the same clothes as themselves. The children were sitting silently, waiting for permission to start their meal of bread and dripping with a mug of water. A few looked up when Matthew, Joe, and Amelia were shepherded to the nearest table, but most showed little interest, for they were too intent on the food in front of them.

"Sit here for today, but tomorrow, you boys will sit on that side of the room, and you, young lady, will sit with the girls."

Amelia, miserable and hungry, reached for her thin slice of bread, but Lizzie swiftly took the plate away.

"There's none for you today, little girl. Nellie will check that I don't give you anything, so you must go hungry. The sooner you learn not to cross Nellie, the better, and don't you two even think of giving your little sister any of yours, or you'll be in trouble too."

CHAPTER 41

Robert felt even more unhappy after meeting with Annie in the churchyard. He now understood why she had married Harry in such haste but imagined images of the rape filled his mind, and he could think of little else. The thought of someone brutalising his beloved Annie was almost more than he could bear, and he was determined to find out who was responsible.

He knew he must be discreet but felt it would be safe to talk to Maisie, and when she came to make his bed after breakfast, he lay in wait for her.

"Hello, Maisie. I know you're busy, but I want to ask you something. I saw Annie the other day, and she told me how she was attacked and why she married Harry. I can see you don't want to talk about this, but I'm so angry that someone should do that to Annie, so please tell me. Do you know who attacked her?"

"No, sir, I honestly don't, and neither does Annie. Didn't she tell you what happened?"

"Yes, she did, but I wonder if she does know who it was and doesn't like to say?"

"No, I don't think she knows. She came to bed straight after the attack and was in a terrible state, but she definitely didn't know who did it. I'm sure she would have told me."

Robert could see she was telling the truth and left her to finish her work, but decided to talk to Mrs Potts. He found her in the kitchen, busy as usual, and asked if she could spare him a few minutes in private. She was somewhat surprised but agreed to take a short walk in the gardens with him.

"Mrs Potts, I'm hoping you can help me with something that's troubling me."

"Why, Master Robert, you know I would do anything for you. Just tell me what it is, and I'll gladly help."

"Well, I saw Annie in the churchyard on Sunday, and she told me what had happened. I understand why she married Harry Rudd, but I can't leave it there. I need to find out who did this and see they're punished."

"Oh, Master Robert, I'm sorry you've found out about this because I know you have feelings for Annie, but there's not much I can tell you. She was late for work that morning, which was unusual for her, and she had been beaten. She had a black eye and a split lip and looked terrible, but at the time, she insisted she had fallen and it was an accident. She didn't go home that week because she didn't want her mother to see her injuries and worry. It was only later, when it became apparent she was pregnant, that Maisie told me about the rape, but I have no idea who the culprit was."

"It just seems ridiculous that something like that could happen and for her not to know who it was."

"Yes, I know, but according to Maisie, it was dark in the cellar, and the man didn't speak out loud, so she couldn't identify him. I've tried to think who it might have been, but the trouble is the house was full of visitors at the time, and they had all seen Annie about her duties, so it could have been any of them. I suppose the obvious suspect is your friend, Frank because he tried to get the better of her before, but Annie seems to think she would have known if it was him."

"Well, he's no longer my friend, though I understand he's now keen on my sister, more's the pity. Is there anyone else in the house that might know more about what happened to Annie?"

"I don't think so, sir, and to be honest, even if you discovered the culprit, how could you prove anything? I'm sure it was none of the servants, for they all think too much of Annie, and if it were one of the young gentlemen, nothing would be done anyway. It's not the first time this kind of thing has happened in this house, I'm afraid. My advice to you is to try to forget it. It was a terrible thing to happen, but Annie is fine now. She's happily married to Harry Rudd, and I'm sure he'll treat the child as if it was his own because that's the kind of man he is."

"I suppose so, but if I ever find out who was responsible, there will be trouble. Thanks for talking to me about it, and if you ever hear more, please be sure to tell me."

"Of course, I will, sir."

"Now, shall we walk around the lake whilst we're here? I know you like that part of the garden."

"Well, I should get back, sir. I must get on with preparing the lunch."

"Never mind that you deserve a little break, especially as it's such a pleasant day."

Robert took the elderly cook's arm and walked her around the lake before escorting her back to the kitchen. He was frustrated that neither Maisie nor Mrs Potts could give him any information to help him find Annie's rapist, but he seethed with anger and was determined to find the culprit. He could think of no one else in the house who could help him, and after much thought, he decided to visit Frank Eastleigh and confront him.

Telling his parents he wanted a short break between finishing school and running the estate, he made plans to travel to London. As the journey would take so long by stagecoach, he travelled by train and left within the week. In such a short timescale, he had been unable to establish whether Frank was, in fact, at home but could not bear to wait for a letter to get there and back. He also suspected Frank might make excuses not to see him if he knew he was coming, for their last meeting had been far from friendly.

The journey to London went smoothly enough, and he took a room at an inn not far from Frank's residence. The next day, he presented himself at Frank's house and asked to see his friend. The butler led him to a grand drawing room where Frank stood by the fireplace wearing a puzzled expression.

"Well, Robert, I must say this is a surprise. After our last meeting, I thought our socialising days were over. What brings you here unannounced?"

"Yes, I can imagine this is a surprise, Frank, but I must ask you something. If our friendship ever meant anything to you, I hope you'll answer me honestly."

"All right then, what do you so badly want to know that you have travelled all this way to ask me?"

"On New Year's Eve, after the party, did you attack Annie again and rape and beat her?"

"What! Good Lord, you're besotted with that girl, aren't you? Why would it matter to you if I did?"

Robert moved towards Frank threateningly, and his former friend quickly held up his hands and stepped back a few paces.

"All right, if it means that much to you, then no, I didn't attack her, and I would certainly never beat a woman. I may take a few liberties now and then and possibly use a little more force than I should, but I have never hit a woman, I promise you. So, what's happened?"

Robert could see Frank was telling the truth, so he calmed down and told him what had happened.

"Well, I'm not altogether surprised, for she's a real beauty, but what you describe is not my style. The chase is part of the fun for me. I'm not at all secretive, and I would want a woman to know I had got the better of her, and as I say, I've honestly never hit a woman."

"All right, I believe you, but do you know who it might have been?"

"No, I'm afraid not. There were a lot of guests, and quite a few had a bit too much to drink. Does it matter?"

"Yes, of course, it matters. Annie's a friend of mine, and she became pregnant and was dismissed, even though none of it was her fault."

"Well, that is unfortunate, I agree, but you can't be sure the pregnancy is a result of that one night. Goodness knows how many men she had slept with before or after that night."

At this, Robert moved angrily towards Frank again, and the man continued rapidly.

"All right, I'm sorry. I can see this is a sore point, though I'm unsure why. Didn't I hear you've been running the estate since David's death and your father's stroke? If it means so much to you, give the girl her job back, and get the child adopted when it's born. Do whatever you need to do if it makes you feel better."

"Annie has married a local man, and they plan to pass the child off as his."

"Well then, what's the problem? A happy ending after all, though unfortunately, it means I'll never have my wicked way with her now, and that is a disappointment." Frank grinned but, seeing the expression on Robert's face, went on hastily. "Oh, I see, you wanted her for yourself, and now that's impossible. Is that it? Talk about the pot calling the kettle black."

This time, Robert leapt forward, grabbed Frank by the lapels of his coat and pushed him back against the wall. "If I ever find out this was you, Frank, you'll be sorry, but I believe you. While we're having this little chat, though, I'm warning you, if you marry my sister, make sure you treat her right because if you don't, you'll have me to reckon with."

Fortunately, Robert had just released the man when Lady Eastleigh entered the room, but she sensed some animosity between the two former friends. "Is everything all right? You both seem a little tense?"

"Yes, we are fine, Mama, thank you. Robert is in London on business and called to say hello, but he was just about to leave."

Robert exchanged a few pleasantries with Frank's mother and left as soon as possible. He remained in London for a few more days to make good his story of taking a break. He visited some famous landmarks, but his mind was in turmoil, trying to think how he could identify the rapist. On the train home, he realised he would have to take Mrs Potts' advice and try to put the matter behind him. However, he knew this would be difficult.

CHAPTER 42

Within a few days of returning home from London, Robert asked his mother for the keys to his father's desk so that he could go through the estate's finances. Eleanor reluctantly handed them over, feeling somewhat disloyal to her husband. However, she knew someone had to deal with the day-to-day business matters, for it had never been her forte. Robert pored over the books for a few days and was pleased to find that the estate was prosperous but then annoyed when he remembered the terrible state of the farm cottages.

Tentatively, he suggested that to manage the estate properly, he would need to take control formally. For Eleanor, this was a huge step and an acknowledgement that Charles would never fully recover. However, she knew this was the case, and together they visited Mr Billery, the bank manager, who agreed to carry out the necessary paperwork. Mr Billery was an old gentleman who had been in his job for a long time. Robert had met him once when, as a child, he had accompanied his father to town, and he now shook Robert's hand warmly.

"Hello, young man. My goodness, the last time I saw you, you were barely knee-high to a grasshopper. Your father is lucky to have you to take over and spare him the worry. I'm sure you're a great comfort to your dear mama, too, following the sad demise of young Master David."

"Thank you; yes, it's been a worrying time, Mr Billery. I never expected to inherit and certainly didn't want to under these circumstances. I hope I can count on your help, at least with the financial side of things?"

"You certainly can, my dear boy. I'll be only too pleased to advise you, for your family has dealt with this bank for donkey's years. I must say, you're the spitting image of your grandfather in his younger days. We were firm friends, and it was such a shame he died so young. Now, please sit yourselves down."

Robert and Eleanor surveyed the dusty room. The walls were panelled in oak and bore numerous shelves bowed under the weight of the books and papers piled on them. There were chairs around the room, but they were also laden with documents, maps, and books, and it didn't look as if the room had been cleaned for years. Robert swiftly held out the one empty chair for Eleanor and cleared one for himself, stacking the papers on the floor.

"Now, you just need to sign this document, Lady Fellwood, as we already arranged for you to deal with your husband's affairs when he first became incapacitated." Mr Billery pushed a document towards Eleanor. "How is Lord Fellwood, by the way?"

"He's made some small progress, thank you, though Dr Luckett thinks it unlikely he'll ever make a full recovery. It's been such a difficult time, with David getting killed and Charles being so ill. We're lucky to have Robert ready to take responsibility for the estate, but I am concerned he's too young. Ideally, Charles would have liked to continue for at least a few more years until David, or now Robert, was a little older."

"Well, he seems to be a sensible young man, and I am more than willing to provide advice should it be needed; you have only to ask. However, may I suggest that he only takes complete control when he reaches the age of twenty-one? That's what usually happens."

"Yes, that sounds like an excellent idea. Should Charles make a full recovery, then I'm sure he would want a say in matters, and what you suggest provides more time for that to happen. Thank you so much for all your help with this."

"It's a pleasure, Lady Fellwood, thank you. Now, Master Robert, please come and see me again in a week or two to sign some other papers I need to get drawn up."

Two weeks later, Robert revisited the bank to sign the necessary documents.

"I'd like to run a few ideas past you, Mr Billery, if I may. I plan to survey the tied farm cottages to see what repairs are required. Some of the dwellings are in a terrible state, and I think it makes sense to keep them well-maintained."

"Does your father know of your plans?"

"No, and I don't want to trouble him. He's ill, and to be honest, I know he would disapprove, so I don't want to upset him. I don't like doing this behind his back, but it's something I've wanted him to do for a long time, and he wouldn't hear of it. I want to do it for the sake of the inhabitants, but surely it must make sound business sense?"

"I can only agree with you, Robert". A small smile played around the bank manager's mouth. "I have often discussed this with your father but could never convince him to do the work. As you say, keeping the dwellings in good repair will save more expenditure later. The families concerned will be grateful and healthier if their roofs are not leaking. However, I'm afraid the repairs will be extensive, for nothing has been done since your grandfather died. We've had some harsh winters and wet summers for the last few years, making maintenance even more important. You remind me of your grandfather, I have to say; you even have his mannerisms. The tenants are fortunate you are of this mind."

"I've studied the accounts, and I think they're in good order, but I'm relying on you to advise me, Mr Billery. Can we afford these repairs?"

"Oh yes, indeed, young man, most certainly, and as you say, it would be money well spent."

"Excellent, because our herd would benefit from some new blood. I want to buy a bull for breeding and a few bullocks to rear for meat. I intend to buy only the best stock, so it might take some time, depending on what's available at the market. I shall attend the cattle market in Barnstaple with Jack Bater over the next few weeks to see what's on offer. I don't have his expertise when it comes to livestock, and I need to learn. What do you think?"

"I think that sounds sensible, sir. Your grandfather had an excellent eye for livestock, though your father preferred to leave that kind of thing to Jack, whom I must admit is efficient. However, there is nothing better than an owner being hands-on and dealing with these matters himself."

Robert shook Mr Billery firmly by the hand and thanked him for his advice, promising to return and let him know how his plans were proceeding.

The following day, Robert mentioned his plans to Jack, who frowned.

"Does your father know of this, Master Robert? He's never been keen to spend money on repairs."

"No, Jack and I doubt he would be this time, but there's no need to worry him with it. If he were well, I would discuss it with him, but then, if he were well, we wouldn't be having this conversation. With David dead and my father ill, I've inherited the estate and must do as I see fit. I've seen Mr Billery, and he approves of my plans, so I hope you will too?"

"Well, I'll be glad to see the cottages repaired, and that's a fact. They're in a terrible condition, and many of my friends live in them, but your father would never hear of it. He'll be annoyed when he finds out."

"I see no reason why he should ever find out. I sincerely hope he fully recovers, but according to Dr Luckett, it's unlikely. Anyway, we'll cross that bridge when we come to it."

The following Friday, Robert and Jack took the horse and cart to the cattle market in Barnstaple. They took Dodger with them in case they needed help getting the animals home. The market was on the edge of the town and next to the slaughterhouse. Many animals made the short walk from the market to the slaughterhouse, where they met their end and were then delivered to one of the butchers in the town. There were numerous pens housing the sheep, pigs, goats, and poultry, all of which were making a loud racket. The horses, cows, heifers, and bulls were in the larger fenced-off areas. The animals were driven into an arena so the farmers could view each animal and bid for it. Although Robert had visited the market before, he still marvelled at how quickly the auctioneers spoke as they tried to get the best price for each animal. It was as if they were singing the words.

Robert intended to buy at least half a dozen bullocks, but unfortunately, few of the beasts shown that day were of the quality he desired, and so, in the end, they only bought one. However, they also purchased a dozen goslings and a dozen ducklings, as Robert thought fattening them up for Christmas would be profitable.

"There's no rush, Master Robert. It's better to wait until the right beast comes along, and there's a market every week."

"Yes, I know you're right, Jack, and we'll try again next week as you say. As we only have one bullock, could you drive it home on your own, Dodger? We can take the ducks and geese on the cart."

"Aye, sir, I'll be fine. It's only twelve miles or so."

"Thank you, Dodger. Here, get yourself a pie to tide you over until you get home for your tea." Robert tossed a few pennies at him.

"Come on, Jack. Let's get some dinner in The Golden Fleece; we might as well make a day of it. I want to show my face and get to know a few people. We can load up the poultry after we've eaten."

Dodger enjoyed his pie, washed down with a half tankard of ale, and then went to collect the bullock. The drover helped him to get the animal onto the road towards Hartford. The bullock was glad to be out of the pen and set off briskly, forcing Dodger to jog to keep up. He puffed and panted, thinking he would be tired out long before he got even halfway home. However, they'd gone barely a mile when the beast slowed down. Another mile and Dodger had to start prodding it with his stick. The animal trotted on happily enough, and Dodger was pleased, for this pace suited him better. They went over a small bridge, and the bullock, smelling the water, rounded the bridge and stumbled down the bank to the water. It waded in, drinking deeply. Dodger let the animal drink its fill and then tried to shoo it back up the bank from the opposite side, but it ignored him.

Sighing impatiently, he removed his boots, tied the laces together, and slung them around his neck. He waded in, brandishing his stick menacingly. The bullock lumbered reluctantly up the bank, but instead of continuing along the lane, it lay down on the grass. Dodger could not believe it. He prodded it with his stick, but it completely ignored him. He decided to have a rest himself and get it moving in a little while. However, half an hour later, the bullock still refused to move, and Dodger was at a loss to know what to do. Then he spotted a gypsy wagon coming towards him. It was driven by an old man wearing a flat cap. The bright yellow wagon was decorated with hand-painted red flowers and green leaves. A dappled grey pony pulled it, and a small collie dog ran alongside. Dodger waved at the old man to stop.

"Hello, Mister. I don't know if you can help me, but I'm driving this bullock home from the market, and he's laid down and won't get up. Do you think you could try to get him moving?"

The man grinned, showing blackened teeth. "All right, lad, just let me pull in a bit, and we'll see what we can do."

The gypsy walked determinedly up to the animal and kicked its backside with his boot. "Come on, get up, you lazy bugger."

The bullock flinched and widened its eyes but didn't move.

"Hmm, a stubborn beast you've got there, and no mistake. He knows his own mind right enough, but there's one sure way of making him move, and I've never known this to fail."

He disappeared into the wagon and returned with a cup, which he filled with ice-cold water from the stream. He grasped the bullock's ear firmly, held it upright, and quickly poured in the cold water. The animal immediately leapt to its feet and ran down the road, fortunately in the right direction.

The old man doubled up with laughter as Dodger quickly ran after the bullock. The gypsy got back on his wagon and followed the boy and animal for a while, laughing whenever they came into view, for they were travelling faster than he was. It was with some reluctance that he turned off at the four-cross way, for the sight was entertaining. The bullock was no trouble for the rest of the way, except it was going faster than Dodger would like, and they completed the journey in no time.

CHAPTER 43

News of Robert's purchases soon reached his mother's ears, and she questioned him. "Robert, I hear you have bought a new bullock and some ducks and geese?"

"Yes, Mama, Jack and I went to the Barnstaple market. I wanted to buy half a dozen bullocks, but the rest were of poor quality, so we are going again next week."

"Is that necessary? I'm not sure your father would agree, and it doesn't do to spend too much money, you know."

"Mama, I know this is difficult for you, but if you want me to run the estate, I must do it my way and make my own mistakes. I've discussed my plans with Jack and Mr Billery, who both approve. I promise I won't waste money, but I've scrutinised the accounts, and we are a wealthy family; we can afford to spend some money, and, believe me, we need to. I'm going to buy some young bullocks and rear them for beef, and in a few months, we should make a decent profit. I'm also going to buy a bull because we've plenty of fertile grazing land, and I want to build up a new herd. Jack and I went to the Golden Fleece after the market and chatted to old Farmer Houle, Alfred Chugg, and one or two others. They were delighted to discuss farming matters and gave me some sound advice, all of which Jack agreed with. We'll fatten up the poultry for Christmas and sell most of it in the market. The ducks and geese won't cost much to keep because they eat almost anything, and there's plenty of waste from the kitchens."

"I just don't think your father will approve."

"Let's not tell him, then. Mama, I'm not intentionally trying to deceive him, but he isn't well, so why worry him? I don't think he'll ever be able to take control again, do you?"

"No, it's unlikely, but you won't get us into debt, will you, Robert?"

"I promise I'll discuss all my plans with Mr Billery, and you can talk to him yourself if you want to. We got on rather well, and he approved of my intention to repair the farm cottages. They're in a terrible state, and if something isn't done soon, I think some could fall down. If the dwellings are weatherproof, I'm sure there will be less illness amongst the workers, and it's the ideal time to do the work now during the summer."

Eleanor sighed, for she knew Charles would certainly not approve of this measure, and whilst she could see the sense of Robert's argument, she felt a traitor in not telling her husband what was going on. On the other hand, she could see there was no point in worrying him, so she nodded and smiled at her son.

Robert gave her a quick peck of a kiss on her cheek. "I'm going for a ride now, Mama, so I'll see you later. Jacko wandered off yesterday, and he still hasn't come home, so I want to look for him. It's not like him to stay out, and I'm a bit worried.

Sabina was washing some blankets that she hoped would dry quickly in the hot August sunshine. She was rosy-cheeked as she pounded the washing to get it clean, and wisps of her red hair and one or two grey ones were escaping from her bun. They had no spare bedding, so the opportunities to wash it were rare.

She was wringing out the last blanket to take to the mangle when Willie, Edward, and Mary appeared out of the woods. They were fresh-faced and tousle-haired from helping with the harvest for a few extra pennies.

"Hello, Mum, it looks like you're busy; will we have any blankets on our beds tonight?"

"Probably not, Mary, but it's so hot you won't miss them. They were filthy; see the colour of that water. We had such a rainy summer last year that I couldn't wash them, but thankfully, the weather is better this year. Have you finished carrying the straw?"

"No, not yet, but we're hungry. Can we have some dinner?"

"Well, there's fresh bread on the table and some dripping or a lump of cheese. Have some pickled onions with it, if you like. Liza made them with the shallots you grew at school."

"Lovely. I'm so hungry."

"Mary, you're looking a bit red; wear a bonnet when you go back out, or you'll be sore with sunburn. Willie and Edward, please wear your caps and roll down your sleeves to protect your arms. I'm afraid we redheads can't take the sun for long. I got badly sunburnt when I was a girl, and I can tell you it was extremely painful, so be careful."

As they entered the house, they heard the sound of a horse's hooves and turned to see who it was.

"Hello, Master Robert, what brings you here? I haven't seen you for a long time."

"Hello, Sabina. How are you?"

"I'm fine, thanks. Would you like a drink?"

"Yes, please, I'm hot and thirsty." Robert followed her into the cottage and explained he was looking for Jacko, who had been missing for a few days. None of the Carters had seen the dog but promised to keep a lookout for him. Stephen, Helen, and Danny were playing with some old wooden bricks, and Robert assembled the bricks into a tall tower and enjoyed the wicked glint in Danny's eyes as he quickly flicked out his arm and knocked them down. All three children laughed and, of course, wanted Robert to build them up again. Robert was pleased to see that Danny had recently started to crawl and was thriving.

"I'm so glad you're looking after him, Sabina, and I see Helen's walking now. I wonder if Danny ever will."

"Yes, I think he will. He's sturdy, and he can pull himself up and stand. Oh, be careful, Helen."

Walking near the table, Helen wobbled and bumped her head on the corner. She screamed, and Sabina picked her up and rubbed her head, where a lump was swiftly forming.

"Come on, it's all right. Let's rub some butter on it to make it better."

Helen had just settled down when Mary suddenly shrieked and leapt up from the table.

"Ouch, something stung me. Is it a bee or a wasp? Ouch, it did it again."

Sabina put Helen down and went to her other daughter. "Quickly, take off your top. It's all right; you've got something on underneath. Take it off, and let me have a look."

Mary quickly pulled off her smock, revealing a thin bodice underneath and kept her back to Robert. As she removed the garment, a wasp flew out and escaped through the open window. There were two bright red spots on her shoulder.

"There, it was a wasp." Sabina went to the larder and returned with half an onion. "Here, rub it with this; it's supposed to help."

"It really hurts; I've never been stung before." The tears were bright in Mary's eyes as she tried hard not to cry.

"There are several around now with so much fruit on the trees. Never mind; it will stop hurting soon."

Sabina hugged Mary and helped her to replace her bodice. She then turned her attention to Robert, who had continued playing with the younger children. "Was there anything I can help you with, Master Robert, or did you just call in to see Danny?"

"Oh, I nearly forgot. I'm having the tied cottages repaired. I'll call in again soon with Jack to survey the work that needs to be done."

"Oh, Robert, thank you; everyone will be so pleased. Some of the cottages are nearly falling down."

"I know, and it's high time something was done about it."

"I was sorry to hear about your brother and your father."

"Yes, it's been a difficult time, but at least now I'm in charge I can do some good, though I wish David were still with us."

A little later, Robert scoured the countryside for hours but did not find his dog. Dispirited, he returned to the Manor and entered through the kitchen, a custom that always annoyed his mother. However, Robert liked to chat with Ethel Potts when he could.

"Hello, Master Robert, there you are. It's nearly time for your evening meal, you know; I was just thinking you'd be late."

"Well, I am the squire now, Mrs Potts, so I should be able to come and go as I like." Robert held his head up in a haughty manner but smiled at the cook and winked.

"Aye, that you are, sir, but we all know your mother likes to think she's still in charge. Would you like a cup of tea?"

"Yes, please; I still haven't found poor Jacko, and I can't think what's happened to him. He's getting on a bit now, and it's not like him to wander off like this."

"Well, he might turn up yet; you never know."

CHAPTER 44

Annie saw Robert pass by on his way home from her mother's and wondered where he'd been. She kept out of sight, just peeping around the curtain. For his part, he looked straight ahead, ignoring the existence of the blacksmith's yard and the cottage beside it. She noted the determined set to his jaw. They had both taken great care not to let their paths cross and had not exchanged one word since that day in the churchyard months ago.

Harry was a kind, considerate man who adored her and would do anything to make her happy. Unfortunately, this was sometimes irritating because, try as she might, she could not feel the same way about him. She was fond of him, but he aroused no passion in her, and her greatest sadness was that he knew it, which made her feel guilty.

Harry could not resist glancing up at the bedroom window as Robert disappeared from view. He knew he would see Annie gazing out, and he gave a deep sigh as he saw that, once again, he was right. Annie quickly drew back from the window, annoyed that Harry had seen her. As he returned to work, he saw his father, Ben, leave the house and walk to the garden gate.

"Hey, Dad, where are you going?" Ben ignored his son, unlatched the gate, and started down the lane towards the village.

Harry ran after him and took his arm gently. "Dad, where are you going? You've no shoes on, look. You'll hurt your feet. Come on, Dad, let's get you back inside."

"Get off. I'm going to the inn. Leave me alone."

"All right, Dad, I'll take you to the inn, but let's get your shoes first. Come on."

Firmly, he propelled his father back towards the house. Matilda came downstairs carrying some dirty washing.

"What's the matter?"

"Dad was off to the inn, Mum, but he's forgotten his boots."

"What are you thinking of Benjamin Rudd? You don't go to the inn at this time of day, certainly with no shoes on."

"Well, I don't know how I forgot my boots."

Matilda and Harry exchanged concerned glances. Ben had been forgetful for a while and behaved strangely recently. He stared at regular customers as if he had never seen them before and forgot people's names. That was bad enough, but the other day, he had carefully carried a bucket of water to the bedroom and poured it all over the bed. Matilda had been furious and shouted at him, but then realised he was just as bewildered as she was and had no idea why he had done such a thing. Other incidents had followed, and today, he had gone out with no shoes.

"I think Doctor Luckett should look at you, Dad. You don't seem yourself."

"Ah, I'm all right, just getting old, that's all. Is it time for tea yet?" He had forgotten all about the inn.

"Aye, nearly, Dad; I'll come in as soon as I finish this job."

Harry returned to work, and Evie called to him as she walked past the smithy.

"Hello, Harry. How are you? And how's Annie?"

"Hello, Evie. We're both fine, thanks, and yourself?"

"Yes, I'm well too, thanks, Harry."

Evie continued her walk to Fred's house. She saw him through the kitchen window, and he beckoned her to come in.

"Hello, Evie. It's nice to see you. Would you like a drink?"

"Yes, please, Fred, it's scorching out there today. How are you doing?"

"I'm all right, thanks, busy, but that's better than no work. I miss William now he's gone back to China."

"Aye, I wish he was still here, too. I can't believe Sarah married him and left him with those three little ones. What sort of a woman does that? He can't even take another wife now. I shall give her a piece of my mind when I see her, I can tell you, but I think she's keeping out of everyone's way."

"Yes, it's disgraceful. She always knew William planned to return to China. Anyway, what would you like to drink? I have some cider in the larder, or I can make you a cup of tea."

"Well, I must admit the cider sounds good. Will you join me in a glass?"

"I don't see why not. We could sit outside in the shade."

Fred busied himself, pouring them a glass of cider each, and together, they carried the drinks to a bench under his apple tree.

Evie took a sip of her drink and murmured her approval at its taste. "How's Lucy? Any chance she might come home soon?"

"I don't think so; she barely knows me. She stares into space and ignores me. Sometimes, there is just a flicker of recognition when I walk in; otherwise, I think I'd stop going, but I can't, you know? We had some happy years together, and I love her, so I can't just abandon her. It seems pretty hopeless, though, and to be honest, if she did come home, how could I leave the children with her after what she did? I was getting ready to visit her; would you like to come?"

"Oh, I don't know, Fred. Would they let me in?"

"Yes, I think so. They don't encourage visitors, but maybe she'd speak to you."

"Well, I do feel sorry for her."

"So, will you come? Please, Evie? I hate going there, and I'd be glad of your company."

"All right then, but I must tell George because I only nipped out of the shop for some fresh air during my lunch break. He probably won't be pleased, but never mind, eh."

"Shall we take the pony and trap, or do you want to ride? It's about ten miles, but the evenings are light, so it won't matter what time we get back."

"All right, I'll tell George, and then I'll get changed at the inn, and we'll ride. It should be most enjoyable on a day like today."

Evie drained what was left of her cider, then hurried off to George's shop. As she suspected, he was not best pleased but could see she was determined to go. He was slightly mollified when she promised to go to work early the following day. By the time she returned to Fred, he had saddled the horses, and they set off in high spirits. However, when the asylum came into view, they would both have liked to turn back. It was an imposing building, and the sight of it raised the hairs on their necks. They dismounted, and Evie glanced anxiously at Fred. He smiled at her and winked.

"Come on. I promise I won't leave you in there."

"Oh, Fred, that's not even funny. Poor Lucy must have been terrified when you left her here."

"Aye, she was. Come on, then, let's get it over with."

Fred rang the doorbell and gave his name to the maid. She showed them to a waiting room and said she would fetch the doctor. Fred was surprised, for usually, trying to speak to a doctor was incredibly difficult. They waited twenty minutes before a middle-aged man with greying hair entered the room.

"Mr Carter, how do you do? My name is Doctor Maloney, and I've been looking after Lucy for the past few weeks. Who is this?"

"This is my sister, Evie. I thought it might be beneficial for Lucy to see someone other than me. She's been so withdrawn for the last few months; it's difficult to get any response from her."

"Indeed. Good afternoon, ma'am. I have to say it is most fortunate that you have accompanied Mr Carter here this afternoon, as I have some sad news. I'm sorry to tell you that your wife has passed away. I was making arrangements to contact you, as it only happened during the night."

"What do you mean? She wasn't ill, except in her mind, was she? What happened?"

"I'm afraid your wife took her own life. It was completely unexpected, I must say. I've been carrying out some new treatments on her recently and had high hopes of improvement, but it's difficult to predict what is going on in the mind of one so ill."

"How did she…?"

"She somehow got hold of a knife and cut her wrists. We will, of course, be investigating how this happened, but deranged patients can be so devious."

"Did no one check on her through the night? You were supposed to be looking after her."

Fred's voice shook with emotion as he tried to keep his temper.

"Well, there was no need. Lucy was locked in a cell alone, and there was no reason she should come to any harm. We've kept her isolated for several weeks, as she had become violent towards the other patients, not to mention the staff. Why, she even bit me last week, and I still bear the tooth marks." Doctor Maloney displayed a circle of bruises and teeth marks on his hand.

"Can we see her, please?"

"Are you sure you want to?"

"Of course, I want to see her. She's my wife, and I have to say goodbye."

"Yes, of course. I'm sorry, but I should warn you that some treatments we use can leave marks. It's nothing serious, but her appearance may not be all you would hope for, and, of course, she did bleed to death."

Fred put a hand over his eyes, and Evie took his arm. "Steady, Fred".

"Just take me to her, man, and save your excuses."

A nurse escorted them to a side room. The body lay on a table and was covered by a sheet. The nurse reached for the top of the sheet, and at a nod from Fred, she slowly pulled it back. Neither was prepared for the sight that greeted them.

"Oh, my God; what have you done to her?"

Lucy was once pretty, with dark curly hair, laughing eyes, and a fair complexion. She had been slightly plump but was now little more than skin and bone. Her head was shaved and covered with burn marks; her cheeks and eyes were sunken, and her skin was the colour of parchment. She was naked, her ribs stuck out painfully, and there were livid bruises on her torso and upper arms. Two gaping, bloody cuts ran across each wrist.

Evie, too, gasped. "When did you last see her, Fred? Was she like this?"

"No, but she was clothed, of course, so I couldn't see how thin she was, and she was wearing a mob cap so that I couldn't see her head, but no, she didn't look anything like this."

"When did you last see her?"

"Well, I suppose it could be six weeks ago because they didn't like me coming too often. They said it unsettled her for days, and what with working all the hours God sends and trying to help Mum with the little ones..." Fred's voice trailed off, and he held his head in his hands. "God forgive me. How could I have let her get to this? My poor darling."

Silently, he stroked her white forehead and kissed her blue lips tenderly. Evie put her arm around him.

"Come on, Fred. You did all you could for her, and now you must say goodbye. Do you want to be alone with her for a few minutes?"

He nodded, and Evie waited outside. He came out looking shaken.

"I want another word with that doctor before I go."

They knocked on the door of the doctor's office, and he bade them come in.

"Mr Carter, ma'am, please accept my condolences. I'm so sorry you had such sad news to greet you."

"Never mind all that. What have you been doing to my wife? Have you seen the state of her? She's as thin as a rake; she looks half-starved, and she always liked her food. What are the burn marks on her head? Have you been torturing her?"

"Now, Mr Carter, naturally you're upset, and I agree her appearance is disturbing; that of the dead often is, but no, of course, we haven't tortured her. The results of the new electrical treatment have been promising, but unfortunately, it can cause minor burns. As to how thin she is, I'm afraid Lucy has been difficult to manage recently. She's been violent to the staff and other patients and was resisting treatment, so on some occasions, her food was withheld, but not without justification, I assure you. As I mentioned, she even bit me last week."

Fred was on his feet. He grabbed the doctor by his collar and pinned him against the wall.

"Those are not minor burns, and I'd say she's not eaten in weeks. You should be ashamed of yourself, and I think you've been experimenting on her."

"No, I can assure you the treatment we use is recognised in many asylums as being efficacious, and she has missed no more than the odd meal, though she has often refused to eat. Now, take your hands off me; this is not helping. Would you like us to arrange the funeral for you, Mr Carter?"

"No, I would not, and the sooner I can remove her from this hideous establishment, the better. I wish I'd never allowed her to come here."

"Well, as you know, it was that or the jail."

"Just get out of my way before I hit you. I'll hire a cart and return within the hour, so please make sure her body is ready."

"As you wish." Doctor Maloney spoke coldly.

Fred and Evie rode into town, where Fred hired a cart. They returned to collect Lucy's body and take her home for the last time. They spoke little on the journey, Evie sensing that Fred wanted to be alone with his thoughts, and when they got home, he went straight to his shed.

"I keep a coffin or two made up in case they're needed in a hurry, but I never dreamt this one would be for my Lucy."

Together, they bathed Lucy's emaciated body and put her in her best dress. Evie found one of Lucy's bonnets and put it on her head to cover the angry weals. They placed her gently in the coffin and stepped back to see how she looked.

"There, that's better, Fred. She looks much nicer now, doesn't she?"

Fred couldn't answer but nodded, and together, they went to the inn to tell Betsey and Ned.

Betsey put her arms around her son. "I'm so sorry, Fred. Stay here tonight, lad. You'll have to tell Llewie, and he'll be upset, but the little ones are too young to understand."

"No, I'll tell him tomorrow. Tonight, I'll stay at the cottage with Lucy. I'm not leaving her alone; she's had enough of that, and it's the last thing I can do for her."

"Of course, if that's what you want. Fred, you mustn't blame yourself for any of this. There was nothing you could have done differently, and though I'm desperately sorry for what's happened, I can't help but be glad God has shown mercy and that poor lass will suffer no more."

"Well, I suppose there is that to it, but I always hoped she might get better. I'll have to get the ferry to Wales and tell her family tomorrow."

"Right, have a bite to eat, and then go home and spend some time with her. The funeral arrangements and everything else can wait until tomorrow."

CHAPTER 45

Lucy was laid to rest a few days later, and the wake was held at The Red Lion. The inn was crowded, for although Lucy had kept much to herself, Fred was well-liked. Many villagers attended the funeral to show their support for him, and some of Lucy's own family had travelled from South Wales. A man entered the inn and squeezed through the crowd to get to the bar. Betsey glanced up from pouring a pint of ale and then looked again.

"Why, it's Bill, isn't it, our William's friend?"

"Aye, that's right, Missus. It's nice to see you again, though I wish it were under happier circumstances."

"Why, what's wrong?"

"I was in these parts again and wanted to offer my condolences. I'm so sorry for your loss."

"That is kind of you, but I didn't know you'd even met Lucy. It's a sad business."

"I don't know anyone called Lucy. Oh, is it her funeral today? Is that why the inn is so busy? No, I've come about William."

"What do you mean, you've come about William? The ship got to China all right, didn't it?"

"Is there somewhere we could talk more quietly, perhaps with your husband?"

"Aye, of course, come through." She shouted to Ned and asked Evie to keep an eye on things.

Once they were sat in the back parlour, Bill looked at them solemnly. "I'm so sorry, but I thought you must know by now that William passed away. Didn't his wife tell you when she returned with the children?"

"What? No, you're mistaken. Sarah changed her mind about going to China, but William sailed with the children, and he should be there by now."

"No, I'm afraid he didn't. I've been travelling on business, but I went to the Customs Office in London last week, and they told me about William dying. I understand the poor man was ill with pneumonia and never recovered. His wife reported the death to them and cancelled the voyage to China. I had to come to Devon again before I sailed to China, and you were both so kind when I called before that I just had to come and pay my respects."

"I don't understand why Sarah came back alone. She told me herself that he had sailed to China with the children. Why would she do that?"

"And where are the children? I'm going to her house to find out what's going on."

"Wait, Ned, I'm coming with you."

Ned opened his mouth to suggest Betsey stay at the inn, but one glance at her face told him he would be wasting his breath.

"Perhaps you should come too, Bill, so we can clear this up. I hope to God it's you that's got it wrong, Mister. It was hard enough waving William off to China, but I'd rather he was there than dead."

"Well, I wish I was wrong, but I'm afraid I'm not, and I'll gladly come with you."

They left by the back door so as not to attract the attention of the mourners, and as they went along the lane, Ned realised that Sarah had not attended Lucy's funeral as would have been expected. Sarah opened the door, and the colour drained from her face when she saw Betsey and Ned. Bill, she had never met.

"Sarah, this is Bill, a friend of William's, and he has some strange news. He tells us William died and never sailed to China. What do you have to say about that?"

"No, sir, you must be mistaken. William sailed with the children, and I came home because I couldn't face leaving England."

Betsey and Ned looked anxiously from Sarah to Bill, not wanting to believe their son was dead, but Bill spoke indignantly. "No, I'm sorry, but there's no mistake. The manager at the Customs Office told me you reported the death to him yourself, so what's going on? If the children are not here with you, then where are they?"

At this, Sarah began to sob, and her father stepped forward.

"Now then, lass, come on, out with it. I thought something wasn't right when you came home alone, and I want the truth. Just tell us what happened. You'd better come in; we can't sort this out on the doorstep."

"I'm so sorry, Betsey. I've done a terrible thing, and I'm so sorry."

"Never mind all that, Sarah, just tell us what's happened."

"Well, we stayed at an inn for a few days until the ship was due to sail, but William became so ill he couldn't leave his bed, and the ship sailed without us. He had a terrible fever, and I got a doctor for him. We did everything we could, but he died of pneumonia."

"Well, all right, that's not your fault, but where are the children?"

"That's just it. I couldn't cope with them. William had promised to get a nanny when we reached China. I did my best after he died, but they didn't like me, and I couldn't face bringing them up alone. That's why I decided to let you think he'd gone to China. He was never much of a letter writer, so I thought you'd just think he hadn't written."

"So, where are they? What did you do with them?"

Betsey grabbed Sarah by the shoulders. "Where are my grandchildren, you wicked girl? Where are they? William would have wanted them looked after."

"I left them with the innkeeper's wife, and I'm sure she'll look after them. Her own family had grown up and left home, and I could see she took to them, and they to her. I thought it was kinder to leave them where they were happy."

"How could you leave them all alone? You knew I would take them in if you didn't want them. What would William say? First, they lose their mother, and now their father, and you leave them with a stranger. Did you think so little of him that you couldn't care for his children after his death? You'd better hope they're safe and sound, or I'll swing for you. By God, I will."

Sarah did not attempt to fight back, and when Betsey released her, she sank to the ground. Her father had said little but now looked at his daughter with contempt.

"You can pack your bags and get out; you're no daughter of mine. Even I would never abandon three little children. Go on, get out, and don't come back."

"No, Dad, please, I've nowhere to go."

"No, and neither had those poor children, but you didn't worry about that, did you? Go on, get out. I never want to see you again."

"Please let me stay. I've regretted what I did ever since I got back, and there's something else you should know. I'm having William's baby."

"Are you sure, or are you just saying that so I'll let you stay?"

For an answer, Sarah pulled apart the light shawl she was wearing.

"See, I've been keeping it hidden, but you can see I'm telling the truth. Dad, please let me stay. You can't turn me out now, surely?"

"Well, I suppose not, but what about these children you left in London."

"Yes, where is this inn in London? We'll have to fetch William's children and woe betide you if any harm has come to them."

Ned glared at Sarah as she scribbled the address on a piece of paper and gave it to him sheepishly. She kept her eyes on the ground, and he snatched it angrily.

"Come on then, let's get home and decide who will go to London. You've not heard the last of this, my girl, and that I can tell you."

They returned to the inn and found Sabina was leaving with Willie.

"Oh, there you are, Betsey; I wondered where you were. I'm off to the smithy because Annie's baby's on the way. She didn't come to the funeral as she wasn't feeling well, and now we know why, but what's wrong? You seem upset?"

"Oh, Sabina, you'll never guess what terrible news we've had." Tears ran down Betsey's cheeks. "This is Bill, a friend of William's, who came to tell us that William died in London. He never went to China at all."

Sabina put her arm around the old lady. "But I thought Sarah said…?"

"Oh yes, that woman. She's a liar. It makes my blood boil to think about what she's done. She buried William in London and left his children with an innkeeper's wife. Anything rather than bring them up herself, and now she tells us she's having William's baby. I don't know; what a time we're having of it lately. First, we lose Tom and Alice, and now Lucy and William. Where will it end?"

"Betsey, I'm so sorry about William, and what will you do about the children? We'll have to find them, won't we?"

"Yes, of course, we will. I know it's what William would have wanted; he doted on those children. Someone will have to travel to London with Bill. He's kindly offered to help because he knows the inn where William and Sarah stayed. I hope the couple looking after the children doesn't want to keep them because they belong here with their family."

"I'd better go, Betsey; I want to see how our Annie is. Tilly's delivered scores of babies, but I'm her mum."

"Yes, of course; I hope it goes well for Annie; let us know, won't you?" Betsey forced a smile onto her face.

Sabina nodded as she released Betsey, and Ned put his arm around his wife and silently hugged her for a few moments before they both went inside the inn. His eyes, too, were bright with unshed tears.

"Hello, Sabina, thanks for coming; Annie hoped you would. I've been banished to wait down here, but if there's anything I can do, you will come and get me, won't you?"

"The best place for you is down here, Harry. Men are not welcome when babies are born; they just get in the way." She squeezed his arm as she passed. "It could be a while; it often is with first babies. Annie kept me waiting nearly two days before she put in an appearance. I didn't think she was ever going to be born."

Sabina went up the stairs and found Tilly sitting beside the bed, chatting with Annie.

"Hello, here's your mum; come to see how you're doing. I'll leave you two to talk whilst I get us something to eat. Would you like some supper, Sabina? I think the baby could be a while yet."

"No, I've just eaten at the inn at Lucy's wake, thanks, Tilly, and I've heard some terrible news. It seems our William died and never sailed to China. Sarah left the children behind in London and came home without them. There's all hell to pay now it's come out. Betsey and Ned are furious and determined to find their grandchildren. Oh, and the other news is that Sarah's in the family way, so more business for you, I expect, Tilly."

"If that's how she's behaved, I don't want anything to do with her. I suppose for the sake of William's baby, I might help, but what a thing to do."

Sabina chatted to Annie, holding her hand when the pains came, and by the time Tilly returned with a tray of food, her contractions were coming about every five minutes.

"Well, young lady, if you keep this up, it won't be long before you're a mother. Now, could you eat some supper, or maybe it would be best to get this over with first?"

"I can't eat, but I'll have a drink, please." Annie gasped as another strong contraction seized her body. "I need to push."

"Just let me look and see how you're doing; try to pant for a minute. That's it, hold on. Oh yes, you're right; I can see the head. When the next pain comes, you push as hard as you can."

Annie found the desire to push overwhelming and pushed as hard as she could. Her pains were coming rapidly now, and she felt she had never worked so hard.

"Is it nearly here?" She gasped. "How much longer will this take?"

"Well, it can take hours, especially with a firstborn, but I don't think it will be long now. Try to rest a little between contractions and save your strength." Tilly spoke reassuringly and glanced anxiously at Sabina, who seemed to be suffering as much as if she were giving birth herself. "I think your poor mother's in a worse state than you are. She's doing fine, Sabina. Don't look so worried."

Sabina smiled and winced as Annie squeezed her hand tightly in a vice-like grip, as another contraction contorted her body. However, a small and wrinkled little girl was crying lustily within the hour.

"My goodness, she's small, but what a pair of lungs, and she has a birthmark on her shoulder. There, see? Nothing to worry about, and at least it won't show. Not like it's on her face." Tilly expertly tied and cut the cord, wrapped the baby in a sheet, and handed her to Annie.

"There you are, my love. What a gorgeous granddaughter you've given your Mum and me, and so quickly, too. Sabina, she puts us to shame; it must be a record time for a firstborn. Fancy us being grannies, eh Sabina? I'll get Harry."

Harry had heard the baby's cries and was already outside the door. He went to the bed and took Annie in his arms.

"Are you all right, Annie?"

"Yes, of course, I'm all right, Harry. What do you think of our little daughter?"

Only now did Harry bend over the tiny bundle in Annie's arms and gently pull back the sheet. A big grin spread over his face as he gazed at the little girl.

"Oh, Annie, she's beautiful and has your hair. What shall we call her?"

"Well, if you don't mind, I'd like to call her Selina. What do you think?"

"Yes, Selina Rudd. Selina Matilda Rudd. What do you think, Annie? Could we give her Mum's name as a middle name? I don't think Selina Sabina would work, do you?"

"No, perhaps next time. Yes, I like the sound of Selina Matilda; that's what we'll call her."

CHAPTER 46

Sarah stayed inside the house for a whole week after the news about William's children came out. She was afraid to show her face, for she knew how the villagers would react to this kind of news. Her father was no comfort, for as far as he was concerned, she had brought it all on herself, and eventually, he lost patience.

"You have to go out sometime, so why don't you go to the shop and get some candles?"

"I'd rather not, Dad. Oh, all right, but if I don't come back, come and look for me, will you?"

She hurried to the shop, keeping her head down. She was aware of people glancing her way and whispering. She prayed the shop would be empty. However, Doctor Luckett was leaving, and Sabina was waiting to be served.

Sarah murmured, 'Good morning,' to the doctor, but he gave her a stern glance and walked past her with his nose in the air. Sensing a change in the atmosphere, Sabina turned around.

"I don't know how you have the cheek to come in here as bold as brass as if you've done nothing wrong. You should be ashamed of yourself, leaving those children with no one to turn to. How could you? Harriet, don't you dare serve her."

Harriet looked uncomfortable, but taking courage from Sabina's presence, she joined in.

"That's right, you can get out. I'm not going to serve you. Go on, get out."

Sarah turned swiftly on her heel, opened the door, and gasped in dismay. Outside, a small group of women was waiting for her, and clearly, the word was spreading, for more were arriving.

"What do you want with me? I've only come to buy candles."

A couple of the younger women moved closer and spat in her face.

"It's you, we want. We want to show you what happens to people like you. We know what you did, leaving those poor little ones behind with no one to turn to. How could you do it?"

"I left them with the innkeeper's wife because I knew she would care for them. They're better off with her; they didn't like me."

"You should have brought them back here to their family, and you know it. You even lied to Betsey about William dying; what a thing to do. Come on, girls, let's teach her a lesson she won't forget in a hurry."

They grabbed Sarah, punching and kicking her and pulling her hair as they dragged her through the village. Her father heard the commotion and looked out of the window. Horrified, he put his hands over his ears to muffle her screams. Eventually, they reached the village pond, and, with no hesitation, four of them took a limb each and threw her into the middle.

"No, don't, please don't! I can't swim."

They took no heed, and there was a huge splash as she hit the water. She sank and then came up, spluttering.

"Please, please help me!"

She sank again, and the women looked uneasily at one another. The water was deeper than they'd thought, and they began to worry now that she would drown. Annie was nursing her new baby near the bedroom window and saw what was happening. She ran downstairs shouting to Harry.

"Harry, quick, they've thrown Sarah into the pond, and she can't swim. Can you help her?"

"Serves her right, but yes, I suppose so."

He ran swiftly to the pond and jumped in and, with a few strokes, was beside the terrified woman. She grabbed wildly at him, almost pulling him under the water with her. He calmly slapped her hard across the face and hauled her to the water's edge, where he left her lying half-stunned and walked away without a backward glance. As the women walked away, one or two spat at her again. Sarah lay where she was and sobbed, and it was some time before she could muster enough strength and courage to get to her feet and stumble home. Her father said nothing but put a blanket around her shoulders and let her get to the fire to get warm.

News of the attack spread through the village and soon reached the ears of Betsey and Ned. They were glad Sarah had been taught a lesson, though Betsey hoped William's baby would be all right. Evie and Fred were to accompany Bill to London to find the children. Evie had been willing to go alone, but Fred wouldn't hear of it and insisted she would be safer if he accompanied her.

"Besides, Evie, I could do with a change of scenery. I know Lucy's not been living here for some time, but it's different knowing she'll never be coming back. Anyway, I owe it to William to find his children."

Evie and Fred travelled to London with Bill. Neither had been before and although they wished it was under happier circumstances, they were excited about visiting the big city. When they reached London, the number of people milling about in the streets fascinated them; there seemed to be thousands from all walks of life. Back home, you rarely saw a dozen people walking through the village unless it was market day.

Many children were running errands or selling matches and flowers, and small outstretched hands thrust their wares towards Fred and Evie when the stagecoach slowed momentarily. The children were dressed in filthy rags and looked half-starved. In contrast, many of the adults were wealthy, the ladies wearing elaborate bustle dresses in bright colours, the men in top hats and suits, with gold watches hanging on chains from their pockets.

On a street corner, two men were talking together, engrossed in their conversation, and Evie noticed a little girl of about five watching them. One of the men had a blue silk handkerchief poking out of his coat pocket, and the little girl was eyeing it up. Eventually, she made her move, skilfully stole the handkerchief without the man noticing, and ran off swiftly. Evie smiled at Fred, who had also seen the theft, and he grinned.

"Well, a girl's got to eat, and he can afford it."

As the stagecoach meandered through the streets, they saw sights they had only heard about, like St Paul's Cathedral, the Houses of Parliament, and Big Ben. They were amazed at the size and the number of buildings seemingly crammed so closely together, with no trace of a green field in sight. Eventually, the stagecoach reached the inn where William, Sarah, and the children had stayed. Bill introduced them to Betty and Jim and explained what had happened.

"What a thing to do," said Betty. "I couldn't understand what had happened to Mrs Carter when she never returned. We made enquiries and even called a policeman, but we couldn't find out what had happened to her. She told the man at the Customs Office that she was taking the children to Bristol to live with her family."

"So, where are the children, then? Are they all right?"

"Oh, my dear, I'm so sorry, but they aren't here. We couldn't keep them, you see, although we wanted to. Oh dear, I've felt so guilty about it ever since. I'm so sorry."

"So, where are they?"

"I took them to Moorfield Workhouse, and I cried all the way home, but we felt we were too old to take on three youngsters at our time of life; it takes us all our time to run this place."

"That's all right, Betty, we understand. Is it far to Moorfield?"

"No, it's not far, but please have something to eat first. It's getting a bit late, so perhaps it would be best to leave it until the morning? You must be tired after such a long journey, and they might not let you in at this time of day."

"Thank you, but I think we'll go now; we want to see the children as soon as possible."

Betty directed them to the workhouse, which was only a fifteen-minute walk from the inn. It was easy to find, and, like Betty, they found the exterior of the building depressing. They felt anxious as they waited until a young maid opened the door.

"We'd like to see whoever is in charge, please. Our niece and two nephews were brought here a couple of months ago, and we want to take them home to live with us."

"I'll see if Matron can speak to you because Mr Parsons, the Beadle, isn't here now."

With this, she turned on her heel and left them sitting on the same bench where Betty had waited with Joe, Matthew, and Amelia. It was half an hour or so before the matron graced them with her presence.

"Good evening, I'm Florence Williams, the matron. How can I help you?"

"Well, our brother, William, came to London a few months ago and died of pneumonia. He was staying at an inn, and Betty Drew, the owner's wife, brought his three children here because she could not contact his family. We come from Devon and have only recently received news of his death. We want to take our nephews and niece home with us."

"I'm afraid you'll have to return tomorrow when Mr Parsons is here. I do not have the authority to release the children into your care. What are their names?"

"Joseph and Matthew are twins, and their sister is Amelia Carter. If we can't take them tonight, could we see them? I'd like them to know we're here to collect them."

"No, that's out of the question, but if you care to come back at eleven o'clock tomorrow morning, Mr Parsons should be able to see you."

Fred and Evie were disappointed, for they longed to see the children, but Fred thanked the woman for her time, and they returned to the inn and told Betty what had happened.

"Maybe I should go with you tomorrow, just in case there's any problem. After all, it was me that handed them in."

"Thank you, that might be best, Betty. With so many children to care for, you'd think they'd be glad for some to be taken in by relatives, but you never know."

The following day, Mr Parsons listened to their story and vaguely remembered Betty handing in the children. He warned them the children could not be returned to the workhouse. If they were from a Devon village, that parish was responsible for their care. Fred and Evie assured him that was not a problem, and he asked the matron to fetch the children.

What a shock they had when the children walked into the room. Fred and Evie could hardly believe they were the same children they had waved goodbye to just a few months ago. Their hair was only an inch long, even Amelia's, and they had lost a lot of weight. Their limbs stuck out of their coarse clothing like sticks, and Matthew was sporting a nasty black eye. They stood silently, their hands folded and their faces downcast, avoiding eye contact.

"Good heavens; what have you done to them?"

Evie rushed over and knelt before them. "Joey, Matt, and Amelia; It's Aunty Evie. Do you remember me? I made you a dolly, Amelia, and gave you boys some sweets; do you remember?"

Amelia gave a huge sob and hugged Evie, who put her arms around all three children and pulled them close. She drew back to look at them.

"We've come to take you home to see Nanny Betsey and Grandad Ned, and Aunty Sabina, and everyone. Would you like that?"

Joe found his voice first. "Oh yes, please, Aunty Evie. Can we go right now?"

"I think we arrived none too soon," said Fred. "Look at the state of them. Do you feed the children in your care, Mister?"

"Of course, we do, Mr Carter, but there are hundreds of children here. They're lucky to have been looked after at all, and you'd do well to remember that."

"Aye, well, I feel sorry for the poor little blighters still here. Do they have any belongings to take with them?"

"No, anything of value is sold to help towards their keep, and we provide a uniform."

"What about my dolly? You know, the one you made for me, Aunty Evie."

"No, your doll will have been sold," said the Matron, with some satisfaction.

"No, she's not! Lizzie's looking after her for me. Please, can I have my dolly?"

Mr Parsons looked at the matron with cold eyes. "Please ask Lizzie Bevan to come here, and if she has this child's doll, to bring it with her."

Lizzie appeared carrying the doll and looking apprehensive. The Beadle nodded to her to give the toy to the child, and Amelia took the doll in delight.

"Oh, thank you, Lizzie. Thank you for keeping her safe for me."

"Why was this doll not sold? You know the rules, Bevan."

"I'm sorry, sir. The little girl was so upset at being separated from her brothers that I said I would keep it in the storeroom and let her see it sometimes. I'm sorry, sir, but I thought it could be sold later."

"Indeed, well, I'll leave Matron to deal with you, but this must not happen again. Do you understand? That doll would have fetched a good price."

Fred listened to all this and reached into his pocket for a couple of shillings.

"Here, take this for the doll, but promise me you will not punish young Lizzie. It sounds like she's the only one here to have shown any kindness to my niece."

"Very well, but Bevan, never let this happen again."

"Come on, then, children, it's time for us to go," said Evie. "Thank you for being kind to Amelia, Lizzie."

When they arrived back at the inn, Betty fed the children a meat pie. They fell on the food as if they hadn't eaten anything as tasty since they last sat at her table, and, in truth, they hadn't.

CHAPTER 47

They let the children rest for a day or two before travelling home. Bill had already taken his leave, as he was due to sail to China. They thanked him warmly for his help; without it, they might never have seen the children again. Betty led them to William's grave in Highgate Cemetery, where the children said goodbye to their father, and Fred arranged for a stonemason to erect a gravestone. He asked Betty to send word by the stagecoach driver to let him know when the work had been completed.

A few days later, they returned to The Red Lion Inn with a warm welcome from Betsey and Ned and a hot meal. As they chatted, they realised they must decide what would happen in the future, and Fred took the lead.

"Right, now listen up. I gave this a lot of thought on the way home from London, and I have a suggestion. It's not only Joe, Matthew, and Amelia to consider here; it's Llewie, Rosie, and Eddie, too, so we have six children to care for. Mum and Dad, you've both been as good as gold caring for my three, but I know it's too much for you, and you can't possibly take on William's three children as well. Now, it would be a bit of a squash, but I wondered if you, Evie, would like to come and live at my cottage and look after all of us? I could take on more work if I didn't have to worry about the children, and you seem so fond of them all; what do you think? You'd have to give up working in George's shop, of course, but I might be able to afford some help for you once I get the business on its feet again. It's suffered since Lucy took ill."

"I think that's the perfect answer, Fred. You have four bedrooms anyway, so one for you, one for me, then one for the boys, and the other one for the girls. I'll never marry or have a family now, but this would be the next best thing. I think it's a great idea."

Betsey smiled with immense relief. She was not far off seventy, and the thought of raising six children had kept her awake at night.

"George will miss you in the shop, Eveline, but he must find someone else. At least you've spent a few months with Harriet, so she knows the ropes. You never know; perhaps Mary Ann could go back there to work part-time."

"I doubt Mary Ann will want to do that, especially now they're getting married soon. I think she was relieved to escape from the shop in the first place."

George had been courting Mary Ann for several months, discreetly at first, then gradually more openly. Surprisingly, considering she had been treated as a hired servant before her sister's demise, Mary Ann had kept George firmly in his place, allowing him no liberties, and he began to realise that she had a more forceful personality than his former wife. However, it was just over a year since Alice had died from diphtheria, and he had recently proposed. The wedding was to take place in a few weeks.

The next day, Fred helped Eveline move her things to the cottage. The children were excited, and for Joe, Matthew, and Amelia, it was a dream come true after the trauma of living in the workhouse. They savoured every mouthful of every meal and left nothing on their plates.

Eveline went to have a word with George at the shop. He had not wanted her to go to London, and it was apparent that, as far as he was concerned, the children could have stayed there despite the fact they were his brother's offspring.

"Hello, Eveline, I'm glad you're back safely; did you find the children all right?"

"Yes, we did, thanks, George; they were in the workhouse and are in a sorry state, but no doubt they'll pick up with care and plenty of food."

"What will happen to them now you've brought them home? I'm sure William would be grateful if he knew, but surely, it will be too much for Mum to raise them and Fred's three children?"

"Yes, of course, it will, but Fred came up with a solution last night. I'll move in with him and the six children and look after them all."

"You'll never manage all that and work here in the shop."

"No, and that's why I've come to see you; I'm going to stop working in the shop and concentrate on looking after the children. They've all lost their mothers and Joe, Matthew, and Amelia, their father, too. They need someone to love and care for them, and I'm looking forward to it."

"You can't be serious? What do you know about looking after children? It's not as if you've ever had any of your own?"

"No, and that's exactly why I'm looking forward to it, George. I've thought about it carefully, and I'm sure this is the right thing to do."

"But, Eveline, I need you here. When you're here, I can safely leave everything to you. I'll never find someone as reliable and trustworthy as you. Please think again."

Eveline smiled, for she had expected this reaction from George. How typical of him to think only of the inconvenience it would cause him if she left the shop. He gave no thought about her happiness or that of Fred and the children. She knew her worth, and he was right; he would not replace her easily. Paying her a better wage over the years wouldn't have hurt him.

"Yes, you will miss me, George, but my mind is made up. I'm sorry it's short notice, but I'm moving into Fred's cottage with the children today, so I've come to stock the larder. How are the wedding plans coming along, by the way? Only a couple of weeks now, isn't it?"

George was silent for a moment, a deep frown upon his face. "Oh, Evie, I wish I could persuade you to change your mind. Yes, the wedding plans are all in place, but without you, I don't see how we can have a honeymoon, and we had planned to go to Cornwall for a week. Could you delay your plans until after the wedding?"

"No, I'm sorry, George, but the children need looking after now. Perhaps Harriet could manage if you got her some help? I'm not far away, so she can always ask me if she's not sure about something."

"Maybe; I'll think about it."

Eveline was still amused as she carried her shopping back to the cottage and told Fred what had happened.

"That's typical of George. He's always thinking of himself, but Mary Ann could return to work until they find someone else. I'm so glad you liked my suggestion, Evie. Knowing the children are well cared for will be a relief. I've not had my mind on my work for a long time. After we've had a bite to eat, I thought perhaps we'd visit Sabina and tell her our news. We'll send the children to school tomorrow, and I'll get back to work, but we'll spend today tying up a few loose ends."

Naturally, Sabina was thrilled to see the children again and hugged them all.

"I'm so pleased to see you, and this is just what your daddy would have wanted: you living with your Aunty Evie and Uncle Fred. "She picked up the little girl. "And you, young lady, must grow those pretty curls again."

She spoke quietly to Fred and Evie. "Looks like you found them just in time; what a state they're in. Never mind, they'll soon put on weight with plenty of food."

Whilst they were at Sabina's, Annie arrived, pushing Selina in the new pram Harry had bought for her. The baby was thriving, though Annie was looking tired. The children took turns holding the baby until she'd had enough and started to cry.

"She's hungry, so I'll feed her before I go home and get Harry his tea."

"Is she good?"

"Well, Uncle Fred, if you mean does she sleep at night, then no, she doesn't. I've barely had more than two or three hours together since she was born. Now, all day long, oh yes, she'll sleep then, but at night she wants to play."

"I'm afraid you were no different, madam, so it's probably justice. Don't worry, sleep when she sleeps; at least you can do that with your first. You'll find it's not so easy when you've got two or three. She was early, too, so she needs regular feeds."

"How's married life then, Annie?" said Eveline. "Are you happy with Harry?"

"Yes, he's as good as gold to me, so I can't complain." She glanced at Sabina as she spoke and was rewarded with a knowing look. "We're worried about Ben, though. His mind seems to be going, although he's not that old. He wanders off and does strange things. He puts things where they don't belong and can't remember customers he spoke to just the day before. It's difficult for Matilda and Harry to keep an eye on him and Jacob. He's a willing lad but can't think for himself."

Eveline nodded. "Matilda mentioned Ben and his antics to me the other day, and I think it may run in the family. His father went the same way and handed the business over to Ben when he was quite young, and there's always been something not quite right with Jacob. Tuppence short of a shilling, my granny would have said. Not a nice thing to say, but it's true nevertheless."

Selina had been sucking hungrily at Annie's breast, and she put the baby over her shoulder to bring up her wind. The baby was promptly sick and then disgraced herself further by pulling an incredibly red face and filling her nappy. They all laughed and then moved away as an unpleasant smell emanated from the child.

"Oh dear, I ate some plums yesterday, which may be affecting my milk. This is the third dirty nappy I've had today." Annie started to change the baby. "Oh, you are in a pickle, young lady. I'll have to change everything you've got on this time. Thank goodness I brought some spare clothes."

Annie undressed Selina and laid her naked on a piece of blanket. Sabina fetched a bowl of water for her to clean the baby. As all this was going on, someone knocked on the door.

"Oh, now, whom can that be? I'd not seen anyone for days, and now everyone is visiting. Oh, it's Master Robert; I wonder what he wants.

"Hello, Sabina. Jack and I are surveying the cottages to see what needs repairing. I hope it's convenient?"

"Why, yes, of course, come in, Master Robert, though I have rather a houseful at the moment."

"Goodness me, what's the occasion? Shall I come back later?"

"No, it's fine, Master Robert. We were going anyway." Fred got up from his chair.

"Are you sure? I can easily do the other cottages and come back later?"

"No, please come in, sir. We're delighted you will repair the cottages, and goodness knows they need it."

"Oh, hello, Annie, this must be the new baby, then? What's she called?"

Annie blushed at the sound of Robert's voice, a matter not unnoticed by her mother.

"Yes, this is Selina. I'm afraid she's got herself into a bit of a state."

"And who are all these children? They can't all be yours, Sabina?"

"No, this is Llewellyn, Rosella, and Eddie, and they belong to my brother-in-law, Fred, and these three are Joseph, Matthew, and Amelia, and they are the children of my brother-in-law, William, though sadly he died recently. Evie and Fred have just collected them from London, and they are all going to live together in Fred's cottage. And, of course, you know my three youngest, Stephen, Helen, and Danny."

"Quite a gathering; I'm so sorry to intrude."

"No, it's fine. Have a chat with Annie, and I'll be with you in a few minutes."

Sabina went outside to say goodbye to her visitors, and Liza tactfully remembered something she had to do upstairs.

Robert squatted beside Annie and looked at her closely for the first time in months.

"Oh Annie, you're so beautiful, you've broken my heart, you know. Why didn't you wait until I got home before marrying Harry?"

"Please don't start all that again, Robert; you know it's no good. I've settled down with Harry, and you've got the estate to think about now. How is your father anyway?"

"He's a bit better, but he's still paralysed and can't speak properly, though he tries to write things down. How are you?"

"Yes, I'm fine, thanks; just tired. This little madam doesn't let me get much sleep. Right, let's get you dressed, young lady. Now you're clean again."

As Annie picked up the child to put her clean gown on, her back came into view, and Robert drew in his breath sharply.

"What's that on her shoulder?"

"Oh, it's just a birthmark; nothing to worry about. Why do you ask?"

"It's rather an unusual shape, and I just wondered what it was, that's all."

Annie lifted Selina's gown again, and they both peered at the reddish-purple birthmark.

"Tilly said it might disappear as she gets older, but I don't think it will. It doesn't matter anyway because it doesn't show."

As Annie finished dressing the baby, Sabina came back in. "Did you find your dog, Master Robert? I know you were concerned."

"Yes, I did, thanks, though not until the next day. I'd ridden for miles and was nearly ready to give up when I heard him barking. I followed the sound, and he had his front paw caught in a rabbit snare. He'd struggled so much the wire was embedded into his foot, and I thought he might bite me when I tried to remove it, but he just sat there with his tail wagging and let me free him. It's healing nicely now."

"Oh, that's good. Poor dog, I know people must catch rabbits, but they should check the snares regularly."

Sabina was anxious to give Annie and Robert as little time together as possible and suggested she take him upstairs to show him the leaking roof, the broken windows, and the rotten floorboards.

"Goodness. One thing at a time, Sabina; it was nice to see you, Annie. Take care of yourself, won't you?"

"Of course, you take care too, Robert. Right, I'm off, Mum; I'll see you tomorrow." She touched Robert's arm lightly. "Thanks for repairing the cottage."

"I always said I would if I had the chance, and now I have. Bye, Annie."

CHAPTER 48

It was mid-November, and Annie was sitting in bed feeding Selina, who was now six weeks old. The baby was sleeping better but still liked one feed during the night. Annie knew she spoilt her little daughter, never letting her cry for long. She ran immediately to her beck and call, for she wanted Harry to get his sleep because he worked so hard. His father was little help to him these days, and his brother, Jacob, needed constant supervision. She gathered her shawl around her, for it was cold.

"Come on, then, never mind all that smiling; we must get back to sleep."

Annie nuzzled the baby's soft neck as she put her over her shoulder and patted her back. Selina gurgled happily and gave an enormous burp.

"Oh, that's a big one."

Annie suddenly sniffed the air, for she thought she could smell smoke. Putting the baby back in her cot, she opened the window, and her heart sank, for next door, the smithy was alight, and the flames were licking at their cottage. She screamed, waking Harry and frightening Selina so that she started to cry.

"Harry, the smithy's on fire! See if Jacob and your mum and dad are all right."

Harry leapt out of bed and quickly pulled on his trousers, boots, and coat. He ushered Annie and Selina down the stairs and out of the back door. He told her to fetch help and then ran to the smithy.

The blacksmith's cottage and outbuildings were ablaze, and Harry quickly doused himself in water from the water butt. Wrapping a sack around his head, he ran up the burning stairs, but halfway, they collapsed, and he fell amidst a shower of flames and sparks. Hastily, he beat out the fire, taking hold of his trousers.

"Mum, Dad, Jacob, wake up. There's a fire; you must get out."

He heard something and shouted again; this time, he could hear his mother.

"Mum, go to the window, and I'll get a ladder."

His voice faltered as the smoke thickened, and he choked, unable to breathe. Coughing violently and tears streaming down his face, he ran to the shed to fetch a ladder. By this time, other villagers were coming to help, and Robert galloped up, having seen the fire from the Manor House. He leapt from his horse and shouted for buckets, which they filled from the village pond. They made a line, handing the buckets along swiftly and throwing the water on the flames, but the fire had a strong hold, and their efforts made little difference.

Harry raised the ladder to his parent's bedroom and started to climb, but Robert tried to pull him back. "Harry, you'll never get past those flames. Where are Annie and the baby?"

"Don't worry, they're safe."

Ignoring Robert, Harry ran up the ladder, and through the smoke, he saw the scared face of his mother peering through the window.

"Don't worry, Mum, I'm coming. Hang on."

He pulled his mother through the window and put her over his shoulder. He almost fell down the ladder in his haste, but willing hands took her from him and away to safety. He could hear her coughing as he hurried back up the ladder despite many protests that it was useless.

He reached the top and clambered through the window, falling over a body that lay just inside. Flames were creeping across the floor, and the thatched roof was burning fiercely. In the thick smoke, he could see nothing but realised it was his brother, Jacob. The body was heavy, and Harry struggled, gasping for oxygen. By this time, Robert, too, had climbed the ladder. He took Jacob from Harry and descended, calling Harry to follow him. The crowd below could see Harry at the window, his silhouette lit by the flames behind him, and they shouted to him to get out, but still, he hesitated, wondering if he could save his father. At last, he realised it was useless, but just as he raised his leg to climb out of the window, the entire floor gave way beneath him, and he was engulfed in the flames.

The villagers gasped, knowing there was nothing they could do to save the young man. They switched their attention to Harry's cottage next door, for there was no hope of saving the smithy. It was a race against time, for the wind was fanning the flames towards the cottage, and the heat was intense. They worked tirelessly, throwing bucket after bucket of water onto the fire, but eventually, they could see it was futile and that the fire would run its course and devour the cottage.

All this time, Annie watched anxiously. She had left Selina with Eveline and returned with Fred to help. She watched Harry descend the ladder with Matilda and went forward to help care for her. She screamed at him to come away, but he ignored her and returned to rescue Jacob. She could only watch in horror as she saw him fall to his certain death.

Kind villagers led her back to Fred's cottage, where they told Eveline what had happened.

"Is Fred all right?"

"Yes, he's coughing from all the smoke, and he's burned his hands, but he'll be all right."

They took Matilda and Jacob to the inn, where Betsey and Ned provided drinks for the firefighters. The Rudds were in a bad way, particularly Jacob, who was severely burnt and unconscious, though still breathing. Matilda was beside herself with worry about Ben and Harry, and the neighbours promised to bring her news as soon as they knew anything.

The fire burned throughout the night until only the shell of the smithy and the cottage were still standing. The buildings were still smouldering at dawn, and no sign of Ben or Harry had been seen. It was not until later in the day that the men dared to venture into the ruins and found the charred remains of two bodies.

Jacob had regained consciousness but was seriously injured. Apart from a hacking cough, Matilda was unhurt, and she tended to her son, reassuring him and dressing his wounds. She was in shock and had not quite grasped the fact that she had lost her husband, son, and home.

Annie stayed the rest of the night at Fred's house and visited Matilda in the morning. They clung to each other and wept, for both had lost their husbands and Matilda, her son, too.

"Oh, Annie, what are we going to do? I can't believe they're both dead. Thank God you and the baby are all right, but how I wish He had taken me instead of them. Where shall we live?"

"Ssh, we'll be all right." Annie tried to comfort her mother-in-law but had no idea what they would do. "Gran's said you and Jacob can stay here for now, and I'm sleeping downstairs in Uncle Fred's house."

The bodies of Harry and Ben were burnt beyond recognition, and Fred hastily made coffins and nailed down the lids. The funerals were held a day or two later. There was much debate about the cause of the fire, and most people suspected that Ben, in his fragile mental state, was probably responsible. Matilda insisted it must have been a spark from the fire but conceded that Ben was not in the bedroom when she awoke.

Whatever the cause, the smithy was no more, and after a couple of weeks at the inn, Matilda rented George's cottage by the sea for Jacob and herself. Jacob was making a slow recovery, for his burns were extensive. Ben had hidden some savings in a tin under a loose floorboard in the kitchen of the smithy, and fortunately, the money was unharmed, so at least Matilda was not penniless.

CHAPTER 49

It was a mild Sunday in early December, and Annie found her footsteps leading her once again to the graveyard. Leaving Selina in the pram on the path, she filled two jars with water from the stream, arranged the holly she had picked in them, and placed one on her father's grave and one on Harry's. There were no wildflowers around so late in the year, but she thought the bright green leaves and the red berries looked perfect against the grey of her dad's gravestone. There was no stone on Harry's grave yet, as the ground needed time to settle.

Since that awful night when Harry and Ben had lost their lives, Annie had been living at her mother's cottage. She was so sad that Harry had lost his life, for he was a kind and gentle man, and she had been fond of him. Though their marriage had been short, he had given her respectability, and for that, she would always be grateful. She also felt incredibly guilty because although she did not want to admit it, even to herself, a small part of her was glad she was no longer his wife. Not for the world would she have wished for him to die, and certainly not in such a horrible fashion, but she no longer had to pretend to love him, which was a huge relief.

Matilda had aged ten years since the night her husband and son died. Her youngest son, Francis, had left his job at the Manor House to rebuild the smithy. The money Ben had saved would not last long, and the sooner they could return home, the better. Matilda had sold some land to George Carter to finance the project, as he wanted to expand his shop. Francis had started clearing the site and would begin rebuilding soon. He was hoping that in a few months, he could get the business up and running again, and Jacob would again be able to help when he fully recovered from his injuries.

Annie returned to the pram and found that Selina was still fast asleep. She decided to walk around the churchyard, for she was not ready to return to the overcrowded cottage. As she walked around the back of the church, she saw Robert approaching her.

"Hello, Annie. How are you?"

"I'm fine, thanks, Robert. How are you?"

"I'm well too. Is your mum pleased with the repairs to the cottage?"

"Yes, she's delighted; the new roof and the windows have made such a difference. It was always so cold before, and the rain came in, but it's cosy now, and I'm sure we've had fewer coughs and colds than usual. Thank you so much for getting all that work done."

"It should have been done long ago." Robert smiled back at her, but then his expression changed to one of concern. "How are things since you lost Harry?"

"Well, quite difficult. I've gone home to live, but it's pretty cramped, as you can imagine. Matilda wants me to live with her when the smithy is rebuilt, but I don't feel I belong there now that Harry is gone. We weren't married that long, but, of course, she still thinks Selina is Harry's baby and her granddaughter."

"I'm so sorry for what happened to Harry, Annie. We didn't get on, but he didn't deserve that. We just both wanted the same thing, and unfortunately for me, he got it. I know it's no time since you were widowed, Annie, but I'd love to see more of you. Could we spend some time together, like we used to?"

"No, it's far too soon after Harry's death. It would be disrespectful, and anyway, we both know it's pointless, so let's not stir up feelings that are best left buried."

"You still have feelings for me, then; that's good. I run the estate now and can do as I like, and you're not married anymore, so why can't we see each other?"

"Oh, Robert, we've discussed this so many times. No doubt my family would welcome you, but if you married me, your family and friends would disown you."

"You know, I rarely socialise with my own class these days, so none of that would be any loss to me. Annie, I'm genuinely sorry that Harry died, especially in the way he did, but it does mean we could be together now if you would just let it happen. In fact, you should know I won't take no for an answer."

"You make it sound so easy, Robert, but there's Selina too; your parents know Miss Wetherby sacked me. They'd never let you marry someone who got in the family way before she was married."

Robert's face clouded, and his mouth was pressed into a thin line.

"You needn't worry about that, either, Annie; I know who raped you."

"I don't know myself, so how could you know?"

"Does Selina still have that birthmark on her shoulder?"

"Yes, of course, I think it will always be there, but what has that to do with anything?"

"I noticed the birthmark when you undressed her at Sabina's that day. Victoria has the same birthmark in much the same place."

Annie's brow wrinkled as she frowned. "I don't understand. How could they both have the same mark, and how does that tell you who attacked me?"

"Think about it; those marks often run in families, and that one is a peculiar shape. Who is Victoria's father?"

"Your father, of course, but no, surely it couldn't be him." Annie gasped, her eyes wide. "Oh no, you can't be serious? He wouldn't have done that to me; he's a gentleman."

"I tell you that birthmark runs in our family. David wasn't here when the attack happened, and neither was I, so the only man in our family who had the opportunity was my father."

"No, I can't believe he'd do something like that, and even if he did, how would that help us to marry? We can't prove it, and if we accuse him of raping me, surely he'd be even less likely to consent?"

"After Danny was born, my mother wouldn't let him anywhere near her, which wouldn't have helped, but it's no excuse. I've given this a lot of thought, and it has to be him, Annie. That birthmark is too distinctive for it not to be. I'm going to tell him I know what he did, and if he doesn't give consent for us to marry, I'll tell Mother about it and where Danny is living, too, if he's difficult."

"Oh, I don't know, Robert. It would cause so much trouble, and your father's not in the best of health. He might have another stroke, and then how would you feel? And what about your mother? It would be the end of their marriage."

"There is a risk he could have another stroke, and it would be hard on Mother to hear what happened, but if he agrees, I'm hoping we can spare her the truth. If he gives his approval for us to marry, there's little she can do, even if she doesn't understand why. Can we at least start seeing each other again?" He looked her in the eyes, his face full of hope. "We can take it slowly and be discreet. We'd have to wait at least a year following Harry's death anyway. Come on, let's go for a walk to our favourite place."

Reluctant but unable to resist, Annie agreed to walk with him, though she refused to let him hold her hand. However, as soon as they were some distance from the village, he tucked his arm in hers. The pram bumped across the grass, but Selina slept on regardless, and when they reached the old mazzard tree, he drew her to him and kissed her tenderly. He held her tightly, breathing in the smell of her hair. His eyes were closed as he savoured the moment he had thought would never come.

"Oh, Annie, how I've missed you. It drove me crazy to see you living with Harry."

Annie clung to him and wept, unable to speak. She had been so unhappy for such a long time that this was almost more than she could take. Selina started to cry, and Annie picked her up. The baby was sucking her fist and turning her head towards Annie, seeking her breast.

"She's hungry; do you mind if I feed her?"

"No, of course not. Let's sit under the tree like we used to. I'll put my coat down because the grass is damp."

They sat down, and Annie discreetly unbuttoned her dress and put Selina to her breast, where she gulped hungrily.

"She's always liked her food. As long as she's got her belly full, she's content, but if she's hungry, then she lets you know all about it."

Robert watched in fascination. "She's lovely, Annie, and she's got your eyes. Now, what are we going to do? You still love me, don't you? Surely you couldn't kiss me like that if you didn't?"

"You know I do, stupid. I've never stopped loving you and never will, but I don't know what we can do about it."

"Will you just leave it to me? Please, Annie, I can make this happen; really, I can, but there is just one thing I need to know."

Although she was still feeding Selina, he shifted somewhat awkwardly onto one knee before her.

"Annie Rudd, will you marry me?"

She opened her mouth to protest again, but he put his finger to her lips.

"Shh, all I want to hear is one word. Just one word is all you're allowed to say. Forget everything else, and just let your heart speak. Now, I'll ask you one more time, and please say what you truly feel. Annie, my darling, will you marry me?"

A wide grin made dimples on her cheeks, and her eyes sparkled as she gently set the child to one side and closed her dress. She took his face in her hands and kissed him on the lips.

"Yes, I will."

He hugged her tightly as if he would never let her go.

"That's all I wanted to hear; you can leave the rest to me."

AUTHOR'S NOTE

I hope you enjoyed reading this book as much as I enjoyed writing it. If you believe this book is worth sharing, please consider posting a review on Amazon or Goodreads

An honest review is the highest compliment you can pay to any author and much appreciated.

You can find me on Facebook or Twitter. If you would like to find out more about me and my books and keep up to date with new releases; please visit https://marciaclayton.co.uk/ to join my mailing list.

Thank you.

Marcia

About The Author

Marcia Clayton writes historical fiction with a sprinkling of romance and mystery in a heart-warming family saga that stretches from the Regency period through to Victorian times.

A farmer's daughter, Marcia was born in North Devon, a rural and picturesque area in the far South West of England. When she left school at sixteen, Marcia worked in a bank for several years until she married her husband, Bryan, and then stayed at home for a few years to care for her three sons, Stuart, Paul and David.

As the children grew older, Marcia enrolled on a secretarial course which led to an administrative post at the local college. There, she seized the opportunity to obtain more qualifications, including two Management Diplomas and two A levels, one in History and the other in English Language and Literature. Marcia progressed through various jobs at the college and, when working as a Transport Project Co-ordinator, was invited to 10 Downing Street to meet Tony Blair, the then Prime Minister. Marcia later worked for the local authority as the Education Transport Manager for Devon County Council and remained there for nine years until her retirement.

Now a grandmother, Marcia enjoys spending time with her family and friends. She's a keen researcher of family history, and this hobby inspired some of the characters in her books. A keen gardener, Marcia grows many of her own vegetables. She is also an avid reader and enjoys historical fiction, romance, and crime books.

Marcia has written five books in the historical family saga, "The Hartford Manor Series". You can read her free short story, "Amelia", a spin-off tale from the first book, "The Mazzard Tree". Amelia, a little orphan girl of 4, is abandoned in Victorian London with her brothers, Joseph and Matthew. To find out what happens to her, download the story here: https://marciaclayton.co.uk/amelia-free-download/ In addition to writing books, Marcia produces blogs to share with her readers in a monthly newsletter. If you would like to join Marcia's mailing list, you can subscribe here: https://marciaclayton.co.uk/

If you enjoyed *The Mazzard Tree,* you may be interested in the other books in *The Hartford Manor Series.*

Betsey

The Prequel to the Hartford Manor Series

1820 North Devon, England

Betsey, a sadly neglected child, is shouldering responsibilities far beyond her years. As she does her best to care for her little brother, Norman, she is befriended by Gypsy Freda, an old woman whose family is camped nearby. Freda's granddaughter, Jane, is also fond of the little girl and is concerned about her.

Thomas, the second son of Lord Fellwood, happens across the gypsy camp and becomes besotted with Jane. However, Jasper Morris, the local miller, also has designs on the young gypsy, and inevitably, the two men do not see eye to eye.

Betsey is drawn into their rivalry for the attention of the beautiful young woman, and she finds herself promising to keep a dangerous secret for many years to come.

The Angel Maker

Book Two in The Hartford Manor Series

1884 North Devon, England

When carpenter, Fred Carter, finds a young woman in dire straits by the roadside, he takes her to the local inn where she gives birth to a daughter. Charlotte Mackie is an unmarried mother and has run away from home where she would have no sympathy from her strict parents. A few days later, Fred takes Charlotte to her aunt's house and does not expect to see her again.

When their paths unexpectedly cross, Fred finds Charlotte distraught as her aunt has arranged an adoption behind her back. Charlotte is desperate to find her baby, and Fred promises to help. However, they are unprepared for the sinister discoveries that lay before them. Set alongside the absorbing detail of country life and budding village romances, dark forces are at work which ultimately test the bravery and resourcefulness of the whole community.

The Angel Maker is the sequel to The Mazzard Tree and the second novel in a compelling series that follows the lives and loves of the villagers of Hartford. A rare treat for lovers of historical fiction

The Rabbit's Foot

Book Three in The Hartford Manor Series

1885 North Devon, England

Mr Edward Snell was more than a little curious when Robert Fellwood, the heir to Hartford Manor, and his elderly aunt, the Lady Margery, begged an audience on a Saturday morning. However, being such valued clients, the solicitor was happy to oblige. As his clerk showed the visitors in, he was intrigued to see them followed by an old man who, though respectably dressed, had something of a vagrant about him. The crisp suit in which he was attired could not disguise his weather-beaten face or his missing teeth.

Robert introduced his Uncle Sam and explained he had come to claim his inheritance. The solicitor was old enough to remember the extensive search for Thomas Fellwood when his father, Ephraim, died in 1840. However, that was some forty-five years ago and the young man had never been found. Yet, here was Sam, who claimed to be Thomas Fellwood's son, and even more surprising, was the fact that the Fellwood family appeared to have accepted him as such.

The Rabbit's Foot is an intriguing and compelling novel with many unexpected twists and turns. Set in the small seaside village of Hartford, it tells the tale of how an old man, who has spent his life with barely a penny to his name, suddenly finds himself rich beyond his wildest dreams. However, there is only one thing that Sam Fellwood truly wants and that is to be reunited with his son, Marrok, whom he abandoned at the age of five. Will Sam find the happiness that has eluded him for so many lonely years?

Millie's Escape

Book Four in The Hartford Manor Series

1885 North Devon, England

It is winter in the small Devon village of Brampford Speke, and a typhoid epidemic has claimed many victims. Millie, aged fifteen, is doing her best to nurse her mother and grandmother as well as look after Jonathan, her five-year-old brother. One morning, Millie is horrified to find that her mother, Rosemary, has passed away during the night and is terrified the same fate may befall her granny, Emily.

When Emily's neighbours inform her that Sir Edgar Grantley has also perished from the deadly disease, the old woman is distraught, for the kindly gentleman has been their benefactor for many years, much to the disgust of his wife, Lilliana. Emily is well aware that Sir Edgar's generosity has long been a bone of contention between him and his spouse, and she is certain Lady Grantley will evict them from their cottage at the first opportunity.

As she racks her brain for a solution, Emily remembers her father came from Hartford, a seaside village in North Devon and had relatives there. Desperate and too weak to travel, she insists Millie and Jonathan leave home and make their way to Hartford before the embittered woman can cause trouble for them. There, she tells them, they must throw themselves on the mercy of their family and hope they will offer them a home.

With Emily promising to follow them as soon as possible, the two youngsters reluctantly set off on their fifty-mile journey on foot and in the harshest of weather conditions. Emily warns them to be cautious, for she suspects Lady Grantley may well pursue them to seek revenge for a situation that has existed between the two families for many years.

A Woman Scorned

Book Five in The Hartford Manor Series

1886 North Devon, England

Lady Lilliana Grantley has been seriously ill with typhoid, a disease that recently claimed her husband Edgar's life and that of his long-time lover, Rosemary Gibbs. Now recovering at last, the lady wastes no tears on her husband but is determined to wreak revenge on his two illegitimate children.

Embarrassed for years by his affair with Rosemary, a childhood sweetheart living nearby, she has falsely accused Sir Edgar's daughter, Millicent, of the theft of a precious brooch and wants to see her jailed or hung.

Fortunately for Millie and her little brother, Jonathan, their granny, Emily, insisted they leave home as soon as she heard of Sir Edgar's death, for she knew his widow would seek revenge. The old lady was soon proved right, and Lady Lilliana, furious the two youngsters were nowhere to be found, evicted the old woman despite the fact she, too, was dangerously ill.

After a long and hazardous journey to North Devon, Millie and Jonathan were united with some long-lost family members who made them welcome and gave them a home. However, aware that Lady Lilliana has put a price on Millie's head, they know they are not yet out of danger. Despite this, they are determined to find their granny, Emily, who seems to have disappeared.

Aided by her long-time lover, Sir Clive Robinson, Lady Lilliana is determined to find Millie and Jonnie and get them out of her life once and for all, but how far will the embittered woman go?

www.ingramcontent.com/pod-product-compliance
Lightning Source LLC
Chambersburg PA
CBHW020722310726
48979CB00004B/1020

* 9 7 8 1 8 3 8 3 2 5 9 4 7 *